Hello there!

I'm absolutely over the moon that you've chosen to read *Belle of the Back Streets*. It's my first novel, the first time I've had a story of my own published in this way. It's something I have dreamed about ever since I was a little girl. And now I'm a (little!) bit older, being a published writer really is a dream come true. That's why it makes me so happy that you've chosen to read my work, and I do hope you enjoy it.

I grew up in the village of Ryhope, which is where the book is set, and I hope that I've done justice to the village and the colliery in bringing the setting alive.

Thank you from the bottom of my heart.

Glenda Young

Praise for *Belle of the Back Streets*:

'Glenda has an exceptionally keen eye for domestic detail which brings this local community to vivid, colourful life and Meg is a likeable, loving heroine for whom the reader roots from start to finish' Jenny Holmes

'I found it difficult to believe that this was a debut novel, as "brilliant" was the word in my mind when I reached the end. I enjoyed it enormously, being totally absorbed from the first page. I found it extremely well written, and having always loved sagas, one of the best I've read' Margaret Kaine

More praise from online readers:

'I loved this book. The characters capture you . . . I would highly recommend' Lisa K

'Wow what a debut from Glenda. The way this book was written you'd think Glenda was a veteran in sagas. I fell in love with the characters and was totally captivated in the ups and downs of their lives. I look forward to *The Tuppenny Child* next' Diane C

'Loved this book! A great lead character with a fantastic story, full of highs and lows. Very well written and Belle's character really drew me in' Sally A

'I so enjoyed this book . . . Can't wait to read more from this author. A brilliant read' Tracy R

'Give this book a read as I loved it and can't wait for the next one from this author. Five stars' Sandra B

'A beautiful and poignant story. You will have tears and smiles throughout. A deserved five stars' Brid C

'Excellent book with a great storyline. Characters that are so well written. I would highly recommend this book to anyone!' Stephanie C

GLENDA YOUNG

Belle of the Back Streets

HEADLINE

First published in Great Britain in 2018 by
HEADLINE PUBLISHING GROUP

First published in paperback in 2019 by
HEADLINE PUBLISHING GROUP

7

Cataloguing in Publication Data is available from the British Library

ISBN 978 1 4722 5658 4

Typeset in Stempel Garamond by Avon DataSet Ltd,
Bidford on Avon, Warwickshire

Printed and bound in Great Britain by Clays Ltd, Elcograf S.p.A.

FSC
www.fsc.org
MIX
Paper from responsible sources
FSC® C104740

Headline's policy is to use papers that are natural, renewable and recyclable products and made from wood grown in well-managed forests and other controlled sources. The logging and manufacturing processes are expected to conform to the environmental regulations of the country of origin.

HEADLINE PUBLISHING GROUP
An Hachette UK Company
Carmelite House
50 Victoria Embankment
London EC4Y 0DZ

www.headline.co.uk
www.hachette.co.uk

Grace Emily Foster

'The bonniest bairn in three collieries'

My thanks go to:

Sunderland Museum & Winter Gardens; Sunderland Local Studies Centre; Durham Records Office; Durham Light Infantry Museum; Beamish Museum; Sunderland Antiquarian Society; Ryhope Heritage Society; June Tipling; Theresa Bradbury; Reverend David Chadwick, vicar of St Paul's church in Ryhope; my friend Lynn Stacey-Kears; my nephew Adam Young for inspiring the idea; Sunderland Women's Centre for their 'Wonderful Words' course, which gave me the kick-start to writing creative fiction; Barry, as always, for his love, patience and kindness and the endless cups of tea when I locked myself away in our spare room to write; my agent Caroline Sheldon and my editor at Headline, Kate Byrne.

Chapter One

Reunion

Summer 1919

'Meg! Come quickly! There's a man in the house!'

'Is it Dad?' asked Meg, hardly daring to hope.

Tommy shrugged his shoulders. 'Come on, we have to run, we've got to get home. He might be a thief.'

Meg smiled when she saw the serious look on her brother's face. 'Tommy, we've got nothing in our house to steal. He might just be a tinker who's come in from the street to get warm. Evelyn's mam had a tinker walk into their house once. He sat by the fire and had a snooze, and when he woke up she gave him a bite of stottie bread, a mug of tea and off he went. She never saw him again.'

'Meg, please, come on! I saw him sitting in Mam's chair in the kitchen!' Tommy urged, starting to run now.

'Did you speak to him?' she asked. 'Did he see you?'

Tommy shook his head and his long brown fringe flopped down over his excited face. 'He was fast asleep.

I only saw him from the back door.'

'Come on then, let's go and find out who it is.'

Meg gathered the bottom of her skirt in one hand and lifted the heavy cloth above her knees to allow her to run as fast as her brother. In her other hand she held tight to the wicker basket with which she'd been sent to buy eggs from High Farm. She knew Mam wouldn't be happy if she returned home without eggs, but she'd never seen Tommy so agitated before. He was usually such a calm lad, happy, with a face that always wore a smile, but there'd been a fearful look about him when he spoke of the strange man at their house. She just hoped that there'd be time to get the eggs later, before Mam finished work.

'Have you told Mam about the stranger?' she asked as the two of them ran home.

Tommy shook his head. 'You know she doesn't like us disturbing her in the pub. The landlord docks her wages when she's not behind the bar. But what if it is him, Meg? What if it's Dad?'

'If it is, then leave everything to me,' Meg said firmly. 'I'll go down to the Albion and fetch Mam. But let's get home first and have a look at him, then we'll decide what to do.'

Meg and Tommy ran all the way from High Farm along the main village road. They passed the big house on Ryhope Green, where one of the gardeners, an elderly man who was busy staking a climbing shrub around the front door, called out harshly to them both.

'Oi! Colliery kids! Get back up to the pit heap where you belong!'

But his words went unheard as Meg raced past with her skirt and basket flying. Tommy ran after her, holding his cap in his hand for fear it would blow off his head. They ran past St Paul's church, leaving the village behind them, heading up to the colliery, towards the lime-washed cottages laid out in rows like rotten teeth. Their home was in Tunstall Street, right at the end of one of the rows. It wasn't nestled in the terrace amongst the others, where it would have been cosy from the warmth of coal fires roaring in the cottages to either side. Instead it was stuck on the end, smaller than the rest of the row. Meg's mam always said she would cheerfully throttle the builder if she ever got her hands on him.

'It's as if he finished building Tunstall Street and then thought to himself, I can make more money if I stick a little bit at the end.'

Meg and Tommy rounded the top of Tunstall Street and ran all the way down the back lane to reach their home at the far end.

'Hey! Meg Sutcliffe!' a voice called out. 'What's your hurry? House on fire?'

Meg didn't stop running, but turned to see her friend Evelyn's older brother Adam. He was standing at one of the taps in the shared yard of the back lane, his tall frame bent as he filled a bucket of water. He smiled at Meg, his deep brown eyes trying to catch hers.

'Can't stop, Adam!' she shouted as she and Tommy flew past.

Just before they reached home, one of the lavatory doors in the back lane swung open. When Meg saw who it was, she stopped running and stood stock still. Her breath was coming fast and her face was flushed after running all the way from High Farm. She pulled Tommy protectively to her and put her arm around his shoulders. He too was panting after their run, and Meg felt his body heave under her touch.

'Is your mother in?' Hawk Jackson growled.

Meg shook her head.

Hawk let the toilet door slam behind him. Pulling his trousers together around the waist and fastening his buttons, he strode towards them. Meg could smell the ale on him the closer he got to her, and she could see the stains on his jacket and trousers, no doubt from ale too. Hawk was a big man, not particularly tall, but wide and heavy-set. His face ran to an unruly black beard and his small eyes were set deep in dark sockets. The hair on his head was as coarse and black as wire wool.

'You can tell your mam I've come for the rent. And you can also tell her she can pay me any way she likes.'

His face broke into an evil smile that sent shivers down Meg's spine.

'She's at work,' Meg said quickly. 'Anyway, rent's not due until Friday.'

'I was passing,' he said, cocking his head towards the toilet behind him. 'Needed the netty and thought I'd call in on your mam. See how she is, like. I was just about to knock on at the back door for her. I always enjoy my little visits to your mam. She's one of my favourite tenants.'

He glanced from Meg to Tommy and back again. 'By, lass, you're turning into a little beauty, aren't you?' he said, walking closer. He reached out a gnarled finger and scraped it across her cheek. 'Got your mam's looks, that's for sure.'

Meg took a sharp step backwards and Hawk's hand dropped to his side. He glared at Tommy. 'And what about you, little fella? Got nothing to say for yourself?'

'Get lost!' Tommy shouted. 'Leave us alone! And leave Mam alone too!'

Meg pulled him tighter to her side. 'We'll tell Mam you called.' She nodded to Hawk.

'Aye, you do that, lass,' he said, his voice deep and menacing. 'Be sure you do.' And with that, he turned and strode away along the back lane.

'I hate him!' cried Tommy as he watched Hawk in his big black, heavy coat and boots shuffle away along the back lane.

'Come on,' Meg said softly, heading towards the back door. 'Let's go and find out who this fella is in our house.'

From an upstairs window in the next-door house, Meg's neighbour Lil Mahone stood watching. Lil was a small woman, bird-like, with piercing blue eyes that missed little of what went on in Tunstall Street. She had been intent on giving her bedroom a good clean, but had stopped in her tracks when she caught sight of Hawk from the window. And when she saw him reach out to stroke Meg's face, the sight chilled her to the bone.

'Not Meg,' she whispered. 'Please, not Meg.'

With Meg leading the way and Tommy behind her, they walked into their back yard, past the coal house and the tin bath hanging on the brick wall. Meg turned to her brother and put a finger to her lips. Tommy nodded: he understood. Meg stood on her tiptoes to reach the small window, but when she looked inside, she saw the kitchen was empty.

'He's not there,' she whispered. 'He's not sitting in Mam's chair like you said.'

She pointed at the back door and Tommy followed as she gently pushed it open. She peered around the door into the darkness of the kitchen.

'What can you see?' Tommy whispered. 'Can you see him?'

Meg didn't reply. With her heart in her mouth, she pushed open the door a little further, this time poking her head all the way around. The coal fire was raging in the hearth, as it always did no matter the warmth of the day, ready to boil up water whenever it was needed. The oven next to the fire looked untouched. Mam's wooden chair with the sagging seat sat next to the fireplace, her knitting bag with its needles and wool tucked away beneath. The dark, heavy sideboard looked undisturbed and the three-legged cracket stool was in its usual place. On the windowsill stood Mam's white enamel bowl. Everything was as it should be.

'He's not here,' she said again.

'Look in the sitting room,' Tommy suggested, but Meg was already inching her way along the passage. The sitting room door was open and she gasped with shock when she saw the bulk of a man sitting in the chair nearest the window. She sank to the floor in the passageway, indicating to Tommy to sit next to her as she peered around the door.

'He's there,' she told him, her eyes bright with excitement.

'Who is it?' Tommy asked.

Meg allowed herself the bravery of staring straight at the stranger, hearing his snores and knowing he was sleeping.

'What's he like, Meg?' Tommy whispered impatiently.

Meg took in the big, heavy brown coat the man was wearing. There were large buttons down the front and its collar was turned up, but not enough to shield his face. There was a gentleness about him, Meg thought, a defeated look, his face soft with sleep and his head slumped forward.

'Is he a tinker?' asked Tommy.

Meg looked at his boots, which were polished to a shine. She shook her head. 'I don't think so.'

She looked at the man's hair, the same dark brown as her own.

Tommy shuffled along the passageway to try to peer into the sitting room, but Meg held him back.

'What does he look like?' he pleaded.

Meg was silent for a few seconds before she gave her reply. 'He looks sad,' she whispered, without taking her eyes off the man. 'He looks really sad.'

'Is it Dad?' Tommy asked. 'Is it, Meg?'

'I'm not sure,' she replied, turning to her brother this time. 'He looks different to how I remember him, but . . . I thought I'd remember him, Tommy, I was certain I would. But now . . . I'm not sure.'

'But it *could* be Dad?' Tommy said hopefully.

'Well, he doesn't look like a tinker,' Meg said. Just then, a thought struck her and she grasped Tommy's arm. 'What if he works for Hawk Jackson and Hawk's sent him?'

Tommy's eyes narrowed with hatred at the mention of the name. 'Then I'll kill him,' he spat. 'I'll kill him while he's sleeping.'

Meg held her brother tightly. 'Don't be daft, Tommy. You'll do no such thing,' she hissed.

'Well, what are we going to do about him?' Tommy whispered, his body slumping against the passageway wall.

'I'll stay here,' Meg decided. 'I'll keep a watch on him, make sure he doesn't escape. You go and get Mam. Run like the wind all the way down to the Albion and tell Mam we need her. Tell her we've captured a strange man in the house.'

Tommy stood at once and readied himself for a sprint back through the colliery to the village. Meg shot her brother a look before he left.

'Tell her . . . tell her we think it might be Dad.'

Tommy ran like the clappers all the way along the back lane of Tunstall Street and then down the colliery past the mine. The further he ran and the more distance he put between himself and the pit belching out smoke and steam, the brighter the air became. When he reached the village green, there was even a patch of pale blue sky. At the bottom of the green stood the Albion Inn, the public house where his mam worked serving at the bar. And beyond the Albion were fields giving way to cliffs standing guard over the expanse of the moody, grey North Sea.

Tommy knew full well that the landlord at the Albion, Jack Burdon, wouldn't be happy to have Mam called away. He had already threatened to sack her when she'd had to give up work to look after Tommy last winter. He'd been playing on the ice with Micky Parks, the two of them skidding down the colliery bank in shoes that were too worn. Both lads ended up falling and smashing into the stone wall near the tram passing place on the bank. Micky had escaped without a bruise, as he always seemed to, no matter what scrape he got himself into, but Tommy ended up with a broken arm.

'Hey, lad, you shouldn't be in here. Jack Burdon will have your guts for garters if he catches you in his pub!'

Tommy put his hands on the bar to steady himself after his run. 'Hetty, where's Mam?' he asked.

Hetty was in the middle of doing a crossword, concentrating on it hard with the end of a pencil tapping against her lips. Seeing the state of the lad, she quickly tucked the pencil into her auburn hair that was loosely piled on the top of her head.

'She's serving in the other bar,' she replied. 'You all right, Tommy?'

Tommy didn't answer; he just belted through the door that led into the smaller bar of the pub. 'Mam! Mam!' he yelled.

Sally turned at the sound of her son's cry. Her hand flew to her heart when she saw the state of him with his face flushed and his eyes bright. She gripped tight hold of the glass she was filling with stout.

'Mam! You have to come home!'

'She's going nowhere. She's got work to do.' Tommy heard a voice behind him and turned to see the tall, thin figure of Jack Burdon, a man who seemed to be made up of long limbs and sharp angles. He stood tall at over six feet, and he was as thin as a lamp post too, with his brown hair always brushed smartly. He rarely had a good word to say about anyone and was never ready with a smile for any of his customers. His dark, heavy eyebrows moved to exhibit more emotion and feeling than he ever spoke out loud.

'What is it, son?' Sally asked, ignoring the warning from her boss. 'Is Meg all right?'

Hetty walked through from the main bar, determined to find out what all the commotion was about. She knew that whatever it was, Sally was going to need some help, as Jack wouldn't take kindly to any interruption to his business of selling beer and ales.

'Mrs Sutcliffe,' he began, 'I'd be obliged if you could deal with your domestic problems in your own time. May I remind you that while you're under my employ, you're being paid to work behind the bar.'

'Just give her a minute, Jack. You can see the state of the lad. Something's clearly wrong,' Hetty pleaded, but she knew her words would have little effect. Jack Burdon was a man of commerce and business who ran the Albion with nothing more on his mind than a healthy bank balance. He liked routine and order in all areas of his life. Most of the pub landlords in Ryhope were welcoming and genial, but not Jack Burdon of the Albion.

'Is it Meg, son? Is she all right?' Sally asked again, holding her son by the shoulders.

'No, Mam, it's . . .' Tommy glanced between his mam and Hetty. He hated to tell lies, really hated it. All his life his mam had brought him up to stand tall, be polite and tell the truth. But Hetty's kind eyes and concern meant he couldn't, he just couldn't. It wouldn't be fair, he thought, if the man turned out to be Dad safely home from the war when Hetty's son Philip had been killed in action. He didn't want to tell Mam, not in front of her best friend, that their dad might be waiting at home. He had seen Hetty's tears and heard her cries after the telegram arrived. She had brought the dreaded piece of paper to their home, where Sally had cried with her over the news that Hetty's son Philip had been killed in France. Ever since the day of the telegram, lines had settled into Hetty's features that had never been there before. The grief over losing Philip had aged her.

'It *is* Meg, Mam, she's . . . she's hurt herself. She needs you,' Tommy lied. And then, just in case there was a tiny bit of Jack Burdon's heart that wasn't as black as stone and might be lenient to giving Mam time away from her work, Tommy yelled towards Jack: 'And I think she might die!'

'Oh my God!' Sally cried.

'Heaven help us,' Hetty said, reaching out to hold Sally's arm.

'Thirty minutes,' Jack Burdon said, tapping his watch. 'You can have thirty minutes to check on your daughter, Mrs Sutcliffe. Thirty minutes without payment, I should add. And you'll come straight back here to finish your shift afterwards.'

'Go on, love,' Hetty told Sally as she gathered her shawl around her shoulders and took Tommy's hand. She followed mother and son to the door of the Albion. 'And you know where I am if you need me,' she said.

Sally and Tommy raced across the main road and headed up the hill to the pit. Back inside the Albion, Hetty squared her shoulders and then raised both hands to the back of her head, where her long auburn hair was coming loose from its pins. She tied it back, then stormed across the bar to where Jack stood, his face like thunder.

'By, you're a hard man, Jack Burdon,' she told him. 'My mother always said I should never have married you. I wish to high heaven that I'd listened to her now.'

Jack pretended to ignore his wife's words, but they cut deep within. Since the telegram had arrived, since Philip's death, he and Hetty had drifted further from each other with each passing day. His only solace now was the Albion. He might not have been able to keep his only son alive, but by God, he was going to keep a tight ship at work. It was the one thing left in his life over which he had some control.

* * *

'Mam . . . Meg's all right. I had to tell a lie,' Tommy confessed as soon as they were out of the pub. 'I had to make it sound more serious than it is to get you out of work.'

Sally slowed her steps. 'What do you mean, son?'

'No, don't slow down, Mam. We have to get home as fast as we can. Meg's there, but she's all right. She's not dying. She's not even hurt. But she's keeping watch on someone, there's someone in the house – and we think it might be Dad.'

'Oh, bloody hell!' Sally muttered under her breath, but not quietly enough.

Tommy turned and stared at his mam. He'd never heard her swear before. She glanced at him as the two of them picked up their pace again, walking as quickly as they could back up the hill to Tunstall Street.

'May God forgive me,' she said as they passed St Paul's church.

His mam's anger confused Tommy. He wasn't sure what he'd expected her to think about Dad coming home from the war, but he certainly hadn't anticipated such cross words from her.

'Have you spoken to him?' Sally asked carefully.

'He's asleep,' Tommy replied. 'He was snoring and it might not be Dad . . . but it might be, and what if it is, Mam? What if it's Dad come home from the war?'

Sally pushed a strand of her long fair hair behind her ear and started striding faster still.

'If it is, then just mark my words. He's got some explaining to do.'

Back at Tunstall Street, Meg was still in her place on the passage floor. She had barely moved, transfixed, watching the sleeping stranger, who looked out of place, too big for their sitting room, too heavy for their furniture. She turned when she heard footsteps out in the back yard.

'He's here, Mam,' Meg said, not caring to whisper any longer, for surely Mam would have to wake up the man now.

Sally paused in the passageway before allowing herself to look into the front room. She was still wearing the green-checked pinny that Jack Burdon insisted she and Hetty wore for work in the pub. Her hands flew over it, smoothing it at the front, then she pushed her hair back from her eyes and walked straight into the room, determined to face whatever was to come. She stood in front of the sleeping man, took in the sight of him and then gave a sharp nod to her children.

'It's your dad,' she said matter-of-factly before turning to Meg and Tommy, who were hovering at the doorway, not daring to enter. 'Now then, you two, make yourselves scarce for the afternoon. Meg, did you get the eggs like I told you to?'

'No, Mam.'

'Well, go and get them now. Tommy, you get yourself back to school for the rest of the day. See if they can teach you something useful in the last few days before term ends. Something that'll save you from a life working in the hell of the coal pits like the rest of them round here.'

'Yes, Mam.'

'And both of you, listen now. I don't want anyone knowing that your dad's back, all right? Don't go telling people just yet. If anyone saw him arriving, well, the news might be out. But I want to tell folk in my own good time, all right?'

'Yes, Mam,' they chimed.

Sally reached out and placed a hand on the brown coat that her husband was wearing. 'I just want to get used to having him back for a while,' she said, more softly. 'Before everyone comes calling.'

Meg picked up her wicker basket from where she'd dropped it earlier, and she and Tommy headed out to the yard. They paused at the back door, hoping to hear their dad speak, to prove it was definitely him.

'I think I'd recognise his voice,' Meg said. 'I think I'd remember it.'

'I can't remember much about him,' sighed Tommy. He kicked the wall as he walked out of the back yard and scraped one of his old, battered shoes along the bricks as they headed slowly along the back lane, walking in silence past the shared wash houses and netties and the taps where water was collected each morning and night. Dark clouds hung above them, cushions of coal dust and muck from the pit.

'I remember . . . I remember the horse he used to have,' Tommy said at last.

Meg smiled. 'Davey Scott's got it now. I see it sometimes when he takes it out with the cart selling his fruit and vegetables.'

'It was brown, wasn't it?'

Meg shook her head firmly. 'Black.' She touched her nose. 'With a white patch just here. Dad always said the white patch was the shape of a star. That's why he called her Stella.'

When they reached the edge of the village green, Tommy said ta-ra to his sister and turned to walk through the doors of the school. He braced himself for a telling-off from Miss

Barnes for disappearing at dinner time without so much as a word. But he'd promised his best friend Micky he'd return the comic to him that Micky had loaned him earlier that week and he'd had to run home at dinner time to fetch it. Now he'd have to think about what to tell Miss Barnes to explain his absence, and his stomach twisted when he realised he'd have to tell another lie. And to top it all off, in all the commotion over finding the strange man at the house, the comic still lay forgotten under his bed. Well, his mam had told him not to tell anyone that his dad was back home, and he had to keep her secret. It was one thing to get on the wrong side of Miss Barnes, but Tommy knew from experience that it was much, much worse to get on the wrong side of Mam.

After Meg waved off her brother at the village school, she continued on her way to High Farm to collect the half-dozen eggs for Mam. But as she walked towards the farm, she saw Micky Parks by the wall of the cattle market, scrapping with a much taller boy she recognised as one of the Finlay lads. She ran up to them, threw her basket to the ground and shoved her arms between them to break up the fight as best as she could.

'Stop it!' she yelled. 'Just stop it!'

Ron Finlay took a step backwards, taken by surprise. Micky used the opportunity to dart to one side, away from Ron's fists.

Meg turned to the bigger boy. 'What's a lad like you doing picking on someone the size of Micky Parks?' she demanded. 'And you . . .' she said to Micky, 'you should be in school.'

'He started it,' Ron snarled, spitting on the ground.

'No, I didn't,' Micky said. 'I was on my way back to school after dinner and he started on me for no reason when he came out of the Albion.'

'You've been drinking?' Meg asked Ron. 'And then you start picking on school kids? You Finlays are all the same with your fighting and drinking. You should be ashamed of yourself. You were a waste of space back when you were at school with me, Ron Finlay, and you've not changed for the better now. And you, Micky, get yourself back to school now, go on.'

Micky quickly glanced at Ron and then looked pleadingly at Meg.

'But they'll all know I've been saved from a fight by a girl. He'll tell everyone.'

Meg shook her head. 'He won't be telling anyone, will you, Ron? Not if he wants his secret keeping about being out drinking when he should be at work in the pit.'

She bent down to pick up her basket, pushed it on to her arm and squared her shoulders. 'Now go on, get yourself home,' she told Ron.

He spat again before slowly turning and walking away, back in the direction of the Albion.

'Thanks, Meg,' smiled Micky once Ron was out of ear-shot. Then he ran off towards the school, leaving Meg to continue to the farm.

In the kitchen at Tunstall Street, Sally put a kettle of water on the coal fire to boil, leaving Ernie sleeping in the front room. She'd spotted what her children hadn't seen: four ale bottles – empty bottles – lying on the floor. She made no effort to be quiet about her preparations; if the noise woke Ernie up, then so be it.

It had been four years since she'd last seen him. Four years in which worry lines had settled around Sally's eyes and a heaviness had crept in around her once carefree face. Four years since he'd been called up for war to serve with the Durham Light Infantry. And in all that time, he hadn't been in touch once with a letter, not once. Oh, there had been cards, cards that the army had provided him with, that they provided all the soldiers with who didn't know what to write, or didn't have the time or inclination. All that the soldiers had to do with those cards was cross out the bits that weren't relevant to them.

I am quite well, Ernie's cards always said in official military print. Underneath that, but thankfully always crossed through in pencil, was *I have been admitted to the hospital*. Then, infuriatingly, another pencil line through the card's final words too: *Letter follows at first opportunity*.

There never had been any letters and Sally doubted that it could have been because of lack of opportunity. Other wives she knew, other mothers, sisters even, had received letters from the front. But nothing came from Ernie Sutcliffe. All that had arrived at Tunstall Street, twice a year, three times at most, were the small postcards with their standard words crossed through or left untouched, depending on what he wanted her to know. His signature and the date were at the bottom of each card, but he never added the words *love from*, and never the *X* of a kiss.

When the kettle had boiled, Sally prepared a pot of tea in the heavy brown teapot that had been handed down from her mam, covering it with a red knitted cosy, one that she'd made herself. When the tea was ready, she poured two mugs and took both into the sitting room. She placed Ernie's on the table beside him, then sat down in the chair opposite, taking in the full extent of him, wondering what to say to him when he awoke.

Ernie had been handsome once, making Sally the envy of her friends when she'd first met him. He wasn't smooth handsome like the movie stars who smiled out from the posters outside Ryhope's Grand Electric Cinema, but rough-hewn and rugged. The man that Sally had fallen for was a strapping fella, broad-shouldered and powerfully built. He looked thinner now, thinner than she ever remembered, his face sunken and worn, his mass of dark wavy hair clipped short.

Ernie woke with a hacking cough that Sally was sure could be heard all the way down to the next village at Seaham. He didn't look at her at first, as his body convulsed with the barking and coughing. When it finally eased, he stood and walked to the kitchen, where she heard him spit into the fire. She followed him and found him slumped in her kitchen chair with his head in his hands. She stood in front of him with her feet wide and her hands on her hips. 'Slept your hangover off yet, have you?'

Ernie lifted his gaze. 'What sort of welcome home's that supposed to be?'

'I saw the bottles, Ernie. One or two beers I could understand. But four? I daren't even think where you got the money from. That's money that could've bought us some ham for tea tonight. But instead I'll be boiling up bones again for soup with a bit of stottie bread.'

Ernie's head dropped and his body rocked again with the cough.

'Have you seen a doctor about that?' Sally asked.

'Saw the quack at the army dispersal centre. He said it's

bronchitis. It's the pit air here, makes it worse. All that smoke and muck pumping out like black vomit. I thought things would've changed while I've been away. But it's still the same old mucky Ryhope that it always was.'

He stood, and Sally took the tiniest step backwards as he reached his arms out towards her.

'Anyway, never mind all that,' he said. 'I'm home now.'

'And you stink of booze.'

'You're not going to deny me a celebration drink, are you? Not today of all days.' He pulled her close, kissing her neck, but Sally didn't respond.

'You never wrote, Ernie. Four years and not one letter from you. You never asked about the bairns, you never asked about me, not one letter, not one lousy letter.'

'I sent you the cards, didn't I? You know I'm not good with words, Sal. But I can show you now how much I missed you. Come on, let's go upstairs.'

Ernie pulled Sally towards him and wrapped his arms around his wife. Sally tried to resist, but her husband's touch proved too much. It was the first time she'd been held by a man in years, and she gave in easily to the arousal. She allowed herself to soften and put her hands to the buttons on Ernie's coat.

'Let's get you out of this first. Where on earth did you get a coat like this anyway?'

'The army let me keep it, the boots too.'

He watched as Sally unfastened his coat for him.

'You're still a good-looking woman, Sally Sutcliffe. You've kept your figure too.'

'Aye? Well if I have, it's because what little food we can afford has had to keep the three of us going while you've been away.'

'Come on, Sally, don't be like that,' he said. 'You've still got that same sparkle in your eyes that you had when I met you. You're still the same pretty-as-a-picture Sally that I fell in love with back then.'

'And you're still the same old Ernie,' she sighed. 'Beer first and family second.'

She helped him out of the coat, enjoying the feel of his body underneath his shirt.

'You haven't even asked how the bairns are yet,' she chided.

'That's because I know they're all right.'

'And you're sure about that, are you?'

Ernie smiled. 'You would've said so if they weren't. I'm home now, Sal. I'm safe . . . and I'm home.'

She pulled back a little and looked at his face, really looked at him properly, and it was when she saw his tears threatening to fall that she threw her arms around him and kissed him with a strength of passion that took them both by surprise.

Sally couldn't remember the last time she'd been in bed in the afternoon, but this wasn't any ordinary afternoon. When she woke, Ernie was no longer by her side and she could hear the sound of his coughing coming up the stairs from the kitchen. She dressed quickly and hurried down to find him sorting through a black canvas bag.

'Medals!' he said proudly, holding up three for her to see. 'Bet you didn't know they gave me medals.'

'You never wrote, Ernie. I didn't know anything,' she replied quickly.

'Thought I'd give them to the lad if he wants them, like.'

'What about Meg? You can't be giving stuff to Tommy without giving anything to Meg.'

Ernie nodded, serious. 'I've been thinking about Meg. She still a bright lass?'

'The best,' Sally replied. 'Far too clever for her own good, that's what the teachers used to say at school.'

'Is that the school Tommy goes to now?'

'He's not got long to go there – only a couple of days till term ends,' Sally said. 'He's not as far on as Meg was at his age, not with his books and reading, but he's happy enough. Oh, but the temper on him sometimes . . .' She nodded towards Ernie. 'He gets that from you.'

'And what's Meg doing now? She got herself a job in one of the shops or the pubs on the colliery?'

'She looks after the house,' Sally replied. 'She does everything, all the cooking and the cleaning while I'm earning. I'm working down at the Albion now.'

'Jack Burdon still running that place?' Ernie asked.

'Jack and Hetty, yes. They lost their son, Philip. He got caught up in some fierce fighting in France, they say.'

'So I heard,' Ernie said softly. 'There were a lot of our battalion that didn't come back.'

Sally moved to sit next to him.

'Was it . . . What was it like, love?' she asked.

Ernie lowered his gaze to the stone floor. 'There were things . . . things I wish I'd never seen. Things I wish I'd never had to do.' He shook his head, as if to shake off the memories. A few moments of silence passed between them, and Sally reached out her hand, placing it on Ernie's own.

'It was hard, Sally, really hard,' he said softly. 'And now I come home and all I see is the same as what was here four years ago. What was it all for? Is this what I fought for? What young lads died for? I'm back to the same black and stinking pit village I left before the war. We were promised new houses, you know. Homes fit for heroes, they said, but I didn't see much building work going on when we drove here from the dispersal centre down south.'

'Ryhope's our home, Ernie. It's not as bad as some places and better than most round here. We don't need to pay the tram fare to fancy places like Roker or Seaburn when we've got a beach at the end of the village. They say that down in the Sunderland slums by the docks, there's bairns that go to school with newspapers wrapped round their feet for shoes. Our bairns have never suffered that bad.'

'And nor will they,' Ernie said decisively. 'As I said, I've been thinking about Meg. How old will she be now? Fourteen?'

'She's fifteen.'

Ernie nodded. 'I was thinking about getting Stella back from Davey Scott and—'

'No!' Sally yelled, jumping up. 'No! You are not putting my bairn out on the street begging with that manky old horse. It's ready for the knacker's yard!'

'Sally, listen, please . . .'

'Ernie, just listen to yourself. You're talking out of your backside. You've not been back five minutes and you think you can tell me what's best for my daughter?'

'Our daughter.'

'*My* daughter, Ernie. They're my bairns that I've been looking after for the last four years. My bairns that I've been up through the night with when they've been sick or they've fallen or they needed love when they were missing their dad and they had no clue if he was dead or alive! My bairns, Ernie, and don't you forget it. I am not having Meg out on the streets collecting rags and bones and selling them down the markets like you used to do.'

'I'll show her the ropes; she can help me get used to life back here. We'll go together for a while, it'll be fine.'

'For a while, you say? Are you going to be handing over the business to her then?' Sally demanded.

'What else is she going to do?' Ernie said. 'Go into service down in that London like all the other bright lasses from round here? Run around after Lord and Lady Muck in some big house? Is that what you want for the lass?'

'She could get a job at Ryhope Co-op,' Sally replied. 'They're always taking on staff.'

'And how many colliery kids are working there?' Ernie replied. 'You know what Ryhope's like, Sal. I bet it hasn't changed a bit while I've been away, stuck in its own bloody-minded ways. One rule for the village kids and another for those of us who live up by the pit. It's always been the same. If you tell me things have changed, I'll forget all about Davey Scott, and he can keep the flaming horse.'

Sally sank into her chair by the fire, defeated. That morning she'd gone to work at the Albion as she'd done every morning while Ernie had been away. She'd had no clue that her world would be turned upside down by teatime. And as for her job at the Albion, well, she could probably go and whistle for it now. She doubted that even with Hetty putting in a good word for her that Jack Burdon would take her back on, not now. He'd only given her thirty minutes away from the bar and she'd taken the whole afternoon.

They sat in silence, the only sound the crackle of the coal fire as it burned in the fireplace.

'Why can't you do it yourself?' Sally said at last. 'Why put Meg out on the horse and cart? Why not you?'

'Like I said, I'll teach her all she needs to know . . . while I still can.' Ernie's body convulsed into another hacking coughing fit. When it was over, Sally heard a scuffle in the back yard and Meg appeared at the door.

'I want to do it,' she said, looking fixedly at her dad. 'I'm not going into service in London, I want to stay in Ryhope with Mam . . . with you. And I don't want to work in the Co-op, they're all stuck up in there.'

'How long have you been stood there listening?' Sally asked sharply.

Meg strode into the kitchen and placed her basket with the eggs in it on the sideboard. She walked towards Ernie and perched on the arm of his chair, putting one arm around his shoulders. He reached up and kissed her on the cheek.

'I want to do it, Mam,' she said again, this time looking at Sally.

'It can bring in good money, you know that,' Ernie added, he and Meg making their case together now to bring Sally round to the idea. 'We could have ham every teatime. No more boiling bones up for soup as thin as dishwater.'

Sally sighed. 'If I agree to this, Ernie . . . *if* I say yes . . . promise me you'll keep her safe. Promise me. You've seen how she's turned out. She's got a beauty about her and she needs protecting from people, from fellas who might see her as an easy target.'

'I promise you, Sally, cross my heart. I'll teach her everything I know,' Ernie replied. He turned towards Meg. 'When we get Stella back from Davey, I'll take you around the streets, show you where to go, who to see . . .' he glanced at Sally, 'who to avoid.'

'I must be stupid to be even thinking of agreeing to this,' Sally said.

'I'll tell you where the richest pickings are, or at least where they used to be – things might have changed while I've been away. And I'll show you the markets where you can sell the rags and bones.'

'Not the markets, Ernie?' Sally said.

Ernie brushed off her concern. 'She'll be fine.'

'She's only fifteen. You know the sort of fellas who work down those markets. You know fine well what they're like.'

'And they'll know she's my daughter and they're to leave her alone. No one ever messed with Ernie Sutcliffe and no one's going to mess with my Meg.'

'When will we start, Dad?' Meg asked, excited now.

'The day after tomorrow suit you?'

'Why not tomorrow?' Sally wanted to know. 'What's happening then?'

'There's a lot of catching-up I want to do,' Ernie said. 'Starting in the Colliery Inn, then the Forester's Arms . . .'

Sally shook her head. 'Beer first, as always.'

'And then the next day . . .' Ernie continued.

'With a hangover the size of the Miners' Hall, I'd bet!' Sally said angrily.

'. . . the next day, we'll get Stella back and have a flit about the streets with her, see where we get to and see who's about.'

'A flit about?' Meg laughed.

'Aye, we'll flit hither and thither.' Ernie smiled at his daughter. 'Up the colliery and down the village. We might even flit as far up the bank as Silksworth or down south to Seaham and get some sea air. We'll flit about like a couple of pigeons, us two.'

'I don't think I want to be a pigeon, Dad,' Meg said. 'How about a butterfly?'

Ernie kissed her cheek once again. 'Then a butterfly you'll be. My beautiful butterfly of the back streets.'

Chapter Two

Work

'Micky Parks?'

'Yes, miss!'

'Jeanie Rushford?'

'Here, miss!'

'Tommy Sutcliffe?'

'Here, miss.'

'Evelyn Wilson?'

There was no reply.

'Anyone seen Evelyn?' Eva Barnes asked, glancing around the classroom.

Tommy raised his arm. 'She's had to start her new job today. She's working now, miss.'

'At the Co-op?' Eva asked hopefully, but Tommy shook his head.

Eva returned to the register in front of her. 'Vic Young?'

'Yes, miss!'

She put a tick against the last name and closed the hard-backed green book in front of her.

'Well, it's the last day of school today . . .' she began, but the remainder of her words were drowned out by the sound of the class cheering and clapping. Eva knew she shouldn't, but she couldn't resist allowing herself a smile before she brought the class to order.

'Children, please!' she cried, standing now in front of them all. 'You'll be out of the classroom soon enough.'

Another cheer went up.

'But before you go, we've got just one small piece of work to complete.'

'Aw, miss, do we have to?'

Tommy didn't need to turn around to see where that comment had come from; he knew immediately it was the voice of his best friend Micky Parks.

'Yes, Micky, we do.' Miss Barnes smiled.

'Is it maths, miss? I hate maths!'

'No, Micky, it's not maths. We're going to finish off our geography project that we started last week.'

Eva Barnes unrolled a map of the north-east coast and carefully pinned it to the wall behind her.

'Now then,' she said, looking expectantly out at the sea of faces. 'Who can tell me where Ryhope is?'

'Why, miss? Are you lost?'

The class erupted into laughter at Micky's joke. Eva had guessed she'd have trouble keeping them under control today of all days, when they were excited and relieved to be leaving school. She looked at the children in front of her; she doubted she'd see any of them again after today. At the age of twelve they were free to leave school, the girls expected to help at home while the boys went to work above ground at the pit until they were old enough to be sent into the hell of the dark underground.

'Micky, come up here and show the class where Ryhope is on this map,' she said, holding out a short wooden stick.

Micky walked to the front of the class and took the stick from her hand. Eva always felt slightly embarrassed when one of the schoolchildren stood beside her, for she was barely taller than they were, even when she wore her best shoes with the heels. She was plump, too, short and plump with a round, kind face.

Immediately Micky pointed the stick at a spot on the map just south of Sunderland, right on the sea.

'And while you're here Micky, you can show the class where Seaham is, too.'

He moved the wooden stick further south to the fishing and mining village along the coast road from Ryhope.

Eva turned towards the class. 'Now, can anyone tell Micky where he'd find the city of Durham on the map?'

Tommy's hand shot up first, but Eva pretended she hadn't seen it. She was hoping for one of the others, one of those who always sat at the back of the class, to answer her question. When no one else spoke, Tommy started waving his hand impatiently.

'Miss, I know! Miss!'

Eva sighed. 'Tommy Sutcliffe, come on up and show the class where Durham is.'

Tommy walked to the front. 'It's there!' he said, pointing to the city that sat ten miles inland to the south-west of Ryhope.

'And what do we know about Durham?' Eva asked the class.

Nellie Hardwick raised her hand at the back. 'It's got a church, miss, a really big church.'

'That church is called Durham Cathedral,' Eva told her.

'And it's got a castle, hasn't it?' Micky Parks added.

'It has indeed.' Eva smiled. 'Durham has a fine castle and a cathedral. Is there anything else we know about it?'

'It's where the miners go, miss,' Tommy said. 'For the gala. Mam says I can go one year.'

'I'm going, miss,' Micky said. 'I'm going with Ryhope Colliery brass band. My uncle Chris says I can help hold the banner and march with them through the streets.'

'Now that the war's over, this year's gala should be quite an event,' Eva said. 'It hasn't been held for the last four years.'

She doubted that she'd ever get to see the spectacle of the miners' gala herself, as her father frowned on such gatherings, disapproving of the spouting of any politics that ran counter to his own. Eva would have loved to see the gala, just once; to hear the stirring brass band music and see the miners' wives dancing in the streets.

'I'm going next year, when I'm a miner,' Tommy said proudly.

'Is that definitely what you're going to do then, Tommy?' Eva asked. 'Go and work down the pit?'

Tommy looked at her, puzzled. 'What else can I do, miss?'

Eva looked out to her class. 'And the rest of you boys? Are you all going to work up at the colliery?'

'Jeanie Rushford's got herself a job as a pit pony,' Micky Parks joked, and the class erupted into laughter again. All except for Jeanie, who turned and glared at Micky.

While Tommy was spending his last day at school with his friends, back at home in Tunstall Street Meg was helping Mam scrub the kitchen clean.

'Your dad said he'd be up and out by now,' Sally huffed as she worked her cloth around the brass fender of the fireplace. 'The lazy beggar's still lying in his bed, sleeping off his hangover after two nights of drinking. He didn't come back till the early hours of this morning. He might as well not have bothered coming home from the flaming war at all if he's going to spend all his time down the pub or in bed.'

'He promised that he'd take me to get Stella from Davey Scott when he wakes up today,' Meg said softly, wanting to believe that the day wouldn't disappear before she saw her dad again.

Sally shot her daughter a look. 'Well your dad promises a lot of things. You do know that poor horse is on its last legs, love?'

Meg shrugged.

'Here, take this,' Sally said, handing her daughter a big bowl of mucky water. 'Go and get some clean water from the tap.'

Meg walked out of the kitchen, through the yard and across the back lane to where the shared tap and the brick building housing the netty stood on a worn and muddy patch of ground. As she filled the bowl, a skinny white dog spotted with black approached her slowly.

'Shoo!' she spat at it. 'Go on, shoo!'

The dog lowered its head and took a step backwards before shyly raising its gaze again.

'I've told you!' Meg said, holding tight to the bowl of water. 'Now go!'

This time the dog skulked away and Meg watched as it turned the corner at the end of the lane. Out of sight, it slumped against the outside wall of their kitchen, enjoying the warmth from the coal fire seeping through the wall into its cold bones and hungry stomach.

When Meg returned to the kitchen, she saw her mam on her hands and knees, scrubbing the kitchen floor.

'It's our turn to clean the netty today, Meg,' Sally told her daughter, as if she needed reminding. 'The night-soil men have been. I heard your dad singing to them when he stumbled home at God knows what time this morning.'

The much-hated cleaning job was one that was shared with the neighbours from their end of Tunstall Street. Meg and her mam always kept to the schedule, which was more than could be said of their next-door neighbour, Lil Mahone. Meg often had to go and remind Lil of her turn to clean it out. In all the years since Lil had moved in next door, they'd never been able to work out if she was forgetful or just plain lazy when it come to her netty-cleaning duties. What they didn't know was that Lil was a woman whose whole world was centred around her husband, Bob. And if Bob wanted his meal on the table or his shoes cleaned or his tobacco brought from the shop, then Lil had little choice but to do as she was bid. Bob wasn't a bad sort, not really, but he was traditional in his ways and had high expectations of how his wife should behave. He was a big man, overweight through drinking too much ale, although the drinking never stopped his jewel-like blue eyes from twinkling from his chubby face. For Lil, though, running around after Bob meant that cleaning the netty was often the last thing on her mind.

'I'll do it today, Mam,' Meg offered.

'You're a good lass.' Sally smiled. 'Remember to knock long and hard at the door first, just in case any of the fellas have fallen asleep in there. You know what they're like round here.'

After soapy water had been sloshed around and Meg was certain she'd made as good a job of scrubbing the shared toilet as she could, she stood guard outside the door as routine dictated she should.

'You can't come in here yet. It's just been cleaned and it's still wet,' she shouted when she saw a group of five men in dark clothes and flat caps ambling towards her along the back lane. As they drew closer, she realised that one of them was Adam, walking home from his shift at the pit. Every exposed bit of his skin – his hands with their long, delicate fingers and his gentle, tired face – was black. But she recognised him immediately. She'd know him anywhere, whether he was covered in coal dust or not. Adam and his sister Evelyn had grown up along the same street as Meg and Tommy. But while Tommy and Evelyn were the same age, Adam was two years older than Meg and no longer a boy.

When he saw her, his face broke into a smile and his eyes and teeth shone white from his coal-black face.

'Hey, Meg Sutcliffe,' he called. 'Netty-cleaning day? Must be your favourite day of the week!'

'See you tomorrow, Adam!' the men shouted as he stopped to talk to Meg.

'See you, lads,' he replied.

Meg smiled, happy to see him. 'It's every bit as horrible and stinky and nasty as you think – worse even,' she told him. 'But I still wouldn't swap jobs with you for all the tea in China.'

'Don't reckon I'd be much good at cleaning, me,' said Adam. 'I can do a bit of gardening, though. I've been helping Dad dig a patch of land over behind the Blue Bell pub. We're going to grow some vegetables, leeks and that. Dad wants to get a few pigeons too, homing pigeons, you know. He can let them fly out and they'll fly straight back home. Some go as far as South Shields before they turn around.'

'When do you get time to do your gardening?' Meg asked, surprised to hear about this hidden talent. 'Aren't you at work at the pit all the time?'

'Not all the time,' Adam replied. 'I like to make the most of the fresh air when I can after spending all day down the mine. Your Tommy's joining us above ground there, I've heard.'

Meg nodded.

'I'll keep an eye on him, Meg, don't you worry. I'll look after him for you and your mam.'

'Thanks, Adam.' Meg smiled.

'And I hear your dad's back safe and sound, like?'

'Word's out already, is it?' asked Meg, surprised. She cast her eyes to the window of her mam's bedroom, where the curtains were still tightly shut.

'You're lucky,' Adam continued. 'Not all of them came back, you know. A lot of the lads sent from Sunderland were killed or wounded. The word down the pit among the men is that a lot of the soldiers who did come home, well, they're broken men now, haunted, they say, by what they've been through.'

'Dad's all right,' Meg said quickly.

'Glad to hear it.' Adam smiled. He lifted his flat cap and doffed it with a flourish that made Meg giggle.

'And now, if you'll excuse me, Miss Sutcliffe,' he said in a pretend hoity-toity voice, 'I'm off home for my tea and a bath in front of the fire. Oh, there's to be a Peace Parade this weekend, did you hear? To celebrate those who returned. Maybe I'll see you there. And I might do a bit of gardening later, if you want to come and watch. You can keep me company while I'm pulling out the weeds.'

Meg glanced again up at Mam's bedroom window, and this time the curtains were open.

'I can't, Adam,' she cried, running across the back lane towards the house. 'I'm going out for the day with Dad!'

Adam shouted goodbye, but his words were lost as Meg disappeared into the kitchen.

Her dad was sitting in the chair by the fire, bent double as he tried to catch his breath. Sally stood in front of him with her hands on her hips.

'I won't tell you again, Ernie, you need to see the doctor,' she said sternly, but he just shook his head before his body convulsed in another coughing fit.

'I'm not seeing no doctor,' he wheezed. 'I've told you, I've just got a bad chest. It'll sort itself out soon enough.'

'There's Spanish flu rife in the town at the minute,' Sally warned him. 'Jack Burdon told me he's been reading about it in the *Sunderland Echo*. The Spanish Lady, that's what they're calling it – it's killing people off. The last thing you want is a wallop of the flu on top of that bad chest.' She turned away. 'And all that drinking won't be helping either.'

Ernie chose to ignore the remark. 'What's there to eat, Sal?' he asked.

Sally wiped her hands on her pinny. 'There's some of yesterday's stottie bread I made, and we've eggs from the farm.'

'That'll do,' Ernie said, nodding at Meg. 'And the same for the lass.'

'I've had my bread this morning,' Meg told him.

'You'll need more, Meg. We've got a heavy day ahead of us. The first thing you're going to need to do every morning is to have a proper breakfast. It might be the only time you eat all day. You're going to be lifting stuff, heavy stuff, working the horse too, carrying and fetching all manner of odds and sods.'

'She's not built for work like that,' Sally said. 'She's just a bairn, Ernie. And what does she know about horses?'

'I'll learn, Mam,' Meg said decisively. She walked to stand next to her dad. 'I want to learn.'

'Look at you, you skinny thing,' said Ernie, stroking her hair. 'We'll have you built up soon enough with your mam's bread and eggs every morning and a day out in the fresh air on the horse and cart.'

'And I'll still look after the house for you, Mam,' Meg said.

Sally sighed. 'I can do it now, love. I don't think I'll be welcome back at the Albion after running out yesterday, will I? Jack Burdon isn't the type to forgive, even if I am his wife's best friend. And no doubt he'll be passing word on up to the colliery pubs that I'm not reliable enough to be taken on elsewhere.'

'Don't you think you could even ask him if he'd give you your job back?' Ernie said.

Sally shook her head. 'I know him too well. I've seen him bad-mouth his other staff in the past; why should he treat me any different? Anyway, we'll have a bit of money coming in once Tommy starts at the pit. And you'll have money, won't you, Ernie? There must be some work you can find to do in Ryhope. I'm sure someone will be willing to take an old soldier on.'

Ernie gazed into the fire while Sally continued talking.

'We should be able to make ends meet and at least pay the rent.'

'Does Jim Jackson still come collecting the rent every Friday?' Ernie asked.

'Not any more. Things have changed while you've been away. It's his brother, Hawk, that we pay now. There was some sort of fight between them, by all accounts, and Hawk took over a couple of the cottages along here from Jim.'

'There's always been bad blood between those two. Nasty beggars, that Jackson clan,' Ernie said darkly. 'We'd do best to keep up with the rent. Wouldn't want to be getting on the wrong side of that bunch.'

'You know the rent's always been the priority, Ernie,' said Sally. 'I've managed to keep the roof over our heads the last four years while you've been away, and I'm damn sure I can continue to do so in the future.'

'But what kind of place is this, eh?' Ernie spat. 'What kind of crumbling, rotten little house is it where there's no space to swing a cat, never mind for a man to bring up two kids and do the best for his wife?'

Sally glared at her husband, furious. Then she began to speak, slowly, spitting out every word.

'I have washed . . . and cleaned . . . and scrubbed . . . and looked after this crumbling, rotten little house, as you call it, all the time you've been away, Ernie Sutcliffe! I have paid the rent, on time, every single week, out of my wages at the pub. I have kept the bairns warm and safe, and by God, if this place doesn't meet the lah-di-dah expectations that you've brought back from abroad with you, then you know exactly what you can do.'

She stood with her hands on her hips, her face flushed with anger. But she wasn't finished yet.

'This little house might not be the house fit for a hero that you thought you were coming back to. It might not be the biggest house and it's certainly not the most fancy, but it's our house, our home, and it's all we've got.'

Ernie stood, ready to challenge his wife, but as soon as he started to speak, his body convulsed again in another coughing fit. This time, Sally left him to it.

'Bread and eggs it is then,' she said, busying herself at the range next to the fire, trying to calm herself. 'I'll make enough for three of us. I'm so hungry I could eat a scabby horse.'

After breakfast and a mug of tea, Ernie and Meg headed out to the back of Tunstall Street. As they turned the corner, the skinny white dog lying by the kitchen wall stood and followed on.

'Get away with you, man!' Ernie shouted at it, and it stopped, briefly. But as they walked on, the dog picked up its pace and followed them again.

'Ignore it, it'll go away,' Ernie told Meg. But every time Meg turned around, the dog was still there, close behind. It followed them all the way up the bank to where Davey Scott lived beside the rhubarb field. And when they disappeared into Davey's house, it slumped outside the door and curled up as if to sleep.

'All right, Davey?' Ernie greeted his old friend. 'How's business?'

Meg watched as Davey shook hands with her dad for what seemed like forever. Davey was as tall as her dad, but older and heavier, with a full belly too. On his head he wore a flat cap to shade his face from whatever sunlight might get through and cause his pale skin to turn redder than it already was. And under the cap were the remains of the auburn hair that had given him the nickname Ginger when he'd been a lad at school. His shirtsleeves were rolled up, displaying a spread of freckles on his arms.

'Ernie Sutcliffe as I live and breathe!' he cried. 'I heard you were home. Some of the lads said they saw you last night at the Forester's Arms, enjoying a pint or two. How are you?'

'Not so bad.' Ernie smiled. 'And how's yourself and Gert? Got any more new grandbairns while I've been away?'

'A whole horde of them, Ernie. I've lost count!' Davey laughed. 'But you know what Gert's like. She's in her element with all the bairns around her. She's always got her arms open for a cuddle from one of them.'

'Glad to hear it. And you're looking well on it. Running around after all those kids must be keeping you fit! Well, you'll know what I'm here for, Davey.'

'Stella, eh? She's been a massive help to me on the fruit and veg cart the last few years. I haven't worked her every day, mind, and I've looked after her, just like I promised you I would. I even had new shoes put on her at the forge just a few weeks ago.'

'I'm looking forward to seeing her, truth be told,' said Ernie. 'I'm taking our Meg out on the streets today, showing her the ropes with the rag-and-bone collecting.'

A shadow passed over Davey's face. 'Are you sure, Ernie? Meg's just a lass; do you reckon she can handle the work . . .' he glanced at Meg and then back to Ernie, 'and everything else that's involved?'

Meg stood firm and crossed her arms. 'I'm tougher than I look, you know!'

'She's right an' all,' Ernie said. 'She's got what it takes, always has. I wouldn't be taking her out on the cart if I didn't think she could manage it.'

Davey led Ernie to the back of the house and Meg followed. There was Stella, their old black horse with the white star on her nose, standing under a wooden canopy on a rough patch of ground. She was tethered to an old fence post.

'You can keep her here if you like,' Davey offered. 'She's happy enough. I get the hay from High Farm now – it's cheaper there than that fella you used to use before. And I've started selling the shi—' He glanced at Meg again. 'I've started selling the horse muck to Henry Wilson and his lad Adam. You wouldn't believe it, Ernie, but you know that patch of land out the back of the Blue Bell? Bob's started digging it over, determined to grow vegetables. You'll remember the state of that land? He'll have more luck prospecting for gold than growing leeks and potatoes on there. But if he's daft enough to buy Stella's muck for manure, then I'll gladly take his money off him.'

'And that money will go to Meg from now on,' Ernie said sternly. 'Stella's her horse now.'

'Of course, Ernie,' Davey said. 'And you can have the cart back too. I'm done selling fruit and veg now, getting too old to wander the streets, too much competition from the young lads down the market. I'm fully intending to finally enjoy my retirement with Gert.'

'Bit of peace and quiet, eh?' Ernie smiled.

Davey shook his head. 'Far from it. With all the grandbairns we've got, we never get a minute to ourselves.

They spend more time at our house than they do at their own. And our kids are living all over Ryhope now, some down the village, some up the bank, I'm just happy me and Gert are fit enough to enjoy having the family around us.'

'You'll have more time once I get this horse from under your feet,' said Ernie. Then he laid his hand gently on Meg's arm. 'Stay back, pet. Let me and Stella have a minute to get to know each other again.'

Meg watched as her dad inched his way forward, gently calling Stella's name. She saw the horse's ears twitch slightly at the sound of his voice.

'You remember me, Stella,' Ernie said softly. 'You remember me, don't you, girl?'

The horse's ears pricked up fully when she caught sight of him.

'That's my girl. That's my Stella,' said Ernie.

Stella made a slight nickering noise in her throat.

'Well I never,' Davey said. 'Four years gone and it's like he's never been away.'

Ernie inched closer to the horse. 'Who's my Stella? Where's my Stella?' he cooed. He placed a gentle hand on her mane, and Stella lifted her black head.

Ernie stood to one side of the horse, looking deep into the serene blackness of her eyes. Stella moved her head again, nudging towards him, and that was when Ernie began gently to sing.

'*My Stella, sweet Stella. What fella could want a finer horse?*'

'Listen to your old dad there,' Davey said to Meg. 'Been away fighting for his country and he comes home singing to an old nag. One of the hardest men in Ryhope and he's as soft as muck at heart.'

'Don't you be going spreading that nasty rumour around, Davey Scott,' Ernie smiled. 'Or there'll be hell to pay!'

Davey laughed under his breath.

'Come, Meg.' Ernie motioned to her with his hand. 'Come and get to know Stella properly. You two are looking after each other from now on.'

For the rest of the morning, Meg listened and watched as Ernie showed her how to handle Stella, how to put on the bridle and reins and how to fasten on the cart. She felt a strange mix of excitement and nervousness as she followed her dad's instructions, grateful for his confidence in her and the skills he was passing on. Stella allowed herself to be stroked by Meg's unfamiliar hands, guided by Ernie's reassuring ones. And when Ernie felt the time was right, he helped Meg up on to the front of the cart to sit with him. Meg tucked her skirts tight under her legs so that the wind wouldn't lift them when the cart started to move.

'Will I see you at the Peace Parade on Saturday?' Davey asked his friend as he prepared to bid farewell. 'We'll be meeting in the Colliery Inn for a pint before the parade goes down to the village, if you want to join us. And I hear your lads from the Durham Light Infantry will be marching through too. All the bairns have been planning their costumes and floats for weeks now. It should be a good day.' He looked to the sky. 'If it stays dry.'

'Can we go, Dad?' asked Meg.

'We'll see, pet,' Ernie said flatly. 'I'm due to be marching with my old battalion – what's left of us, anyway. Davey, if I'm there, I might see you after the parade in the Guide Post Inn.'

'Bye, Davey!' Meg cried as her dad urged Stella out to the main road of Ryhope Street South, the cart wheels scraping and rolling over the uneven ground. Behind them, unseen by Meg and Ernie, the skinny white dog ran to keep up.

'Ready for your first day at work, Meg?' Ernie grinned at his daughter.

Without taking her eyes off the road ahead, Meg nodded. With every step that Stella took, with every turn of the cart wheels, her smile became wider. She felt the wind brush her cheeks as the cart made its way past the rhubarb field. She'd never known such speed, such spirit. Out on the cart with her dad by her side and Stella leading them on, she felt a freedom that she'd never felt before.

'Where are we going first, Dad?' she asked.

Ernie's face broke out in a mischievous grin. 'Oh, I think we'll take a turn around the village green first. What do you say, Meg?'

But before she could answer, his body shook as a coughing fit took him over. His hands flew to his chest as if to steady himself and Meg immediately snatched up the reins, pulling back on them to slow Stella down as her dad had told her to do earlier. They came to a stop at the bottom of Nelson Street, and Ernie turned his face from Meg while he spat on to the road.

'Don't tell your mam,' he warned her, but it was too late, Meg had already seen the blood.

With the reins still in Meg's hands, they carried on along Ryhope Street South, with men waving and cheering at Ernie as they saw him pass by on the cart.

'Welcome home, lad!' they shouted. 'Welcome home!'

Meg smiled each time her dad was recognised by his old pals. She wished that he could always be this happy, as contented at home in Tunstall Street with Mam as he was out on the horse and cart. But then she thought about how Mam had suffered from Dad's neglect over the last few years, and how she was having to put up with his drinking now that he was back. It was little wonder that her mam wasn't as happy about her dad's return as those who were shouting their greetings to him in the street.

Meg let Stella carry on down the main road, past St Paul's church and the school, until they were at the top of the village green.

'It's the big houses you want to go to here, Meg,' Ernie told her. 'Ryhope Hall and Coqueda Hall; they're the places you'll get your quality rags from. All the old clothes and linens the village people don't want, they chuck them out, see? And that's where you come in. All these houses round the green, the big houses, they'll all have something for you to collect.'

'But how will I let them know I'm here, Dad? Do I leave Stella in the street and knock on their front doors?'

Ernie shook his head. 'Oh lass, you've got a lot to learn. Rule number one is never knock on doors. Rule number two, whatever you do, is never, ever go to the front door at one of these big houses, always the back. Be invisible. Remember what we said about being a butterfly? Flit about, never stay in one place too long. And rule number three, my darling Meg, is that you're going to need to develop a strong pair of lungs.'

'What for, Dad?' she asked.

'There's only one way you can let people know you've come calling for rags. You've got to make yourself heard, you've got to shout, Meg, shout. Just listen to this . . .'

Meg watched as he stood up on the cart while Stella kept

moving slowly forward. He cupped one hand around his mouth.

'Any old rags!' he shouted, as loud as could be. Then he turned his head to the right and shouted again. 'Any old rags!' before sinking back down into his seat, the exertion of the cry bringing on his cough again.

'Now you try,' he said once the coughing subsided.

Meg stood and put her hand to the side of her mouth as she'd seen her dad do. But even though she called out as loudly as she could, her voice didn't carry like his.

'Try again,' Ernie said, still holding his chest.

'Any old rags!' Meg shouted, louder this time, she hoped. 'Any old rags!'

'You'll get there.' Ernie smiled. 'You just need to practise, that's all.' He glanced up at a first-floor window at Ryhope Hall. 'Come on,' he said. 'We've been given the nod.'

'What do you mean?' Meg asked, sitting back down on the cart.

Ernie pointed to the big house. 'See that window up there? If the maids or the gardeners have got any old rags they want rid of, that's where they'll give you the signal from. If no one comes to the window when you call, that means there's nothing for you.' He paused while he took the reins from Meg and pulled them to make a right turn. 'Now we can go around to the back of the hall to pick up what they've got.'

'But how do we pay them for it, Dad?'

Ernie tapped the side of his nose. 'We don't, lass. That's the beauty of it. They get rid of stuff they don't want and we take it away.' He leaned in conspiratorially and whispered, 'And the best bit of all? We get to sell it and make ourselves rich.'

'You mean we don't pay them at all?'

Ernie shook his head. 'Some of the tatters in the town—' he began.

'What's a tatter?'

'A tatter? Why, it's you, it's me. It's a rag-and-bone man, collecting tats and scraps.'

'Are there any rag-and-bone women, Dad?' Meg asked, excited.

Ernie thought for a few seconds. 'There's one or two, or at least there used to be, before the war. But you, Meg, with your looks, you'll be the queen of them all.'

Meg smiled up at him, wishing he could always be like this.

'Anyway, some of the tatters in the town give out wooden pegs in exchange for rags. Wooden pegs for washing day like those your mam's got. And if there are children in the house who bring out the rags, some of them offer balloons in exchange, even goldfish I've heard.'

Meg's eyes widened. 'Goldfish? Where do they get them from? Not from round here in the sea?'

Ernie laughed. 'No, lass. There's a fella down the docks used to sell them. It's been a long time since I've been down there, but if he's still there we'll meet him when we go to the market today.'

He pulled Stella to a stop at the back gate of Ryhope Hall and got down from the cart. He held out his hand to Meg, but she managed to jump off on her own.

'See, you're a natural!' Ernie smiled.

Meg couldn't help but stare at the back door of the hall. It was very grand, she thought, far bigger, wider and fancier than any door she'd seen on a colliery house, front or back. Not that their own front door was ever used; everyone came and went into their cottages through the back doors in their yards. There was a saying in Tunstall Street that only twice in your life did you leave your house through the front door. The first was on your wedding day, when you were on your way to St Paul's church, and the second was when you were being carried out in a box, heading to the same destination.

The back door opened and Meg was stunned to see a familiar face.

'Evelyn!' she cried. 'I didn't know you worked here!'

'I've just started today,' Evelyn replied, smiling. 'I'm helping them prepare for a big party tonight before the Peace Parade tomorrow.' She glanced at the horse and cart. 'What's this then, what are you up to?'

'Dad's showing me how to be a tatter,' Meg said.

Evelyn screwed up her nose. 'A what?'

'I'm collecting stuff nobody wants any more and selling it on the market.'

'Not just the market, Meg,' Ernie added. 'We'll be selling to the paper mill too.'

'Is this your job now, then?' Evelyn asked. 'I thought you were looking after the house for your mam.'

Meg shrugged. 'I want to work with Dad and Stella now.'

Evelyn pulled at the heavy blue skirt of the pinny she was wearing. 'Like my new outfit?' she said, giving a twirl. As she turned, Meg saw that her long brown hair had been pinned up into a small white hat. She looked older somehow, in her working clothes, older and more sensible. No longer was she the girl that Meg used to play with in the back lane when they were children. Evelyn was a young woman now.

Meg looked up at the high walls and windows of Ryhope Hall. 'Are they treating you all right in here?' she asked.

Evelyn was about to say something but thought better of it and just nodded her head.

Meg reached out to her friend and took hold of her hand. 'You be sure to let me know if anything's not right here, okay?'

'Are you two going to stand here chatting all day?' Ernie asked impatiently. 'There's work to be done.'

'Sorry, Mr Sutcliffe,' said Evelyn. She turned and picked up a small pile of linen and passed it to Meg.

'Upstairs says you can have these; we don't need them any more.'

Meg took the items in her arms. 'What's it like then? Upstairs?' she asked.

'Cold mainly,' Evelyn replied. 'There's a coal fire in each room, but not even that will heat all the way up to the ceiling. But oh, Meg, the food, you should see it. The party tonight, there are hams a size that I've never seen before. And the fruit, the colours on it, it's come all the way from the docks at South Shields. And as for the wine and the fancy crystal glasses—'

'Evelyn Wilson!' a voice barked from the darkness of the passageway behind her.

Evelyn stood to attention in silence before slowly turning around. Meg saw the stern face of a stout middle-aged woman, lips pursed, ready to unleash her anger on the nearest person to her.

'You, girl,' she said to Meg. 'What's your business here?'

Ernie stepped forward, but it was Meg who spoke first.

'We're collecting rags from your maid and we were just about to leave.'

'Be gone with you then,' the woman said. 'And take your filthy animal with you.'

'Our horse isn't filthy!' Meg cried.

'I wasn't talking about the horse, although I am quite sure it must carry every parasite known to man, and some that man has not yet become aware of.' The woman pointed behind Meg. 'I'm talking about your dog there, that mangy beast of a thing. Get it away from the gardens now.'

'But that's not our dog . . .' Meg protested.

'Come on, Meg,' Ernie said, walking back to the cart.

Meg turned to leave. 'Bye, Evelyn . . .' she began, but the door had already been slammed in Meg's face.

As she walked away, she heard the woman shouting and Evelyn beginning to cry. She marched back up the path and banged with her fist on the door, determined to give her friend the help she needed. But her knocking went unheeded and she returned reluctantly to the cart. The dog that had followed them all day sat gazing up from the pavement with a hopeless expression on its skinny face.

'It's a persistent little brute, I'll give it that,' Ernie said thoughtfully.

He jumped down from the cart. The dog didn't move an inch.

'And it's not flighty, see?' he told Meg. 'You could do a lot worse than have a dog like this with you on the cart.'

'As a companion?' Meg asked.

'As protection,' Ernie replied. 'You'll see things doing this job, Meg. You'll see things and you'll hear things and you'll get a glimpse behind the doors at all sort of places, rich and poor. And not all of what you'll see you'll like. But pay no mind to any of it, you hear?'

Meg nodded.

'Your job is to collect the rags, put them on the cart and sell them. Got it?'

Meg twisted round to see if she could make out Evelyn at any of the windows of Ryhope Hall, but she was nowhere to be seen.

'Got it?' Ernie repeated.

Meg nodded again. Ernie reached down towards the dog and it allowed itself to be lifted on to the back of the cart. It licked Ernie's hand, then pushed its nose into Meg's back.

'Right then,' said Meg, taking the reins in her hands to get Stella moving again. 'I'm ready to start work.'

Chapter Three

Peace

'Why do they call them rag-and-bone men, Dad?' Meg wanted to know. 'I mean . . . there are rags here that you say we can sell on the market, but what about the bones?'

Meg allowed Stella to keep moving forward, the reins in her hand, as another coughing fit shook her dad. This time he didn't even try to disguise the blood that he was spitting to the street as he knew Meg had already become aware of what his body was trying to rid him of.

'Say nothing to your mam about this, right?' he said once his chest stopped heaving.

Meg nodded and they carried on in silence for a few minutes, heading towards the beach road. As they drew closer to the sea, she could see the iron bridge high above the railway lines. The tracks ran along the cliffs all the way from Seaham to Sunderland, cutting through Ryhope behind the Albion Inn. At the sight of the bridge, Stella's speed picked up and she turned right before Meg could stop her.

'Whoa there!' she called, slowing the horse down. 'What's your hurry, Stella?'

But it all made sense as soon as they saw where Stella was headed. Just at the entrance to Ryhope East railway station stood the Railway Inn. The pub had always been a firm favourite of Davey Scott's when he was selling fruit and veg from the cart.

'That Davey lad's taken you here more than a few times when he was out with his fruit and veg,' Ernie chuckled, then turned to Meg. 'This horse knows its way around Ryhope better than I thought.'

Meg pulled Stella to a halt outside the pub.

'Come on then,' Ernie said. 'You were asking about bones. Let's go and see if John Harvey's inside, and he can tell you all about them.'

Meg looked at the worn door of the mucky limewashed pub. 'But I can't go in there, Dad. I'm not allowed,' she said, not moving from the cart.

'You can,' Ernie said decisively. 'And you will. You're with me, so you've nothing to worry about. And you're going to have to get used to going into places like this and dealing with people like John if you want to make any money.'

From her seat high up on the cart, Meg peered down through one of the big windows of the pub and saw heads turn towards her. She placed the pile of linen from Evelyn in the back of the cart next to the sleeping dog and jumped down, following her dad into the darkness of the inn. Her stomach heaved as the thick smell of beer and tobacco hit her with a force she wasn't ready for. Once inside, the noise of men's laughter and jeers made her stick close to her dad's side. Ernie walked straight to the small bar, where a woman with a mass of fair hair piled up on her head was working a cloth around an earthenware jug.

'John Harvey in?' he asked her.

The woman stopped what she was doing and stood stock still. 'John Harvey?' she said sharply. 'He hasn't been in here for years.'

'Do you know where I'll find him?' Ernie asked.

'I know exactly where you'll find him,' she replied. 'Six feet under in the cemetery up the lane. He died in a pit accident a couple of years ago.'

Ernie dropped his head and took a deep breath. 'I'm sorry, love,' he told her. 'I've been away . . .'

'Who's come looking for John?' a voice behind them demanded.

Meg swung round and saw a thickset man with a round, jolly face, a flat cap on his large head. She also noticed that the checked waistcoat he was wearing, stretched across his fat stomach, was missing most of its buttons.

Ernie turned slowly, and when he saw who it was, stuck out his hand in greeting.

'Big Pete!' he cried.

'It's you, Ernie lad!' Pete said, taking both of Ernie's hands in his own. 'I'd heard you were home. Here, let me buy you a drink.'

Ernie glanced at Meg. 'I'm not stopping. I've got things I need to get done today.'

'You've got to stay and have a pint,' Pete pleaded. 'Can these things you've got to do not wait until tomorrow?'

Ernie shook his head. 'You know me, Pete. If I could, I would. Another time, though, right? Listen . . . who's buying the bones now that John Harvey's gone?'

'It's me now, Ernie. But what do you want to know that

for? Man, you're not going back on the rag-and-bone, are you? A good soldier like you coming back home needs a decent job.'

'Not just me, Pete. It's our Meg here. She's taking it on too.'

Big Pete turned to Meg. 'A lass?' he cried, eyeing her up and down and taking in the size and shape of her. 'Best of luck to you, pet. You're going to need it.'

Meg pushed her feet forward in her boots and clasped her hands in front of her skirts. She looked up into Big Pete's friendly, open face.

'You're buying the bones now, Pete?' she asked, her gaze unwavering.

Pete looked at Ernie and smiled. 'She's got your spirit, I'll give her that. And she's got her mother's good looks, that's for sure too.' He turned back to Meg. 'Yes, pet. I'll buy any bones from you that you bring in here. You can find me in here most days, except for Sunday, when the wife drags me to church. And if I'm not in here, I'll be down at the Albion. Just ask for Big Pete, everyone knows me. And your dad knows I'll give you a good price.'

'Anything else you want, Pete, apart from the bones?' Ernie asked.

'Wood's always good, even driftwood off the beach. I can always do a bit of trade with wood. Oh, and sea coal, of course.'

Ernie nodded. 'Of course.'

Big Pete removed his cap and lowered his head. 'It'll be a pleasure doing business with you, Meg,' he said, giving a friendly wink.

Meg stuck out her hand as she'd seen her dad do earlier

and shook Big Pete's hand a little more forcefully than he was expecting.

'Keep that strength in your handshake, lass, if you want to show the fellas around here you mean business,' he said.

'When she comes in here selling, you'll keep an eye on her?' Ernie asked. It wasn't so much a question as a statement of fact.

Pete put his cap back on before he replied. 'Course I will. You know that. Now, are you sure I can't buy you an ale while you're here?'

Ernie shook his head and led Meg away from the smoke and noise of the dark pub. She emerged blinking into the light and the two of them clambered back on the cart.

'When folk give you bones they want rid of, Meg, they'll be beef or mutton bones from the boiled dinners that some of them have round here, them that can afford them anyway. Bring them down here for Big Pete and he'll sell them to the knacker's yard down the docks and give you a cut of the price.'

Meg tucked her skirts under her again as Stella set off at a slow trot. They left the railway station and the noisy pub behind. As the cart wheels trundled across the cobbles, the dog let out a soft whine.

'Mam's going to kill us when we take that dog home, you know,' Meg said. 'She can barely afford to feed me and Tommy, never mind a dog.'

'You just leave Mam to me,' Ernie said. 'You'll have money coming in soon enough from selling clothes on the market, rags to the paper mill and bones to Big Pete. And you've got Stella's manure money from Davey Scott too.' He smiled at her. 'You'll be living the life, Meg.'

With Ernie guiding her, Meg directed Stella away from

the cobbled street and on to the main road leading to Sunderland. For a long while they sat in silence. The road ran parallel to the railway line as they travelled along. On their right-hand side were the cliffs and the grey North Sea. To their left was Ryhope itself, with the spire of St Paul's church and the tall, thin chimney of the water pumping station puncturing the dirty sky above.

'You'll keep your work to the daytime, Meg,' Ernie said at last. 'No going out after dark. And you'll need to wrap up for the weather and the rain. Not every day's going to be as warm and dry as today. You'll take care of yourself, you hear me?'

Meg looked at him, puzzled. 'But we're going to be doing this together, aren't we? We'll be taking care of each other.'

Ernie chose not to reply, for he knew there was nothing he could say that Meg would want to hear. From the corner of his eye he could see that Meg kept glancing at him, expecting him to say something, expecting him to explain himself.

'Aye, we'll take care of each other, lass,' he said finally, staring ahead at the road. But his words disturbed Meg, for he had spoken them without feeling, without giving her the reassurance she needed.

They rode on in silence until they reached a flat red-brick building with a tall chimney at either end.

'This is the paper mill,' Ernie explained. 'See that door there? That's where you take the rags you collect, but only the good stuff, the linens and cottons. And if you separate them into colours first, whites and browns, they'll thank you for it too. Come on,' he said, hopping off the cart. 'Let's go and see if Ruth still works here, or if she's gone the way of John Harvey and passed on while I've been away.'

Fortunately for Ernie and Meg, Ruth was very much still there working at the paper mill, and as large as life as ever. Meg stuck out her hand for her to shake, and although the woman looked surprised by the young girl's action, she returned the handshake with a smile.

'Ruth, this is my daughter, Meg,' Ernie said proudly. 'I'm showing her the ropes; she'll be helping me out on the rag-and-bone.'

'She's never your daughter,' Ruth laughed. 'She's far too bonny for that! She's clearly got her mother's looks, because thankfully she hasn't taken after you, Ernie.'

'Just you make sure you give her your best price,' Ernie warned her. 'I know what you girls can be like here, cutting corners where you can and keeping the pennies for yourself.'

Meg ran back to the cart, leaving her dad talking business with Ruth at the back of the mill. She picked up the pile of linens that Evelyn had given her earlier, but when she turned to head back, she saw Ernie on his knees on the dusty ground, fighting for breath. She flew to his side and Ruth bent down to attend to him too, the pair of them helping him stand as his body shook with every cough.

'Home . . .' he wheezed when at last he could speak.

Ruth tried to help Meg get him up on to the cart but it wasn't without difficulty, as Ernie kept insisting that he didn't need any help. Finally he relented and let the women guide him into his seat. The two of them rode home slowly, with Meg's hands guiding Stella along the road back to Ryhope. As they neared the village, she glanced at her dad's worn face, his body lost inside the army coat that he wore. When the first houses came into view, she slowed Stella down and cupped her hand around her mouth.

'Any old rags!' she shouted. 'Any old rags!'

The noise of her cry started the dog barking from the back of the cart, joining in with the call.

'You'll have to do it louder than that, Meg,' Ernie told her. 'You're here to make a living, not get a sore throat.'

'Any old rags!' she cried again, louder still, competing with the barking of the dog.

As Stella led the cart around the village green, the bells of St Paul's began to chime the hour, ringing out over and over, long and loud across the village and halfway up the colliery too. Meg looked at her dad and the two of them exchanged a smile, both knowing what she needed to do.

'Where am I going to get a bell from, Dad?' she asked. 'I could ring it and shout at the same time and then they'll hear me when I come calling.'

Ernie laughed and turned round to where the skinny white dog was standing now, charged up after barking with Meg. He scratched the animal behind its ear and it nuzzled into his hand.

'We'll get you a bell, pet. There's bound to be someone in Ryhope knows where to get one. And with your bell ringing, your dog barking and you shouting, I think they'll hear you well enough.'

Ernie smiled and pointed to the old water trough at the edge of the village green, and Meg let Stella walk forward to take a cooling drink. Then they made their way back up the bank to the back of Davey Scott's house, where Ernie showed Meg how to settle Stella into the makeshift stable that had become the horse's home.

'Will we leave the dog here too, Dad?' she asked once Stella was feeding. Ernie thought about it for a second before he replied.

'No,' he said, shaking his head. 'It'll come home with us

and live in the yard. You'll need to get to know it, Meg, make sure it understands you're the boss.'

'Will we give it a name?' she asked.

'You choose. It's yours from now on,' he replied. He stood behind the dog and lifted its front paws from the ground, exposing its stomach and back legs. 'And it's a he, by the way.'

Meg giggled. Ernie got down on his knees, feeling the dog's legs and hindquarters. The animal sat quiet and still as he lifted its ears to check for infection.

'Looks a decent dog, Meg,' he said finally, standing. 'Must be half Dalmatian, that'd account for the black spots, although I'm not sure what the other half might be.'

'I'll call it Spot,' Meg decided.

'Come on, lass,' said Ernie, coughing again. 'We need to get home.'

The two of them walked back to Tunstall Street with Spot following behind. When they reached the back lane, Spot hung back until Meg slapped her hand to her side and encouraged the dog to follow her into the yard. But when she reached the kitchen door, she turned and put her hand in front of the dog. 'No,' she said firmly, and Spot sat obediently in the yard.

When Meg followed her dad into the kitchen, she saw her mam sitting in her chair by the window, knitting. Next to her was Hetty, sitting on the cracket stool by the fire, blue wool wrapped around her hands, which were held upright, palms together. As Mam knitted, Hetty turned her hands towards the needles, allowing the wool to flow. Tucked behind one of Hetty's ears, sticking out of the messy pile of hair on the top of her head, was one of Mam's knitting needles. The sight of it made Meg smile. It seemed that Hetty always had something stuck in her hair, whether it was a needle, a pencil or a fork; something useful, just in case.

Meg stood in the kitchen doorway, doing her best to shield the dog from her mam's eyes until her dad had the chance to explain it. But she should have known better, because Mam never missed a thing.

'Hetty, pet!' Ernie said, bending down and kissing Hetty on the cheek. He noticed the lines etched on her face, lines that hadn't been there when he'd last seen her over four years ago. 'I was awful sorry to hear about Philip. He was a good lad, one of the best.'

'Been a long time, Ernie,' Hetty replied, barely glancing up, the subject of her dead son still too raw for her to address in passing conversation. She concentrated on the wool. 'You well?'

Ernie and Sally exchanged a quick glance.

'Aye,' was all he replied.

'Marching in the Peace Parade tomorrow?' she asked.

'Whole village is turning out for it, I hear,' Ernie said.

'And your Tommy's starting work at the pit the day after, Sally's just been telling me.'

Ernie cleared his throat. 'Sally, love—' he began.

'Oh! I always know there's something up when he calls me "Sally, love"!' she said.

The two women laughed and Sally continued with her knitting, her expert fingers flying without her even having to look at her work. She turned her face towards Ernie and waited for him to explain away the dog at the back door that she knew he thought she hadn't yet seen.

'Sally, love, I was thinking—'

She cut him short. 'You were thinking, were you? And

were you thinking about bringing home a scabby stray dog that'll need feeding and cleaning up after?'

'Sally—'

'Don't, Ernie,' Sally said. 'We can barely make ends meet as it is, never mind find the money to feed a bloody dog.'

'Meg will need a bit of protection when she's out on the cart,' Ernie explained.

'I've called him Spot,' Meg chipped in from the doorway, and at the sound of her voice, the dog walked in from the yard to stand by her side. 'I'll look after him, Mam,' she said. 'I promise.'

All eyes turned towards Spot.

'I can send up food slops from the Albion,' Hetty offered. 'They usually go to the pigs at High Farm, but I'm sure we can spare some for the dog.'

Sally sighed deeply. She really didn't want to start a fight over the dog, as she guessed it would be one she would lose, not just with Ernie but with Meg too. And Tommy had always wanted a dog, ever since he'd been little, and now that he was starting work, the animal might walk with him to the pit and back, a bit of protection for him as well as Meg.

'All right, it can stay,' she said. 'But I'm not spending any money on it, got it? If you want to keep it, you feed it from your earnings, Meg.'

She returned her concentration to her knitting, missing the smile exchanged between Ernie and Meg.

On the morning of the Peace Parade, all of Tunstall Street was awake early. All, that is, apart from Ernie Sutcliffe. Sally had got up to make an early start on baking the day's stottie bread and left him sleeping. She didn't want to waste a minute of the warm summer day. Tommy hadn't slept well; he was too excited for the parade, bursting with pride to see his dad marching later. He was also looking forward to spending the day with his friends in the village in their fancy dress costumes on the floats. And Meg was up early too, eager to see Spot and feed Stella before the parade began. The Sutcliffes' next-door neighbours Bob and Lil Mahone were already shouting at each other, their swearing and yelling easily heard through the too-thin walls. It was at times like this that Meg was glad they lived at the end of the street, so that they had only one set of noisy neighbours to overhear. Sometimes it seemed to her that all the residents of Tunstall Street ever did was fight.

'Can I take a bit of bread for Spot, Mam?' she asked when the stottie bread was out of the oven, cooling on the kitchen windowsill.

'If your lazy beggar of a father doesn't get up soon, you can give his portion to the dog,' Sally huffed. 'He didn't come in until the early hours of the morning again. I don't suppose he said anything to you about where he was off to, did he?'

Meg shook her head.

'And I don't know where he's getting the money to buy beer from,' Sally continued. 'Unless it's his friends treating him after hours with a lock-in at the Blue Bell. Anyway, he's going to have to get up soon. He's due at St Paul's to meet the regiment, and in full uniform too, for the march.'

Sally pushed loose strands of her long fair hair behind her ears and strode towards the bottom of the stairs.

'Ernie!' she yelled. 'Are you up yet?'

After a few seconds of silence, there were three knocks from the bedroom floor above.

'At least he's stirring,' she sighed. 'Although I dread to think what his hangover's going to be like.'

She tore off a chunk from one of the cooling flatbreads and handed it to Meg. 'Here, make sure you eat most of it before you give the remains to the dog.'

'Thanks, Mam,' said Meg.

'I see it slept in here last night. I told you, I don't want it sleeping in the house. Keep it in the yard, I said.'

'Dad must have let it in when he came home from the pub,' Meg replied, feeding bread to Spot.

'Just look at the state of the thing!' Sally sighed. 'It's as soft as muck, that animal.'

She moved to the stairs again and shouted up once more for Ernie. In reply this time there was just one thump from the bedroom floor.

'Here, Meg,' Sally said, handing her daughter a knitted blue flower. 'Pin this in your hair today; you'll look a treat at the parade. I've knitted Tommy a blue badge too. He's already gone down to the village to help them set up the floats.'

Their conversation was halted by the sound of Ernie's coughing from the bedroom above, and after a few minutes they heard his heavy footsteps coming slowly down the stairs.

'You two get yourselves to the parade,' he said when he entered the kitchen. 'I'll walk on behind you to meet the regiment, and I'll see you when we march past.'

'You want some breakfast?' Sally asked, but Ernie shook his head.

'Go on, both of you,' he said, almost in a whisper.

'Will you wave, Dad, when you march past?' Meg asked.

'I'll wave,' he replied, smiling at his daughter.

Sally ushered Meg out of the kitchen and Spot followed. As they were heading into the back yard, Ernie said: 'Got you a bell, Meg.'

Meg turned. 'Who from, Dad?'

Ernie looked sheepishly at Sally before he gave his reply. 'Best not to ask, pet. Let's just say that the next time they do an inventory at the Co-op, they might find their stock a little light.'

'Out! Now!' Sally cried to Meg before turning back to Ernie with her face full of fury.

'You should be ashamed of yourself, Ernie Sutcliffe!' she spat at him. 'You were a thief and a drunkard before you went away to war and you've come home still a thief and a drunkard! You're not fit to march with the army today. You're not fit for anything.'

And with that, she was gone, striding out along the back lane, hoping that the warmth of the sun on her face would dry her tears as they started to fall.

Meg had never seen Ryhope looking so pretty. All the shops along the colliery had triangles of red, white and blue cloth strung outside their windows in preparation for the parade. The Co-op store looked magnificent, the outside decorated with bunting and flags, and the pubs opposite the pit had balloons flying too. There was excitement in the air and the pavements were bustling as Meg and Sally walked up the hill to the Colliery Inn, where the parade was due to start. Even so early in the morning, the doors to every pub were flung open, and drinking had already started.

From outside the Colliery Inn, Meg and Sally could see through the coal dust belching from the pit all the way down the bank to the village, and out to the sea beyond.

With the sun in the sky, there was even a sparkle of blue on the water that fringed Ryhope's smoke-begrimed cottages and narrow, straggling streets. Meg smiled when she saw Tommy and Adam walking towards her, Tommy with his knitted badge pinned to his flat cap.

'Dad's going to wave as he marches past,' she beamed as the boys drew near.

'Is he here yet?' asked Tommy, but Meg shook her head.

'Mrs Sutcliffe, can I buy you a beer to celebrate the day?' Adam asked Sally, nodding his head towards the Colliery Inn.

'Go on then, lad. Just a small one.'

'Can I have one, Mam?' Tommy asked with a cheeky grin on his face.

'You'll have no such thing!' Sally replied. 'The last thing I want is you getting a taste for drink in the same way as your dad.'

Adam disappeared into the throng of the busy pub and emerged some time later with the glasses of beer. When Sally had taken her glass and thanked him, she turned to watch the march as it prepared to set off. Behind her, Adam passed his glass to Tommy, who took a mouthful of beer. He screwed his face up as he handed it back.

'That's horrible!' he said.

Adam laughed. 'See! And you think I enjoy myself when I'm out at the pub!'

'I don't know how you can drink it,' Tommy said, shaking his head.

'Lads!' shouted Sally, turning to look at them. 'Come through to the front; the parade's just about to begin.'

From round the back of the Colliery Inn came the first horse-drawn floats, and a huge cheer went up from the packed pavements. The floats were decorated with ribbons and bunting in the same way as the shops and pubs, and on each were children from the school in fancy dress. There were cowboys and Indians, nurses, even young soldiers holding rifles made from cardboard boxes donated by the Co-op. Spectators along the route clapped and cheered as each float went past. Tommy inched his way right to the edge of the pavement and stood in front of his mam, who cradled him to her with an arm around his shoulders. Adam made his way next to Meg, the two of them standing tight together in the squash of people peering to watch the parade.

After the children's floats had gone by and were making their way down the bank, past the pit and the church and into the village, then came the brass bands. Held by two soldiers in uniform, a banner flew high, and Meg could see the words *Great War Ryhope Branch* on it as it fluttered in the wind. A loud banging noise started up and a band of drummers marched by, the crowd now clapping and swaying in time to the music. Meg clapped along too to the stirring sounds of the cornets, trumpets and euphoniums. She clapped louder still when all of those around her let out a huge cheer, the loudest one so far, and the soldiers in uniform began to parade past. Left, right, left, right, they marched in time to the music as the people of Ryhope applauded the boys who had come home safe from the war.

As Sally scanned the soldiers, searching for sight of Ernie, she thought of Hetty, who would have given the world to have her son Philip marching today. And at the end of the parade, after the soldiers had passed, was a flag-covered coffin on a cart pulled by two sturdy black horses, a reminder of all of those who hadn't returned home.

'Where is he, Mam? Can you see him?' Meg asked, scanning the ranks of soldiers for her dad.

As they marched past in identical uniforms with their caps pulled down over their eyes, it was hard to make out who was who at first. Sally looked at each line of men as they walked past in step. She knew she'd recognise Ernie the minute she saw him, the way he swung his arms and the way he held his head. But no matter how hard she looked, she soon began to realise that Ernie wasn't there. Her hand flew to her stomach as the truth hit her like a punch. She wasn't able to speak at first to answer Tommy's questions.

'Where's Dad, Mam?' he kept demanding. 'Where is he?'

'I'll kill him!' Sally hissed under her breath. 'I'll flaming kill him!' She handed her glass of ale to a man behind her. 'Here, take this,' she said. 'Tommy, Meg, come with me. Adam, you go back into the Colliery Inn and see if he's there. I'll try the Forester's Arms, and then every pub in Ryhope down to the Albion Inn until we find him. And God help him when I get my hands on him . . .'

Meg and Tommy followed their mam as she pushed her way through the crowds. At every pub Sally went into, she called Ernie's name, asking if anyone knew where he was. But it was all to no avail. No one had seen him since the lock-in at the Blue Bell the night before, when by all accounts he'd been so drunk he was up on his feet singing the songs he used to sing in the war.

'I'm going to look for him at home,' she told Meg and Tommy. 'You two stay at the parade with Adam.'

'No,' said Meg firmly. 'I'm coming with you.'

Sally crossed the road, pushing through the marching band, blinded by fury, desperate to let Ernie know exactly what she thought of him, letting the family down on today of all days. And it wasn't just his family either, but the whole of Ryhope and his regiment too.

Away from the crowded parade, there was a peace and quiet to the back lane of Tunstall Street. With Meg running to keep up with her, Sally stormed into the yard, pushing the gate so that it would swing loudly enough to wake Ernie from his hangover upstairs. The noise startled Spot, who barked in surprise from his new home in the yard. Sally pushed open the back door. There was no sign of Ernie in the kitchen, no sign even that he'd eaten any of the bread she'd baked earlier. He wasn't in the front room either. She barged up the stairs, holding on to the handrail, Spot bounding after her, caught up in the chase.

'Ernie Sutcliffe!' she yelled from the bedroom doorway when she saw the rounded lump under the bedclothes. There was no response. She strode towards him, intent on waking her husband from his beer-induced coma.

'Ernie!' she yelled again, shaking his shoulder under the blanket. But still there was nothing: no sound, no movement, not even a hung-over groan. It took her a few seconds to realise what had happened. Ernie Sutcliffe was stone-cold dead.

'Fetch Hetty!' she cried to Meg, who was standing at the bedroom door. 'And bring the vicar too.'

In shock, Meg forced herself to turn. She was about to head down the stairs when she spotted three empty ale bottles on the floor at the bottom of the bed. She glanced quickly at her mam, who was bent over her dad's body, then picked up the bottles, determined to get rid of them before Mam found out they were there.

She fled from the house, with Spot barking and running behind her. All the way down the colliery they ran, through the crowds watching the parade, past the bands and the marching and the children on floats. Everything went by in a blur, and it was only when she reached the gates of St Paul's that she allowed herself to stop and to breathe. She saw the vicar standing at the church door beside some of the villagers who had chosen it as their viewing point to watch the parade.

'Reverend Daye,' she said, gasping for breath. 'Please come, please. Mam needs you . . . It's Dad, he's . . .'

'Drunk?' a voice piped up from behind the vicar, but Meg paid it no heed.

'He's dead. Please come. Quickly.'

The vicar held Meg's hands in his own large, cool hands providing a calm that she welcomed. 'My dear child,' he said.

As the Reverend Daye turned to enter the church, pick up his bible and head to Tunstall Street, Meg continued onwards to the village. At the Albion Inn, she had to squeeze through the packed pub to reach the bar and yell to get Hetty's attention.

'What on earth is it now?' Jack Burdon demanded when he saw her at the bar talking to Hetty. But Hetty didn't reply. Without even throwing down her glass cloth or taking off her pinny, she took Meg's hand and left the pub.

The vicar arrived quickly, bringing soothing words, the words Sally knew she needed to hear. The last time she and Ernie had set foot inside St Paul's had been on Tommy's christening day, and she was grateful to him for not mentioning her absence from his flock. Hetty arrived soon afterwards and Sally was glad to have her friend by her side as arrangements were made for Ernie's funeral.

Later, when the vicar had left, the three women sat in

silence in the kitchen. Finally Sally straightened in her chair.

'I shall be grieving for a week, for appearances' sake at least,' she told Hetty. 'I'll wear my black skirt and I'll close the curtains at the windows. I'll do what I need to, even if it's more than he deserved.'

'Now, Sally—' Hetty began.

'No, Hetty,' she said, determined. 'That man as good as deserted me and the bairns when he went off to war. You know he hardly kept in touch all the time he was away. And then he comes home after four years away – four years, Hetty – and is off drinking and roaming around the streets with the old horse and cart.' She decided not to mention the stolen bell for fear Hetty would make Meg return it to the Co-op. 'Well, as I say. I'll do the right thing, but nothing more.'

Hetty nodded. 'You'll be needing ham,' she said. 'I mean, for the funeral. You can't have a funeral without ham. I'll get some off the meat delivery cart that comes to the Albion. And you can have the wake at the Albion at no cost to you either.'

'What about Jack, what will he have to say about that?' Sally asked.

'Never mind Jack. I'll handle him,' Hetty replied. 'I dare say he'll rub his hands with glee at the thought of all the money he'll make from selling ale at the wake.'

Sally held her friend's hand. 'Thanks, love,' she said.

'And what about you, Meg?' Hetty asked. 'With your dad gone, will you be selling the horse now?'

Meg sat firmly in her chair with her hands in her lap and Spot by her side. She took a deep breath, raised her gaze to her mam and blinked back the tears that were threatening. Through all the years her dad had been away in the army, they'd rarely talked about him – she'd had Mam and Tommy and they just had to make the best of things and get along without him. But since he'd been back she'd fast become her daddy's girl, the pair of them as thick as thieves roaming the streets with Stella. There was no question about what she would do next; selling the horse was an option that she would never countenance. She shook her head.

'I'm going to do what Dad wanted me to do,' she said, then looked towards her mam. 'I can earn money, Mam, real money. I can buy Tommy some boots without holes in, and a new shawl for you.' Then, remembering her dad's words, she added: 'We'll live the life, Mam. We can save some of the money and rent a bigger house, a better house.'

'Oh, and where do you propose we go, Miss High and Mighty?' Sally smiled.

Meg shrugged. 'I don't know, but where there's money, there's a chance, isn't there? A chance to change things, make things better. And that's why I'm going to do what Dad wanted. I'm going out working on the cart.'

The day of Ernie Sutcliffe's funeral dawned under a coal-grey sky that didn't brighten all day. For the first time in her life that Meg could recall, their back door was locked. She followed her mam and Tommy as they prepared to leave the house the respectable way, through the front door. And as the three of them set off on the short walk to St Paul's, hidden in the shadows on the corner of Tunstall Street, the shady figure of Hawk Jackson watched on.

Chapter Four

Double Threat

In the weeks following Ernie's death, Meg steeled herself. She became determined to get out to work on the cart, knowing it was what her dad had wanted her to do. But she also felt, more surely than ever before, that it was what *she* wanted too.

As the weather began to cool towards autumn, she wrapped herself up in her dad's army coat to help keep her warm as she worked. The big brown coat with its enormous buttons was the only thing she had to remember him by. She would wear it with pride now, feeling the security of it around her. The coat had protected her dad during four years of conflict and now it would keep her safe as she worked on the cart. She snuggled down into it on days when the wind and rain did their worst, and the coat protected much of her, keeping her skirts dry. Spot was always at her side, another welcome reminder to Meg of her dad keeping her safe as she worked.

Out each day on the cart, Meg became more confident,

not just in handling Stella around the dingy streets, but also in her dealings with Ruth at the paper mill and with Big Pete who bought the bones. But there was still one place that she hadn't yet visited: the indoor market down by the docks. Her dad had told her many times that it was where she should be selling clothes and oddments, but as his death had come suddenly, there'd been no chance for him to take her there himself.

With the clang of the handbell and Spot barking along, she had no trouble making her presence known when she was out collecting rag and bone. She knew to look up at the windows of the big houses on Ryhope Green to see if a maid was waving to her, and she'd exchange their rags for the wooden clothes pegs she carried now. Often at Ryhope Hall it was Evelyn who came to the back door to hand over the rags. The two of them would whisper and laugh, sharing confidences at the back door until the housekeeper came to put an end to their chat, barking: 'Back to work, Evelyn Wilson!'

When the housekeeper had disappeared back inside the house, Meg whispered to her friend, 'Is she always such a dragon?'

'Oh, don't worry. Her bark is worse than her bite,' Evelyn replied. 'And I've figured out how to get her off my back now.' She glanced behind her to ensure that the housekeeper was out of earshot, then leaned close to Meg and whispered, 'I caught her dipping her hand into Cook's cake box in the kitchen when she thought no one was looking. I've promised her I'll keep quiet about it if she stops giving me such a hard time. She only does it because I'm the youngest and she thinks she can get away with it.'

Meg laughed. 'Well, don't let her get you down,' she replied.

Evelyn stifled a giggle before she turned and headed back inside to work.

On the rare occasion when Meg was given woollen clothes or blankets, she would take them home to Mam, who unpicked every stitch and knitted up the wool again. With Tommy now working at the surface of the pit, he welcomed the warmth of one of Mam's hand-knitted jumpers.

As Meg and Stella travelled the streets of Ryhope, Meg heard her dad's words at every turn. It was easy to conjure up his voice in her head, telling her to call out for rags. It was as if he was there with her, right next to her on the cart. She always worked in the daylight, as Dad had told her to do, and as soon as the darkness of the autumn afternoon fell, she headed home to stable Stella at the back of Davey Scott's house.

When Davey heard the cart wheels clatter across the cobbles at the back of his house, he leaned out into the yard over the kitchen half-door.

'How's it gone today, Meg?' he called out, watching her unbridle the horse.

Meg smiled. 'Good, thanks, Davey.'

'You been down the market?' he asked.

Meg bit her lip and took a few seconds before she replied. 'Not yet. But I will . . . I will.'

'Well, just watch what you're doing down there,' Davey warned. 'Listen, Gert's just put the kettle on the fire to boil for tea if you want a cuppa before you go.'

'Thanks, Davey. Tell her I can't stop. I want to get back home to Mam before it's dark. How's Gertie's leg now? If you need me to get more ointment from the doctor in the village, let me know. It's easy enough for me to call in any time for her.'

Davey smiled. 'You're a good one, Meg. I'll be sure to let her know. You would have thought all her years training as a nurse would have made her careful about resting that leg, but she won't sit still, she's always up and doing something.' He disappeared into the kitchen, closing the half-door behind him.

As Meg prepared Stella's bran mash, Spot helped himself to a cooling drink from the horse's water bucket. Once the food was ready, Stella nudged her head towards Meg and rested her chin on her shoulder.

'Good girl, Stella,' Meg said, stroking the horse's nose. Then gently she began to sing, the words coming to her with a warm memory of her dad, a memory strong enough to bring tears to her eyes.

'Stella, sweet Stella, what fella could want a finer horse?'

Spot glanced up and started to whine, joining in with the song. Meg sang it again, over and over, lost in the joy of the moment between the warmth of the horse's breath on her skin and her crazy dog trying to sing. She was so wrapped up in it all that she didn't notice a sound behind them, a sound that made Stella's ears flicker in slight consternation.

Once Stella had been fed and watered, Meg and Spot set off back to Tunstall Street. Meg knew that when she got home, she'd have to help Mam with her chores before tea. Tommy was working the day shift at the pit and was due home for his bath. It was Sally who would fetch and heat up the water to fill the tin bath. Then they would allow Tommy the privacy of the kitchen, where he'd have his bath in front of the fire, scraping off the black of the coal from his skin. Once he was done, the soapy water would be chucked for Meg to swill out the back yard. Only after the bath and the yard cleaning were done would the preparations for tea begin.

It was a routine that the Sutcliffes had settled into since Ernie died and Tommy had started at the pit. Sally always made sure that Tommy's bath was ready for him at the end of his shift, no matter what time of day or night he came home. And Meg turned over to her mam any cash that she'd made on the cart. Some days there was enough for the luxury of a fish supper for the three of them from the chippy by the cinema. But on other days she earned nothing at all – and today had been another nothing day.

As Meg turned the corner of the back lane at Tunstall Street, the smell of baked fish and freshly cooked bread coming from Mam's kitchen made her realise how hungry she was. But as she entered the back yard, she heard raised voices within.

'Leave her alone!' a voice roared. 'Get off her!'

It was Tommy. Meg flew to the kitchen door.

'Or what? What are you going to do about it?' replied a voice that Meg knew only too well.

'Hey! What's going on?' she cried, storming into the kitchen.

Hawk Jackson turned towards her.

'What's happening?' Meg demanded. 'Mam?'

Sally was slumped in her chair with the front of her pinafore torn. The tin bath lay on the floor by the fire, empty.

'I've just come in,' Tommy said, gasping for breath, beads of sweat appearing on his coal-blackened forehead, 'and I found him here. Meg, he was . . . he was hurting Mam.'

'Get out, Hawk,' Sally hissed. 'Get out of my house and never come calling again.'

Hawk laughed. 'I'll come calling any time I like, Sally Sutcliffe, and don't you forget it. I own this house and you owe me the rent.'

'She said get out!' Tommy yelled, but Hawk didn't budge.

A low growl started up in Spot's throat.

'And you can shut that mutt up for a start!' Hawk said to Meg. 'You must be making a pretty penny on the rag and bone, young 'un. If your mam's not paying the rent, maybe I should come and collect it from you and you can pay me in kind. Much as I like my rent money, I always enjoy a bit of kind.'

He blew a kiss towards her and then began to mimic the song she'd been singing earlier outside Davey Scott's house.

'*Meg, my sweet Meg now, don't make a fella beg now.*'

Sally launched herself from her chair and threw herself at him, her fists pummelling hard against his thick black coat. 'Get out, you bastard! Get out of my house now!'

'Not without my money,' Hawk growled, standing firm.

Tommy moved to stand between his mam and Hawk. 'You heard what she said. Get out!'

Hawk bent to Tommy's height and stared straight at him, right in the eyes. 'Make me,' he whispered.

Tommy's breathing turned shallow, throaty and noisy like a bull getting ready to fight. The whites of his eyes flashed with anger from his coal-black face. His hands flew out and his feet kicked but he was no match for Hawk

Jackson, who stopped every punch with one of his own. He held Tommy's hands tight in his big callused fists.

'Now you just listen to me,' he said, turning to Sally, 'the lot of you—'

'No, Hawk!' Meg spoke from behind him. 'You're going to listen to me!'

Hawk dropped Tommy's hands and turned to face her. She was holding Mam's knitting needles tight with both hands, the pointed metal just inches from Hawk's cheek.

'God help me, I'll shove these right into your fat face if you don't leave us alone,' she said, fighting tears.

Hawk roared with laughter. 'What are you going to do, Meg? Knit me to death?'

He took a swipe at her arm and the needles went flying across the kitchen, clattering to the stone floor. Tommy and Meg both ran at him at the same time, determined to push him out of the house, but it was Spot who reached him first.

'Get it off! Get that bloody dog off my leg!' Hawk yelped as Spot held on with his powerful jaws.

'Spot! Leave!' Meg called, and the dog obeyed immediately.

Hawk Jackson took a few seconds to compose himself and stand up straight.

'You've not heard the last of this,' he growled before he turned and left the kitchen. Spot chased him, jumping and barking, until Hawk was out of sight.

'Did you hear that, Bob?' Lil whispered.

Bob looked up from his newspaper but said nothing in reply.

'You must have heard it,' Lil continued. 'All that yelling and fighting next door. It sounded like Hawk Jackson, and you know what a nasty piece of work he can be. Everyone knows what he's like. We should go and see—'

'We'll do no such thing,' Bob said sternly. 'You know as well as I do that what goes on behind closed doors is no bugger else's business. I've told you before – no good will ever come out of gossip. And maybe if you paid less attention to your neighbours and more to your husband, then you and me wouldn't end up arguing so flaming much!'

Lil sighed deeply. She knew she had a reputation as a gossip – always wanting to know what was going on, and sticking her nose in where it wasn't wanted. But this was different. She tried again. 'But Bob—'

'No, Lil,' Bob said, taking up his newspaper again. 'We're not getting involved and that's that.'

Meg flew straight to her mam's side, knelt down by her chair and took her hands in her own. Tommy stood in front of them both.

'What happened, Mam?' Meg asked.

Sally quickly glanced at Tommy. 'You arrived home at just the right time, son, and I'll always thank you for that.'

'Is it true, Mam?' Meg asked. 'Are we behind in the rent?'

Sally slowly nodded her head. 'Just one week. I begged him to give me a few more days, but he wouldn't hear of it. Money's been tight since I had to pay for your dad's funeral.'

'But he was hurting you, Mam. I saw it when I came in!' Tommy said.

Sally's hand went to the ripped cotton of her pinafore. 'It's nothing, love,' she lied. 'He'd been drinking, that's all.'

Meg saw the worried look on her mam's face and knew instinctively that there was more to the tale than she was letting on. She'd noticed that Sally had been looking pale and drawn recently. And through the too-thin bedroom wall she'd heard her mam being sick into a bucket over the last few mornings too.

'Can we not go back to paying rent to Jim instead of Hawk?' Tommy asked, but Sally shook her head.

'This end of Tunstall Street is Hawk's now, son. Anyway, Jim's just as bad, worse even. They say he killed a man in a fight at Silksworth village not long since.'

'We've got to keep him out, Mam,' Tommy said. 'When me and Meg are out, you'll keep the doors locked and the windows shut and—'

'I'll do what I can,' Sally said softly. 'I'll do what I can.'

Spot trotted back into the kitchen and headed straight towards Sally, laying his head on her lap and gazing up with his glassy black eyes. Meg stood and thrust her hands into the pockets of her skirts, where she found a penny, a single penny, caught up in the lining of the heavy cloth. Tomorrow, she decided . . . tomorrow she would visit the market for the first time. Tomorrow would see the end of her nothing days. Tomorrow was the day when she would make a start on making proper money, enough to get her mam out of Tunstall Street and away from Hawk Jackson's rough and evil grip.

'Come on then, Meg. Come and help me fetch the water,' Sally said finally. 'We've got baked cod for tea tonight; Adam dropped it in on his way to work this morning after fishing on the beach last night. He said his mam's got plenty and it would just go off if it wasn't eaten soon.'

'Sounds lovely, Mam,' said Meg, her stomach rumbling. Tomorrow would be her new start.

The next morning, as the Sutcliffes were huddled around the fire eating the remains of the fish for breakfast, there was a knock at the back door. Spot immediately rose and walked to the door, standing guard and giving a soft growl.

'It'll be Adam,' Tommy said. 'He said he'd knock on for me this morning. We're working the same shifts this week.'

He unlocked the back door, and sure enough, the tall, thin frame of Adam Wilson came walking into the kitchen. He was dressed ready for work, his three-quarter-length trousers tucked into long pit socks pulled up to his knees. In his hand he carried his bait box with sandwiches in it prepared by his mam, and an empty water bottle to fill at the pit head before going underground.

'Hey, Spot!' he said, stroking the dog's head. He politely removed his flat cap. 'Morning, Meg. Morning, Mrs Sutcliffe.'

'Thanks for the fish, Adam,' Meg said.

'The cod are jumping down the beach at the minute. If you ever want to come down one day with me, Meg, I'd be happy to show you how to fish.'

Meg wrinkled her nose at the thought.

'Stella all right?' he asked her, and she nodded, unable to speak with a mouth full of bread and fish.

'If you need any help with her, you know, just ask. I'm quite handy with the pit ponies now at work.'

'He's in charge of three of them,' Tommy beamed.

Meg swallowed hard. 'And do they all live underground?' she asked.

'They do,' Adam confirmed, 'but I look after them well. Tam's my favourite, he's a real character, lovely black-and-white coat and a proper friendly face. He's just like a little old man. And then there's Dart and Mack, too.'

'If I had a pit pony I'd call it Empire,' Meg laughed.

'You wouldn't, you know, not if you worked down the pit. They've got to have short, sharp names we can yell quickly in case the dreaded three blasts go up. Mind you, we haven't heard those for some time.'

Sally made the sign of the cross on her chest. 'And nor do we want to,' she said.

'Everything going well on the rag-and-bone cart?' Adam continued.

'I'm going down the market today,' Meg said, not daring to look at her mam.

'You'll be careful down there, right?' Adam said.

'They're just people, selling and buying stuff same as me, aren't they?'

'That's as may be. And it's true there's good and bad in everyone, but you know full well the market by the docks isn't the place for a young lass to be going on her own.'

'I'll not be on my own. I'll have Spot.'

'Well just you watch out.'

Sally stood, clearing away the remains of their breakfast. 'Now come on, you two,' she said to Adam and Tommy. 'Get a move on, you don't want to be late for work.'

Tommy slung his flat cap on his head and Adam replaced his too. Their caps were the only protection they would have against the rigours of working at the pit. Tommy picked up his bag of bread and cheese that Sally had made for him to eat at dinner time, and kissed his mam on the cheek, then the two lads left, with Spot following behind until they'd disappeared along the back lane. After they'd gone, Sally said quietly: 'He's a nice lad, that Adam.'

Meg didn't reply; there was no need to. Everyone knew Adam was nice.

'What I mean is, Meg, you could do a lot worse.'

'What? Me and Adam?' Meg laughed.

'He's kind, he's gentle, he's hard-working and his mam thinks the world of him.'

'But he's . . . why, he's just Adam. He's like my older brother.'

Sally playfully pulled Meg towards her and took her daughter's hands as if to waltz around the kitchen with her.

'You're almost sixteen, Meg. Sweet sixteen and never been kissed.'

'Mam!' Meg laughed. 'You're crazy.'

'I have to be, pet, because if I don't laugh I'd cry,' Sally said.

Meg pulled away and looked at her intently. 'Why didn't you tell me things were bad with the rent?' she said. 'I've been gathering a pile of clothes in the bedroom upstairs that are too good for the paper mill and I know I can sell them down the market. I could have done it earlier, if only you'd told me you needed more money.'

'We'll get by, Meg, don't you fret,' Sally said. 'Now go. Go and make the most of the day. I'm not even going to try to talk you out of the market today because I know what you're like. You're as stubborn as your dad always was and you'll pay me no heed. But watch what you're doing there, and take Spot with you.'

Meg hugged her mam tight, then set off with Spot by her side to get Stella and the cart. Once she had gone and the house on Tunstall Street had fallen silent again, Sally ran out of the kitchen door, through the yard and across the back lane. When she finally reached the netty, her stomach heaved with the waves of nausea that had threatened her since she woke.

Out on the main road to Sunderland, Meg saw the paper mill ahead to her right-hand side, and beyond it, the white froth of the sea. The mill had been the extent of her travels so far and she knew Stella would be expecting to turn at their usual place.

'Keep on,' she said to Stella, gripping the reins tightly to ensure the horse tracked straight ahead. 'Keep on.'

On the opposite side of the road, a tram came towards them. Meg read the advertising banner emblazoned across the front of it. *Shop at Binns*, it declared. She knew of the Binns store in Sunderland, and she also knew that no matter how much money she earned, she could never afford to shop there, no matter what the tram said.

A few minutes' ride past the paper mill, the road became a little more confusing. It wasn't obvious to Meg which was the main road any more as a straggle of streets joined it. More and more buildings and houses came upon her quickly as she entered the unfamiliar area. Keeping the North Sea to her right-hand side, as her dad had told her she must, she followed the road towards the water.

The houses down by the docks were bigger than those at home, taller and thinner, some even with three floors. But none of them looked any grander than those back in Tunstall Street. In fact, they looked worse, worn and grimed with seagull muck. Some had windows that were jagged and smashed, and the closer Meg travelled to the river, the blacker and more ruinous the buildings became. Finally she slowed Stella down. The road split left and right along the riverside and she had no notion of which way to turn. Spot stood on the cart behind her, sniffing the stench from the river, thickly covered with coal dust.

An old man, bent double, pushing a barrow filled with coal, walked towards them.

'Where's the market?' Meg called to him.

The man let his barrow down gently to the cobbles. Without a word, he pointed behind him, then picked up his barrow and continued on his way.

The first thing Meg noticed about the market was the long glass roof that arced into the sky atop red brickwork the like of which she had never seen before. And the size of it too: it went all the way back from the river's edge, at least three streets back as far as she could tell. She directed Stella towards a piece of rough ground where she could see horses tethered to posts at the market's edge. From her cart, she watched as men, one after the other, shouldered wooden boxes from the market and dropped them down on their carts. For a long time she sat watching, unnoticed and unremarkable, her long dark hair tucked inside her dad's army coat. She watched the men loading up boxes of fruit, vegetables, bloodied meat and fish to their carts and then with a cry they were off, their horses' hooves echoing along the cobbles as they disappeared to sell their wares.

'Hey! You, boy!' Meg heard a voice call. 'What do you think you're doing? Move on. You've no business waiting there.'

She turned and saw a stocky man with thick black hair. He was in white shirtsleeves covered by an apron with its straps tied around his neck and bulging stomach. The apron fell almost to the ground and Meg could see a pair of black boots poking from underneath. The white of the apron was streaked with the red and brown of what she quickly realised was blood.

He waved his hand at Meg, dismissing her. 'We can't have you hogging the butchers' entrance, we've got work to do, meat to move. Now shift!'

Meg stood her ground. 'Where can I tether my horse?' she asked politely. 'I have business here today.'

'You're a lass?' he cried when he heard her voice. He walked closer to take a good look at her. 'What business has a lass like you down here?'

'Selling clothes,' she replied, indicating the pile of rags in the back of the cart.

'Clothes, is it?' he laughed, taking in the sight of Stella. 'You'd make more money selling me your old nag to make into chops for tea.'

'Ernie Sutcliffe sent me,' said Meg, taking courage from using her dad's name.

'Never heard of him,' the man replied quickly. 'Get yourself round the back,' he told her, pointing the way. 'Ask to see Florrie Smith. She sometimes buys clothes. Now shift it, go on.'

Meg entered the market through the back door, leaving Spot on the cart with the clothes. The first thing that hit her was the smell, the sick, heady stench of raw meat and blood, fish guts and ripe fruit. She walked slowly, taking care where she put her feet on the wet floor streaked with animals' blood. Pigs' heads and trotters were laid out in a row on a wooden table, under a line of skinned rabbits and chickens hanging from hooks above. She read a sign that offered *Ox Tail – Best Price on the Market!* and next to it another sign offering low prices on a bloodied pile of knuckles and joints. It was all a far cry from the food hall at Ryhope Co-op, where she had seen meat and fish laid out for sale on marble slabs in neat rows.

Oh, and the noise! Men shouting and barrows clattering up and down as women in shawls with a basket across an arm and a crying baby at the hip shuffled from stall to stall looking for food they could afford. The stalls were pushed tight together in narrow aisles, and the place was so big Meg could scarcely see where it all ended. Above her, the glass roof let in the only light. In all the noise and bustle, she wondered how on earth she was to find Florrie Smith.

She continued in a straight line down the aisle, past the stinking meat stalls. When she reached the end, she saw two men sitting in the corner at a small table, their heads bent in concentration over a square board. It was only when she drew near that she saw they were playing cards. Both men wore identical flat caps and shapeless jackets, and their roughened hands cradled the cards towards their chests. As she approached, the man facing Meg nodded towards her, his grotesque features forming themselves into an expression that reminded her of the pigs' heads she'd walked past seconds ago.

'Well now . . . what have we got here then?' he said, his lecherous smile exposing broken and blackened teeth. 'Aren't you just the prettiest little thing we've seen in here this morning. You looking for me, love?' he laughed.

Meg stood stock still and thrust her hands into the pockets of her dad's coat. The other man, who'd had his back to her, now turned to see what the fuss was all about.

'As if a nice lass like that would be looking for you, Billy Shillen,' he laughed at his friend. 'We haven't seen you in here before, have we?' he asked Meg, standing now and extending his hand towards her. She shook it firmly, as Big Pete had told her to do that first time at the Railway Inn.

'It's nice to meet you,' he said, his eyes shining as he smiled warmly at her.

'I'm Meg,' she said. 'Meg Sutcliffe. And what's your name?'

'Clarky,' he replied, holding on to her hand a little too long. 'Just Clarky.'

'I'm looking for Florrie Smith,' Meg said. There was something mesmerising about Clarky's face and the way he looked at her. She couldn't help but return his gaze, attracted immediately to his rugged features and deep brown eyes.

'Aisle five,' Clarky replied. 'All the clothes hawkers are in aisle five. This your first time here?'

Meg nodded. 'My dad told me to come,' she said boldly. 'He was well known at the market before he went off to war.'

Clarky brought her hand to his lips and kissed it gently before releasing it. The touch of his lips on her skin took her by surprise.

'Your dad, you say? What was his name?'

'Ernie Sutcliffe,' Meg said proudly. 'From Ryhope.'

'I know Ernie,' Billy announced from the table. 'He's a smashing fella, one of the best. How's he doing these days?'

'He died . . .' Meg said, the words still difficult for her. 'A while back. It was the effects of gas, they say, from the war.'

'Ah now, that's a shame and I'm sorry to hear it. God bless Ernie Sutcliffe. We miss old Ernie down at the market, don't we, Clarky?'

Clarky didn't reply; instead he held Meg's gaze for what seemed like a very long time. 'Aisle five,' he said again at last. 'Any of the women up there will tell you where you can find Florrie.'

'Thank you, Clarky,' Meg said.

He raised his cap, revealing a mop of curly black hair. 'I'll be seeing you here again then,' he said. 'Or at least I hope so.'

Meg felt a warm flush around her face. She lifted her gaze to meet his. 'I hope so too,' she said.

She turned to head off across the market in the direction that Clarky had indicated. As she walked away, she wondered if he was watching her, and found herself hoping that he was.

After Meg had gone, Clarky took his seat at the table, ready to resume the card game. 'Did you see her, Billy?' he asked. 'What a beauty she was, eh? But who's that fella she mentioned, that Ernie Sutcliffe bloke?' He glanced at his cards again, certain this was a game he could win.

'I've got no idea,' Billy said. 'I've never heard of him. But she doesn't need to know that, does she?'

Away from the meat aisle, across the fish aisle and right at the very end of the market, Meg finally found the stalls selling clothes. If anything, aisle five was even more crowded and busy than the other parts of the market she'd already seen. Clothes were piled high on tables as a pulsating mass of shoppers pressed in, not afraid to snatch or grab at the bargains. Meg saw women using their elbows as weapons to keep others away from the items they wanted to buy. High above the tables there were more garments hanging from hooks – jackets, long skirts and dresses, and even, Meg saw, a fur coat.

As the women picked over clothes and fought at the tables, Meg attempted to catch the eye of one of the stall-holders to ask where she'd find Florrie Smith. She tried waving to get their attention, but they had more important things to be doing than tending to Meg, when there was money to be taken at their stalls. Meg knew there was only one way to find Florrie Smith and that was to make herself heard above the chattering din. She took a deep breath, cupped her hand to her mouth and yelled: 'Florrie Smith!'

A few women glanced up before returning to their task of hunting through the mountains of clothes.

'Florrie Smith!' she yelled again.

This time, an older woman in a buttercup-yellow hat looked up. 'She's over there!' she said, pointing further along the aisle.

Meg looked where the woman was indicating, but all she could see was another tangle of shoppers pushing and shoving at a table piled high with clothes. As she inched her way forward, she spotted a woman standing behind the counter, facing out to the crowd of women and orchestrating each handful of clothes grabbed from her stall.

'That'll never fit your Stevie,' she told one of the customers, throwing her a grubby blue shirt. 'Here, have this one instead. You'll need to stitch a couple of buttons on, but if you give me full price for the shirt I'll give you the buttons for free.'

'Florrie Smith?' Meg asked, pushing her way to the front of the crowd.

Steel-grey eyes shone from under a black velvet hat around which wisps of brown curls fell. 'Who's asking?'

'My name's Meg. I was told to come and see you. I've got clothes to sell.'

'A lass as bonny as you out working as a pedlar?'

Meg returned Florrie's stare, hoping there was kindness behind the woman's eyes. 'I work on the rag-and-bone and I've got a pile of clothes to sell. I was told you might buy them.'

'I'll buy that coat from you,' Florrie said.

Meg dug her hands in her pockets. 'It's not for sale. I have other clothes to sell though, if you want to buy them?'

'I might . . . and I might not. Depends on what they are. I'd have to see them first, of course.'

'Of course,' said Meg. 'I've got them with me on the cart outside.'

Florrie was just about to reply, but something caught her attention.

'Put that back, Maisie Duggan,' she said to a woman beside Meg. 'Think you can take advantage of me when I've got my eye off the stall? I've told you before about stealing from me.'

'I need something for the bairns,' Maisie said. 'Please, Florrie. It's not for me.'

Meg watched as Florrie ducked down behind the counter. When she reappeared, she gave Maisie a handful of rags that Meg wouldn't have thought decent enough for her to sell at the paper mill.

'They'll need stitching,' she told her. 'You ought to get

yourself down to the Salvation Army, Maisie, get the bairns some proper food there too.'

'I might not have much but I've still got my pride,' Maisie huffed. 'I'll not be needing charity yet.'

'And you'll not be stealing from me either, got it?'

Maisie nodded and disappeared into the throng of women in the aisle. Meg stood to one side and watched as Florrie deftly and quickly sold her wares. Shirts, dresses, hats, socks, even underwear was taken from the pile in exchange for pennies and shillings, which Florrie kept in her bulging skirt pockets. With each sale she made, she handed over the clothes with a kind word to the woman who had bought them.

Within an hour, everything had been sold, and not just on Florrie's stall. All along aisle five the tables were bare. The only items remaining were those on hangers above the stalls, the fancy dresses and the fur coat that no one could afford.

'Right then,' said Florrie, as she tidied away behind her stall. 'Give me a minute to put my takings in the tin and I'll come and have a look at these clothes of yours and see if we can do business.'

Carrying her tin of cash wrapped in an old sheet, Florrie led the way and Meg hurried to follow her, down aisle five, past the fish and the fruit and vegetable aisles and towards the meat aisle. Florrie was a woman who meant business; she liked to get things done as quickly and efficiently as she could and Meg had to step up her pace to keep from losing her in the crowd. She felt a surge of excitement as she headed back to the meat aisle, her eyes scanning the corner looking for the table she'd seen earlier. She was hoping to spot Clarky again, but he was nowhere to be seen.

'How long have you had your stall here?' she asked Florrie when she finally caught up with her. She wondered if she might know anything about Clarky.

'Feels like I've been here forever,' Florrie replied. 'My mam used to run the stall, and when I was old enough I came in and helped her. I've been here ever since. It's a good market. Folk bring pillowcases with them some days to shop here, filling up on cheap stuff, you know. They come in from the pit villages as far away as Hartlepool on a Saturday. That's the cheapest day – knock-down Saturday they call it. Everything sells off then.'

They left the market at the spot where the hawkers tied up their horses and carts.

'So,' Florrie said, looking over at the horses. 'Which one's yours?'

But Meg couldn't reply. She couldn't speak at all when she caught sight of Stella and her cart. Not only was Spot missing, but her pile of clothes had gone too.

Chapter Five

Birthday

Meg felt a sudden coldness hit her hard. She walked slowly to her cart, relieved at least to see that Stella was all right and in no distress.

'Spot!' she called out when at last she found her voice. 'Spot!'

'What is it, lass?' Florrie asked. 'You seem a bit shaken.'

But Meg didn't hear Florrie's words as her head raged with anger at her own stupidity for leaving the dog and the clothes behind while she'd been inside the market. She reached down under the seat in the cart and pulled out the handbell, then cupped her hand around her mouth, swung the bell hard and called as loudly as she could for her dog. Over and over she called, but there was no sign of him anywhere. Finally, the tears that had threatened started to fall. Florrie moved towards her and put an arm around her shoulder.

'Hey now, come on. It can't be that bad, can it?'

'Everything's gone,' Meg sobbed. 'All the clothes I was

going to sell . . . and my dog, Spot, he's gone too.'

'You mean you left a pile of clothes out here on the cart while you were in there with me?' Florrie asked.

Meg nodded her head.

'Oh lass. You've got a lot to learn.' Florrie turned Meg to face her. 'Listen to me. The rogues round here will take anything that's not nailed down. You're going to have to chalk this one up to experience and learn your lesson from it.'

'But what about my dog? Have they taken him too?' Meg cried, wiping her eyes on the sleeve of her dad's coat.

Florrie didn't answer; she didn't want to cause Meg any more distress. Instead, she pulled the girl towards her in a gentle hug.

'Come on. I think you could do with a hot drink inside you before you set off home.'

Florrie led the way, now carrying her tin of cash tucked inside her jacket, and Meg followed her along the sloping alleyways that ran between the houses down to the murky water's edge. At every turn she called for Spot, hoping to see a flash of white running along a lane, looking for her in return. Turning right along the cobbled river road, she heard a cry go up from a deep and husky voice.

'Morning, Florrie!'

She looked across the cobbled road to see two women walking towards them, each carrying a large, flat straw basket on her head.

'Morning!' Florrie nodded. 'Sell it all today?'

'Don't we always?' the women replied.

Meg stared at them as they bustled past. The older one was stout and hard-faced, her large frame wrapped tightly in a black shawl. On her feet were wooden clogs, poking from under a mass of black skirts. The younger one wore the same sullen expression but there was a lightness to her features. Meg noticed the resemblance and realised the pair were daughter and mam. But it was the baskets on their heads that intrigued her. She'd never seen anything like them in Ryhope.

'What's in their baskets?' she whispered to Florrie.

'By, lass, you really do have a lot to learn, don't you?' Florrie smiled. 'Have you never seen fishwives before?'

Meg shook her head.

'Well, their baskets are empty now, but earlier they would have been full of fish. Lasses married to fishermen have to sell the fish, you see. Mind you, some of them get more joy out of chasing you with a sweeping brush than they ever get out of selling anything. They're hard women, Meg; they have to be, living and working down here.'

Meg turned to watch as the women disappeared into one of the alleyways.

'You're not from round here, are you?' asked Florrie as she bustled ahead along the cobbled street.

'I'm from Ryhope,' Meg replied proudly, walking quickly to keep up. 'And . . . well, it was my dad who said I should try selling some of the clothes down here on the market. But I'm not sure I want to come back after what's happened today.'

'Where's your dad now?' Florrie asked.

Meg dug her hands deep into her coat pockets. 'He died not long since,' she said quietly. 'He went off to war, and when he came back he took ill, so I'm looking after the rag-and-bone business for him now.'

Florrie thought for a moment. 'From Ryhope, you say?'

Meg nodded.

'I knew a fella from Ryhope once who worked on the rag-and-bone. Mind you, this was some years ago now. Nice fella he was, but he didn't half like his drink. We did a bit of business at the market over many years, on and off. Ernie . . . Ernie Sutcliffe I think he was called.'

Meg's face lit up. 'That's my dad!' she cried. 'Ernie's my dad! I mean . . . he was my dad. I'm Meg Sutcliffe.'

'Well I never!' laughed Florrie. 'Little Meg! I can remember your dad bringing you here as a young 'un. He used to sit you on his knee and wrap you up in his jacket. He had a black horse, a beautiful thing it was. And there was another bairn too that he used to bring with him, a little lad?'

'Our Tommy,' Meg smiled. 'And the horse is still the same one, just a lot older now. Stella, she's called. You mean Dad used to bring us here to the market? I've been here before?'

'Just once or twice,' Florrie replied. 'It's not a place for bairns, but he was ever so proud of his little 'uns and he wanted to show you off. So, you're Ernie's daughter? My word . . . and just look at you now. What a beauty you've turned out to be.'

'I'll be sixteen in a couple of weeks,' Meg said.

'Ah, now you're making me feel old,' Florrie smiled. 'Come on, let's see if we can find a cup of tea somewhere along here. We'll have a chat and I'll put the word out about your dog and the missing clothes, see if anyone's heard anything.'

'Thank you, Mrs Smith,' Meg said. 'I really appreciate your help.'

'That's as may be,' replied Florrie. 'But if we're going to be friends, then there's one thing I insist on.'

Meg's smile froze on her face. 'What?' she whispered.

'That you drop the Mrs Smith and call me Florrie.'

Over mugs of hot, salty beef tea in a shop that boasted a counter and two stools, Florrie and Meg got to know each other. Florrie told Meg about the sort of clothes she could sell at the market and what she was willing to pay. And when she found out how much Meg was paying for the wooden clothes pegs she gave away in exchange for the rags, she told her where to buy them cheaper on the market.

'Dad said there was a fella on the market selling goldfish too,' Meg remembered, but Florrie shook her head.

'Can't say I've seen goldfish being sold there for years,' she replied. 'But there's balloons to be bought, for when bairns bring out the clothes.'

In return for the older woman's advice, Meg found herself confiding to Florrie about her dream to move out of Tunstall Street, taking her mam and Tommy away from the coal-blackened streets. And after their tea was drunk, true to her word, Florrie called at every pub and shop along the riverside letting it be known that she was on the warpath after whoever had stolen a white dog and a cartful of clothes.

With everything that had happened since, Meg had all but forgotten her encounter with Clarky earlier that day. But as the two women headed back to the market, she decided to ask Florrie about him.

'You'd do well to stay away from that one,' Florrie warned her. 'But you're a grown lass and you'll do what you want. Heaven knows, I did the same at your age. Just remember, Meg, you're a long way from Ryhope now, with its pretty village green and all the pit families who know each other. Down here there are dockers and shipyard workers, hard women and even harder men. People come and go. Drifters, chancers, buying and selling all manner of things in the dark. When you come to the market to see me, make sure that's all you do. Bring your clothes in off the cart next time; don't leave anything out there you don't want thieves to get their hands on.'

'What about Stella?' Meg asked. 'Will she be all right?'

'Yes, love.' Florrie smiled as they reached the back of the market, where Stella stood waiting. 'She'll be all right. I can't see anyone wanting to make off with an old nag like that.'

Meg walked towards the horse and stroked her protectively. Just then, Spot appeared, bounding around the corner of the market. There was a flash of red at his throat and Meg's hands flew to her chest.

'It's Spot! He's bleeding!' she cried. But as the dog came closer, she could see that the crimson around his neck wasn't blood at all. It was a piece of torn material trapped in his jaws.

She bent down to greet him, hugging him tight and kissing his nose.

'Where have you been, boy?' she cried, hugging him to her as he nuzzled into her neck. 'Where have you been?' Gently she lifted the scrap of red from Spot's mouth and held it in her hands, puzzled.

Spot jumped aboard the cart and Meg readied Stella to leave. As Florrie waved her off and headed back into the market, Meg spotted Clarky coming towards her. She took a deep breath and sat up tall in her seat, trying to keep as calm as she could while her heart was going nineteen to the dozen at the sight of him.

'I'm glad I caught you before you left,' he said, walking up to the cart and stroking Stella's nose. 'I was hoping I'd see you again.'

Meg smiled at him. 'Me too,' she said.

Spot's ears pricked up and he pressed himself close to Meg's side. Clarky's dark brown eyes shone and Meg noticed a dimple appear when he smiled.

'How's about having a drink with me down at the Ship Inn?' he asked.

'I . . . I can't,' Meg replied, but even as the words left her lips, she knew that she wanted nothing more.

'Ah, now that's a shame,' said Clarky. 'If you won't come to the Ship Inn with me, perhaps I could come calling on you? Of course, I'd need to know where you lived, though I'd understand if you didn't want to tell me.'

'Ryhope,' Meg blurted out.

Clarky's face lit up. 'Village or colliery?' he asked, eyeing her. 'Let me guess . . . colliery, right?'

Meg nodded.

'I often have business to attend to in Ryhope,' he told her. 'Maybe I'll ask for you next time I'm there.'

'Maybe you will.' Meg smiled at him. 'Thanks for your help earlier, with finding Florrie, I mean.'

'My pleasure,' Clarky said. 'I'm more than happy to help out. And any time you need me, just mention my name. Everyone knows where to find me.'

He put his hand to his mouth, kissed it and blew it towards her.

'I'll see you soon, Meg.'

Meanwhile, down on the riverside, in the Ship Inn, Billy Shillen had become the joke of the day. It was his backside that was causing much merriment, as it was on show to anyone who cared to look. The flabby white mass of it poked through a hole ripped in his bright red trousers. Billy held court at the bar with tales of how he'd fought off the biggest, most evil dog he'd ever seen. And with every pint of beer he sank, his tale became more elaborate, the dog more fierce than anyone had ever seen.

Later, in a dark corner of the pub, over a pint of stout and a pork pie, Billy allowed himself a wry smile. It had been a good day for business after his unexpected find of the pile of clothes. As he'd said to Clarky earlier, if someone was daft enough to leave their cart unattended outside the market, they deserved all they got.

Over the following week, the weather took a turn for the worse, ushering in the full force of autumn with rain and sleet on a harsh, bitter wind. Meg wrapped herself up well in her dad's coat when she went out on the streets with Stella and Spot. And underneath the army coat she wore as many layers of the rags she'd collected as she could manage. But even layers of rags couldn't hide Meg's charm and appeal and there were those she met at the market who commented often on her attractive smile. The men's clothes that she was given on the rag-and-bone round went to Tommy, to keep him as warm and dry as possible in his work at the pit. Mam wouldn't take any of the clothes for herself, saying that Meg needed to sell as much as she could to pay the rent to Hawk Jackson and keep him away from their door. But after almost two weeks of working without a break, she begged Meg to take a day of rest, if not for herself then for Stella. Meg finally agreed to a day spent at home on her birthday.

'Sixteen today, Meg. I don't know where the time's gone,' Sally smiled when Meg came downstairs on the morning of her birthday. 'And you get more beautiful with each passing day.' Meg hugged her mam tight and the two women stood in front of the coal fire, warming themselves, with their arms around each other. Meg noticed that there seemed to be more flesh on her mam's skinny frame now.

'Tommy's shift ends this dinner time,' Sally said. 'I thought that if the weather gave up a little, we could all go for a walk on the beach this afternoon.' She busied herself with the kettle by the fireplace. 'Adam said he might come too if he finishes work on time. And Evelyn's got the afternoon off. If we had the money, I'd throw a proper birthday tea party for you here.'

'A walk's fine, Mam,' Meg said. 'I don't need a party.' At the sound of her voice, Spot came out from under the kitchen table, and lay down on the floor by her side.

'And I was thinking that if the rain stops and we do walk down to the beach, we can call in to the Albion for Hetty. She said she'd enjoy a walk out and some fresh air, if she's not too busy in the pub.'

Meg stroked Spot's head and ears as she looked out of the kitchen window at the grey and darkened sky. She stood and walked to the back door, unlocked the top half and leaned out into the yard. Over the rooftops of Tunstall Street, the sky hung heavy with cloud, but she could see the tiniest patch of white among the grey, and the rain that had fallen fast and heavy over the last few days finally looked to be dwindling away. She returned to sit by the fire with her mam.

'Here, I made you these for your birthday,' Sally said,

handing her a cotton bag. Inside was a hand-knitted dark green scarf with a matching hat and pair of gloves. 'They'll help keep you warm out on the cart.'

Meg leaned over and kissed her gently on the cheek. 'Mam . . .' she began.

'What is it, love?'

'Are you all right, Mam? I mean, you're not ill or anything, are you?'

Sally sat stock still. She knew she would have to reply as calmly as she could. She was still in shock about what was going on with her body and she wasn't yet ready to share the news with anyone, not even Meg.

'Whatever gives you that idea?' she asked.

Meg took a few seconds to reply. 'I . . . I've heard you being sick a few times over the last—'

'It's nothing,' Sally said, shaking her head. 'Nothing at all.' She stood and walked to the sideboard in the kitchen, where she took out two eggs and a bowl. 'Go and get dressed, Meg. Once you've seen to Stella, I'll make us eggs and bread for breakfast with a nice hot cup of tea.'

Sally turned her back as she began to whisk the eggs, putting an end to further talk.

When Tommy returned home at the end of his shift, the women left him to the privacy of his bath in the kitchen. A pan of broth that had been simmering away all morning was served up for dinner, and once the pots were cleaned and put away, preparations were made for an afternoon at the beach.

As Meg fastened her boots, there was a knock at the back door. Spot trotted to the door and sniffed, his tail wagging when he saw that it was Adam and Evelyn.

'Happy birthday, Meg!' they chimed.

Adam handed over a small, heavy parcel wrapped in newspaper and tied with string.

'I made you this. I hope you like it.'

Meg slowly untied the string bow and removed the paper to reveal a glass jar.

'I picked everything in there myself, see,' Adam explained. 'When I've been fishing on the beach, I've been collecting things.' He pointed to the jar. 'There's shells in there, little shells at the top and bigger ones at the bottom. There's a couple of bits of sea coal and a gem of a piece of sea glass too.'

Meg held the jar up to the light of the kitchen window.

'And see there, those little orange stones wash up every now and then, striped they are. I thought you might like them.'

'Adam, it's beautiful. Really beautiful.' She smiled. 'Thank you.'

Evelyn thrust her hand forward. 'And I made you this,' she said.

It was a birthday card, a folded sheet of yellowed paper with pressed blue and lilac petals on the front.

'I made it for you ages ago, when the flowers were out in the garden at the big house.'

'Evelyn, it's gorgeous, thank you,' Meg said, hugging her friend.

'And I've got you this too,' Evelyn said shyly, handing over a bar of sweet-smelling pink soap. 'I thought you might like a bit of something that doesn't smell of old clothes and the docks,' she laughed. 'They won't miss it at the big house. They've enough soap to last them till kingdom come.'

Meg turned the soap over in her hand. 'You stole it?' she whispered.

'Not really,' Evelyn said quickly.

'I've already told her she should take it back,' Adam said. He turned to his sister. 'The last thing you want to do is get into trouble with the housekeeper again.'

Before Evelyn could reply, Tommy and Sally entered the kitchen.

'Everyone ready?' Sally asked.

'Just about,' Meg replied, pulling on her new green knitted hat.

'Make sure you lock the door, Mam,' Tommy said as they all trooped out of the kitchen. But Sally didn't need reminding; her key was already in the lock. Not that it would stop Hawk Jackson from entering if he felt like it.

Spot ran ahead of them as they walked down the colliery bank to the village. Every now and then he would stop, turn and wait for them to catch up, then run ahead again. At the village green, Sally went into the Albion Inn and returned a few minutes later with Hetty. After Hetty's birthday greetings and a hug for Meg, the small group set off again, heading towards Beach Road and the narrow track that led down to the sea. Before the sights and sounds of the ocean could be enjoyed, however, the track led through the muck of the farmer's field. Meg brought her new scarf up to her nose to mask the smell. Once they were across the field, the beach road opened out in front of them, a winding curve sweeping down to the sea under fierce cliffs that fringed the coast. And there in the distance, at the end of the road, was the grey of the ocean, and in front of it, the best thing of all, the expanse of the sands.

'The tide's out!' Tommy cried, running ahead with Spot galloping at his side.

Evelyn and Meg walked together with Adam a little way behind. And last of all came Sally and Hetty, arm in arm and deep in conversation. When they reached the sands, the cliffs provided shelter from the remains of the wind and a tiny bit of blue appeared in the sky.

'It's turned out to be not such a bad day after all,' Sally said.

Tommy and Spot ran to the water's edge, leaving footprints in the wet sand. Ryhope beach was dotted with large stack rocks giving way to rock pools and caverns on sands blackened with sea coal. Craggy limestone cliffs stood high along the coast all the way to Hendon in the north and Seaham to the south. Meg and Evelyn followed Tommy, who was now throwing stones into the water and watching the waves splash on the shore.

'Are you collecting driftwood today, Meg?' Adam asked as he too picked up a stone and skimmed it across the water. Meg watched as the stone jumped, not once, not twice, but three times.

'Not today,' she replied. 'I'm having the whole day off work.'

She watched as Adam picked up another stone and threw it into the sea. This time it skipped just once before disappearing.

'They call this the German Ocean, you know,' he said, gazing out across the waves.

'Who does? The Germans?' Meg laughed. 'It's not Germany's, it's ours. It's Ryhope's North Sea.'

'Our freezing-cold North Sea. It's bitter out there, even in the summer, and treacherous too. Did you know there was a shipwreck here once, Meg? *The Unicorn*, it was called, a boat smashed to pieces right here on Ryhope beach.'

'How do you know all this?' Meg asked.

Adam shrugged. 'I read a bit,' he said, looking out to sea.

'There's a lot of sea coal today,' Meg noted, kicking at the stones with her boots.

'I'd be happy to come and help you collect it one day, when you're working, that is,' Adam said. 'Dusky diamonds, they call the sea coal. I've seen fellas picking it off the beach and taking it home in carts, on bikes, even in baby's prams, when I've been down here fishing.'

'What sort of fish do you get?' Meg wanted to know, an idea forming in her mind.

'Cod mainly,' he replied. 'A bit of mackerel and whiting in the summer, haddock in the winter if I'm lucky. Crabs I can get all year round. But I couldn't catch much on a day like today: the tide's too far out, it's too calm. I need a rough sea with a good swell, that's the best for fishing.'

'Are any of the fish really small?' she asked.

Adam shook his head. 'What do I want small fish for? The bigger they are, the more meals Mam can get out of them.'

'I wasn't thinking of eating them.' Meg smiled. 'I was thinking of giving them away. Some of the rag-and-bone men in Sunderland give goldfish in jars in exchange for rags. But I've not been able to find anyone who sells them here. I think I could take in more rags if I could offer goldfish; the bairns would love them.'

Adam laughed. 'Maybe you could offer small crabs instead?'

Meg wrinkled her nose at the thought.

'Or I could . . .' he glanced at her, 'I could fill more jars with shells and pebbles and you could give them away instead. If you'd like me to, I mean. I don't want you to feel obliged, of course.'

'That's a lovely idea, Adam,' she replied, smiling at him. 'Just lovely.'

They walked along the water's edge in silence, enjoying the sound of the sea as the waves broke on the shore. Soon Evelyn caught up with them, out of breath after chasing Spot and Tommy on the damp sand. Adam hung back and waited for Tommy to catch up, leaving Meg and Evelyn to walk on ahead. Evelyn linked her arm through Meg's and leaned in to her friend.

'I didn't steal it, you know. The soap. He gave it to me.'

'Who did?' Meg asked.

'Michael.'

'Mr Patterson's son?' Meg said, alarmed. 'What's he doing giving you things? You're only thirteen, Evelyn. You watch what you're doing.'

'We're friends, Meg, just friends, and he's the same age as me. Besides, he's the only one in that house who's nice to me. I can't do anything right by the housekeeper, she's always on at me. "Work quicker, Evelyn," she says. "Be quiet, Evelyn. Less talk, more work, Evelyn."'

Meg smiled.

'And Michael's just the same as me, really,' Evelyn continued. 'I'm the only person in the house who's nice to *him*, he says. Mr Patterson is never home. I think he works in Sunderland; he's something big in the River Wear Commissioners. And Michael's mam is ill in bed, so it's the housekeeper who looks after him and—'

'Michael Patterson is not the same as you, Evelyn,' Meg

said firmly. 'And you mustn't forget it. Tunstall Street and the village are all part of Ryhope, but they might as well be a million miles from each other. You know full well that colliery kids like us have no place making friends with those in the village, especially those who live in the big house. If I were you, I'd do my job, keep my head down and leave Michael Patterson well alone.'

They walked on in silence for a few moments, the only sound the rhythmic pulse of the sea.

'I'll take the soap back,' Evelyn said at last. 'But do you mind if I tell you something, Meg?'

Meg glanced at her friend. 'Go on.'

'If I take it back, would you let me buy you some from the Co-op instead?' Evelyn dropped her gaze to the sand as they walked. 'It's just that . . . you know I joked earlier about the smell of the rags and the docks?' She lifted her head and looked directly at Meg. 'Well, it wasn't really a joke.'

Meg stopped, took a deep breath of sea air and stood, hands on hips, looking out to the waves. She tasted the salt air on her lips. Evelyn reached out to touch her arm.

'I'm sorry, Meg. I didn't mean to upset you.'

Meg felt her eyes prick with tears and turned her face away from Evelyn.

'I thought you should know,' Evelyn said. 'I thought you'd like to know . . . I didn't mean to hurt you, Meg.'

Meg gazed out towards the sea and watched as the waves tumbled towards her, rolling over themselves in their hurry to reach the shore.

'Working every day with a horse and a dog brings a freedom,' Meg said finally. 'And it's a freedom that means I can roam where I choose.' She turned towards her friend.

'Working on my own . . . well, I need you to say such things to me, Evelyn, because there's no one else who would tell me. Mam's too busy with the house, and with Tommy working hard at the pit, he needs his bath every day when he comes home. There's only ever time for me to have a cat lick of a wash in front of the fire. I hadn't really thought about nice things like soap and . . .' she smiled ruefully, 'I just want to say thank you.'

'There's no need to thank me,' Evelyn said. 'I'm your friend, that's what I'm here for. I won't mention it again . . . not if you don't want me to.'

'I'm glad you did,' Meg replied. 'It might be about time I started thinking about how other people see me.' She turned and hooked her arm through Evelyn's and they continued on their walk.

'A bar of Co-op soap would be lovely, Evelyn, thank you. And if you ever need anything from my cart, let me know. I even get underwear; some of the bras are as good as new.'

'What's it like, Meg? Being out with Stella and Spot?' Evelyn asked. 'Do you get scared on your own?'

'Well, I'm not on my own, not really,' Meg replied. 'If I stay in Ryhope, I've got Big Pete to visit. If I go to the paper mill, I see Ruth. She's really nice, you'd like her. She's a bit bossy, but she has to be because she manages all the girls at the mill. And if I go to the market, I've got Florrie to look after me. There's someone else at the market, too . . .'

Evelyn looked at her. 'Who?'

'A boy!' Meg whispered. 'Clarky. Well, he's a man really. About the same age as Adam, but he's darker, with curly hair.'

'What do you sell to him?' Evelyn asked.

Meg shook her head. 'Nothing. But he seems really nice, and he helped me when I was first at the market.' She decided not to mention Clarky's kiss on her hand, or the warm rush she'd felt in her stomach when he'd smiled at her.

'Meg! Evelyn!' It was Adam, shouting for them both. They turned and saw him waving them towards him. 'Tide's coming in!'

They retraced their steps along the beach, kicking sea coal and pebbles as they walked. Spot and Tommy were making the most of the exposed sand, running around and chasing each other before the tide came in fully to put an end to their fun.

Sally and Hetty hadn't moved all afternoon from their spot on the rocks in the shelter of the cliffs.

'You know as well as I do what the gossip round here is like,' Sally told her friend. 'It runs more freely than the ice-cold water from the tap in the back lane.'

'I could make enquiries,' Hetty said. 'There's a woman I know in Seaham that could help. It might not be too late.'

Sally shook her head. 'I couldn't, Hetty. I just couldn't.'

'Well if you're going to keep it, you can't keep it quiet for much longer, pet.' Hetty laid her hand gently on Sally's arm. 'Everyone's going to know soon enough. But first, you've got to tell the bairns.'

'Tell us what, Mam?' Meg said as she approached the two women. She looked from Sally to Hetty and back again. 'Tell us what?'

Sally glanced up at Meg and Tommy. Adam and Evelyn were close behind.

'Sit down, the lot of you,' she said. 'I've got something I need you to know.'

'Pregnant?' Meg said quietly, letting the weight of her mam's words sink in.

'And it's your dad's, just in case you hear otherwise on the colliery once the news is out,' Sally said firmly.

'But he wasn't back from the army long before he died,' Tommy said, confused.

'He was back long enough,' Hetty said gently.

Tommy poked a piece of driftwood into the sand. 'A baby?'

Hetty forced a smile. 'A baby brother or sister for you both.'

Meg and Sally exchanged a look.

'Hetty's offered me some work at the Albion, cleaning work, until the baby comes. She's going to square it with Jack. We'll make ends meet, love, we always have.'

'Come on, we should be getting home now,' Hetty said, pushing herself up off the stones. She held out her arm to help Sally stand too. Then in silence they all walked back along the beach to the winding track that cut through the cliffs to the village.

Two weeks after Meg's birthday, she had collected enough clothes on the cart to make a visit to both the paper mill and the market worthwhile. As she travelled along the main road to the mill, a heavy mist inched its way inland from the sea and she felt the damp air on her face. She pulled her green scarf up, but that too was cold from the sea fret. She kept the sound of the ocean to her right-hand side as she made her way, but the mist became heavier until all she could see as she approached were the tops of the landmark chimneys. She slowed Stella until she was sure of the turn in the road, and headed towards the mill.

The mist cleared, just a patch of it, as she clambered from the cart with the parcels of rags and knocked hard at the door. When it finally flew open and Ruth appeared, a cloud of white dust billowed out from behind her.

'Come on in, love,' she said.

Meg followed her inside, grateful to be out of the cold. The air was thick with dust and it took her a while to focus. When she could finally take stock, she saw rows and rows of girls and young women sitting at long tables, all of them cutting up rags with scissors and knives.

'Welcome to the rag house,' Ruth said. 'Or as I like to call it, my little palace.'

'And I'm her little princess!' one of the women shouted from a table, causing the others around her to burst into laughter.

Meg watched as the women worked. Many of them were coughing as they cut and tore, and the dust was starting to catch in Meg's throat too. She looked around the huge room, the rags piled high on the long tables that ran the length of it. The cloud of dust never stopped moving, expanding upwards with nowhere to go. There were no windows, she noticed, no ventilation at all, just the door through which she had entered, which was now tight shut behind her.

'What've you got for me, Meg?' Ruth asked, eager to get her hands on the rags.

Meg handed over two separate piles. 'There's white cotton in this one,' she said. 'And canvas and cord in here.'

'Smashing,' Ruth said, running her expert eye over the goods. 'These will go to make both white and brown paper.'

She handed over the payment to Meg and then took a notebook and pencil from her apron pocket, marking the transaction in the book.

Curious, Meg asked: 'Have you always worked here, Ruth?'

'Always,' Ruth replied. 'Are you interested? It's hard work, but you'll be used to that after being out on the horse and cart. The girls start at six thirty every morning and work until six at night. They even get a full day off once a week. It's good money too.'

Meg glanced at Ruth, who was clearly waiting for her reply. It was generous of Ruth to offer her the work. But being stuck inside, six days a week, from dawn to dusk? After the freedom of being outdoors on the cart, working in the dusty rag room was much less appealing than Ruth could have known.

'I'll bear it in mind.' She smiled.

Ruth nodded and walked back to the door, and Meg followed, grateful for the release from the dust and noise of the rag house.

After Ruth had said goodbye and disappeared back into the cloud of white dust, Meg breathed deeply of the damp misty air outside the mill before clambering back to the cart. As she took up the reins and Stella began to trot forward through the dark drizzle of the day, Spot nuzzled his head against her shoulder.

'Good boy,' she said, leaning towards him. 'Good girl,' she called to Stella.

When they reached the junction in the road where Meg needed to turn right to return to the road to the market, she slowed Stella to a walk. The mist was thicker now and she heard a foghorn blare from the coast. Slowly and carefully Stella walked forward, and only when Meg was certain there were no cars or trams to be heard did she allow Stella to move on to the road. The fog was drifting in patches: at some points Meg could see in front of her clearly, while in others it was becoming difficult to see past Stella's ears. She took the road slowly and Stella seemed only too happy to walk rather than her usual trot. Meg noticed the horse giving a slight nod of her head with every step, but she put it down to the fog.

As they neared the river, the fog began to lift, revealing the blackened houses and alleyways, the whole place as decrepit as Meg remembered from her first visit. At last they reached the market. Meg found herself looking forward to seeing Florrie again, and she even allowed herself to hope that she might see Clarky too. He'd been much on her mind since the first time they'd met. She wondered what he did when he wasn't at the market, where he went and how he spent his time. She was surprised by how much she was hoping they would cross paths again.

She walked in carrying the clothes she was taking to Florrie, with Spot following behind this time. There was no way she was going to leave her dog on the cart, not after he'd gone missing last time. She was prepared for the sights that had horrified her the first time at the market. She walked straight past the pigs' heads and the rabbits with their stomachs slit open, all the while scanning the stalls for the sight of Clarky's smile and his dark curly hair. And at the end of the meat aisle, there he was, sitting at the card table, turning over cards in his hands and laying them out in front of him. He was sitting with his back to her, but she knew it was him, she just knew. He wasn't wearing his flat cap this time, and his hair fell to the collar of his grey jacket. She took a deep breath to calm herself before she walked alongside him. Spot stayed tight to Meg's side.

'Hello, Clarky,' she said, beaming down at him.

Clarky's face looked like it was about to split in half with the smile that appeared when he saw her. He stood at once.

'Here, let me take those,' he said, and Meg handed over the pile of clothes. He placed them on top of the card table, and once his hands were free, he lifted one of Meg's into his own and quickly brought it to his lips for a kiss. He was fascinated by Meg, by the way she looked and held herself in contrast to the rags she wore. He'd seen nothing like her among the girls who lived down by the docks. There was something special about this one; she really was a knockout.

'Now then,' he said. 'This is a lovely surprise. I didn't know you were coming in today.'

'Thought I might have seen you in Ryhope before now,' Meg said. 'Or at least I'd hoped I would.'

'Ah, well, you see . . .' Clarky started to say. 'I've had to look after my mam, that's why I've not been able to come. She's not been well, bad with her nerves, the doctor says. Anyway, I couldn't get away. I've had to stay local, just in case she needs me. You understand, don't you? It's not that I didn't want to come and see you, Meg, it's just that my mam needed me, and with me being her only child, I couldn't desert her now, could I?'

'Of course not,' Meg replied. 'You've got to look after your mam. I didn't mean to tease. What's she called?'

'Beattie,' he replied.

'And is she getting better now?'

'She's on the mend,' Clarky said quickly.

'So, will you come to see me in Ryhope when she's well? Will you come to ours for tea one day?'

'I'd like nothing more,' Clarky smiled.

'What about tomorrow?' Meg asked hopefully. She'd have to square it with Mam, of course, but she felt sure she could do so if she brought him into a conversation as breezily as she could.

Clarky nodded. 'Sounds good to me.'

'Will I write down my address for you?' Meg asked.

'No need,' Clarky replied. 'I'll ask around and find you. Ryhope's not a big place.'

'See you then.' Meg smiled.

Clarky laughed. 'Not if I see you first.'

Meg picked up the clothes and walked away. Spot followed but not without baring his teeth at Clarky first. Meg turned back to see if he was still watching her. She caught his eye and he gave a cheeky wink before his attention was caught elsewhere.

Meg turned the corner at the end of the aisle and walked past the fish aisle and the aisle piled high with apples and potatoes.

'Meg! Over here!' a voice called. It was Florrie Smith, leaning out from behind her stall. This time her head was covered with a small, round green hat with two red cherries to one side. She gratefully accepted the clothes from Meg's hands, and began sorting them into two piles. When she glanced up, she caught Meg staring at her hat. She playfully tapped her hand against the side of her head.

'Perk of the job, these hats.' She smiled. 'I get to wear them, and if I like them, I keep them. If I don't, then I sell them, see?'

Meg nodded with approval. 'It's pretty,' she said.

As Ruth had done earlier at the paper mill, Florrie took a book from her coat pocket and marked the transaction with the date and the amount paid.

'Should I do the same?' Meg asked. 'Keep a record like that?'

'You mean you're not doing so already?' Florrie asked her, surprised. 'Yes, lass, get yourself a book from John Stuart over there, back of the market; he sells paper and pens. You should be making a note of your spends and your takings. How else do you know if you're making any money at your work?'

Meg shrugged. 'I know I've had a good day when I can treat Mam and Tommy to a fish-and-chip supper.'

'Did your dad not tell you how to keep your records?' Florrie asked, and Meg shook her head. 'Well, he never was one for being organised, if I remember correctly. But I can show you if you like. Mind you, I'll need a favour in return.'

'Thank you,' said Meg, wondering what on earth she could possibly do that would help someone like Florrie Smith. 'What sort of favour do you need?'

'A ride on your cart into town. I've got to take my money to the bank, see, and with the fog the way it is, it's best if I don't walk in today. You never know who's lurking in the alleyways round here. I had my takings robbed once before and I have no intention of letting it happen again.'

'Your bank's in town?' Meg asked. 'Sunderland town?'

Florrie nodded. 'Which other town did you think I meant?'

'It's just that . . . I've not been there before.'

'I'll keep you right, don't you worry,' Florrie reassured her, sensing Meg's unease. 'It's one long road into town from here and the bank's close by the Binns store. I'll be straight in and out of the bank and then you can take me home.'

'Binns?' Meg cried. 'I've never seen it before!'

Florrie smiled. 'Then you and me are going to have an adventure.'

Chapter Six

Clarky

'What's wrong with your horse, lass?' Florrie asked.

Meg was puzzled. 'There's nothing wrong with her, she's just old. Dad bought her as a foal, and she's an old lady now.'

'No, love,' said Florrie. 'See the way she's dipping her head there every time she puts her front hoof down? You need to get her looked at.'

'Is she ill?' Meg asked, trying to mask her alarm. 'I just thought it was the fog affecting her vision.'

'She could be lame,' Florrie replied. 'Is there somewhere you can take her when you get home? Someone who could have a look at her?'

Meg thought for a moment. 'There's the forge by the village green where she gets shod, they'll help.'

'Then I'd take her there on your way home after we've finished in town,' Florrie said firmly. 'With no horse, you've got no business. You've got to look after your assets.'

The cart continued slowly along the main road towards

the town centre, with Meg at the reins and Florrie sitting beside her. In the back of the cart Spot stood alert.

'Keep straight on,' said Florrie, pointing ahead. 'Just keep on this road all the way. Follow the tramlines and it'll bring us into Fawcett Street, where Binns is. My bank's on the next corner.'

As they neared the town, the fog began to lift and through the mist Meg saw the outlines and shapes of buildings appear, buildings that were tall and proud and strong. Buildings the likes of which she had never seen before. Some were three and four storeys high, made of solid stone, a world away from the dingy lime-washed cottages of Tunstall Street.

'It's all so grand!' she said, looking around, taking in as much as she could through the wisps of fog. 'Do people live here?' she asked Florrie.

'They're offices mainly,' Florrie replied. 'Lots of banks and legal offices round here, and there's the town hall, of course.'

Meg pointed to her right, eyes wide. 'Oh . . . what's that?'

At the side of the road was a building that dwarfed those around it. It stood alone, not as part of a terrace, and Meg could make out a lake at its edge. Shining curves of glass domes, one after the other, looked out over the water.

Florrie laughed. 'Don't tell me you've never been to the museum and winter gardens, lass?'

Meg couldn't take her eyes off the building and slowed Stella to take in the sight.

'You should get yourself in there one day,' Florrie told her. 'They've got plants and flowers from all over the world. They've even got a lion.'

'A real one?' Meg asked.

'It's stuffed,' Florrie said. 'They call it Wallace, would you believe? And there's more stuffed animals in there too.' She laid her hand gently on Meg's arm. 'There's lots to learn, Meg, about the world, about life outside of Ryhope. And the museum's a good place to start.'

Meg pointed ahead of her. 'Is that Binns?' she cried. 'Is that really Binns?'

Florrie nodded. 'That's Binns all right.'

The gleaming white stone building stood handsome and proud, looking out on to Fawcett Street with its smart black window frames.

'See that window there?' Florrie said, pointing. 'That's where the haberdashery department is.'

Meg looked at her blankly.

'They sell buttons and threads, laces, zips, that kind of thing. And the best dress material you can find anywhere in the north-east. Silks and furs too, for those who can afford them.'

Meg gazed at the windows of the store as the cart trundled past, trying to take in as much as she could of the colours and clothes on display.

'Come on,' said Florrie. 'Get a move on, there's trams coming behind. You can't stop and stare from the middle of the road, not when you're in the town centre. Drop me at the bank and there's a place you can tether Stella at the back.'

She hugged the old sheet with her cash tin wrapped in it to her chest.

'I'll be in the bank for a few minutes, Meg. I've got a bit of business to do. While I'm gone, go and take yourself a look inside Binns.'

Just then Spot poked his wet black nose between Meg and Florrie and laid his head on Meg's shoulder.

'And leave him on the cart,' Florrie told her. 'They'll not thank you for taking him in.'

After leaving Stella at the back of Florrie's bank and tying Spot with a length of rope to the cart so he wouldn't follow her, Meg headed towards Binns. The lights from the store let out on to the street, making it all the more inviting. She stood for a while at the entrance, peering through the glass doors. She could see clothes for sale that she knew she could never afford, modelled on life-size dolls. All manner of clothes were on display along rails and on counter tops.

'Are you coming in, pet?' an older woman asked as she swept past Meg.

Meg nodded. 'Yes, thank you,' and she stepped through the door that the woman held open.

There was a gentle hush inside the store, a calm that helped quell the panic Meg felt building inside her. She wasn't sure where to go first or what to look at, there was so much to see. The Ryhope Co-op was the grandest store she'd set foot in so far, but Binns made the Co-op look drab. Uniformed assistants, women all, stood to attention behind their counters, some wrapping outfits, some talking to customers, helping them choose what to buy. Meg stood stock still, unsure of which way to turn.

'Can I help you?' A woman appeared at Meg's side, tall and thin with a nipped-in waist to her uniform. A name badge was pinned to her breast that read: *Miss Nicholson, Floor Manager*. But it was her perfume that Meg noticed most, as if the woman had floated in on a cloud of heady, sickly scent.

'I'm just . . . I was looking . . .' Meg began, not really knowing what she was doing.

Miss Nicholson eyed Meg all the way from her green knitted hat and her dad's too-big army coat down to her black skirts and muddied boots. She glanced again at Meg's face, taking in her clear, bright eyes and her engaging features, which were at odds with the rags she wore.

'I've just come for a look around,' Meg said at last.

'And were you intending to make a purchase?' the woman asked.

Meg shook her head.

The sales assistant fixed a smile on her face. 'Then perhaps madam would like to return at a time when she is able to do so.'

'Couldn't I just take a look?' Meg pleaded. 'I've never been here before and I've heard so much about it and I've seen all the trams with the adverts and—'

'Madam, please,' the assistant said. 'I doubt very much there is anything in our emporium that will be to your . . .' she paused and breathed in sharply through her flared nostrils before spitting out the word, 'taste.'

Meg felt her anxiety give way to a hot stab of anger. 'Are you saying you want me to leave?'

The assistant grabbed hold of her arm and marched her back to the door she'd just walked through minutes ago. 'If madam would allow me to escort her out of the store . . .'

'But I haven't done anything wrong!' Meg insisted.

Within the clothing department, a few heads turned at the sound of her cry. A customer at the underwear counter raised an eyebrow towards Sue Pegg, the assistant, and whispered, 'Oh, those dreadful urchins.'

'Yes, madam,' Sue Pegg replied, as she'd been trained to do, without passing further comment. She kept her eyes firmly on Meg, admiring the girl's appeal and spirit, if not her choice of coat.

Outside on the street, now free of the floor manager's grip, Meg rubbed her arm. The heavy glass door had swung shut with Meg on one side, outside in the cold and the mist. On the other side, inside the light, warm shop, stood Miss Nicholson, hands on hips, waiting for her to walk away. Meg stuck her hands deep into the pockets of her dad's coat, took a deep breath and squared her shoulders. She stood for what seemed to be a very long time, long enough for Miss Nicholson to make the first move away from the door. It was a tiny victory, but one that Meg relished. However, instead of walking back to Stella and Spot, she put one foot firmly in front of the other and marched straight back into the store, walking up to Miss Nicholson and tapping her on the shoulder.

A look of horror passed over the floor manager's face when she turned around to see who was demanding her attention in so impertinent a way.

'You again!' she hissed. 'Do I have to call the police to have you thrown out?'

'There's no need,' Meg said quietly. 'I'm going to walk out on my own this time. But before I do, I want to let you know that I'll back here one day. It may not be soon, and I may or may not make a purchase. But when I return, you will give me the respect I deserve.' And with that, she turned and walked away.

Miss Nicholson stood open-mouthed with shock. And from her position at the underwear counter, where she had watched the exchange, Sue Pegg allowed herself a smile that didn't go unnoticed.

'You, girl. Back to work!' the floor manager barked at her.

'Yes, Miss Nicholson,' Sue said, bowing her head slightly. But as soon as her boss was out of sight, she looked out of the window and watched Meg disappear along Fawcett Street.

Back on the cart, Meg waited for Florrie to return from her business at the bank. The encounter with the shop assistant in Binns had rattled her a little and she didn't much like the way it made her feel inside. There was a sinking feeling in the pit of her stomach. She breathed deeply and straightened her back, ready to greet Florrie when she returned, then prepared herself for the long ride home, pulling her scarf up to her ears and tucking it inside the collar of her dad's coat. When Florrie finally clambered aboard, they set off once more.

'Am I going back the way I came, on the same road?' asked Meg.

'Yes, lass. I'll tell you when to turn off so you can get me safely back home. And I'll not forget my part of the bargain, Meg. Whenever you're ready to learn about keeping records for your business, you just let me know.'

They travelled in silence away from the town centre. The fog that had thinned while they'd been in Sunderland started to build as they travelled back towards the coast. Finally Florrie issued directions and Meg steered Stella from the main road into a cobbled lane, one side of which was lined with tall trees. Fallen leaves paved the way along the lane.

'Anywhere here will do for me, Meg. You can turn around at the end,' Florrie said.

Meg pulled Stella to a stop.

'That's mine, number ten,' Florrie said, pointing at a red wooden door surrounded by stone the colour of straw. Red-painted window frames looked out from each side of the door and there were more windows above it, too.

'But . . . it's beautiful,' said Meg, taking in all she could see of Florrie's house. 'I never knew you . . .'

Florrie gave her a friendly wink. 'What? You didn't know I lived here? Well, there's a lot about me you don't know.' She hopped off the cart. 'I'll see you at the market soon, Meg,' she said. 'And thanks again for the ride. You want to be going straight home now. Looks like the fog is getting worse.'

Stella took a little more encouragement than usual to begin the journey back to Ryhope. The fog came at them thick and fast as soon as they joined the coast road, and Meg did her best to keep a fluttering of anxiety at bay. It was the sea that helped her navigate through the foggy darkness of the late afternoon. The sound of the waves lashing up to her left-hand side reassured her that she wasn't far from home and the blare of the foghorn guided her.

Suddenly Spot let out a bark. It was just one bark to start with, then a whole series of them, short and sharp, one after the other.

'What is it, boy?' Meg said. 'What is it?'

The dog quietened at the sound of her voice, but Meg was alarmed. Had Spot picked up on something hidden in the mist? The fluttering in her stomach returned, and to help calm her fears, she began gently to sing.

'*Stella, sweet Stella, what fella could want a finer horse?*'

Taking courage from the words and from Spot now quiet behind her, she sang the line over again, slightly louder each time. But despite her soothing words, Stella slowed to a walk. Behind her, Meg heard a low growl start up deep in Spot's throat.

'Steady, Spot,' she said quietly. 'Steady.'

And then, through the ghost grey of the fog, she saw a dark shape appear, moving towards her. Panicked, she tried to encourage Stella to move faster, then gasped as a hand appeared through the fog and grabbed her coat. She tried to scream, but no sound left her mouth. Spot barked again, louder this time. Her hands left the reins and her fists pummelled against the hands grabbing at her.

'Meg! It's me!' a voice panted. 'It's Adam!'

Meg slumped with relief.

'Let me jump up,' he said.

She did as instructed and moved along the seat. As Adam mounted the cart, she saw that he was still in his pit clothes, his face as black as coal, with only the whites of his eyes shining through the fog.

'Your mam sent me out looking for you,' he explained. 'We've all been worried sick. She said you were supposed to be home hours ago.'

'It's Stella,' Meg told him. 'There's something wrong with her, she's walking slow.'

'Let's get you home and I'll take a look at her in the morning,' he replied.

Meg let him take the reins and they continued on their way with the toll of the bells from St Paul's guiding them safely home.

The following day, the fog had lifted. Down at the Railway Inn there was a stir of excitement when two strangers strode into the pub, headed for the small bar. Big Pete was in the middle of a game of dominoes with four others when the men walked in. He kicked his pal Robbie under the table and nodded towards the bar. Robbie turned and eyed the men up and down before turning back to Big Pete with a shrug.

'Young 'uns these days, eh?'

'Where'd you get them trousers from, son?' Big Pete shouted towards the bar. 'Steal them off a clown?'

'He *is* the clown,' Clarky shouted back, and the dominoes players erupted into laughter while Billy Shillen put his hand to the black patch of cloth that now covered the hole in his red trousers.

'And is the circus coming to Ryhope?' Big Pete laughed. 'Or are you two just passing through?'

Clarky walked towards the table.

'I'm looking for someone, a lass by the name of Meg. She runs a horse and cart and lives up the colliery. You wouldn't know where I might find her?'

Big Pete laid his dominoes face down on the table. 'And why's a fella like you looking for a quality lass like Meg?'

'We're doing business together,' Clarky said. 'Market business. She said I was to come and find her in Ryhope.'

Big Pete nodded slowly. 'Well, I'll tell you what, lad. You get yourself back to your clown there, and when you're ordering your ale, get another in for me and I'll let you know where you can find her.'

'Much obliged,' said Clarky, heading back to Billy at the bar.

With his tongue loosened over another pint of Vaux ale, Big Pete told Clarky how to find his way to Tunstall Street.

'And if she's not there, you'll likely find her at the back of Davey Scott's place with her horse,' he said, giving directions to the rhubarb field and Davey's house.

Clarky finished his own pint and leaned over to Billy. 'You stay here,' he told him. 'You'll have to get yourself home without me. I don't know how long I'm going to be.'

He swaggered out of the Railway Inn and walked towards the village green. At the corner, he turned right past the school. In front of him was St Paul's church with its pathway sweeping up through the gravestones towards the impressive arched oak door. He paused on the pavement by the wall that protected the church from the road and looked up at the leaded roof. Then he pushed open the iron gate and walked up the path. But instead of heading towards the church he walked around the back of it, looking from side to side to ensure no one else was around, then glancing up at the roof again. A plan began to form, but it was one that would need Billy's help, and he decided to leave it for now. Besides, he had tea at Meg's house to see to first.

He walked back round the church, through the gravestones. Just as he was about to head down the path again, he caught sight of a flash of colour on top of one of the graves. He walked over to it and smiled as he picked up the small floral tribute that had been left. He gave it a gentle shake to knock a spider from one of the leaves, then, with another glance around to ensure he wasn't being watched, he opened his jacket and slid the flowers inside.

Clarky walked on, up past the Guide Post Inn as Big Pete had instructed, keeping to the right-hand side of the road. The honey-coloured stone of the large houses in the village gave way to smaller, grubby rows of cottages opposite the large Co-op store. He made his way into the maze of terraces, looking for Tunstall Street. It was Meg's dog he spotted first in the back lane, the same dog that had tried to bite a chunk out of Billy Shillen's backside. At the sound of Clarky's footsteps, Spot's ears pricked up and his nose sniffed the air. He turned and headed to his own back yard, and Clarky followed.

'Is this it, boy?' he said. 'Is this where she lives?'

At the entrance to the yard, Clarky gave a quick look up and down the back lane, and when he saw the coast was clear, he kicked the dog hard in its back leg. With a yelp, Spot fell against the kitchen door.

'That's for biting Billy's arse, you bloody stupid dog,' he hissed.

He gave three sharp knocks at the back door. While he waited, Adam bounded into the back yard. He glared at the stranger, but before either of them could ask who the other was, the top half of the kitchen door was pushed open. Clarky's face cracked wide in a smile at the sight of Meg. She really was an eyeful, by far the best-looking lass he'd ever come across.

'I found your dog,' he said. 'It was crying in the lane there. Think it might have trodden on glass or something.'

Adam glared at Clarky. 'Who's your friend?' he asked Meg.

Meg pushed loose strands of her long hair behind her ears. She didn't know where to look first. 'Adam, this is Clarky.'

Adam stood stock still and Clarky nodded to him without a word.

'Stella's fine, if you're interested, Meg,' Adam said at last, trying to keep his voice firm. 'I just came to tell you that. She had a stone in her hoof, that's all. I've taken it out.'

'Thanks, Adam,' Meg said.

'I've cleaned the hoof too,' he continued. 'You should be all right to take her back on the road tomorrow.'

'Thank you,' she repeated, raising her gaze fully to him this time.

Adam turned to Clarky. 'And you, lad. What business have you got with the Sutcliffes?'

'I've been invited,' Clarky replied with a smile at Meg.

'Oh, have you now?' Adam asked sharply.

Clarky nodded. 'Meg asked me to come to tea, and here I am, coming for tea. Is that a problem for you . . .' he paused and stared hard at Adam, 'lad?'

'Adam works down the pit,' Meg said quickly. 'He works with the pit ponies and he's been helping me with Stella, she had a bad foot.'

'Pit ponies?' Clarky sneered.

Meg watched as Adam shot Clarky a look. She had known Adam all her life, but she had never seen such an expression of hatred on his face.

'There's nothing wrong with honest toil down the pit,' he said forcefully. 'We're hard workers in Ryhope. We might not have much, but we get what we want by working for it, not taking other people's—'

'What?' Clarky said. 'Taking other people's what?'

Adam shook his head. 'Nothing. I've said enough. I've got better things to do than pass the time of day with the likes of you.' He turned to Meg. 'I'm going home,' he said sternly. 'If you need me, you know where I am.'

He turned to leave and Spot followed him into the lane. Meg called after him. 'Adam . . . please, Adam . . .' but he didn't stop, he just kept on walking away.

Meg pushed open the door and Spot ran into the house past Clarky, taking up position by the coal fire in the kitchen, licking his wounded leg.

'So, you found me then,' she said.

'Said I would, didn't I?' Clarky replied.

He followed Meg into the kitchen, where she fell to her knees to tend to Spot, who was rubbing his head against her.

'Where does it hurt, boy?' she said. She lifted each paw in turn to inspect them, but the pink pads were intact, with no sign of injury. Spot moved from the fire and settled under the kitchen table, from where he kept a watchful eye on events.

Meg indicated Mam's chair by the fire. 'Have a seat,' she told Clarky. 'Get yourself warm. There's been a frost in the air today.'

Clarky looked around the room. It was a shabbier place than he'd imagined a beauty like Meg would live, but it was still more luxurious than the attic room he and Billy shared at the docks.

He reached into his jacket. 'I brought you these,' he said.

Meg gasped when he handed her the small bouquet. 'No one's ever given me flowers before.'

'Well, you deserve them,' Clarky said. 'Nice girl like you deserves nice things.'

Meg lifted the flowers to her nose and took a deep breath, but the only smell from them was that of damp earth.

Just then, Sally walked into the kitchen. As soon as Clarky saw her, he stood to attention from his seat.

'So, you must be Clarky,' she said. 'I've heard a lot about you from our Meg. And I'm grateful to you for looking after her while she's been at the market.'

'It's a pleasure to meet you, Mrs Sutcliffe,' Clarky replied. He extended his hand and Sally looked at him hard for a moment before she shook it. 'And thank you for inviting me to tea.'

Sally quickly glanced at Meg but kept quiet about being told that Clarky was coming to tea – and at such short notice too.

'Sit down, lad,' Sally said. 'No need to stand on my account. And there's not much for tea, just a bit of bread and fish.'

'Mam, Clarky brought me these flowers,' Meg said, showing her the bouquet.

Sally nodded. 'Very nice they are too. I've got a jug we can put them in. Give them here and I'll sort them for you.'

Meg handed her mam the flowers and Sally busied herself locating the pottery jug and filling it with water.

'Do you want them on the windowsill, Meg?' she asked. 'There's not much room on it, though.'

Meg reached over and picked up the glass jar that Adam had given her for her birthday, the jar he'd filled with pebbles, sea glass and shells. She placed it on the floor under the sideboard, then took the jug of flowers from her mam and positioned it where Adam's jar had stood.

'They look lovely, don't they?' she said, glancing at Clarky.

Sally handed Clarky and Meg a cup of tea each and then took a seat at the kitchen table.

'What do your mam and dad do, Clarky?' she asked.

'Dad's a fisherman, one of a crew, and Mam's a fishwife. She sells the fish down by the docks and at the market, or at least she used to, before she took poorly.'

'And you help them, do you?'

Clarky shook his head. 'I do a bit of fetching and carrying at the market with my mate Billy. Life on the sea as a fisherman isn't for me. I like being on dry land.'

'And is your mam all right now?' Meg asked. She looked at Sally. 'She's not been well, Clarky said.'

Clarky shifted in his seat. 'Oh aye, she's fine now, fine, thank you. I'll tell her you were asking after her.'

'And do you have any brothers or sisters?' Sally quizzed.

'Just one older sister, Barbara.'

'But I thought you said you were an only child?' Meg asked him, puzzled. 'That's why you couldn't leave your mam when she was poorly.'

Clarky took a long sip of his tea before he replied. 'I don't see her much, our Barbara. That's why I didn't mention her.' He flashed a smile at Sally. 'Smashing tea, this, Mrs Sutcliffe.'

Sally sipped her own tea and watched Clarky as he sat by the fire. When she met new folk that she liked, she always asked them to call her Sally and never Mrs Sutcliffe, once introductions had been made. Adam was the only person she knew who kept on calling her Mrs Sutcliffe, out of respect, although she often told him to call her by her first name. But there was something about Meg's new friend she didn't feel sure about. Oh, she'd be hard pressed to say what it was that made her feel uncomfortable, and she wouldn't mention anything to Meg, not yet anyway. But for now, Mrs Sutcliffe was what he could call her.

'What time will tea be ready, Mam?' Meg asked. 'Have I got time to take Clarky to see Stella? I could do with going up there to feed her.'

'Go on, get yourselves out for a walk and be back in half an hour,' Sally replied.

'But it's cold out,' Clarky said, wrapping his hands tight around his mug of tea.

'You can borrow my scarf if you like,' Meg offered.

Clarky pulled on his jacket and turned up the collar to give him as much protection as possible. He took the scarf that Meg held out to him and wrapped it tight around his neck. Meg thrust her arms into her dad's army coat and pulled on her green knitted hat, and with Spot following behind, the two of them headed out of the house.

'You'll like Stella, she's an old horse but a good worker,' Meg said brightly. But Clarky's ready smile of earlier had disappeared into the warmth of the fire they'd left behind in the house.

They walked towards the rhubarb field, now just a mess of muck as the plants lay dormant under the soil for the winter. When they reached the back of Davey Scott's house, there was no greeting from Davey or Gert and their kitchen door remained closed. Meg led Clarky into the makeshift stable at the back of the house, kicking through the straw on the ground.

'She's an old lady, this one,' she explained as she tended to Stella. Clarky remained silent and stood at the edge of the stable, away from the horse. Meg nuzzled into Stella's neck and the horse nudged her for more attention.

'Do you like horses, Clarky?' she asked.

He forced a smile. 'Course I do.'

'I'm glad she's out of pain now,' Meg said softly to herself.

'Look, Meg,' Clarky began. 'I was hoping we might have some time on our own, you know . . .'

'We *are* on our own,' she replied.

He waved his hand towards Stella. 'No . . . I mean, just the two of us. Not with your horse and the dog.'

Spot let out a soft growl at the tone of Clarky's voice.

'Just you and me,' he said more softly.

He walked towards her and she turned from the horse. Clarky wrapped an arm around her, pulling her to him, and she didn't resist.

'I want to get to know you, Meg,' he breathed, stroking her face with his hand. 'I want to know all about you.'

He kissed her softly, pulling her lips gently with his own. She responded eagerly, a flurry of gentle kisses falling around his mouth. She didn't want to stop but knew that she must and reluctantly pulled away.

'Clarky . . .' she breathed. 'We need to get home, Mam's waiting. But there'll be other times.'

Clarky raised his eyebrows. 'Other times? Is that right, now?'

'Just you and me, alone next time,' Meg said. For whatever she had felt kissing Clarky just now, she knew she wanted it again.

They walked in silence back to Tunstall Street, where Sally had the table set for tea with the jug of flowers in the middle. All through their meal of stottie bread and baked cod, she asked Clarky questions about his home life, determined to find out more about the young man that her daughter was clearly smitten with. She had always worried that Meg's beauty would bring the wrong type of fella to her door, and meeting Clarky made her worry all the more. A fella from the market with no proper job and no proper home life to speak of was definitely not the type she would have chosen for her daughter. But Meg seemed keen and so Sally chose to give him the benefit of the doubt, for now.

Some of her questions Clarky answered readily – those about his work at the market and his life at the docks. But Sally noticed a hesitancy in his replies when she asked him about his family, his sister and his mam, although there was no denying his politeness. After tea had been eaten, he offered to bring in the buckets of water from the back lane and coal from the coal house so that Meg and Sally didn't need to do it before Tommy came home for his bath.

'I'll walk you out,' Meg said when he finally took his leave.

'Bye, Mrs Sutcliffe,' Clarky said, putting on his cap and pulling the collar of his jacket up again.

Spot stood from his place by the fire and followed them to the back door. And as Clarky waved his farewell to Meg and left the back yard, the dog stayed tight by Meg's side, growling softly until the visitor had disappeared.

Clarky retraced his steps from earlier that day, walking down the colliery bank until he reached the Guide Post Inn. Lights were on inside and he made his way into the noise of the pub. Unlike the Railway Inn, no one in the Guide Post stared at a stranger walking into their midst. No one noticed, or cared, that an outsider had entered. Card games were under way at tables around the pub, with a small crowd of onlookers standing round. When a good hand was played, a cheer went up; when a bad hand was played, a long sigh. Clarky bought his pint and positioned himself to watch one of the games, which was being brought to its end.

'I'm out,' one of the players said, standing from his chair. 'My wife'll not be happy when I've told her how much I've lost to you boys.'

Clarky eyed the empty chair. 'May I?' he asked an old man at the table who was shuffling a deck of cards.

The man glanced around. One by one each of the players nodded their assent.

'Sit down, lad,' the dealer said. 'What's your name?'

'Johnny,' Clarky said without missing a beat. 'Johnny Hunt.'

'Well then, Johnny. Put your shillings on the table and you can join in the fun.'

'I was hoping we could play for higher stakes than shillings,' Clarky said.

One of the men at the table let out a whoop.

'We've got a high roller here, boys!'

'How much were you thinking?' the dealer asked him.

'It's not how much I'm willing to wager, but what I can trade instead,' Clarky replied.

The dealer cocked his head to one side, intrigued to know more.

'I've got a horse,' Clarky said.

Another whoop went up.

'It's an old horse, but a good worker. Healthy, too.'

'You're prepared to gamble your horse on a game of cards?'

Clarky eyed the pile of coins in the middle of the table. 'Winner takes all, right?'

The old man leaned back in his chair for a moment, shaking his head in disbelief. Then he started dealing the cards, cutting Clarky into the game.

Chapter Seven

Christmas

Clarky watched carefully as the cards were dealt to the four players around the table. It was the dealer's left hand he was interested in; not the hand that was dealing the cards, but the one that was holding the pack. As he had hoped, it wasn't as steady as it would have been had the dealer been sober. He had picked this table deliberately, having watched these particular players for a while before moving in to take the empty seat. And while he'd been watching, he'd noticed that the pints that had been supped had made their already rheumy eyes grow redder and their speech more slurred.

Once the cards were dealt, each man lifted them to his chest so that only he could see what they revealed. But the players weren't as sharp as they thought they were. The many pints of ale they'd downed in the course of the afternoon had turned them sloppy when they should have been careful, especially with a stranger at their table who'd offered no stake apart from the promise of a horse. They were so drunk they hadn't even bothered to quiz him further; they'd simply taken him at his word.

Clarky spotted a flash of red on a card held by the player to his left. His eyes flicked across again, and he saw on the corner of the card a diamond and the number four. He glanced at his own cards, pulling them tight towards him, not allowing anyone else at the table to see. He kept his smile hidden, giving nothing away. This was going to be easier than he could ever have guessed. Playing with slow-witted drunkards for a pile of cash in a back-street pub was child's play for him. His years spent playing cards at the market had honed his skills to perfection.

'You ready to play, Johnny Hunt?' the dealer asked, and Clarky simply nodded in reply.

An hour later, Clarky walked out of the Guide Post Inn with his jacket pockets heavy with coins. He headed back to the village, intent on spending some of his winnings on the price of a tram ticket to take him home to the docks. As he walked past St Paul's church, he glanced up again at the lead roof, wondering when he could put his plan into action. Not yet, not now. Now he was planning to head home back to the poky room he shared with Billy.

But as he rounded the corner of the village school and headed towards the tram stop, the welcoming lights of the Albion Inn proved too hard to resist. Within seconds, he was at the bar, being pulled a pint of Vaux stout by Jack Burdon. And while it might have been the first time Clarky had been served a pint in the Albion, it certainly wasn't the last. Within hours, he had been relieved of his winnings in exchange for pint after pint after pint. Drunk and penniless when Hetty finally called last orders, he was left with no option but to walk all the way home in the cold.

* * *

As the weeks went by, Meg called often at the market to offload the clothes she'd collected on the cart. Her business there was with Florrie, and the two women were becoming firm friends. But it was Clarky that Meg really looked forward to seeing there. Since their kiss, he was constantly on her mind, the last thing she thought about before falling asleep at night and the first thing she thought of when she woke. He wasn't to be found every time she went to the market, but she searched for him anyway, just in case he was in his usual place playing cards, on his own or with Billy. If he was there, she'd sit with him a while after she'd finished her business with Florrie, answering his questions about her life on the cart. But when she asked questions about *his* life – what he did outside of the market, where he lived, about his family – he always managed to turn the talk back to her.

'What's been happening in Ryhope, then?' he asked her one day as they sat together. 'Any news?'

Meg thought for a moment and then turned her gaze to meet his. 'Micky Parks has started working at the pit with our Tommy,' she said.

'Who's Micky Parks?' Clarky asked.

Meg shrugged. 'Just a friend of my brother's – they went to school together. Oh, and the vicar's on the warpath down at St Paul's. Someone's been stealing the lead off the roof, he says.'

'Is that right, now?' Clarky said slowly.

Meg nodded. 'He's asked me to keep an eye out in case anyone offers me lead when I'm out on the cart, and if they do, I'm to let him know.'

'Shocking news, that,' Clarky tutted, shaking his head. 'You can't trust anyone these days.'

A barrow trundled past them along the stone floor of the market, followed by a large man in a butcher's apron and heavy boots.

'Where do you want these turkeys?' the butcher shouted up the meat aisle.

'Up here, John!' a yell came back.

Meg watched as the featherless birds were unloaded from the barrow and strung up in rows across a stall.

'They're getting them in for Christmas,' Clarky said. 'Have you ever tasted one?'

Meg shook her head.

'Would you like to?'

'You can afford to buy one?' Meg asked, surprised.

'I might be able to. I was thinking . . .' He paused, then took hold of Meg's hand and raised it to his lips. Meg dared to let her hand rest against his face, to prove that she welcomed his touch and wanted more. 'I could bring one, like. A turkey, I mean. I could bring one for you and your mam and your Tommy this Christmas, to Ryhope.'

Meg drew her hand away. 'You mean you want to come for Christmas dinner?'

'Well, it was just a thought,' Clarky said, unable to bear the thought of yet another Christmas spent alone. Even Billy Shillen's mam cooked for her son once a year, but it was a meal to which Clarky was never invited. Clarky's own mam, Beattie, sent word to the market to say he was welcome to go home for Christmas dinner. But while his dad still lived and breathed, Clarky refused to go for fear of another drunken beating.

'I'd have to ask Mam,' Meg said quickly.

Clarky smiled.

Meg thought about Mam and her growing belly with the baby inside, and how much she'd enjoy eating the white meat of the turkey. They'd never had turkey before, not at Christmas, not ever. She raised her hand again and placed it gently on the side of Clarky's face, then her other hand went around his back, pulling him towards her.

Clarky couldn't believe his luck with Meg. Not only was she a beauty, but she believed his every word. It was proving a powerful combination and he knew just how to work his way in with her. First he had to get his feet under the table at her mam's house. Then he'd take his pleasure with Meg. He smiled at her and his eyes shone as she leaned in for a kiss.

There was just one problem now that Clarky had to resolve. But after he and Billy had risked life and limb stripping lead from the roof of St Paul's, how hard could stealing a turkey be?

In the days before Christmas, there was little work for Meg out on the horse and cart. None of the big houses on the village green had any linens or rags for her. Evelyn had told her that they were busy preparing for the Christmas dinners and parties. And as Meg travelled past the houses with Stella, she could see through the windows to where lights sparkled and even, in some houses, real trees stood, decorated with baubles. She saw living rooms and hallways decorated with paperchains of all colours. And when the snow began to fall, she saw snowmen standing proud in front gardens, wearing flat caps atop their heads, with pieces of coal for their eyes and carrots for their noses.

The snow made the village look pretty, enchanted, the snowflakes delicately dusting the village green. But back at

Tunstall Street, it made the pit rows look even worse than before. Grey slush banked up against the end of the rows, and in the back lane the melted snow mixed with muck from the netty and became stuck on boots and shoes. The taps in the back lane froze solid and only one of them, right at the far end away from Meg's house, remained able to work. It meant an even longer walk to collect water in the freezing cold.

Christmas Eve came around quickly and Meg set to cleaning the house for the following day, when Clarky would arrive with the turkey. Mam wasn't initially struck with the idea of him coming for Christmas dinner, although she wouldn't exactly say why, and it took some pleading from Meg to change her mind. It was only when Meg mentioned the turkey that she gave in.

Meg collected the water from the back lane and filled two buckets of coal for the fire. Then she set to helping Mam boil up toffee on the stove, with the two of them taking it in turns to stir the mixture in the blackened cast-iron pan. Home-made toffee had always been their yearly Christmas treat when she was a child, but during the war years of sugar rationing, it had become a luxury that they could ill afford. This year, though, with the turkey and then the toffee for after, there'd be a proper Christmas dinner for the very first time. Adam had called in earlier with the offer of a bag of sprouts from his allotment behind the Blue Bell, and Sally had enough potatoes to add to the meal too.

Needing a break from being on her feet all morning, Sally sank into her chair by the fire and tried to make herself comfortable. She put one hand to her belly.

'I swear I don't know how we'll manage when this little one comes along,' she sighed.

Meg looked up from the toffee pan. 'I'll help, Mam. I'll do what I can, you know that.'

Sally reached her hand to Meg's shoulder. 'You're a good lass, Meg.'

'I was thinking, I could start keeping any baby clothes I get given on the cart . . . I mean, if we wash them, they'll be all right, won't they? And the wool, we can unpick the jumpers that don't fit Tommy any more and knit them up into things for the baby. You can show me how to knit, Mam. I'll do everything I can.'

Sally stared hard into the dancing flames of the fire. 'Do you know what your grandad Sutcliffe did one Christmas when me and your dad were first wed?' she said softly. She didn't wait for Meg to reply before she continued reminiscing. 'He slaughtered his pet rabbit and served it up on Christmas Day. Of course, he told anyone who'd listen that it was chicken that he'd bought at the Co-op, and we never knew it wasn't. I mean, none of us had tasted chicken so how were we to know? It wasn't until months later that we found out the truth. He told us the rabbit had escaped into the field.'

'Do you miss him?' Meg asked, turning her head towards her mam.

Sally smiled. 'Who? Your grandad Sutcliffe or the rabbit?'

Meg laughed. 'You know who I mean. Do you miss Dad?'

Sally straightened herself in her chair. 'Folk tell me that I should. But the truth is, I don't. Your dad had the same problem with the drink that Grandad Sutcliffe had. The beer came before everything else, before me, before you and Tommy. No, love, I don't miss him. I just wish he'd been a better man, a more honest man, a man who loved his family more than he loved his ale.'

She reached out her hand and stroked loose strands of Meg's dark hair back from her lovely face. 'That's why I'm hoping this Clarky lad you've taken to doesn't turn out the same as your dad, pet. And speaking of the devil, what time's his lordship coming tomorrow?'

'His lordship? He's just a friend, Mam. He said he'll start walking from the docks early morning. And he's bringing us our first turkey, remember.'

Sally shot her daughter a look. Meg was entirely unaware of her beauty and how that could attract unwanted attention. 'I'm just worried about what he'll be expecting in return.'

Meg turned her back to her mam and returned to stirring the toffee with a little more vigour than before.

On Christmas morning, Tommy was out of bed first, determined to make the most of every minute of his day off work. After a quick trip to the netty, he brought in a bucket of coal from the yard and got the fire stoked high. Then he half walked, half skidded down the back lane to the one unfrozen water tap to fill a bucket. Spot followed him there and back, the dog's skinny legs slipping on the black ice.

'Merry Christmas!' Bob Mahone shouted from the yard next door when he saw Tommy walking by. 'Will we see you at the service this morning at St Paul's?'

'Merry Christmas, Bob!' Tommy replied, a wide smile on his face. 'We can't make it to church this year, 'cos we've got a turkey coming!'

* * *

Bob Mahone bent down to fill his bucket with coal from the shed in the yard and headed back indoors.

'Lil!' he called as he entered the kitchen. 'Lil! Next-door's having turkey for Christmas dinner.'

Lil looked up from the fire, where she was toasting thick slices of bread on the end of a forked metal stick held to the flames.

'Turkey? How on earth can they afford turkey?'

Bob shook his head. 'Beats me. Perhaps Meg's making more money with her horse-and-cart business than we gave her credit for.'

By the time Tommy walked back into the kitchen, Meg and Sally were up too.

'Are we having the tablecloth on, Mam?' Tommy asked.

Sally nodded. 'Course we are. It's a special occasion. Christmas dinner, turkey *and* a visitor.'

Tommy spread the thin red-and-white-checked cloth across the table. Mam started peeling potatoes at the sink and Meg began washing the sprouts. Tommy sat at the table, watching them, Spot lying by his feet with his head resting on his front paws.

'Can I have a bit of toffee, Mam?' he asked. 'Can I?'

'Go on then, just a bit. We're supposed to be keeping it for after dinner, remember.'

Just then, Spot jumped up and started barking. Immediately there was a brisk knock at the back door, once, twice. Meg and Sally exchanged a look.

'Go and let him in, pet,' Sally said.

Meg wiped her hands on the front of her pinny and all eyes turned to the door as she opened it to reveal Clarky with a parcel wrapped in newspaper under his arm. His face was pinched red from the cold.

'Merry Christmas, Mrs Sutcliffe,' he said, walking into the kitchen. A blast of cold air followed him inside.

Sally didn't fail to notice that he'd addressed her first, his manners impeccable as always, but still, there was something about him she just wouldn't allow herself to trust.

'I brought this for you,' he said, holding the package towards her. She took it from him and placed it on the table.

'Merry Christmas, Meg,' Clarky said, smiling at her.

As Sally fussed over the turkey, unwrapping it from its newspaper and string, Clarky took hold of Meg's hand and gave it a tight squeeze. Tommy stood from where he was sitting at the table.

'I'm Tommy,' he said as assertively as he could.

Clarky shook his hand. 'Merry Christmas, Tommy,' he said. 'And thank you, all of you, for inviting me for Christmas dinner.'

'Thank you for bringing the turkey,' Meg smiled.

'It was the least I could do,' he replied.

Sally appraised the bird, lifting its doughy skin this way and that.

'Should be able to get it into the coal oven, I reckon,' she said. 'It's not too big. Sit down, Clarky, you're making the place look untidy. Meg, put the kettle on, make us all a cup of tea.'

Clarky pulled out a chair at the table opposite Tommy and they watched the women prepare the meal. Spot took up his place at Tommy's feet again, keeping watch on Clarky.

'Would you like to see my medals?' Tommy asked, but before Clarky could reply, he had already disappeared up the stairs. When he returned, he held out his hand and Clarky saw three medals attached to ribbons of striped red, white and blue.

'They were Dad's, from the war. He gave them to me before he died.' He pointed to each one in turn. 'British campaign medals, see? This one's the Star, the one in the middle's the British War Medal and this one's his Victory Medal.'

'Pip, Squeak and Wilfred,' Sally piped up. 'That's what they call those three medals.'

Clarky reached out and picked up the medal from the centre of Tommy's hand.

'They're smashing, these, Tommy,' he said, feeling the weight in his own hand. He turned the medal over to look at both sides of it, running the ribbon through his fingers. Then he did the same with the other two. Tommy beamed with pride at his interest.

'I keep them safe, like,' he said. 'Hide them under my bed in a box.'

Clarky handed the medals back, and Tommy put them on top of the sideboard.

'Is there anything I can do to help with the dinner preparations, Mrs Sutcliffe?'

'No, lad. You've walked all the way here this morning and brought us this turkey. Just sit a while and warm yourself up,' Sally replied.

Tommy and Clarky exchanged a smile across the table.

'Meg tells me your old schoolfriend Micky Parks is working with you at the pit now,' Clarky said.

'He's been in that much trouble since he started work, though,' Tommy said. 'He's always cheeking the gaffer and not doing what he's supposed to.'

'I've finished doing the sprouts, Mam. Is there anything else I can do?' Meg asked.

Sally looked at the turkey again. 'I think I'll be able to manage now, love. I know you'll be wanting to go and feed Stella, so get yourself up there now. Give it a couple of hours or so and dinner should be ready to serve.'

'Do you want to come, Clarky?' Meg asked. 'And then we can have a bit of a walk around Ryhope, if you're not too tired from your walk here this morning.'

More walking was the last thing Clarky wanted, especially out in the cold, but time alone with Meg proved too hard to resist. It was the one reason he was here, after all. Forcing a smile, he stood and put his coat back on, while Meg thrust her arms into her dad's army coat, turned up the collar and pulled on her green hat.

Outside in Tunstall Street, the pit rows were deserted, the women indoors cooking whatever meagre rations they had for Christmas dinner, the men in the pub. Few of those from the colliery would be in the congregation at St Paul's singing Christmas hymns. Meg and Clarky walked up to the rhubarb field and round the back of Davey Scott's house, where Stella stood calmly in her stable. There was no light from Davey's house, and neither he nor Gert came out to greet Meg with Christmas wishes. Meg wondered if they were at church, or out visiting relatives.

Stella's stable was dry, the straw on the stone ground making it smell earthy and warm. Clarky stood to one side while Meg fed the old horse, watching the way her body moved inside the army greatcoat as she tended the animal.

With Stella munching contentedly, Meg turned towards him. 'Shall we walk around the village?' she asked. But she knew even before she suggested it that a walk was not what she really wanted at all. Ever since she'd first set eyes on Clarky, she had felt a connection between them. When she was with him at the market she felt alive inside, alive and wanted and loved in a way that she'd never felt before. And when they were apart, she spent her time thinking about him, wondering where he was and how he spent his days. If she felt it so powerfully then he must do too, surely? She turned her face towards him. 'Did you want to have a walk?' she whispered.

Clarky stayed quiet. He gestured with his hand for her to walk towards him. Meg eagerly did as she was bid. When she reached him, she lifted her face, her lips meeting his.

'A walk sounds good,' he breathed. 'But it's warmer in here.'

She snuggled closer into his body. 'Do you remember the first time we met at the market?' she asked him.

'Course I do.'

She raised her eyes to look deep into his. 'Well, I wasn't going to tell you this . . . it sounds silly when I say it out loud. But something happened that day . . . I can't say what it was, not really, but I felt it in here . . .' Her hand flew to her heart. 'And I need to know, Clarky . . . I need to know if you felt it too.'

There was a beat, just a moment, before he allowed himself to reply. 'Yeah. I felt it all right.'

Meg pushed herself further into Clarky's embrace and he wrapped his arms around her. They stood in silence for a couple of minutes, enjoying the heat of each other's bodies, before he spoke again.

'Your mam said she wants us back in a couple of hours. We could go for that walk you said you wanted to take.' He tilted Meg's face towards his own. 'Or we could stay here, get to know each other properly. Maybe you can tell me more about that feeling you said I gave you the first time we met?'

'Is it love, Clarky?' Meg asked softly, laying the side of her face on his coat. 'Is this what love feels like inside?'

Clarky gazed around the stable. 'Course it is,' he replied.

He didn't move; he didn't need to. Meg wanted his kiss. And she wanted more, wanted his touch on her body. Who was there to see them? Here in the stable on a cold Christmas morning, with no one around, not even Davey and Gert, who would know if she kissed him? Who would know if she allowed his touch on her body?

Clarky's strong hands twisted the buttons on Meg's coat and it fell open at the front. He slowly pulled off her woollen hat and then knelt down and laid it on the straw. Meg followed him to the ground, the two of them pulling at each other's clothes now, desperate to find contact, to find skin. She lay down on the straw and pulled him to her, their bodies hot and urgent, until finally Clarky released inside her with a shudder. She tried to kiss him again, but he rolled away and then stood.

They dressed quickly and quietly as Stella continued eating, and left the stable together acting as if nothing between them had changed. They walked to the village and Meg reached out to hold Clarky's hand. He allowed it to be taken for all of five steps before dropping it back to his side. Anyone who saw them would never have known them to be lovers, or even friends, just two people out together on a Christmas Day stroll.

They walked around the village green and Meg pointed out Ryhope Hall, where Evelyn worked. She hoped to see Evelyn at the window, so that her friend would see Clarky and she could show off her very own fella from the market. She desperately wanted to hold Clarky's hand, to cuddle up to him again, but he'd already shaken her off once since they'd left the stable and she didn't feel confident about trying again. If this was love, it was confusing, that was for sure.

As they passed Ryhope Hall, Meg looked through the huge bay window at the front of the house and saw Evelyn in her black-and-white maid's uniform and cap, serving at a table around which sat at least twelve, maybe fifteen people. She waved in the hope that Evelyn would see her, but the other girl was too busy to glance out of the window today of all days.

They walked in silence back to Tunstall Street, and as they stepped in through the kitchen door they were greeted by a strong, savoury smell the likes of which Meg had never known.

'It smells wonderful, Mam,' she said, taking off her coat and hat.

Underneath the table, Spot lifted his eyebrows and sniffed.

The table was laid now with plates, knives and forks. A white stone dish in the middle held thick brown gravy that sat underneath a curl of steam.

'Sit down, everyone,' Sally said.

Meg, Tommy and Clarky took their seats as Sally brought the bird to the table, followed by the potatoes and sprouts. Tommy carved the turkey and laid out the juicy white meat in thick slices on the four plates. Sally spooned out the vegetables.

'Help yourself to gravy, Clarky,' she said, pushing the bowl towards their visitor. 'And thank you again for this meal.'

She took her seat at the table and watched as Clarky tipped the gravy bowl to his plate. He took a little more than she would have liked – it meant there wasn't enough remaining for the three of them now, but she'd go without; the bairns had to come first. As he leaned across the table to pass the gravy bowl to Tommy, she spotted something unusual about the way his shirt was hanging at his neck. She was certain it had been buttoned correctly when he first arrived that morning, but now it looked all skew-whiff.

She glanced towards Meg and noticed for the first time – properly noticed – the flush in her daughter's cheeks and the tiny wisps of straw caught up in her hair. Her gaze dropped to the plate of food in front of her and she picked at the white meat with her fork. The Christmas dinner had been cooked to perfection and she'd been looking forward to eating it ever since she'd seen the turkey this morning. But now her heart sank with the realisation of what had happened between Clarky and Meg. If she hadn't been so hungry, she would have pushed her plate away. But the meal looked delicious and she needed the nourishment inside her, no matter how hard it might be to swallow. Because the last person she would have chosen for her daughter to lose her heart to – the very last person – was some fella from the market she knew nothing about.

In the cold, dark days after Christmas, Sally made the most of the turkey bones, boiling them up for thin soup on the kitchen stove. Tommy returned to work at the pit, with Adam calling at the kitchen door to collect the younger lad on his way to work his shift underground. And Meg, wrapped in layers of second-hand clothes under her dad's army coat, headed back out to the streets with a slow-moving Stella ahead of her and Spot sitting by her side.

Sally noticed that Meg stayed out of the house longer than usual on the days when she went to the market. She didn't need to ask why. It was Clarky, of course; her daughter's infatuation with him was clear. Sally wished for some time alone with Meg, just an hour, just the two of them, for the talk that every mother should give. She hadn't yet told Meg about the birds and the bees; she hadn't felt the need to. She knew that Meg had a good head on her shoulders, but as for knowing what went on in the dark between a woman and a man . . . well, it seemed she was learning it from Clarky instead.

Would her daughter listen to her now? Would she even need to? Sally wondered. She knew Meg had always had her dad's stubbornness within her and would do whatever she wanted, no matter what her mam or anyone else said. Speaking her mind at this stage might do more harm than good, and could even push Meg away from her.

On the morning of New Year's Eve, Tommy was already at work on the early shift when Meg left with Spot on the cart. With the house quiet, Sally took to cleaning the small cottage. The nesting instinct was upon her, she knew it; she'd felt the same way when she'd been pregnant with Meg and Tommy. She seemed to have an excess of energy she needed to get rid of. She wanted to enter the new year in as clean and ordered a fashion as she could.

She set to filling the poss tub, the large metal tub where dirty clothes were beaten clean with soap and water, carrying buckets of water along the back lane from the only tap that wasn't iced shut. She rolled up her sleeves as she brought bedsheets and pillowcases downstairs to be sloshed about in the water heated by the coal fire. Once she was certain the bedding was clean, then came the back-breaking task of running it through the mangle in the yard. Only then could it be hung to dry in the kitchen on the wooden rails of the clothes horse. In warmer weather, the washing would go up on the clothes line in the yard to blow about in the breeze. But on winter days like today, crisp with cold and ice, there was no option but to dry it indoors, steaming up the whole house.

Hours later, with the sheets still drying in front of the fire, Sally had a sit-down with a cup of tea and a piece of the day's stottie bread. Then she worked her way upstairs, sweeping the wooden steps one by one with a hard wire brush that banged and clattered as she worked. As she climbed ever higher up the stairs, sweeping the muck and dust into a small dustpan in her hand, she didn't hear the kitchen door behind her click open. And when she reached the top of the stairs to enter the bedroom that Meg and Tommy shared, she didn't hear the footsteps that landed on her kitchen floor. So engrossed was she in her work that when she finished tidying the bairns' bedroom and her own and came downstairs at last, she gasped with shock at the sight waiting for her in the kitchen.

'What . . . what are you doing here?' she said, trying to sound more assertive than she felt. She gripped the wire brush tightly in her left hand and the dustpan in the other, ready to use them as weapons if Hawk Jackson made a move.

'Bit early for a spring-clean, isn't it?' he growled from the chair by the fire where he was slumped.

'It's none of your business when I do my cleaning,' she spat.

There was a silence between them as Hawk eyed Sally from her boots all the way up, his gaze lingering on her pregnant belly. She glared back at him, trying to keep her breath as even as she could. She would not allow her fear to show, not to him. She noticed a redness in his cheeks that she would have put down to the cold of the day if it had been anyone but Hawk. But that redness, combined with the easy way he sat in the chair, was familiar to Sally. Hawk Jackson was drunk. She recognised the signs too easily from the days when Ernie had been in his cups. But although Ernie had been a drinker, he'd never been violent. He'd never so much as laid a finger on her or the bairns. After her last encounter with Hawk Jackson, though, she couldn't say the same of him.

'What do you want, Hawk?' she demanded, gripping the brush and pan tighter still.

A nasty smile played around Hawk's mouth. 'Oh, I think you know what I want, Sally Sutcliffe,' he grinned.

'I've told you, the rent's coming. I'll get it to you. You know that,' Sally said. But her words didn't come out as easily as she would have liked. She'd never been a good liar.

'So you say,' Hawk slurred. 'But you owe me . . . oh, let's see . . .' he started counting on his fat callused fingers, 'one, two, three, four weeks rent now, missus. Or is it five? Or even six? Can't say I remember all that well, but it's a lot of weeks, and do you know what that means?' He stood from the chair and inched towards Sally, bending slightly as he breathed the words in her face. 'It means a lot of money.'

Sally could smell the ale on him now, on his breath and on his clothes. There was another smell too, a stench coming from his filthy trousers. She took a step backwards, just one step, intent on taking another, then another, then running out of the kitchen into the back yard and yelling to Lil and Bob next door for help. But drunk as he was, Hawk saw the movement. His right arm shot out and his fist landed heavily on the side of Sally's face. The force of the blow pushed her back against the sideboard, the pain in her hip causing her to cry out. The brush and dustpan clattered to the stone floor.

'You bastard!' she howled. 'You absolute bas—'

His fist connected again with her face, and the shock of it this time, the intensity, left her gulping for breath.

'It's about time you cleared your debt, Sally Sutcliffe,' Hawk hissed. He pressed his body to hers so that she was trapped between his bulk and the sideboard behind her, and his hands went to the buttons of his trousers, working them loose. Sally twisted to get away from him, but he pressed against her harder still. Desperate, she screamed for Lil and Bob, hoping they were home, hoping they could hear her through their shared cottage wall.

Next door, Lil and Bob were indeed home and could hear Sally's cries, but Bob was as impassive as ever. He refused to acknowledge his wife's pleas to intervene in whatever horror was taking place on the other side of the thin wall.

'It's not our business, Lil!' he barked. 'How many times must I tell you? Leave well alone.'

Lil cast a nervous glance towards her husband. 'But it's Hawk Jackson again,' she said. 'I can tell it's him . . . Just listen, will you?'

Lil would recognise Hawk's voice anywhere. She had a hard time forgetting it, if truth be told. She knew only too well what Hawk was capable of, but Bob had no idea of what had gone on in the past between her and the evil landlord.

'Lil, I won't tell you again,' Bob said sternly. 'It's not our business to interfere. Just because we have the misfortune to live on top of each other in these shoddy little houses doesn't mean we're not entitled to some privacy. Now leave it well alone!'

Sally continued to scream over and over, but no one came and each cry just excited Hawk more. The dirty pink flesh in his trousers strained towards her. When his hands slid under her skirts, she pushed against his chest, but she was no match for him, no match at all. As his fat fingers worked their way up her bare legs, there was a noise behind him, and the back door was flung open to reveal Tommy standing there, black from head to toe after his shift at the pit.

'Son!' Sally yelled. 'Tommy! Get him off me!'

Tommy reached instinctively for the nearest weapon to hand, something that he could use to get Hawk away from his mam. The cast-iron pan in which Sally had made the turkey soup was standing on the sideboard – the very same pan that Sally's mam had given to her and Ernie on their wedding day. She'd scrubbed it clean that morning and it was waiting to be put back on its shelf. Hawk was lost in the moment, too drunk to care now, too lost in his urgent need to know or concern himself with what Tommy was doing. With both hands Tommy picked up the pan, feeling every muscle in his arms, every sinew, as he raised it above Hawk's head and brought it down heavily. The pan glanced off Hawk's shoulder and the pain and shock were enough for him to release his grip on Sally and shudder backwards, his trousers dropping around his thighs.

'You whore!' he screamed at Sally and raised his fist towards Tommy.

Tommy brought the pan down again with both hands, with more force than before. Hawk stumbled backwards, knocking the wooden clothes horse and the damp, steaming sheets to the floor. Tommy didn't move. He stood, trembling, with the pan in his hands, ready to strike him again.

'You'll regret this, you and your whore mother!' Hawk growled. Slowly he started to raise himself from the floor, trying to yank his trousers back up. But one of his feet caught in the filthy material, and as he tried to stand, he stumbled again. Drunk and weakened by Tommy's blows, he tumbled backwards, all the while swearing at them both, bitching and cursing until his head connected with the brass fender of the fireplace . . . and then there was nothing but Sally's tears and the roar of the coal fire to be heard.

Still Tommy didn't move. He stood ready for Hawk to get up and come at him once more, the pan held tight in both hands, like a cricketer waiting for a ball to be bowled. But there was nothing, not a sound, not a movement. Not a breath. Finally, Sally bent down to Hawk's body and laid a hand on his chest. It felt warm but was still. She laid an ear close to his mouth, but there was no sigh from his lips. She sank into her chair by the fire, watching for signs of life. Despite it all, she even prayed for signs of life. But Hawk lay still in front of the coal fire, with only the flicker of the flames reflected in his lifeless eyes.

Chapter Eight

New Year's Eve

Tommy fell into a chair at the kitchen table. His hands, which had grasped the cast-iron pan tightly just moments ago, began to tremble and the pan clattered to the floor. Neither he nor Sally could look at each other; both of them stared at the dead body of Hawk Jackson sprawled on the floor in front of the fire. A trickle of blood oozed from the back of Hawk's head and the fender was splattered with blood from his fall. The damp sheets and the clothes horse lay where they'd landed when Hawk fell.

Sally gasped, breaking the silence, and at first Tommy thought his mam was crying. But when he looked, he saw she was bent double, holding her stomach.

'What is it, Mam? Are you hurt?' he cried. He stood and walked over to her and laid his arm around her shoulders. Sally shook her head and tried to straighten her back against the chair.

'It's nothing, son. I'll be all right.' She smiled wanly.

'Did he . . . did he hurt you, Mam?' Tommy asked.

Sally raised her hand to the side of her face. 'Just here, son. Nowhere else.' She was too afraid yet to mention the dull ache in her back that had come on when Hawk had first slammed her against the sideboard.

Tommy took his seat again opposite his mam, Hawk's body lying between them.

'What are we going to do, Mam?' he asked at last.

Sally stared hard into the flames. She needed time to think.

'Shall I go for Hetty?' Tommy asked, but Sally shook her head.

Tommy tried again. 'The vicar, then? We need to tell someone, Mam, we need to let someone know what's happened.'

'We need someone we can trust, lad,' she said. 'Someone who'll help us.'

'Help us do what?'

Sally nodded to the body on the floor. 'Get rid of him.'

'Mam! No!' Tommy gasped in horror.

'Who'll miss him, eh? Who'll miss a nasty piece of work like him? Even his own brother wanted him dead not so long ago, the two of them fighting in the street up at Silksworth, I heard. Well, we've done them all a favour, haven't we?'

'Mam, you're in shock, you're not talking straight,' Tommy pleaded. 'You've brought us up to tell the truth. Stand tall, be polite and tell the truth, that's what you've always said. We have to tell someone, Mam, we have to go to the police. I killed him–'

'No, Tommy!' Sally snapped, pointing her finger straight at her son. 'He fell, never forget that. You did not kill him and this is not your fault. It's *my* problem. But do you think anyone will believe my word against a landlord like Hawk Jackson when I tell them that he died from a fall in my kitchen with his trousers around his knees?'

Tommy's shoulders sank.

'If we go to the police, they'll quiz us both, Tommy, and I'm not having you brought into this. It's my mess and I'll get us out of it. Now listen . . . was there anyone out in the back lane when you came home from work earlier?'

Tommy shook his head.

'Right then,' said Sally. 'Then here's what we're going to do . . .'

As Sally gathered her thoughts and outlined her plan to Tommy in the kitchen at Tunstall Street, Meg was making her way home with Stella and Spot. She'd had a good day, the sort of day she wouldn't mind having more of, despite the bitter cold. It had been so good that she'd been able to buy a small piece of ham for their New Year's Eve tea. She'd even sat with Clarky at the market for a little while, the two of them chatting and kissing when they thought no one was looking. Spending time with Clarky made her feel good. It made her feel special having a fella of her own. Clarky was someone she could confide in, and she told him everything, about life in the tiny cottage with her mam and Tommy. Every now and then, though, when she'd been talking to him, she'd caught him looking elsewhere, watching the women as they walked past with their baskets on their arms. And she was further confused by his actions when he had to leave suddenly to go out on business with Billy Shillen, leaving her sitting in the market alone.

She'd sold rags and linens to Florrie Smith, who had taken her down to the quayside and treated her to tea and a bun. Even Spot was given cooled tea in a bowl on the floor. While they ate and drank, Florrie had explained a little more to Meg about how to keep her accounts book. She'd showed her how to create columns to keep a note of how much money she was spending and how much she was taking in.

Meg was taking in precious little money yet, as she paid for food not just for Mam and Tommy but also for Stella and Spot. Not every day was easy, and sometimes she made no money at all after calling for rags and bones on the streets around Ryhope. But there were days when she was given clothes to sell at the market and rags to sell at the paper mill. There were days when she was given plenty of bones to sell to Big Pete in the Railway Inn. And when she added in the pennies she earned from selling Stella's manure to the allotment lads, on those days Meg knew what her dad had meant when he'd told her she'd be living the life.

It might be a mucky kind of life for a girl of her age, but it gave her a freedom she would never have had, she knew, if she'd gone into service like some of her friends from school. Her time would have been restricted by the demands of the big house, just like Evelyn's was. In fact, since Evelyn had started work at Ryhope Hall, Meg and Tommy hardly saw her any more. And if Meg had gone to work at the Co-op, she knew that her colliery ways wouldn't have come up to scratch in such an emporium.

She thought of the shop assistant at the Binns store that she'd had a run-in with, and a shiver went down her back. No, that life was not for her. Out here on the cart, although her cheeks might be ruddy from the wind and the cold, the rest of her body was warm. Underneath her dad's army coat, she wore any old rags she was given that would fit.

Her dad's army boots were Tommy's now, worn at the pit to give his feet some protection from the rigours of his work. Tommy balled up old pages from the *Sunderland Echo* that the lads at the pit gave him and stuffed them into the toes of the boots to make them fit.

As Meg travelled along the coast road to Ryhope, her heart lifted, as it always did, when she saw the spire of St Paul's church looming high above the fields. Dusk was falling quickly, and although she had less fear now of being out in the dark on the cart, she was looking forward to getting home and showing Mam the meat she'd bought. If Mam had baked earlier, there'd be stottie bread to eat with it too. Her stomach rumbled at the thought. The church bells chimed the hour and Meg realised that Tommy would be home by now, his shift over for the day. She imagined the look on his face when he saw the piece of ham.

As the cart trundled slowly into Ryhope, Stella slowed down, heading to the trough on the village green. Spot jumped off the cart to take a drink too, the two animals side by side with their heads bent, licking up the icy-cold water. When he'd finished, Spot jumped back up to sit behind Meg in his usual place, and Meg moved Stella slowly on. As they travelled past Ryhope Hall, she looked up at the window on the first floor, and there was Evelyn, dressed in her black-and-white uniform, waving at her. Meg smiled and waved back, then watched, stunned, as another figure, a boy no taller than Evelyn herself, appeared at the window. Meg saw Evelyn turn to him and point, and the boy waved too. Was that Evelyn's friend, Michael Patterson? she wondered. He wasn't dressed in a servant's uniform but a smart suit and tie. It must be him, she thought; who else could it be?

'Look, Spot!' she said to the dog behind her, pointing up at the window. 'It's Evelyn, up there, look!'

Spot followed the direction of Meg's hand and barked at the figures at the window, making Evelyn and the boy beside her burst into laughter. And then the cart moved on, leaving Evelyn and the village and the big house behind as Meg made her way up to Davey Scott's house to stable and feed Stella.

Once the horse was settled in, Meg gave a cheery wave to Davey and Gert through their kitchen window, where she saw them standing side by side. They always looked comfortable together, she thought, settled and happy. They complemented each other perfectly, both of them being short and a little overfed but cuddly with it too. They had been together for so long that it was almost as if they'd turned out looking like each other. When folk talked of Gert and Davey, it was always as a couple.

Never was it just Gert or just Davey, it was always both of them talked about in the same breath. She smiled when she saw them still watching her from their kitchen window. Gert's hair was piled high on her head, as if it would fall at any time, although it never did. Gert was too organised for that and her hair was always pinned in place. Davey was in his shirtsleeves, and without his flat cap on, Meg could see the remains of the reddish hair that he usually liked to keep hidden. She liked the Scotts, with their large family of grandbairns, and she felt safe when she was there. Gert and Davey liked her too, always ready with a hug and a smile for her.

She picked up the piece of ham wrapped in butcher's white paper and stuck it into her coat pocket. Then she and Spot made their way home to Mam.

* * *

'Meg Sutcliffe!' she heard when she reached the back lane of Tunstall Street. She recognised the voice immediately and turned to see Adam walking behind her. Spot recognised it too and happily sauntered up to Adam, who rewarded him with a scratch behind the ears. Meg stood and waited for Adam and Spot to catch her up so that they could all walk together. Adam swung a small paper bag in his hand.

'Got some more sprouts for your mam from the allotment,' he told her. 'Did you enjoy the ones I brought last time?'

'We had them with our Christmas dinner,' Meg replied. She felt a heat start in her neck and rise to her face as she remembered what had happened between her and Clarky on Christmas Day. She quickly turned her head away from Adam.

'Are you coming in to see Mam?' she asked. 'If we're lucky, she'll have the kettle on and you can stay for some tea.'

Adam whipped his flat cap off his head as they entered Meg's back yard. She pushed down the handle on the back door, expecting it to open as usual, but it was tight shut. She tried again, pressing her hip to the door this time, thinking the wood had jammed. But it still wouldn't budge. Then she noticed that the red-checked kitchen curtains that her mam had stitched from rags were pulled across the window. She banged on the door with her fist.

'Mam? Mam! It's me!'

She heard a scraping noise from within as a key turned in the lock. The door inched open and Tommy stood there, still black from his work at the pit.

'Leave the dog in the yard, Meg,' he whispered.

'Why? What's going on?' she demanded, trying to peer past him into the kitchen. 'Why are you still in your pit clothes?'

'Just leave him there. Please.'

'Spot. Stay,' Meg instructed the dog, and he slunk away to a corner of the yard, drooling at the smell of the ham in Meg's pocket that had teased him all the way home.

Then Tommy caught sight of Adam standing to one side behind Meg. 'He can't come in,' he told her, trying to keep the panic out of his voice. 'Adam can't come in.'

'What's going on, Tommy?' she demanded. 'Of course he can come in.'

She pushed past her brother and stepped into the kitchen. In front of her, right in the middle of the floor, was what looked like a thick roll of damp bed sheets. Steam was rising around the kitchen from the heat of the fire in the same way it did on Mam's weekly washing day. But there was no rhyme or reason that Meg could fathom to what a lumpy bundle of washing was doing on the floor. One glance at her mam's face told her that something serious was going on.

'Mam? What's happened?' She nodded towards the floor. 'What's . . . that?'

Adam stepped forward. 'Mrs Sutcliffe? Tommy? Are you all right?' he asked.

Sally and Tommy remained silent as Meg inched her way forward and peered down at the bundle of sheets. Hawk Jackson's empty eyes stared up at her. She looked from her mam to Tommy and back again, her mouth open in shock.

'Is he dead?' she whispered at last.

Tommy nodded, his eyes darting from Meg to Adam.

'But . . . why is he laid out on our floor?' Meg asked, trying to make sense of the sight in front of her.

'Is the vicar on his way?' Adam said in a quiet voice.

'I'm sorry you had to find us this way, Adam,' Sally said. She crossed her arms and pulled them tight across her stomach. 'I was hoping to keep this quiet, not get anyone else involved. But you've seen it now and there's no undoing what you know. In answer to your question, the vicar's not on his way because Hawk Jackson doesn't deserve the vicar's words. A man like him doesn't deserve anything at all.'

Meg put out a hand to the kitchen table to steady herself. Adam sank into a chair opposite Tommy.

'Hawk Jackson?' Meg breathed.

'I killed him,' Tommy said, raising his eyes to meet Meg's.

'No, son, you didn't,' Sally said sharply. 'He was trying to rape me. Tommy fought him off and he fell.'

She nodded at Meg.

'Sit down, pet, and I'll tell you and Adam what happened.'

As Sally's words spilled out of her, Meg felt her stomach grow cold and her eyes prick with tears. She sat stock still at the kitchen table, unable to move, still wearing her coat and hat but feeling an icy chill despite the flames from the hearth. Her mam's words came to her as if in a dream, a very bad dream, and she willed herself to wake up from the nightmare. She kicked her boots against the chair legs, angry with Hawk Jackson, angry with herself for not being there to protect Mam, angry at her dad for drinking and dying and not being there to protect any of them, angry at Tommy, so willing to take the blame for Hawk's death.

Meg knew her brother's temper, had seen him fighting alongside Micky Parks against village boys after school. They were fights that Tommy and Micky always won. But she also knew that her mam wouldn't lie to her, and if she said that Hawk had fallen after Tommy hit him to stop him raping her, then that was what she would believe.

When Sally's tale was told, the four of them sat in silence. Meg couldn't take her eyes off Hawk Jackson's body, bound tight in the sheets on the floor.

'Mam wants to get rid of him,' Tommy said at last, looking at Meg and Adam for support. 'I think we should tell someone, though, maybe his brother. That's it, we can tell Hawk's brother that we found him dead in the back lane, that he'd been drinking and—'

'No,' Sally said sharply. 'We tell no one, do you understand? No one.'

Meg and Tommy exchanged a look.

'I agree with Mam,' Meg said finally. 'We need to get rid of him. It was an accident, a fatal accident, and Mam's right. No one will miss him. No one will even know he was here.'

'But how?' pleaded Tommy. Sally too turned to her daughter.

'We need some help,' Meg said, thinking quickly. She looked at Adam. 'Will you help us?'

Adam was still in shock, unable to move, unable to speak. Finally he gave a sharp nod. 'Tell me what you want me to do,' he whispered.

Meg looked down again at the long, lumpy shape inside the bed sheets.

'I'll bring Stella and the cart tonight, but it needs to be before midnight. Before the pubs empty out and everyone's wishing everyone else a happy new year in the street. We'll do it while the pubs are still open and the streets are empty. We'll lift his body up on the cart, me, you and Tommy, and we'll take it down to the cliffs and give Hawk Jackson the only send-off he deserves.'

'Will your mam be expecting you home?' Sally asked Adam.

'She will, aye,' Adam replied, straightening in his chair. 'I'll . . . I'll go now and tell her I'm spending New Year's Eve here with you, and then she'll not worry. She'll not think anything unusual's going on.'

'Good lad,' Sally said.

'And what'll we do until it gets properly dark?' Tommy pleaded. 'Just sit here with the body and wait?'

'We'll move him into the coal house in the yard and shut the door on him for now,' said Meg.

'Come on, Tommy,' Adam said, nodding towards the sheets. 'Let's lift him and get him in the coal house.'

No one moved from their seats. Sally rocked gently forward with her arms around her stomach.

'Are you all right, Mam?' Meg asked.

'It's just a twinge, pet,' Sally replied. 'Now come on, the lot of you: get him out of my house. Just because he's dead doesn't mean he's not still the same evil bastard he was when he was alive.'

Adam stood and nodded towards Tommy. 'You take his feet, Tommy,' he said, positioning himself at Hawk's head. 'Meg, open the kitchen door and get the coal house open too. Make sure there's no one in the back lane first. We don't want anyone peering over the wall and seeing what's going on.'

'Make sure the Mahones don't catch you in the yard,' Sally warned.

As quickly and quietly as they could, Tommy and Adam lifted the body from the kitchen floor. Adam walked backwards, taking tiny steps to cope with the dead man's weight.

'Spot! Stay,' Meg told the dog as it stood to attention when Tommy and Adam brought out their grotesque burden. Spot lay back down in the corner of the yard, watching what was going on, sniffing the icy air.

It wasn't easy, but Tommy and Adam finally bundled the body into the coal house and Meg slid the lock shut on the outside of the door. Adam turned to the wall and stretched out his arms, his palms flat against the cold brick, breathing deeply in and out. Tommy swallowed hard, determined not to let the bile he felt inside rise up again. Finally Adam stood up straight and indicated to Meg and Tommy that they should head back into the kitchen. Once they were all inside, Meg locked the door.

'Don't wash,' Adam told Tommy. 'Leave the pit black on you; we don't want anyone to see our faces if we can help it. Meg . . . it'll be safer if you don't come tonight. Leave this to me and Tommy.'

'I'm coming, Adam, whether you want me to or not,' Meg said. 'Besides, Stella knows me, she'll respond to me better, and she's never been down to the beach before so I need to be with her in case the noise of the sea scares her.'

Adam knew there was little point arguing with her once her mind was made up.

'What if Davey and Gert ask what we're doing?' Tommy said.

Sally shook her head. 'They'll be in the Albion tonight, as they always are on New Year's Eve.'

Adam glanced at the clock on the mantelpiece. 'Tide'll be turning about nine,' he said. 'We need to do it before then, catch the tide when it's in at the cliffs. I shouldn't think anyone will be down there to see us. There'll be no fishermen on the beach tonight; they'll be too busy getting drunk in the pubs. I'll go down to see Mam now, tell her I'll be with you tonight for supper and to see in the new year.'

'You won't tell her anything else, will you, lad?' Sally said, but even as the words left her lips, she knew that Adam would keep their secret. After her own bairns and Hetty, he was the person she trusted most.

Once Adam had left, Meg called Spot into the house, and he went straight to the hearth and lay down in front of the fire. She locked the kitchen door again and the three of them sat in silence until Adam returned minutes later. It was only then that Meg started to remove her dad's coat, and that was when she remembered the ham in her pocket. She pulled out the damp, paper-wrapped parcel and laid it on the table. Spot's nose twitched at the smell of it.

'It's ham. I was hoping we could have it for tea, but—'

Sally cut her daughter short. 'No buts. We will have it for tea. Or at least, the three of you will. You'll need feeding up for what's ahead of you tonight.'

Sally rose slowly from her chair by the fire. She went to the sideboard and lifted the blackened cast-iron pan – the only pan she owned – to cook the meat. Tommy couldn't bear it: he buried his head in his hands and tried to stop the tears. Meg took the pan from her mam's hands.

'Here, let me do it,' she said softly.

Sally gave up the pan easily and sank back into the chair, gasping as a shot of pain circled her stomach and back. She saw the worried looks as all eyes turned towards her, and lifted one hand. 'I'm fine,' she said. 'I'll be fine.'

Meg moved towards the fire with the pan, warming it in the flames. Watching her, Adam remembered his own offering. He thrust the bag of sprouts towards her.

'Shall I scrub these and we can boil them?' he asked. 'I know it's not much of a meal, but it'll help keep our strength up.'

'Good lad.' Sally smiled at him. 'I don't know where we'd be without you.'

They ate their meal in silence, not really tasting the food and certainly not enjoying the luxury of the ham, knowing what was in store for them later. Sally nibbled at a piece of ham and ate a couple of sprouts, leaving the bulk of the meal for Adam and her bairns. Afterwards, tea was brewed and drunk in silence as Adam kept watch on the time. Then, under cover of the dark, he walked with Meg to fetch Stella and the cart from the back of Davey Scott's house, leaving Tommy under strict instructions not to let anyone into the house while they were gone.

Stella moved slowly from her stable, much more slowly than she ever did during the day. Meg pulled up the collar on her coat and brought her hat down over her face as much as she could. She'd lost the scarf that her mam had given her for her birthday, though she seemed to recall she'd had it when Clarky had called for tea the first time he came to Tunstall Street. Adam too pulled up his coat collar and hid his face as best as he could.

When they reached the back lane of Tunstall Street, Meg lined up Stella outside the back yard so that the cart was open and ready to be loaded. Again Tommy and Adam struggled with the weight and bulk of Hawk Jackson's body, which was stiffening now with the cold. Once it was on the cart, Meg threw old rags across it to hide the truth of her cargo.

Before they set off, Adam thrust both hands deep into the coal shed, turning his hands in amongst the black of the stones. Meg looked on but didn't ask any questions, trusting him to know what he was doing. With his hands covered in coal dust, he went straight to Stella and wiped the black all over the white star of her nose.

'Just in case anyone sees us tonight,' he whispered to Meg. 'If they're asked about what they saw, they'll have to say the horse wasn't Stella, because everyone in Ryhope knows that Stella's got a white star on her nose. Got it?'

Adam sat next to Meg on the cart, and Tommy had the task of making sure the body didn't roll out, sitting next to it with his head lowered so that no one saw his face. Spot stayed in the kitchen with Sally, lying by the fire as she started washing the plates from the meal and scrubbing the cast-iron pan clean again.

Adam was right: the streets of Ryhope were deserted on New Year's Eve. Those who could afford it were either sitting in one of the pubs or supping ale at home by way of celebration. Stella's hooves clipped down to the village green, past the big house where Evelyn worked, past the Albion Inn, where Hetty and Jack Burdon were serving on their busiest night of the year. No one noticed the horse and cart as it clattered through the village. Only when they were on the beach road, out of sight of the houses and pubs, did Meg breathe a sigh of relief. But before they could continue on down to the sea, the farmer's field had to be crossed.

'It won't be muddy, we won't get stuck,' Adam whispered when he felt her tense at the edge of the field. 'It's frozen solid.'

Stella walked into the field and the cart bounced behind her, throwing Meg and Adam together. Tommy kept his feet pushed up against Hawk's body in the back and hung on to the side of the cart until the field had been crossed and the ride became smooth again. The moon hung low over them as they made their way down to the sea, spilling silver light on to the water. Adam breathed a sigh of relief at the sound of the waves crashing into the cliffs. He'd timed it right after all.

'We haven't got much time,' he said, pointing to the clifftop. 'Up there.'

Meg pulled Stella to a stop in the gap between the cliffs, the sea just ahead of them. She jumped off the cart, and the three of them pulled the dead body towards them. Without being told, Tommy took Hawk's feet; Adam and Meg struggled to lift the rest of him, and between them they staggered slowly up the grassy bank to the top of the cliff, panting, sweating despite the icy-cold night, their chests heaving with exertion. The bed sheets that Hawk had been wrapped in were coming undone, and in the moonlight Meg could see the darker material under the cotton sheets exposing his trousers, his shirt, his hand.

They took a second to gather their breath, but just a second, for no time could be wasted; they needed to do what they'd come here to do and leave as quickly as they could. Hawk's body lay at the edge of the cliff as the waves pounded below, sending up spray that left its kiss on their faces and hands. The roar as the breakers hurled themselves at the cliff drowned out Adam's cry as he pushed the body into the sea. The crash of the waves also drowned out Meg's gasp of horror and Tommy's tears.

Adam beckoned to the others, pointing to Stella and the cart. Meg followed, but Tommy didn't move; he couldn't. He just stood on the clifftop, looking out to sea, the roar of the waves no match for the roar inside his own head. Adam motioned for Meg to continue down to Stella and the cart, then went back for Tommy, grabbing his arm and pulling him all the way back down to the road. They clambered aboard, and the cart slowly turned as Stella negotiated the track up to the beach road and back through the farmer's field. And as they headed home in silence, behind them, at the beach, Hawk Jackson's body was being picked up by the surging sea, picked up and dropped and smashed into the cliffs, over and over with each crashing wave.

Much later, the three of them walked back from the stable to the cottage at Tunstall Street. Sally was still up, sitting by the fire, waiting for them. Meg knew the minute she saw her mam's face that she'd been crying. She went straight to her and flung her arms around her neck. Sally gripped tight to her daughter and whispered in her ear.

'Hetty . . .'

'What?' Meg said, leaning in closer.

'Get Hetty,' Sally repeated urgently. 'Now.'

A gasp of breath left her lips as she doubled up with the pain that had been coursing through her in the hours she'd been alone at the house.

'I'll go,' Tommy gasped, but Meg shook her head.

'No, let me. Look at the state of you: you're still covered in coal dust. If you go out looking like that, folk will start asking questions. They know you finished at the pit hours ago. I'll go; you stay here with Mam.'

Meg ran like the clappers all the way down to the Albion Inn. It wasn't easy getting Hetty's attention, as the pub was heaving with revellers intent on bringing in the new year with as much ale in their bellies as they could afford. But as soon as Hetty caught sight of Meg in the crowd at the bar, she knew something was up. Jack Burdon complained, of course, when Hetty told him that she had to go. He complained loudly and bitterly and even grabbed his wife's arm to stop her leaving.

'What is it with them flamin' Sutcliffes?' he demanded. 'If it's not one thing, it's another. And I'd ask you to remember it's me you're married to, Hetty Burdon, and your duty is with me behind the bar of our pub!'

'Sally needs me, Jack,' Hetty said. She waved a hand out across the bar. 'None of these need me, and you . . . you don't want me any more, not since Philip died. I couldn't stop our lad from being killed, but by God, I'll do what I can to help my friend out of her pain.'

Jack dropped his hand from Hetty's arm and let her go without another word.

'Shall I go and fetch our mam while we wait for Hetty?' Adam asked Tommy, but it was Sally who replied.

'No, lad, no. Hetty will know what to do when she gets here.'

'What is it, Mam? Is it the baby?' Tommy asked, kneeling now in front of his mam's chair by the fire.

Sally rocked gently forward. 'I fear it might be, pet,' she said softly.

'He hit you much harder than you told us, didn't he?'

Sally didn't reply. She glanced up at Adam. 'I can't thank you enough for what you've done for us tonight, Adam. We'll never forget it and we'll never be able to repay you. We'll be forever in your debt.'

'Mrs Sutcliffe, I—'

Sally held up her hand. 'No need to say anything, lad. But Hetty's going to be here soon. It might be best for you to get yourself home now.'

Tommy stood and followed Adam out of the back door into the yard.

'Will she lose the baby?' he whispered.

Adam nodded. 'She might, Tommy. You'll have to be brave for her.' He turned to leave the yard and then stopped. 'Let me know if I can do anything to help. Anything at all.'

'Thank you, Adam,' Tommy said. 'Thank you – for everything.'

As Adam disappeared into the darkness, Tommy headed back to the kitchen to find his mam bent forward in her chair, gasping for air, a wail of pain coming from her. And that was when he saw the blood on the kitchen floor.

Chapter Nine

Mam

1920

Hetty sent for Dr Anderson immediately when she found Sally in the kitchen at Tunstall Street. But on New Year's Eve, such a night of celebration, the doctor proved hard to find. It was Meg who tracked him down eventually, just about to take his first glass of Vaux in the Railway Inn. But he couldn't save the baby. He found Sally too far gone with pain and contractions as her body rid itself of the child Hawk Jackson had killed inside her. Hawk's blows to her before he tried to rape her had done untold harm. Slamming her against the sideboard, over again, had destroyed the new life inside her.

In the first week of the new year, Hetty came often to the house, boiling up beef tea for her friend and sitting in a chair by the side of Sally's bed reading the news to her from copies of the *Sunderland Echo* left by customers in the pub.

And if Sally started to drift off to sleep, Hetty pulled a pencil from where she'd tucked it into her auburn hair and used it to circle the news stories she would read to her friend when she woke.

At work at the Albion Inn, when Jack's attention was elsewhere, Hetty popped a bottle of whisky under her shawl and took it up to Tunstall Street. She let herself in using the spare key – Ernie's key – that Sally had given her.

'Is that you, Hetty?' Sally called. 'I'm up here. I'm still not feeling up to coming downstairs yet.'

'Hush now,' Hetty said, entering the dark bedroom and taking up her position by Sally's bed. 'You'll be up when you're good and ready and not before.'

'But I feel so useless,' Sally said. 'I need to bathe too. I want to go downstairs.'

'You're not going anywhere, Sally Sutcliffe. You've been through a rotten time and you're to rest. You heard what Dr Anderson said. Some women are weak and ill for months after they lose a baby, and you've just had a few days. There's plenty of time to get up and out when you're better, Sally love. But now you've got to rest.'

Sally winced as she tried to shift position in her bed.

'How are the bairns managing with you laid up?' Hetty asked.

'They come and sit with me every night. Meg brings in some bits of meat from the market for our tea when she's had a good day. And she's looking after Tommy too. But it's not right, my bairns fending for themselves like that. I should be down there cooking for them, getting Tommy's bath ready for him instead of him having to do it himself.'

'They're good bairns,' smiled Hetty. She took Sally's hands in her own. 'You're lucky to have them.'

Sally gently squeezed Hetty's hands. 'I'm weakened inside now, Hetty. Dr Anderson told me yesterday when he called. Oh, if only I hadn't—'

'Now look!' Hetty said sternly. 'Let's be having none of this "if only". None of this is your fault, Sally. None of it. And you must never, ever blame yourself for losing a bairn, you hear me? Never.'

The next morning, Meg woke early. It was her turn on netty-cleaning duties, and with Mam still in bed, she had twice the chores to do. Lil Mahone next door hadn't been much use. Meg was confused and more than a little annoyed as to why their neighbour hadn't offered to assist her in looking after Mam, for she knew she would have helped if Lil had been laid up ill in bed. What Meg didn't know was that Lil had sworn to Bob that she wouldn't get involved in anyone else's business, and it was easier for her to tell him what he wanted to hear rather than risk another fight between them both.

Meg made a breakfast of boiled eggs and took one upstairs for Mam. But Mam wasn't sitting up waiting for her breakfast like she normally did. Meg opened the curtains, letting in what little light there was. Sally's shape under the bedclothes moved, but only just.

'Mam . . .' Meg said gently. 'Mam, I've got you an egg. And the kettle's on for tea.'

'Hetty?' Sally croaked from underneath the blanket.

'She's coming later,' Meg said. 'She'll bring dinner up for you from the Albion.'

Sally struggled to push herself up on to her elbows into a sitting position. Meg put the plate down and helped her get comfortable.

'I must look a fright.' Sally smiled at her daughter. 'I haven't had a bath in God knows how long, and—'

'Don't worry about it, Mam,' Meg said. 'Just eat and rest and get your strength back. There'll be time enough for a bath when you're feeling better and not before.'

'You're a good lass, Meg.'

Sally accepted the breakfast plate from her daughter and lifted the spoon, knocking it against the egg. She tried once, twice, but she couldn't break the shell. 'I haven't even got the strength to knock the top off a flaming egg,' she said.

Meg took the plate and opened the egg for her mam, digging deep into the runny yolk with the spoon.

As Sally ate, Meg went downstairs to make the tea. She filled up Spot's bowl of water on the kitchen floor and then brought up two steaming cups. They drank their tea together, chatting about Meg's day ahead, and about Stella. They talked about the cold of the day outside and the dark of the morning. They talked about Tommy, and Meg assured her mam, as she always did, that she'd have his bath waiting for him at the end of his shift. They talked about Lil Mahone next door and how she'd not even so much as popped in to ask after Sally. But what they didn't talk about was Clarky. Sally didn't press Meg about him, although there was a sadness about her daughter, she'd noticed, a quietness that wasn't usually there. But she knew that if Meg wanted to speak of him, she would. And if she didn't, then it was fine by her not to have his name mentioned again in her home.

With her chores done and Mam settled, Meg set off on the walk to the rhubarb field with Spot by her side to get Stella and the cart. The first thing she had to do was meet Big Pete in the Railway Inn to sell him the stack of bones she'd collected. She pulled the cart to a halt on the corner of the pub beside the serving hatch that was used to sell ale in jugs for those who wanted to drink their beer at home. Next to the hatch was the side door to the pub. Meg jumped down from the cart. She told Spot to stay, and the dog obeyed, as he always did. She pulled the heavy bag of bones from the back of the cart and dragged it along the ground towards the door.

'Oh here she is!' Big Pete called out as soon as she entered. All eyes turned towards her. Once she would have been fazed by this, but now she took it all in her stride. She even smiled at the elderly barmaid, who gave her a nod. One of the fellas sitting with Pete got up out of his seat and helped her drag the bag of bones to Pete's feet.

'Lemonade while you're here?' the barmaid asked, but Meg shook her head.

'Not today. I can't afford it,' she said. But the barmaid was already busying herself with a bottle.

'On the house, love,' she said, pushing the glass across the counter. 'You're looking a bit tired, if you don't mind me saying so. Sit down and have a drink.'

'Thank you,' Meg said, taking the lemonade and positioning herself at a table near the bar.

Big Pete walked over and handed her some money in exchange for the bones. 'You've done well, lass,' he said, tipping his hat to her before returning to his friends on the other side of the pub.

Meg knew she'd have to write up the takings in her little accounts book, but not here, not in the Railway Inn. She'd do it later, away from prying eyes. There was no need for anyone but her to know how much she was earning on the cart. As she sipped at her lemonade, enjoying the fizz on her tongue and the sugary taste in her mouth, she looked across at Big Pete and his friends in conversation and she caught a word, just one word, that made her sit up straight in her seat.

'Hawk?' Big Pete said.

The man to Pete's left-hand side nodded. 'That's what they reckon.'

'I heard that story too,' the man opposite Pete said. 'They say Jim's done away with him good and proper this time.'

'There's always been bad blood between them two brothers,' Big Pete said. 'And Jim's threatened to kill him before. Many's the time Jim and Hawk have been caught fighting, with knives too last time. And it's not as if Jim hasn't done it before . . .'

'What? Killed someone?'

Big Pete nodded and glanced around the pub. When he caught Meg looking over at them, he leaned in close to the table, all heads bent towards him as they carried on their conversation about how Hawk Jackson had gone missing and how his brother Jim was the likely culprit.

The rumours spread quickly around Ryhope that Jim had finally done away with Hawk, and soon reached Lil and Bob at Tunstall Street. Bob never paid any heed to local gossip, whatever the source or topic, and dismissed the talk with a wave of his hand.

'It's best not to speculate on such matters,' he said. 'When you've got two men as hard as the Jackson brothers, it's best to keep well out of such things.'

'But Bob . . .' Lil began. 'That night . . . New Year's

Eve, when we heard Hawk Jackson next door and Sally screaming. You don't think . . . you don't think them next door had anything to do with him disappearing, do you?'

'What are you saying, Lil?' Bob demanded. 'That little Sally Sutcliffe next door got rid of a big brute of a fella like Hawk Jackson? Don't be so daft.'

'But you heard her, Bob. You heard those screams.'

'Aye, and I heard a cuckoo in the clock an' all. I heard the whisper of the breeze and I heard the kettle on the boil. I've told you already, I'm not getting involved in any of this. And if the cops come calling, asking questions about Hawk, I want you to remember what I've said and say nowt to no one.'

'But Bob—'

'No buts, Lil. You know fine well I had a run-in with the coppers when I was younger, and by God, I've got no intention of getting involved with them again. If they come calling, you tell the cops we heard nothing, right? Nothing!'

Sally was confined to bed during much of the first weeks of the new year. Her body recovered much more slowly than her spirit. She was anxious to be up and out of bed, away from the stinking commode in the corner of her room. She wanted to go downstairs, to feel the heat from the coal fire on her skin. But all she felt was the chill from the bedroom window when sleet blew in on the wind. It was dark upstairs too, the tiny window letting in precious little light. And as she lay in her bed, unable to find the strength to get to her feet, little did she know that a secret was being kept from her.

* * *

The secret was one that Meg was keeping to herself, for now at least. It was burning within her, causing her to lie awake at night, staring up at the ceiling, running through all kinds of scenes in her mind. After nights spent tossing and turning, confused and angry, she could hardly keep her eyes open the next morning when she was busy with Stella on the cart. She couldn't bring herself to tell Mam. She couldn't bear to share the weight of it when Mam was suffering so much herself. But she needed to tell someone, to ask for advice from someone who knew about these things. And it had to be someone she could trust.

From everything Meg understood from the whispers in the playground when she'd been at school, there could only be one reason for her periods to stop. She'd waited and waited for her body to do what it had done monthly, regularly, since she was twelve years old. But the waiting had been in vain. She'd been feeling nauseous too, out on the cart each morning. The sickness had been so bad that she'd once had to pull Stella to a halt on the way to the paper mill to heave up on the side of the road.

She toyed with the idea of telling Hetty, of asking for her help, but then decided against it for fear that Hetty would tell Mam. And the last thing Meg wanted to do was give Mam any more reason to worry; she'd been through enough. She dismissed telling Evelyn because of her friend being too young to offer her the kind of advice that she needed. She also ruled out asking Adam's mam for advice for fear that Adam would find out before she wanted him to know. And he'd find out soon enough. And then Meg wondered if she could, or should, tell Florrie Smith. The two of them had become close at the market, but were they friends, real friends? Would Florrie respect Meg's secret if she told it to her in confidence? In her head Meg knew that she needed to get advice from someone who'd been through it. But in her heart, there was someone she needed to speak to first. And so, on a frosty January morning with the sun low in the sky, she decided to look for Clarky.

But as she was finishing her breakfast of hot tea and stottie bread, and feeding scraps to Spot, there was a sharp knock at the back door. Meg opened the door, surprised to see her next-door neighbour Lil Mahone there. She was further surprised when Lil didn't even wait for an invitation to enter, but simply barged past Meg and made her way inside.

'How's your mam, pet?' Lil asked without any preamble. She didn't wait for an answer, just continued straight on. 'Thought I'd call in, like, to see how she was doing, see if you needed anything.'

As she was speaking, she kept her gaze firmly fixed on the back door, as if expecting someone to walk in at any moment.

Meg was confused. 'Lil, if you don't mind me asking, what do you want? You've not come to see how Mam is in all the time she's been ill, and I can't for the life of me think why you're asking now.'

'Just being friendly,' Lil said quickly. 'Neighbourly.'

Meg opened her mouth to reply, but as she did so, there was another knock at the back door, a loud banging this time. When she opened it, a policeman was standing there, his helmet atop his head and a notepad and pencil in his hand.

'Can I come in, miss?' he asked politely. 'Just need to ask a few questions.'

'Yes . . . yes, of course,' Meg replied as calmly as she

could, although her heart was going nineteen to the dozen at the sight of the uniform. This was something she'd been dreading for days. Something she and Tommy had whispered about late at night from their beds. Had their secret been found out? She breathed deeply to calm herself and stepped aside to let the policeman enter. The height and bulk of him almost filled the kitchen.

Lil shrank back towards the fireplace, standing next to Spot, who was warming himself by the flames. The policeman looked from Meg to Lil and back again, and then gave a short cough.

'We're investigating the disappearance of Hawk Jackson,' he began. His deep voice was polite but firm.

Meg felt his words as a punch to her chest, and she couldn't hide the gasp of fear that escaped her mouth.

'A disturbing event, I'm sure, miss,' the policeman said, mistaking her fear for shock about the news. 'Now then, we've spoken to the other residents of Tunstall Street, where we believe Hawk Jackson was last seen on New Year's Eve, and you're last on my list of house-to-house enquiries, being right at the end here. I understand Mr Jackson was on Tunstall Street collecting rent the day he disappeared, is that right?'

'I . . . I . . .' Meg faltered.

'That's right,' said Lil firmly. 'He was here. You've already spoken to my husband next door and he's told you we saw Hawk Jackson leave here on the day he disappeared. I saw him myself when I went out in the back lane to use the netty.'

Meg swung round to look at Lil, but the older woman's piercing blue eyes gave nothing away.

The policeman addressed Meg directly. 'He left here?'

'Yes,' Meg said softly. She grasped the back of a chair with both hands to steady herself.

'And is there anyone else who can vouch for that?' he asked.

'My mam,' Meg replied. 'But she's upstairs in bed. She's ill, you see. Dr Anderson's been to see her and he's said she has to rest.'

'I might need to speak to her, for the record,' the policeman said.

Lil took a step forward. 'The woman's just lost a bairn. Have you no compassion, Officer? She's in no fit state to be questioned.'

The policeman gave another short cough. 'Yes, well, as you say, best leave her to recuperate. And when he left, Mr Jackson didn't give any indication as to where he was headed?'

Meg shook her head. She was gripping the back of the chair so hard that her knuckles had turned white.

'No. I don't think so. I can't remember.'

'He'll have been headed to the pub, Officer,' Lil said firmly. 'He was already drunk when he came to our house for the rent and he'll have been off to spend the money he'd collected on more beer, no doubt.'

'That's as may be,' the policeman sighed. 'And neither of you have heard anything from his brother Jim, have you?'

Meg and Lil both shook their heads.

The policeman tapped his pencil against the notepad in his hand and then stowed both the pad and the pencil in his pocket. Meg loosened her grip on the chair back as he turned to head out of the kitchen door.

'Thank you for your time, ladies,' he said as he left. 'And if you hear anything more, do be sure to call into the station.'

It was Lil who walked the policeman out into the yard and it was Lil who made sure that he'd turned the corner of Tunstall Street and walked away, out of sight. When she returned to the kitchen, she found Meg sitting in her mam's chair by the fire, bent double with her arms crossed in front of her. She stood for a moment, not saying a word. Finally Meg looked up.

'Why, Lil? Why did you lie for us?'

Lil straightened her back and took a deep breath. 'Because he's a bastard, that's why. Hawk Jackson is evil, and whatever happened to him, well, he had it coming. It's been long overdue.'

Meg steadied herself against the shock she felt, a mixture of relief and terror rushing through her.

'He tried it on with me, Meg,' Lil said quietly. 'It was years ago. I had to lie to Bob and tell him I fell over in the back lane when he saw the marks from the beating Hawk gave me. We were behind twice on the rent, twice, and he beat the living daylights out of me for it.'

'Bob doesn't know?' breathed Meg.

'No, and neither will he. I dare say if I'd told him, he would have killed Hawk himself. He's been handy with his fists in the past, has Bob. Oh, never against me, but against other men. He's spent a night or two in jail for his fights and he won't get involved with the police any more than he needs to these days. These thin walls don't hide any secrets, so I know you'll have heard us rowing. But I know Bob, I know how to handle him. He just doesn't like me sticking my nose into other people's business, says I should keep quiet about what I hear and see. You see, pet, it suits all of us to keep quiet about what happened on New Year's Eve. But I'll say this to you now, and I'll say it no more, I'm glad that Hawk's gone. And I'll tell you something else, me and Bob, we won't breathe a word about what we might or might not have heard the night he disappeared. Not a word, you hear me?'

Meg raised her gaze to meet Lil's piercing stare. 'Thank you, Lil. And to Bob, too.'

'We'll take it to our graves,' Lil said. 'And we'll never speak of it again. Oh, and if Bob should ever ask you, I wasn't here. I never called in, got it? He thinks I just nipped out to use the netty.' With that, she turned and walked from the kitchen, leaving Meg sitting by the fire.

As soon as she was alone, Meg's tears fell for a very long time. She kept her sniffling and sobbing as quiet as she could for fear that her mam would hear from upstairs in her sickbed. If the day ahead hadn't been as important as she'd planned it to be, she would have been tempted to stay home with Mam. She needed to tell Adam and Tommy about the policeman's visit and what Lil had done too, but all of that would have to wait. She knew that Adam's mam and dad would have been questioned by the policeman, and if Adam was at home, he'd have suffered having to lie, unless he'd been able to keep quiet while Jean and Henry had done all the talking.

She filled the kettle again and calmed herself with the ritual of making another pot of tea. Only when she felt still and ready did she start to think again about the day that lay ahead. The threat that had been hanging over them all, the tension they'd felt that at any time their secret could be discovered, finally seemed to be lifting. She would tell Mam about Lil's revelation later, as soon as she returned from the market. It might even help her on her road to recovery. But that was all for later; she couldn't put off any longer what she had to do today. She had to find Clarky and tell him her news.

Since the turn of the year, Clarky had spent less time at the market. Meg had gone looking for him every time she was there on business with Florrie, but she'd only seen him once or twice, and even then just briefly before he scuttled away. Where once he would easily have been found at the little table, playing cards with Billy Shillen, now he spent his time elsewhere. At first, she'd been worried, concerned about his disappearance. She'd given him the benefit of the doubt and thought maybe his absence from the market was because he was looking after his mam at home. Hadn't he told her that she'd been bad with her nerves? Maybe she was still ill. But she knew in her heart that she was making excuses for him. There was a reason he was avoiding her, and her initial concern gradually hardened to anger towards him each time she visited the market and he was nowhere to be found.

Everyone at the market knew Clarky – he'd worked there long enough to be one of the regulars – yet no one seemed to know where he was. Or at least that was what they told Meg. But today she was more determined than ever to find him once her business with Florrie was done. She would do whatever it took to make sure she spoke to him, and this time she would take no excuses from anyone who was hiding him from her.

She'd planned in advance what she was going to say to him when she found him, gone over the lines in her head. What his response would be to any of it would never be under her control, she knew that. She decided to give him a chance, just one chance, to make a commitment to her, if that was what he wanted. And if he didn't? Well, she'd deal with that if and when it happened. Being on her own didn't scare her, or so she kept telling herself. She had her dad's fighting spirit, the Sutcliffe fighting spirit, and if Clarky didn't want her, then she would take care of herself in the only way she knew how.

'You're looking a bit flushed, pet. Are you all right?' Florrie greeted her when she handed over the clothes at the stall.

'I'm fine,' Meg replied, hoping that the waves of nausea wouldn't come upon her again.

She took out her accounts book from the pocket of her dad's coat and pencilled in the amount that Florrie had paid her. She drew a line down the page and entered the date too, as Florrie had told her to do.

'You're not normally here so early, Meg,' Florrie said, putting the clothes on a stool behind her stall.

Meg kept her eyes on the corner of the clothes aisle, searching for Clarky still. 'Thought I'd make the most of the day,' she replied. 'And then get home to Mam this afternoon.'

Florrie leaned out across the stall with her elbows resting on a pile of shirts.

'How's she doing, your mam?'

Meg shrugged. 'She's still not up. She's weak. The doctor says there's not much can be done. She just needs to rest.'

'It's a sad to-do,' Florrie tutted. 'Very sad indeed. Losing a baby like that.'

'Florrie?' Meg began. 'I don't suppose you've seen Clarky around today, have you?'

Florrie pulled herself up from the shirts and busied herself behind the stall with the rags Meg had brought her, pulling the garments from the pile one by one, inspecting the seams and the buttons.

'Florrie?' Meg asked again.

Florrie stopped what she was doing. 'I've seen him,' she said sharply. 'You'll likely find him in the meat aisle, if you haven't looked there already.'

Meg turned and walked across the market, taking breath after deep breath to help prepare the words she had rehearsed so many times in her head.

He was there. She stopped in her tracks the minute she caught sight of his dark curls. She stopped so abruptly, so quickly, that Spot, who was following her, carried on walking and bumped into the back of her legs. Meg took another deep breath to try to calm her nerves before she moved towards Clarky. But breathing in the stench of dead flesh from the meat stalls made her stomach turn. She steadied herself, wondering whether to run from the market, but after a few seconds the wave of nausea passed, and she brought her hand to her nose as she headed towards Clarky.

He didn't hear her footsteps behind him. The shouts of the market traders and the rumble of the barrows on the cobbles drowned out all other noise. Spot clung to Meg's side as she made her way around the table where Clarky sat, turning over the cards in front of him. It was the dog he saw first, and then the swish of dark material as Meg's coat brushed past him. Without a word, she took the empty seat at the table, the seat where Billy Shillen usually sat. Clarky didn't look up. He continued playing his game of patience as Meg settled herself, pushing her feet forward in her boots and sitting up as straight as she could in the chair. Spot stood by her side, both of them watching Clarky.

'Haven't seen you for a while,' Meg said, more assertively than she felt.

Clarky laid the pack of cards face down on the table. Slowly he raised his gaze to meet Meg's and then glanced at Spot, who bared his teeth in return, giving a low growl.

'Do you have to bring that dog everywhere with you?' he said.

'You haven't answered my question.'

'Wasn't aware you'd asked one,' he replied with a cheeky smile. Meg noticed the dimple that appeared when he smiled. It was the same smile that had won her over the first time she'd met him at the market all those weeks ago, and yet there seemed to be a harshness to it now. Or was it just her imagination?

'I was wondering where you'd been,' she said. 'I've been to the market loads of times since Christmas . . .'

She let the word hang between them for a few seconds, searching Clarky's face for a sign. But she saw nothing in his eyes that proved that what had happened that day meant as much to him as it had to her.

'I've been busy,' he said, avoiding her gaze.

Meg reached a hand across the table and tried to take hold of Clarky's own, but he pulled away from her. He picked up the pack of cards again and started shuffling it.

'Clarky, I've got to talk to you,' Meg said quietly.

Still he didn't look at her. He finished shuffling the cards and started laying them out in neat rows, setting up a new game for himself.

Meg leaned across the table, scattering the cards, determined to get his attention. Around them the business of the market carried on with the clatter and rattle of the barrows on the cobbles.

'Listen to me, Clarky,' she said. 'I've got something to tell you.'

He dropped the rest of the cards to the table and leaned back in his chair, giving a long sigh.

'What?'

She put her hands to her belly. As soon as he saw the movement, his face dropped.

'No . . . no . . . oh no. You can't do this to me,' he said, shaking his head. 'You cannot do this to me!' He leaned across the table towards her. 'How do I even know it's mine?' he hissed.

Meg felt hot tears spring to her eyes. She had been determined not to cry, but none of the words she'd rehearsed would come now. It wasn't going how she'd planned and hoped.

'I know what you colliery kids are like,' Clarky spat. 'It could be anyone's child. Anyone's!'

'It's yours, Clarky,' Meg said softly. 'It's your baby . . . our baby.'

He pushed his chair back, leaping to his feet. 'No!' he yelled. 'I am having nothing to do with this, you hear me? Nothing!' He thumped the table hard with his fist, sending the cards spinning to the floor.

Meg dropped her gaze as the cards fluttered down. She saw the red flash of the two of hearts landing next to the jack of spades. Without another word, Clarky turned and walked away.

Meg swallowed hard. She would not cry. She had promised herself she would not cry, not here in full view of the shoppers and market traders. She sat at the card table, watching Clarky walk away, staring at the back of his jacket. Confusion raged inside her and she felt a hot rush of anger to her face. She swallowed against the lump that had risen in her throat and blinked back the tears that had found their way to her eyes. How could she have been so stupid as to have been taken in by someone so callous? How could she? She was a Sutcliffe, a strong lass from a strong family. And she'd let herself be taken in by someone who had just treated her like a piece of muck he'd found stuck to his boot. She had offered him the chance to accept her and the baby and he had thrown it back at her. Well, let him walk, she thought, let him walk far away. She knew then that the humiliation she felt meant that she would never allow herself to run after him. Never.

She blinked back the tears that still threatened to fall and bit her lip, determined to keep as much dignity as she could. She reached out and stroked Spot in his favourite place behind his ears, then bent low to the ground to pick up the two of hearts. She ran a hand across her face, tidying loose strands of hair behind her ears. She pushed her feet forward in her boots and pocketed the playing card. Then she got to her feet, lifted her head, thrust out her chin and walked steadily from the market with Spot by her side.

When Meg returned home, she headed upstairs to check on Mam and found her sleeping.

'Have you seen Dad's medals, Meg?' Tommy called out when he heard her footsteps on the stairs. 'I was going to give them a polish.'

Meg peered around the blanket that hung as a curtain between their beds. A rusty nail hammered into the wall at each end stretched it across the room. The grey wool blanket offered scant privacy, but Tommy and Meg had shared the room ever since they were little. They had learned over the years the best way to give each other as much space as they could.

'Can I come through?' Meg asked, and Tommy lifted the blanket to one side. He was on his hands and knees, peering underneath his bed.

'They were here, I know they were. I always kept them under here in that little box Mam gave me.'

'When did you have them last, can you remember?'

Tommy straightened up and knelt by the side of his bed. He bit his lip as he thought. 'I had them downstairs, I think. On Christmas Day, when Clarky came.'

Meg felt her throat tighten and a chill went through her. 'And did you bring them back upstairs and put them away?' she asked. She was certain that Clarky had never been upstairs in their house when he'd visited.

'I think so,' Tommy said. 'I mean, I always bring them back upstairs. But . . . I remember putting them on the sideboard after Clarky looked at them because I thought he might want to see them again before he left.'

He stood and looked at Meg. 'You don't think he took them, do you?'

Meg shook her head. 'I don't know, Tommy. I don't think I know him as well as I thought I did.'

'But you'll be seeing him again, won't you?' he asked. 'At the market? You'll see him and ask him?'

'I'll do what I can,' she said, although she had little confidence in ever seeing Clarky again.

She went to her own bed on the other side of the curtain. She took from her coat pocket the two of hearts card and placed it underneath her hard pillow.

That night, she didn't sleep well. It was a night spent thinking through the events of the day: what she could have said to make Clarky's reaction to the baby news different, better. In her mind, she went over and over the scene in the market, playing it out in all kinds of ways, ways that would have seen Clarky reach for her and take her in his arms and tell her that he loved her. But no matter how many times she thought it through, she knew that he had reacted in exactly the way that she had feared.

He'd disappointed her, certainly. He'd hurt her, confused and angered her, definitely. But had he ever loved her? Oh, she wanted to believe so. When he'd told her on Christmas Day in the stable that he too had felt in his heart what she had felt, that warm rush of love when they'd first met . . . had he been truthful to her then? So many doubts whirled in Meg's mind. Because if Clarky had not been truthful when he unbuttoned her coat and removed her clothes in the stable, then what hope did she have for the future with other men? Would other men tell her lies then leave her too? Would it always be like this? If she fell in love with someone else, someone who would be willing to take on her and the baby, would he turn out to be like Clarky? Was that really what love was about?

The following day, Meg made her way to the market with much on her mind. Since the night of Hawk's death, she and Adam had barely spoken to each other. The truth was, they had no words for what had happened, no way to communicate the enormity of what they had done. She knew that Adam would keep their secret, just like Tommy would, the three of them bound together by Hawk's death. Could she allow herself to feel a sense of relief, she wondered, after Lil had covered for them with the police? Could the pressure finally be off them all after what she'd overheard Big Pete and his cronies talking about in the pub? If Jim was being blamed for his brother's disappearance, then local gossip would soon spread around the village, cementing this as real news, further safeguarding their secret.

Meg knew that if Hawk hadn't fallen and died, if Tommy hadn't returned home when he did, it might have been Mam who was dead, her body cold in the earth at St Paul's churchyard. And now, the miscarriage brought on by Hawk's violence against her had left her too weak to leave her bed. Meg wanted to believe that Mam would get better; she needed to believe it. But the truth was that every morning, when she took her breakfast upstairs, Mam looked more frail and overwhelmed.

There was only one person Meg could turn to for advice now. She urged Stella to trot on, to move a little faster. But Stella was slow now, slower than she'd ever been before. 'Come on, old lady,' Meg cried from the cart, but it made little difference.

When she finally reached the market, Meg looked for Clarky, her eyes darting this way and that, up and down each aisle. Her heart leapt when she saw a figure sitting at the card table at the end of the meat aisle, but it was only Billy Shillen. He denied having seen Clarky when Meg quizzed him, but there was a reluctance to meet her gaze that told her all that she needed to know.

With Spot following, Meg made her way to the clothes aisle, where she knew Florrie would be. The whole aisle was busy with bargain-hunters, women in shawls wrapped around them with baskets on their arms and babies at their hips. Toddlers in shabby jackets, some without shoes, held tight to their mothers' skirts as the women scrabbled through piles of linens and cottons on the stalls. Meg walked slowly up the aisle, watching the children's faces and returning their stares. She looked at the babies being held tight by their mothers, some wrapped up in the women's shawls with just their tiny faces peeking out through the wool. Women pushed and shoved around her, trying to get to the stalls that offered the best bargains and the cheapest clothes.

Up above the stalls were the dresses and coats hung high away from snatching hands that could ill afford such luxuries. The fur coat that had been displayed at the market ever since Meg's first visit was still there, still for sale, although she knew now that it wasn't real fur – Florrie had told her so. But still it was far beyond the means of those who scavenged at the market. Shouts were exchanged across the aisle as the women behind the stalls yelled out their wares. 'Shirts!' 'Trousers!' 'Shoes for the bairns!'

Meg felt the floor beneath her feet move, just slightly, and reached out to grab the woman next to her to steady herself. Her head spun, the floor no longer solid under her feet as she lurched with each step forward. A face in the crowd, the hatchet face of an old woman, loomed into her vision.

'Are you drunk, lass?' the woman asked.

Meg opened her mouth to reply, but no words would emerge. She collapsed to the floor and passed out.

A cry went up for Florrie's help when one of the stall-holders recognised Meg as Florrie's friend. Meg's fine features and beauty meant that hers was a face few people forgot. It was Florrie who helped her to her feet and called for a glass of water. And it was Florrie who helped her to walk to the back of her stall, where Meg sat on the stool with Spot by her side, his head resting on her lap.

'Florrie, can I talk to you when you finish here today?' Meg asked in between sips of water.

'Course you can, love,' Florrie replied, although she already had an inkling of what Meg was about to say. She'd noticed the girl's face and figure filling out over the last few weeks. 'But we'll not talk here, not in the market,' she continued. 'And it might be best for us not to talk down at the café either. If you can take me home on the cart when I'm done here, I'll serve up dinner for us both and you can let Spot loose in my garden.'

Meg's eyes widened. 'You have a garden?'

Florrie laughed. 'By, lass, if you're that excited about a garden, I'm not sure how you'll react when you see what else I've got at the house.'

'What is it?' asked Meg.

Florrie winked. 'Just you wait and see.'

Meg remembered the way to Florrie's house after her first visit there in the autumn. With its warm honey stone, welcoming front door and clean windows with flowered curtains inside, how could she forget such a place? She pulled Stella to a stop in front of number ten.

'Keep going,' Florrie said, pointing to the end of the lane. 'There's a turning you can use to get into the garden from the back. There's plenty of grass there too, Stella would like that, wouldn't she?'

They carried on in the direction Florrie indicated, and as they swung around the back of the lane, Florrie's garden came into view. It looked like a field, with trees around the edges standing tall, spindly and brown.

'She'll be safe enough here,' Florrie said, hopping down

off the cart. 'And Spot too; let them loose, both of them, while we're indoors.'

Meg readied herself to climb down from the cart and Florrie positioned herself to help, holding out her hand to her friend.

'After this morning, I get the feeling you might be needing this,' she smiled. Meg took Florrie's hand, grateful for the support.

Florrie led her to a wooden gate in the stone wall and they entered the back garden together. Spot immediately ran to one of the trees and lifted his leg.

'I'm sorry!' Meg said.

Florrie shook her head. 'No need for apologies, love, that's what dogs do. Now bring Stella in and let her chomp on some of this grass. It'll save me having to call in the gardener to cut it.'

'Do you really have a gardener?' Meg asked.

Florrie smiled. 'No, he's just a friend. A friend who helps me out now and then.'

Meg gazed around her, taking in the sight. There was so much space, so much green, with the expanse of grass that ran from the stone wall at the end of the garden down to the house itself.

'Florrie, this is . . . this is beautiful,' she said. 'But where's your netty?'

Florrie nodded to where the horse and cart stood in the back lane. 'Bring Stella into the garden,' she said. 'I'll go and get the house opened up and then I'll show you around inside.'

Meg did as she was told, and left Stella happily chewing on the grass with Spot running rings around the trees, barking and chasing his tail. Every time he ran too close to

Stella, she swished her tail at him, a warning to leave her in peace as she ate.

Meg had never seen the likes of Florrie's house before. It wasn't as ornate or as stuffed full of furniture as the big houses on Ryhope village green. The curtains at the windows weren't as heavy or as patterned as those she'd seen when she'd collected rags from Evelyn. There was a simplicity that Meg warmed to. And the kitchen was more than double the size of her mam's back at Tunstall Street.

Florrie removed her brown velvet hat and laid it on top of the sideboard. Then she ran her hand through her hair and shook out her short brown curls.

'Sit down,' she told Meg, indicating the chair by the fire. 'Pull the fire guard away if you need more heat. You never know, you might even warm up enough to take off that blasted coat, or is it glued on?'

At Florrie's remark, Meg crossed her arms and hugged the coat closer to her.

'Do you live here alone, Florrie?' she asked.

Florrie kept her back to Meg, busying herself with the kettle, and it took her a long time to answer.

'I do now,' she said at last. 'But I didn't always live alone.' She turned to face Meg. 'Remember that bank you took me to in Sunderland? My husband was the manager there, before he died.'

'In the war?' Meg asked.

'Before that,' Florrie replied. 'It was a long time ago but it feels like yesterday sometimes. Anyway, after he died and his will was read, it turned out I owned this house and I've been here ever since. Working on the market keeps me busy. The money's not great but it puts food in my belly and keeps the wolf from the door.'

Meg watched as Florrie made a pot of tea that she covered with a knitted tea cosy of red and white stripes. While the tea was brewing, she picked up a tea cloth and used it to pull open the oven door next to the fire. Inside Meg saw a large, flat orange pan with a blackened lid and handles on either side.

'Panackelty all right for you?' Florrie asked.

Meg couldn't remember the last time she'd had panackelty. A memory came to her of Grandma Sutcliffe making the potato and onion dish when she and Tommy were very small.

'Thanks, Florrie,' she said.

Florrie ladled the stew on to plates for them both and handed Meg a fork. Meg stared hard at the food, trying to work out what the small brown bits in between the potato and onion were. She'd never seen panackelty made with beef before.

'Here . . .' Florrie said, handing over a chunk of flat white bread, 'have some stottie to soak up the juices.'

Florrie pulled up a chair beside the fire and sat opposite Meg.

'Now then,' she said, gulping down a mouthful of hot food. 'I know you said you wanted to talk to me, but I'll save you the embarrassment. Just answer me one thing – how far gone are you?'

Meg felt tears prick her eyes and a lump rise in her throat. 'Since Christmas,' she whispered. 'I've not needed my monthly towels since Christmas.'

'And it's Clarky's?' Florrie asked.

Meg nodded.

'Does he know?'

Meg lifted her gaze to meet her friend's. 'Yes,' she said

quietly. 'But I haven't seen him since I told him.'

Florrie sighed heavily. 'And it's likely you'll not see him again, pet. I warned you about him, didn't I? A girl as pretty as you, you're easy prey for men like Clarky. You can cover yourself up in that daft old coat you wear, but you can't hide your beauty, Meg, not even if you wanted to. And there'll always be fellas like Clarky willing to take advantage of a girl with a pretty face. But it's too late for all of that now. We've got to think about you and what you're going to do. Do you want to get rid of it?'

Meg shrugged. 'I don't know . . . No . . . I don't know what to do. I haven't thought yet. I haven't had time to think . . .'

'Or you could give it away,' Florrie said. 'I know women who'd offer you money in exchange for a baby, women who can't have their own. It's good money too. Or there are homes you can go to if you want to keep it, places for young girls in your situation. They'll look after you and the baby.'

'No,' Meg said, shaking her head. 'No, I don't want to go into a home. I won't.'

'Good,' Florrie said, stabbing a piece of potato with her fork. 'And I'm guessing your mam doesn't know?'

Meg shook her head. 'I can't tell her, not yet. Not with the way she is.'

'But you're going to have to tell her soon enough,' Florrie said. She bit into a chunk of bread. 'She'll find out, Meg. There's no hiding these things.'

Meg looked at the food on her plate. The smell of it was something else, meaty and savoury. It was unlike anything she had seen or eaten in a very long time. She'd been living on little more than fish from Adam and eggs from the farm for as long as she could remember.

'Eat up,' Florrie said. 'We'll talk more after you've finished.'

'I need the netty,' Meg said.

Florrie nodded towards a door in the kitchen. 'The closet's through there,' she said.

'It's indoors?' Meg cried. 'Is that . . . is that hygienic?'

Florrie smiled. 'Yes, lass, it's indoors. That's what I wanted to show you. Is yours in your yard?'

'It's across the back lane,' Meg replied. 'And we have to share it with the neighbours down our end of the street.'

'Well, this one's private.' Florrie smiled. 'Go on, go and have a look.'

With dinner over, darkness had begun to fall and Meg knew she had to make her way home. Florrie's words had given her much to think about and she realised she had options now. But could she really bear to sell her baby? Or visit a woman who would flush it from her body? One thing she knew, absolutely knew, was that she would not go into a home for girls who had been caught out as she had. She talked it over and over with Florrie after dinner and Florrie told her she would offer her as much support as she was able over the coming months. But she also told Meg that she must break the news to her mam.

'Who knows,' she said. 'It might even perk her up to know she has a grandbairn on the way.'

Meg wasn't sure about that, but she knew Florrie was right when she said that she should tell Mam the truth. On the journey from Florrie's house to Ryhope, she thought about what she would say to Mam when she returned home. She practised saying the words out loud as the cart rattled past St Paul's and up to the rhubarb field. She tried them again in the stable as she settled Stella in for the night. And she repeated them under her breath as she walked with Spot down the back lane at Tunstall Street.

When she reached the back yard, she took her key from her coat pocket to open the kitchen door, which was always kept locked now that Mam was ill in bed and she and Tommy were out at work. But the door was already open and slightly ajar. She pushed at it slowly, scared to look inside. Would it be Hawk's brother Jim in there, come to take his revenge on them all?

'Meg? Is that you?' she heard a voice call.

She ran to the foot of the stairs, where she saw Hetty kneeling on the floor.

'It's your mam, pet,' Hetty said, beckoning Meg to her.

Meg looked down at the thin body cradled in Hetty's arms.

'She must have tried to come downstairs and fallen. I found her here when I brought her dinner.'

Meg knelt on the floor next to Hetty and the older woman wrapped her arm around her shoulder.

'I'm sorry, Meg,' Hetty sobbed. 'I am so, so sorry.'

Meg's own tears fell soundlessly. She cried for her mam and for the child that Hawk's violence had so cruelly taken from her. And she cried for Clarky and her own baby, and for what would become of them all.

Chapter Ten

Light

On the morning of Sally's funeral, Meg and Tommy sat together in the kitchen at Tunstall Street.

'Is it our fault, Meg?' Tommy asked quietly as he gazed into the fire.

Meg turned at his words. 'What on earth do you mean?'

'Is it our fault . . . my fault that Mam died? I keep feeling that it is. That it's my punishment for what happened with Hawk that night.'

Meg went to her brother and crouched down on the floor in front of him. She took both of his hands in her own.

'Listen to me, Tommy. Mam died because of Hawk, because of the complications with the baby after he beat it from her body. You mustn't blame yourself, Tommy. Never.'

Tommy lifted his gaze to meet Meg's. 'Will it ever go away, this pain inside at losing Mam?'

'I don't know,' Meg said. 'But I don't think I want it to, not fully. I always want to remember her, to feel her in my heart, don't you? Maybe one day when we're older, it won't hurt as much, but we'll still feel her around us. One day we'll stop crying, and we'll carry our grief around like a shiny stone in our pockets. It'll always be there to remind us of her.'

Tommy sniffed back his tears. 'Do you think she's with Dad now?'

Meg forced a smile to her face. 'Dad'll be in a pub, wherever he is.'

Tommy sniffed again.

'But you mustn't blame yourself, Tommy. Promise me you won't.'

'I'll try,' he replied.

Meg smiled. 'Promise me you'll try, then?'

'I promise.'

The fire roared in the hearth and the kettle was already filled with water ready for anyone who came back to the house for a cup of tea after. Not that many were expected at the funeral. There'd be Hetty, of course, along with Adam and Evelyn and their parents Henry and Jean Wilson. Lil Mahone from next door would be there, because a funeral was as good a place as any to find out what was going on and she might meet up with folk she hadn't seen in weeks. Bob had expressed his disapproval, but as soon as Lil offered to bring him a jug of ale from the Colliery Inn before she left, he reluctantly came around to the idea.

A sound at the kitchen door caused Meg to glance up, and she smiled when she saw Hetty walking in.

'Are you ready?' Hetty asked, looking from Meg to Tommy.

They both stood, as did Spot, who'd been lying at Meg's feet.

'Spot, stay,' Meg ordered, and the dog obediently lay back down.

Hetty turned to Meg. 'Oh love, is that really what you're going to wear today of all days?'

Meg simply nodded in reply and Hetty didn't question her further. In her grief over her mam's death, Meg wanted nothing more than to wear Ernie's army coat. She needed to feel the warmth and protection of her dad around her as her mam was being laid to rest.

'Listen, both of you,' Hetty said. 'Jack and I have been talking and we'd like you to come and live with us at the Albion.'

Tommy and Meg exchanged a look that didn't go unnoticed by Hetty.

'Only if you want to, that is,' she added hurriedly. 'But the offer's there. We've got a spare room. It's Philip's room, of course, always will be. But I can make space for the pair of you for as long as you need.'

'Thanks, Hetty,' Meg said softly.

Hetty nodded towards Spot. 'There's just one thing, though. Jack's not fond of dogs. He's allergic. He says they bring him out in a red rash. So we wouldn't be able to take in the dog. But the two of you would be welcome. I wanted to make the offer to you both and let you think on it. There's no need to decide just yet, but Jack's asked if you could let him know as soon as—'

'Come on,' Meg said, interrupting her. 'We should be going. Reverend Daye will be waiting.'

Hetty turned and locked the kitchen door at the same time that Meg unlocked the door at the front of the cottage. Out in the street, Lil Mahone was waiting, ready to join the mourning party.

Hetty, Meg and Tommy walked down the colliery to St Paul's church with Hetty in the middle and Meg and Tommy at either side. Lil walked a few steps behind, dabbing at her eyes with one of Bob's old cotton handkerchiefs.

'Jack says we can call at the Albion for a drink after,' Hetty said as they neared the church.

'That'd be grand,' Lil piped up from the back.

Inside the church, in the second row from the front, sat the Wilsons, all four of them. Meg took her place in the pew in front of them, with Tommy sitting next to her, then Hetty. Lil sat in the third row and there was a rustle of paper as she delved into her handbag for a boiled sweet. In the rows behind sat Sally's friends from the colliery, and customers from the Albion Inn who had known her when she worked behind the bar.

The vicar cleared his throat to bring them all to order. Then he began with a speech about Sally being one of his flock, a proud villager and devoted mother. A hymn was sung, just one. It was Sally's favourite, the twenty-third psalm. Lil was in good voice and sang out deep and strong. Meg and Tommy did what they could, half singing, half whispering the words they knew well. When Tommy faltered, Hetty, standing next to him, sang louder still to carry him along with her. All too soon it was over, Sally's pauper's funeral brought to a close with prayers and a blessing from Reverend Daye, and the small group left the church in silence, leaving Sally's coffin behind. Outside in the cold air, the mourners gathered by the church door as the vicar shook everyone's hands and wished them well on their way.

'There's a free drink at the Albion for those who'd like it,' Hetty announced.

'I'd like to go, Meg. Can I?' Tommy asked.

'I'll look after him,' Adam's dad offered.

Meg nodded her assent. 'I think I'll head straight home,' she told them all.

'Then I'll come with you,' Adam said. 'Please, let me walk you home.'

Lil Mahone was first down the church path, leading the group walking to the pub for the wake. Behind her came Adam's dad, Henry Wilson, who looked just like Adam in every way, though his open, honest face was more lined and worn than his son's. Henry was followed by his wife Jean, who was deep in conversation with Hetty. Evelyn walked next to Tommy, her arm linked through his.

Adam and Meg headed in the opposite direction, back towards Tunstall Street.

'Hetty's offered to take us in,' Meg told Adam as they walked up the colliery bank.

'And will you go?'

'We'd have to leave Spot,' she said quickly. 'And I've grown fond of him now. And there's Stella to think about too. I'd be further away from her if I was living at the Albion.'

'But you'd be fed and watered if you lived with Jack and Hetty,' Adam said. 'They'd look after you and Tommy properly. You'd not go without. And I could still come and see you . . . if you wanted me to, of course.'

Meg smiled. 'Course I'd want you to. And Tommy would want to see you too. You're our friend, Adam, our best friend.'

Adam stared straight ahead as they walked along the back lane at Tunstall Street. When they reached the gate, Meg paused before heading into the yard.

'Adam . . . there's another reason I don't want to go and live with Hetty and Jack.'

'What is it?' he asked. 'I know Jack Burdon can be a bit of a stickler for discipline – he runs a tight ship at the Albion, I've been told – but Hetty's all right, isn't she? She'd look out for the two of you.'

'Well that's just it . . .' Meg began. She pushed open the gate into the yard. 'Come on in,' she said. 'I'll make us some tea. There's something I've got to tell you . . . something I need you to know.'

Adam stood in front of the fire warming his backside as Meg busied herself with the teapot and kettle.

'Do you need any coal fetching in while I'm here?' he offered.

Meg shook her head. 'Thank you, Adam, but Tommy will do it when he gets back.'

'The church was cold, wasn't it?' he said, turning to warm his hands at the fire.

'Always is,' Meg noted. 'Even when I've been there in the middle of summer for the church fayre, it's always dark and cold inside. Pretty, though, with the stained-glass windows, isn't it?'

Adam stood watching her, unsure what to do with himself.

'Sit down, Adam,' she said at last.

'In your mam's chair? Doesn't seem right somehow.'

'It's the warmest seat in the whole house; someone might as well make use of it. It'll take the chill off you.'

Adam did as he was told and Meg pulled a chair from the kitchen table to sit opposite. She handed him a steaming mug of strong tea.

'Two sugars, just how you like it,' she said.

Adam placed the cup down on the fireside hearth. 'You said you had something to tell me, Meg,' he said seriously.

Meg swallowed hard from her mug, the hot tea burning the roof of her mouth. She took a few seconds before she began to speak, but once she started, the words tumbled out of her. She was relieved at last to confide in someone who knew her inside and out. Adam sat in silence as she spoke about her feelings for Clarky, her words like bullets to his heart. And when she told him about the baby and about Clarky's disappearance, there were tears in his eyes that he didn't try to hide.

'Do you want me to find him for you, Meg?' he offered. 'I'll go to the market and I'll bloody well kill him when I find him!'

'You'll do no such thing,' Meg said. 'He's made things clear. He doesn't want to know. And I won't go chasing someone who doesn't want me. I might not have much, but I've got my pride. I don't want him found, not now.' She put her mug of tea on the hearth next to Adam's and laid her hands on her stomach.

'Who else knows?' Adam asked.

'Just Florrie, a woman on the market I'm friendly with.'

'Not even Tommy, or Hetty?'

Meg shook her head. 'I'll tell them in my own time. But I want to keep the baby, Adam. I've made up my mind. With Mam gone, I want someone of my own to love now, you know? I'll find a way to keep it. I'll earn more, I'll work harder. Me and Tommy can keep the house going for a while. We'll manage the rent somehow.'

'Hawk's brother Jim is collecting the rent again now, I've heard,' Adam said.

At the mention of Hawk's name, the two of them fell silent.

'My mam will look after you, Meg,' Adam said at last. 'I know she'll want to help . . . when she finds out about the baby.'

'Don't tell her yet, will you?' Meg pleaded. 'I need to tell folk in my own time.'

Adam nodded. 'And I . . . I could help too, if you'd let me.'

'Don't suppose you know much about babies,' Meg smiled.

'What I mean is, well . . . I could marry you.'

'You?' Meg smiled.

Adam shrank back into his chair.

'Are you serious?' she said softly.

'No one need know the baby's not mine. It'd save you having to explain to folk about Clarky,' he said. 'You'll be the talk of Ryhope when the news comes out, and it will, you know. But if I told everyone I was the dad, well, it'd be more respectable, like. I earn a decent wage at the pit. You, me and Tommy could live here, couldn't we? And Mam could come and help out. And our Evelyn loves children, she would—'

'No,' said Meg forcefully.

Adam's shoulders sank and his gaze dropped to the floor. Meg reached across to him and took his hands.

'What I mean is . . . I've made my mind up, Adam. This is my baby and I'm going to bring it up on my own.'

He lifted his gaze to meet hers, and she saw the tears in his eyes.

'It's not that I'm not grateful,' she said quietly. 'It's just—'

'Well, I've said my piece and I've made my offer,' Adam said, dropping her hands. He stood from the chair. 'And now that I know where things stand, I shan't embarrass either of us by offering again. Now if you'll forgive me, I've to get home and get ready for my night shift at the pit.' With that, he turned and walked out of the kitchen, closing the door gently behind him.

Meg sat by the fire a while after Adam had gone, his untouched mug of tea growing cold on the hearth. Had she done the right thing? she wondered. Should she have accepted his offer, if not for her own sake then for the baby's? It just didn't seem right somehow to marry him when she didn't love him, not in that way at least. He'd always been Adam, just Adam, like a brother to her . . . hadn't he? It was hard to think of him as anything other than that. He was sweet, was Adam. He was kind and gentle and good, but he didn't set the butterflies free in her stomach when he smiled at her, not like Clarky had done. But maybe being as different to Clarky as he could possibly be was not such a bad thing after all. When she'd reached out to hold Adam's hand just now, she hadn't felt the way she felt when she held Clarky's hand, felt his skin against hers. But there had been a sense of comfort there, even if she'd had to turn his offer down. For that was what it was, wasn't it? Just an offer to marry her for the sake of the baby. There'd been no mention of love. And yet sitting with Adam, holding hands in front of the fire, had felt reassuring somehow, comfortable and right.

Meanwhile, down at the Albion Inn, Jack Burdon was bristling after Hetty insisted on serving up a round of free drinks to the mourners.

'Don't give me that look, Jack,' she told him as she gathered the glasses onto a tray. 'It's just one round of drinks. You might care more about your finances than your friends, but Sally was my best friend and the least I can do is offer them all a drink.'

'Just one, then,' Jack said sternly. 'Otherwise folk will think I've gone soft.'

Hetty shot her husband a look. 'I doubt there's much danger of that,' she replied.

She took the drinks to the corner of the front bar where the small group of mourners sat, and handed out glasses of whisky to Lil, Henry and Jean. For Evelyn and Tommy there were larger glasses.

'Here, half a pint of shandy for each of you.'

When everyone had their drink, Hetty pulled up a stool and joined them at their table. She raised her own glass.

'To Sally. May her soul rest in peace.'

'To Sally,' they chimed.

'To Mam,' whispered Tommy.

Lil Mahone took a long sip of the dark amber liquid from the heavy glass.

'Is there no food at this wake? I don't usually drink on an empty stomach.'

'No, Lil, there's no food,' said Hetty. 'Just be grateful you're getting a free drink.'

Lil sniffed. 'Funeral's not a funeral without a good spread afterwards. Ooh, the last funeral I was at, there was a beautiful piece of ham there, remarkable it was.'

Jean glanced at Hetty and raised her eyebrows.

'Have a bit of respect,' she told Lil, nodding gently towards Tommy.

'I was just saying,' Lil said quietly, suitably chastised.

'I've offered for Tommy and Meg to move in here,' Hetty told the group.

'Will you?' Evelyn asked Tommy.

He shrugged. 'Don't know. Me and Meg haven't talked about it yet.'

'It's very kind of you, Hetty love,' said Jean. She turned to Tommy. 'It'd give you and Meg the chance to save a bit of money. I've heard Jim Jackson's going to put the rents up now that Hawk's disappeared.'

'Oh, speaking of Hawk . . .' Hetty said. She stood and walked across to the bar, where she picked up a copy of the *Sunderland Echo*. She brought the newspaper back to the table, licked her index finger and flicked through the pages until she found the story she was searching for.

'Here, what do you make to this?' she said, pointing at two square inches of newsprint at the bottom of a page.

As the others leaned forward to read the story, Tommy sat stock still. His heart was beating every which way inside his chest and he felt sure the others could hear the drumming of it as it tried to escape his body. His brow broke into a sweat as Lil began to read out loud.

Mystery of body washed ashore at Seaham

Sunderland police have failed to identify a man's body washed ashore at Seaham. The body came ashore at Nose's Point during the winter storm of Friday last. It was thought that it may have been that of missing Ryhope man Herbert Jackson, known locally as 'Hawk'. However, Mr Jackson's brother James failed to identify the body when called in by the Sunderland coroner, Mr Edward Harley Esq.

Sunderland police report that the body does not match records of other missing persons in the area. They now believe the dead man could have been a vagrant.

Burial to follow this week.

Tommy took a long swig of fizzy beer and lemonade. His hands started trembling.

'Well I never!' crowed Lil. She swirled the last few whisky drops around the bottom of her glass and tipped them into her open mouth. 'Think I'll be getting myself home for a spot of dinner then,' she said.

She gathered her handbag towards her and said her goodbyes, then headed for the pub door, muttering to herself all the way. 'Who'd have thought it? A funeral without a ham. Wait till I tell Bob about this.'

Once Lil had left, Hetty bought them all a second round of drinks, making a show of putting her own money into the till under Jack's watchful gaze. The newspaper still lay open in the middle of the table when she returned with the tray of glasses. But the story of Hawk and Jim Jackson had been forgotten as talk turned to the new beer from the Vaux brewery on sale in the pub.

When the Albion started to fill with pitmen finished on their shift, Jean and Henry suggested to Tommy and Evelyn that they walk home together. Hetty went to work beside Jack at the bar as the others put on coats, scarves and gloves. Unnoticed, Tommy picked up the copy of the *Sunderland Echo* and slid it inside his jacket before they began the slow walk up the colliery back to Tunstall Street. When they reached the back lane, he bade a polite farewell to the others before turning into the back yard and bursting into the kitchen.

Meg turned sharply when she heard him. 'You'll have that door off its hinges if you're not careful,' she said.

Tommy thrust the newspaper towards her. 'You've got to look at this, Meg! You've got to read it!'

Meg took the paper.

'There.' Tommy pointed. 'Read it, Meg. Read it.'

He stood over his sister as she scanned the words in front of her. Slowly she turned her gaze upwards.

'But it could be anyone,' she said at last. 'If his brother says it's not Hawk, then who's to say Hawk's body won't wash up any day now? Who's to say the police won't come to our door and ask questions we haven't got the answers for?'

'Everyone knows dead bodies in the sea from round here wash up at Nose's Point. And no one else has been reported missing. It's got to be him, Meg, it's got to be.'

Meg laid the paper on her knee. 'I suppose there's a chance,' she said. 'Do you know what this means, Tommy, if it is him? We can stop looking over our shoulder all the time. We can sleep a little easier.'

'We need to tell Adam,' said Tommy. 'Where is he anyway? I thought you two walked home from church together.'

'You go,' Meg replied, knowing full well that Adam would not want to see her again tonight, not after what had just happened between them. 'You go and tell him and show him the paper. But keep it hidden inside your coat so that his mam and dad don't see it. We don't want them to worry. I'll stay here, and when you come back, I'll boil up beef tea for us both.'

Tommy ran from the house along the back lane towards the Wilson house. Left alone at the fireside, Meg took a deep breath, and then another. It was too early to believe that they were out of the woods, and she wouldn't believe it, not yet. But an unidentified body washing up on the tide at Seaham was important news indeed, and something that she would take a scrap of comfort from, for now anyway.

Now, if anyone had asked Jim Jackson what he thought of Edward Harley Esq., he'd have had to say he was a funny-looking fella. The Sunderland coroner was a short man, almost as wide as he was tall, with a round head and an even rounder belly. A pair of specs sat awkwardly on his fat face and a black hat topped his bald head. It was a hat that Edward Harley removed when Jim Jackson went to identify the dead body that had been washed ashore. Jim had reported Hawk missing out of a sense of duty, not from concern or brotherly love. And so when a body was washed up at Nose's Point, he was called in by the coroner to see if he could identify it.

Jim knew the minute he saw the body who it was. Even with the corpse so badly decomposed after being crashed around in the waves for weeks, he recognised his brother straight away. There it was, the strawberry birthmark on Hawk's shoulder, the birthmark Jim used to tease him about when they were kids. But he kept his face straight and his manner passive. Since Hawk had gone missing, gossip the length and breadth of Ryhope had been rife that Jim had done his brother in. Everyone knew of the hate the Jackson brothers had for each other. From the looks they gave him and the gossip he heard, Jim had already been found guilty by Ryhope folk of killing Hawk and doing away with his remains.

Now he stood by Hawk's dead body, aware that the eyes of Edward Harley were watching. If he told the truth to the coroner, that the body in front of him was that of his brother Hawk, then the folk of Ryhope who had already found him guilty would roll their eyes and say to one another: 'Didn't I tell you Jim murdered him? Wasn't I right all along?' The whole village – and beyond – knew of his threats to kill Hawk and had seen the brothers fighting. If he told the truth, he knew the police would pounce on the gossip and the rumours and his freedom would be taken with few questions asked. But if he lied . . . if he told the coroner that the body in front of him was not his brother, that he didn't recognise the bones of him, the skin of him, the hair, the eyes, the nose of him, well . . .

'It's not him.'

'Are you sure, Mr Jackson?' Edward Harley Esq. asked, making a note in his ledger.

Jim nodded. 'I'm sure. I'd recognise my own brother, sir.'

'Indeed,' Mr Harley said drily. 'Then I apologise for having to put you through such a distressing morning as this. You may leave.'

Jim Jackson left the coroner's building and walked straight into the nearest pub, where he spent the rest of the day sinking pint after pint after pint.

When the chief inspector at Ryhope police station received the news from the coroner's office, he was not best pleased. It meant that he still had an unsolved case on his desk, and the chief inspector didn't much like those at all. Besides which, he'd been trying to get the Jackson brothers behind bars for years and had pinned his hopes on the death of Hawk Jackson being his chance to finally put Jim away. The mystery of the body washed ashore at Nose's Point was niggling at him, because he knew full well that any dead bodies washed up at Seaham had been carried down the coast on the tide from Ryhope. He'd seen it before: suicides where tortured souls had thrown themselves into the sea from the clifftop above the beach. He decided to make enquiries around the village pubs to see if anyone had seen anything unusual in or around the cliffs in the weeks and the days before the body had been washed up.

He called in first at the Albion, where Jack and Hetty were polite to him, and even gave him a free drink that he was very grateful for, but they couldn't say whether they'd seen anything unusual. They were always too busy working to notice what was going on in the village, they said. He had more luck with his questions at the Railway Inn, but less luck in getting a free drink. One customer there, an old man with rheumy eyes and a bad chest, said he'd seen a horse and cart go by, on New Year's Eve of all nights, when he was outside the pub having a breather. He was certain, he told the chief, that it was headed to the beach road. But when he was asked if he knew anyone in Ryhope who owned a horse and cart, he shook his head.

'Only Meg Sutcliffe,' he replied. 'And she's just a lass who wouldn't hurt a fly. Besides, Meg's horse, it's got a white star here,' he pointed to his nose, 'and the horse I saw that night was all black. But you could ask Davey Scott, he might know more. He looks after Meg's horse and he might know who else in Ryhope runs a horse with a cart.'

The chief made a note in his book and walked up the bank the next day to see Davey.

'New Year's Eve, you say?' said Davey, scratching his head. 'Horse was here. I couldn't be more sure of it. I fed her myself.'

The chief went away, unsettled by his lack of progress. Maybe there was more to Jim Jackson's statement to the coroner than he'd let on. He was determined to dig up as much as he could about Jim and Hawk, because this case was starting to try his patience.

The next time Meg came to the stable to tend to Stella, Davey made sure that Gert was out of earshot before he said his piece.

'Don't ever do that to me again, Meg,' he warned her. 'I don't care where the horse was or what you were doing with her on New Year's Eve. Me and Gert were down at the Albion celebrating that night so I have no notion of what might have gone on. But I know that when I checked on Stella the next morning, the cart had been moved. Now I'm not saying anything, Meg. I'm not implying. But I never – you hear me – I never want to see the police at my door again. Your dad landed himself in trouble enough with them when he was a lad. I'll cover for you, you know that. And I'll never ask questions. But I will not have the coppers here again.'

Meg turned her face away and tried to busy herself tending to Stella. Her heart began to hammer so loudly inside her chest that she was certain Davey could hear it.

'I hope I never need to mention this again,' he said, then turned and walked back into the house.

Left alone in the stable, Meg felt her legs weaken from the shock of Davey's words. She took a deep breath and laid both hands firmly against Stella to steady herself. How could they have been so foolish as to think that no one would notice the horse and cart on the roads on New Year's Eve? If the police had come asking questions at Davey and Gert's house, then who else were they talking to? Was the truth of that night still in danger of being discovered and their secret revealed? Meg's hands shook as she brushed Stella's coat and she felt her eyes burn with tears.

In the coming weeks, Meg saw less of Adam than usual, although she had heard from Tommy that he was just as relieved as they were about the news in the *Sunderland Echo*. She'd hoped that they could put aside their recent differences, but when Adam called at the house to pick Tommy up on his way to work, his hurt at Meg turning down his proposal was still evident. He hovered at the kitchen door instead of coming in and warming himself by the fire, and although he enquired politely about her health, he was now more distant and formal. If they ran into each other in the back lane, no longer would he call out a cheery 'Meg Sutcliffe!' like he always used to do. He'd walk past her at the water tap or while she was cleaning out the netty, and simply smile and say hello.

Meg had by now told Tommy her news. Her brother was neither surprised nor upset about the addition to the family. Why, lasses had babies all the time, didn't they? His only concern was where the money would come from to feed it. He'd secretly hoped that he and Meg would take up Hetty's offer and go to live above the pub, but once Meg had explained about the baby, he understood why they had to stay put. Jack Burdon wasn't a man who would welcome the noise of a baby's cry in the night, or at any other time of day. Hetty also knew about the baby now after Meg confided to her. Meg was not surprised that the first thing Hetty asked on being told the news was whether the baby was Adam's. Hetty knew how close Meg and Adam were, or had been.

Standing outside Ryhope police station, Jim Jackson pulled the collar of his jacket up to keep the chill from his neck. He took one last drag on the cigarette he was smoking, hoping it would help calm his nerves as he prepared to enter the station, then flung the butt to the pavement, squared his shoulders and walked up to the heavy black door. It opened into a lobby area, where an officer was on duty behind a desk.

'Evening, Inspector,' Jim said, removing his cap.

'Evening, Jim.' The inspector nodded. 'What can we help you with?'

'It's this . . .' Jim said. He dug his right hand into his coat pocket and pulled out a sheet of folded paper. 'It came this morning. Found it on my doormat when I got home not half an hour since and thought it best to bring it down right away.'

The officer took the paper from Jim's hand, unfolded it and slowly began to read. He nodded slightly as he took in the scribbled words.

'I see,' he said once he had finished. 'And it's just arrived, you say?'

'Yes, sir,' replied Jim.

'And you can verify that this is your brother Hawk's handwriting?'

'I can indeed,' Jim said, trying to keep his voice as even as possible.

'You have proof of his handwriting about you?'

'I do,' replied Jim. He reached into his other pocket and brought out a long, narrow envelope. 'Property deeds,' he said. 'For the houses we own between us on Tunstall Street and beyond. You'll find that his signature there matches the writing on the letter.'

'You won't mind if we keep the letter, Jim?' the officer said. 'For the file, you understand. The chief inspector likes his paperwork kept in good order.'

'Of course,' Jim said quickly. 'Is there anything else I need to do . . . about Hawk's letter, I mean?'

The officer shook his head. 'No, lad. You're free to go.'

When the chief inspector was shown the letter, he read it through twice at his desk. Then he leaned back in his chair and sighed heavily. He knew he'd have to resign himself to the fact that the dead body washed ashore had been a vagrant after all, as he'd suggested to the reporter from the *Sunderland Echo*.

It didn't take long for word to spread around the village pubs that Jim Jackson had received a letter from his missing brother. It was said that Hawk's letter was advising his brother that he'd moved away to Dorset, to live with an aunt. The news reached Adam's dad Henry in the Railway Inn one night. When Adam found out what had happened, he ran along the back lane to tell Meg and Tommy. The words flew out of him and they drank the news in. Of course, they knew Jim was lying about the letter, he had to be, for the three of them knew what had really happened to Hawk. But they also knew why Jim had risked the lie. He'd done it to save his own skin, being under suspicion of Hawk's death by no less than the chief inspector himself.

* * *

As winter finally gave up its icy hold, buds began to form on the trees that surrounded the village green. Meg kept the swell of her belly covered by her dad's army coat. When she was out on the cart with Stella and Spot, no one knew her secret and it was hers to keep for as long as she could. In Ryhope, only the Wilsons knew about the baby, as well as Hetty and Jack. Even Lil Mahone next door had gone back to keeping her distance. After she'd covered for them with the police, Meg had expected to see more of her, had hoped for it even, but Lil kept herself to herself as Bob demanded she should.

In the early weeks of spring, clusters of yellow daffodils appeared along the side of the main road from Ryhope to Sunderland. There was a subtle warmth in the air now, a breath of life, as trees came into leaf and blossom. But out on the cart, Stella moved more slowly still. She was an old girl now, getting on. Davey Scott even offered to take her off Meg's hands and sell her to the knacker's yard, but Meg held firm against his offer. She still earned enough working on the rag-and-bone to feed herself and Tommy. And with Hetty offering scraps from the pub, Spot ate well too. Davey helped feed Stella, doing all he could for Meg, calling in favours from High Farm.

Each week Meg put money away to pay the rent. It was money that had been slowly building, because Jim Jackson hadn't called for payment in weeks. Jim's time was now spent in the Albion Inn, according to Hetty. And if he wasn't in the Albion, then he could be found in the Railway Inn or the Guide Post Inn or any of the pubs up and down the colliery or in the village. But Meg was determined never to be in a position where she was behind with the rent, never. Not after what had happened with Mam. So she saved the rent money every single week in a tin box she kept under the bed in her mam's bedroom, where she now slept.

Although Meg was enjoying the luxury of privacy and space in her own room, she missed the closeness she'd had sharing with her brother. She missed the sound of him turning over in bed in the night, the reassurance of his presence on the other side of the blanket that had divided their room. Now, in her mam's bedroom, there was silence, although she could sometimes hear through the wall the sound of Tommy's snores. She often heard him crying too, on the nights he couldn't sleep, when the memories of Mam, and of that night with Hawk, were too much for him to bear. And on those nights, she would creep along the corridor that separated their rooms and tap gently at his door.

'Tommy? Are you all right?' she would ask.

And in return he would simply say, 'Yes.'

But she knew, she always knew, as soon as she saw him the next morning, that he hadn't slept well, that he was still suffering. And she vowed to help him as much as she could. She was going to become a mam to her bairn and she would do what she could to look after Tommy too. She knew in her heart, felt it with every fibre of her being, that it was what Sally would have wanted her to do.

In her mam's bedroom there was a small chest of drawers with Sally's clothes in them – what clothes she'd had: a few blouses and skirts, all worn and mended. Meg was about the same size as her mam and could have worn the clothes had it not been for her growing belly. But it was enough for her to hold them in her hands; to bury her face in them. The bed sheet she changed to a spare one she found in the bottom drawer in Mam's bedroom, but she kept the pillowcase the same. And when she lay awake at night, she welcomed the scent from it, which rocked her with its lullaby as sleep pulled her under.

Under the pillow of her old bed in Tommy's room she had placed the two of hearts card that she'd brought back from the market the day Clarky had shown his contempt for her. But the first time she slept in her new bed, her mam's bed, she removed the card from Tommy's room and threw it into the fire. She watched, mesmerised, as the flames licked around the red hearts until the whole card blackened, curled up and disappeared. Now, in a corner of Mam's bedroom, there was a small pile of baby clothes she had started to collect from her rag-and-bone work. Knitted shawls, tiny white jerkins, mittens and hats that had been thrown out by families who no longer needed them but that she could use when the time came.

As the amount of money in the tin box under the bed grew each week, it began to worry Meg. What if a tinker came in and stole it? She decided to do the decent thing, the honest thing, the thing that she and Tommy had been brought up to do. She had to hunt down Jim Jackson and pay him the rent money she owed.

It wasn't going to be easy. She'd have to face the man whose brother had died in their house and whose body they'd had to get rid of. It took a great deal of thinking through over the course of many days. But she now knew that Jim had secrets to keep too. For his own reasons, he had lied to the police, to the whole of Ryhope, when he said he'd received a letter from Hawk, from down south. Meg took courage from this. And in some small way, paying Jim the rent money before he came calling for it was her way of reckoning her feelings about the night they'd thrown Hawk's dead body from the cliffs.

She walked down the colliery bank, calling at every pub on the way, asking if anyone had seen Jim Jackson. She finally found him in the Railway Inn. She sat quietly beside him and if anyone had seen them, they might have thought Meg was Jim's niece, a daughter, even an alluring young lady companion, so intently did he listen to her words. And when she handed him the cash, wrapped in newspaper, he slid it into his pocket without a word. Meg brought out a small notepad from her skirt pocket, wrote down the amount paid in one column and the date in another. Then she passed it to Jim, who signed his name and added the words *Dues Paid*.

Just two little words they were, in Jim's barely legible handwriting, but they made the world of difference to Meg. As she walked back to Tunstall Street, she felt a lightness about her shoulders, a final loosening of the tension that had lodged there since New Year's Eve.

As the weather warmed and the season turned, life at the market continued as it always had. But there had been not one single sighting of Clarky since Meg told him about the baby. According to Florrie, there had been talk that Clarky had gone to live with his mam. But where they lived or what his mother's surname was, she couldn't say. Even Billy Shillen seemed to have disappeared. And in the corner of the meat aisle where the two of them used to sit and play cards, the table had been taken away.

Each time Meg went to the market to sell her wares to Florrie, there was always a little something for her from her friend. Some days it would be a bag of boiled sweets. 'Got to keep your energy up, girl,' Florrie often told her. Other days it was a blouse she'd come across on the stall. 'This looks about your size. I'll have it back when it doesn't fit you no more.' And every now and then there was a parcel of baby clothes and blankets. 'Let me know if you need anything more,' Florrie would tell her, always refusing to take payment too.

Meg was growing now and it was obvious to anyone who looked at her that she had a bairn on the way. She'd tried to hide the swell inside her dad's army coat, but when the weather changed, she could no longer wear it for fear of sweltering in its warmth. She took another jacket that had been given to her, a man's brown jacket with deep pockets, and put her dad's coat away until the weather turned again.

The new life inside Meg made her bloom. Her cheeks were always flushed from working outdoors, but in the summer of her pregnancy, her face rounded. Her long dark hair curled and waved around her shoulders, her already pleasing features softened and her skin took on an almost translucent glow. She had no idea of how pretty she looked. She just felt tired all the time. Tired and hungry and always in need of the netty, something that wasn't easy to find when she was out on the horse and cart.

She kept working, collecting around Ryhope and the neighbouring villages of Silksworth to the north and Seaham to the south. She stuck to her routine, roaming the streets ringing her bell and calling out: 'Any old rags! Any old rags!' until a door was opened. There'd be a shout – 'Over here!' – and she'd exchange wooden clothes pegs for linens, rags and bones.

It was women, always women, who opened their doors to Meg. The men in the pit villages around Ryhope were either at work, in the pub, or in bed sleeping off the night shift. Most of the women were pleasant to deal with. Some came out with a bowl of water for Spot or an apple for Stella; even a slice of cake or warm bread for Meg too. And when Meg finally felt able to stop hiding her belly underneath her dad's coat, and people realised she was heavy with a bairn, their kindness shone through even more, although one or two of the village women were harsh with their judgement. Not everyone was happy that an unmarried mother – and such a young one as Meg – was flaunting herself, as they saw it. Those women with the sharp tongues Meg avoided as much as she could, and when she did overhear any gossip about her condition, she simply squared her shoulders and held her head high. All that mattered was her growing belly and the bairn inside; she would not allow idle chatter to undermine the love she felt for her baby within her.

But there were other women, kinder women, who laid a gentle hand on hers when they saw her on the rag-and-bone round. Their touch came with a knowing smile and the words 'Take care of yourself, pet,' for there were plenty who had been in her position in the past. Meg was grateful for everything she received from the women in Ryhope and for all the advice given to her. She even noted concern from some who warned her that she shouldn't be spending time around such a mangy horse, not in her condition. But what else could she do? She needed the money and she loved Stella, so there was no way she would stop working, not until she had no choice. Clambering up to the cart was harder for her now. She had to take more care than she ever had before as her body changed shape and size.

* * *

On her way to the paper mill one fine morning in early summer, Meg lifted her face to feel the heat of the sun. Away from Ryhope, the skies were bluer and the air fresh. A light breeze lifted her hair and ruffled Spot's ears as Stella hauled the cart along the main road. Once at the paper mill, Meg went through her usual routine, giving three sharp knocks at the back door. As always, Ruth opened the door and a cloud of white dust escaped from within. It was the first time Ruth had seen Meg out of the big coat that she always wore, and the brown jacket did nothing to disguise how far gone she was. Ruth gasped, staring at Meg's stomach.

'Oh, you poor love!' she said at last. 'Here, let me get the linens from the cart for you.'

Meg watched in silence as Ruth took the rags from the cart. Even Spot was confused. His head turned towards Meg and he gave a gentle whimper.

'There's no need, Ruth,' Meg said. 'I can do it. I'm pregnant, not ill. I'm going to have a baby, not a heart attack.'

Ruth dropped the linens at the doorway and then reached out her arms to wrap them around Meg. Meg didn't move and let the older woman hug her close.

'You poor love,' Ruth said again. 'Oh, what a mess you've got yourself into!'

'I'm all right, Ruth,' Meg said, bemused. 'Really, I'm all right.' Slowly she pulled away from Ruth's arms. 'I'm going to be a mam,' she said firmly. 'There's no need for you to worry about me.'

She delved into her jacket pocket and brought out her notepad and pencil. 'Now then, I reckon you owe me at least double what you paid me last time I was here,' she said.

Ruth laughed. 'By, lass, I've got to hand it to you. You're damn fierce when you want to be. You're a little warrior, that's what you are. That bairn inside you is lucky indeed to be getting you as its mam.'

She stared hard at Meg's stomach again. 'Will the dad be helping much?'

Meg shook her head.

'Didn't think so,' Ruth tutted. 'They're all the same. Some of my girls in here . . . well, the stories they could tell you would make your hair curl.'

She opened the leather wallet she kept in her apron pocket and handed some coins to Meg, which she noted in her accounts book.

'You take care, you hear me?' Ruth said when she waved Meg off.

Meg waved in return and directed Stella to head back home.

She secured Stella in the stable at the back of Davey Scott's house. The rhubarb field was covered in green now. Large flat leaves with stalks of red underneath ran as far back as the Blue Bell pub. She and Spot walked to Tunstall Street, and as soon as she entered the back yard she noticed that the tin bath had been taken from the wall. She stood outside the kitchen door with Spot by her side.

'Tommy?' she yelled.

'Give us a couple of minutes,' he called back.

Meg went into the back lane to fill up Spot's bowl with water, and by the time she'd returned, Tommy had opened the back door. He was dressed now, his face and hands flushed pink from his bath.

'I'll chuck the water out, Meg,' he said. 'You can't be lifting the bath any more. You've got to let me do it.'

Meg didn't argue. She was finding the limits of what she could and couldn't do frustrating. But she also knew she shouldn't push her body, not while the baby was growing within. Her mam had made the mistake of thinking her skin and bones were as strong as her will. Meg wasn't going to repeat that mistake.

'Hey, Meg, do you want to come to Durham next week?' Tommy said as he was carrying the bath into the yard.

'Durham?' she said.

'To the miners' gala. It's next Saturday. Some of the lads are going from the pit. Adam's coming, and Evelyn said she's asked for the day off. Jean and Henry are coming too. There's a charabanc laid on leaving from the Colliery Inn first thing Saturday morning.'

Meg had heard about the miners' gala but had never expected to be lucky enough to see the spectacle for herself.

'And will they let me go on the chara?' she asked.

'I can put your name down,' Tommy said. 'I'll tell the gaffer you're pregnant if you need a comfortable seat, if that's what you're worried about.'

'I'm not worried,' Meg replied. 'It's just . . . You say Adam's going too?'

Tommy nodded. 'It'll be great, Meg, just great. Adam's mam's already baking pies and bread to take. There's going to be a picnic when we get there.'

Meg thought for a moment. A day in the sunshine with friends sounded too good to resist.

'Then I'll come, Tommy,' she said at last. 'Put my name down for a seat on the chara!'

The city of Durham was more beautiful than Meg could ever have imagined. She'd seen pictures of it at school, of course, but to be there, to see it for the first time, almost took her breath away. The River Wear twisted itself in a loop around the small city centre, under bridges heaving with people. Up on a hill stood the magnificent cathedral, and next to it the castle, its ancient stones warmed in the July sunshine. Everywhere Meg looked there were banners from pit villages all over the north-east, held high with pride. Each village had its own brass band marching in front of its banner. There were trumpets, drums, all manner of musical instruments that Meg recognised, and even some she didn't. And behind the banners came the miners, walking with pride and dignity, the workforce that kept the whole north-east region strong.

Meg had her brown jacket laid over her arm as the sun was high in the sky on a beautiful clear day. She wore a blouse the delicate blue of a bird's egg, a blouse that Florrie had given to her at the market. It floated gently down on her stomach, hiding the gap where she could no longer fasten her skirt with the button; instead, a length of string held it closed. On her head was her knitted green hat. She smiled as she marched alongside Tommy behind the Ryhope pit banner, their feet moving in time to the band. Meg swung her arms to the drum beat as the procession made its way through the winding streets of Durham all the way to the field by the river where the speeches would be made. Walking just in front of Meg was Adam, next to his mam and dad. Evelyn hadn't been able to come, her request for a rare day off denied.

Meg and Tommy smiled at each other as they marched over Elvet Bridge. Thoughts of Hawk Jackson, which had plagued them for so long, were further pushed to the back of their minds.

'Mam would have loved this, wouldn't she?' Tommy said.

'She would indeed,' Meg smiled in reply.

Spectators lining the roadside watching the bands march by clapped and cheered, and some even danced in the streets. Tommy lifted his flat cap high into the air, then threw it, spinning, only to catch it again with his other hand. A round of applause went up as other men tried the same trick, with less success.

Meg was so caught up in all the music and laughter and noise of the parade that it took a little while before she noticed there was a woman walking next to Adam. A woman she hadn't seen before. She was tall, like Adam, tall and thin. She was pretty too, Meg noted when the woman turned her head to laugh at something Adam said to her and laid a hand on his arm. Meg's chest felt suddenly heavy.

'Who's that?' she asked Tommy, straining to get a proper look at Adam's new friend.

Tommy shrugged, caring only about the music and the marching, lost in his own happy world.

Just in front of Meg were three women she recognised from the chara. They were marching along to the music, singing loudly. All of a sudden one of them grabbed Meg's hand and another grabbed Tommy's. The third woman pulled at Adam's hand, distracting him from talking any further to the tall woman by his side. All six of them holding hands now, they formed a circle behind the pit banner.

'Come on, to the left!' someone shouted, and off they went, laughing and singing and dancing in a circle. More people joined in and the circle grew bigger, still dancing to the left. After a few steps, some dancers moved out to stand at the side of the road and applaud. People changed position as the circle broke and re-formed each time the music changed. And then suddenly Adam was there, next to Meg, holding her hand behind the pit banner. They stood still, separate from the other dancers, who circled them, happy and laughing and singing. Meg glanced over to the tall woman.

'Are you courting her?' she asked.

'Why? Are you jealous?' Adam smiled.

Before Meg could respond or even begin to process the emotions that were flooding her and what they might mean, a cry went up from the crowd.

'There they are! Up on the balcony!'

There was a loud cheer. Meg looked up at the balcony of the County Hotel, where a handful of well-dressed men in hats and suits were standing waving out to the crowd.

'Who are they?' she asked Adam.

'That one there,' Adam pointed, 'that's Ernest Bevin, trade union leader and Labour politician. And see him, he's Philip Snowden, another politician and a good speaker by all accounts. The one on the end . . . I'm not sure who that is . . .'

'It's another politician, George Lansbury,' a voice piped up behind Meg. She turned to see a woman she recognised from the village school.

'Miss Barnes!' said Tommy. 'I didn't know you were coming today.'

'Wouldn't have missed it for the world,' Miss Barnes said. 'Although if my father finds out I'm here, I dare say I'll have some explaining to do. He thinks I'm at a piano recital. He's not a fan of the type of politicians out in force in Durham today.'

'Are you coming to the field to hear their speeches, miss?' Tommy asked.

'No need to call me miss any more, Tommy. You're not at school now. My name's Eva. How's your pal Micky Parks getting on? Still as cheeky as ever?'

'He's working with me at the pit, miss . . . I mean . . . Eva. But they needed him there today so he's at work. I got the whole day off.'

'Well, make the most of it and have fun,' Eva said. And with that, she ran ahead to where a man with a heavy moustache was waiting for her, holding his hand out for her to take.

The field where the speeches were held was crammed with men in flat caps. Loudhailers attached to wooden stages boomed out the words of dignitaries, politicians and the mayor of Durham himself. The brass bands that had already arrived in the field had their banners proudly on display around the perimeter fence for everyone to see. And underneath the banners, sitting on the grass, were the musicians themselves, tucking into their picnics and bottled beers.

Meg put her hand to her stomach. 'I don't think I want to be going into that crush of people,' she told Tommy when she saw the crowded field.

'Can I go, Meg?' he asked her. 'I want to go.'

'I'll stay with Meg,' Adam said. 'Get yourself away, Tommy. We'll meet you at the Ryhope pit banner when you're done.'

Tommy ran off into the crowd, pushing his way to the front to hear what the politicians had to say about improving working conditions for miners underground.

'Let's go and sit under the Ryhope banner,' Adam suggested, leading Meg by the arm. 'Mam said she'd meet me there and she's been making chicken pies for the picnic.

I'm sure she'll have enough to feed you and Tommy too. Oh, and in answer to your question, Meg . . . no, I'm not.'

'Not what?' she asked.

'Courting that woman.'

Meg cast her gaze to the ground. 'Oh,' was all she said.

'Were you jealous?' he asked her coyly.

'Might have been,' she admitted. 'Just a bit.'

'Oh, a bit, eh?' Adam laughed. 'And would that be a big bit or a little bit?'

'A middle-size bit,' Meg said, making Adam laugh again.

He guided Meg to where the Ryhope banner was propped on its brass poles against a wooden fence. Adam's mam and dad were sitting on the dry grass to one side of it. Jean tapped the ground next to her, and Meg sat down. Jean wrapped her arm around the girl's shoulders.

'Are you all right, Meg?' she asked. 'Not too tired?'

'I'm fine, thank you. It's been a wonderful day.'

Jean opened the picnic hamper and handed round small golden pastry balls filled with chicken. Meg took one and turned it over in her hand.

'You know, I was only your age when I fell pregnant with our Adam,' Jean confided.

Meg turned towards her in surprise.

'Henry and I wed as soon as I found out I was carrying a baby. My mother made sure of that; she didn't want any scandal. But folk knew, of course they did. I know things have changed a little since those days, but people still gossip as much as they always did, especially when a young girl gets caught out with a bairn. What I'm trying to say, Meg, is that Henry and me don't think any the less of you, you know. For what's happened, I mean, with that fella from the market. Adam's told us all about him. And it sounds as if you're well shot of him too. I've known you since you were born, since we first moved into Tunstall Street. I've watched you grow from a little girl into a beautiful young woman. And I just want to say that me and Henry, we're here for you, Meg. I know it can't be easy for you. But if there's anything you need, you just let me know and I'll do my best for you.'

Meg breathed deeply. With the sun on her face, Adam by her side, and the love and support of Jean and Henry, she hadn't felt so warm, safe and happy in a very long time.

Chapter Eleven

Birth

After the Durham miners' gala, the summer flew by quickly. Meg and Adam's friendly familiarity, diminished since Meg had turned down Adam's proposal, began again in earnest, and both were happier for it too. Finally they were able to speak of things they hadn't dared to in a long time, and their shared relief over being in the clear on the matter of Hawk Jackson's death brought them closer still.

On his way to the pit on the days when he worked the same shift as Tommy, Adam would call at Meg's house. But no longer would he hover by the kitchen door. Meg was always sure to invite him in now, and it was an invitation he always accepted. While he waited for Tommy to do up his boots or pick up the lunch pail that Meg had prepared, the two of them would chat as they always had in the past. But there was a line that was never crossed. Meg never asked about Adam's friend, the woman she'd seen him with in Durham, and Adam never raised the question of marriage again. Clarky's name was left unsaid too. What went unspoken between them was much less important than getting their friendship back on track.

With only weeks to go until Meg's baby was due, Hetty came to visit daily, her walk from the Albion to Tunstall Street made all the more enjoyable by the sunshine. Better still was the walk back down to the village afterwards. From up on the colliery bank, heading down to the village, the horizon twinkled, with the sun creating dancing diamonds out on the sea.

It was on days like these that the colliery folk of Ryhope took heart from their industry. Warm days were spent at the beach, paddling in the water after a picnic on the sands. Some of the miners would go straight from work to bathe in seawater instead of going home for a bath. And when baths were taken at home, they were often in the warm air of the back yard instead of indoors in front of the fire. The village blossomed with leaves and flowers of every description. Gardens in the big houses around the green frilled with the blue and pinks of hydrangeas, yellow dahlias as big as dinner plates, and the sweetest scent of roses, to be cut for the table indoors. In the vegetable plots grew potatoes and peas, broad beans and carrots.

Even up at Tunstall Street, in stone pots against brick walls, vegetables grew. Leek trenches were dug in the allotment plots at the back of the Blue Bell. Adam and his dad grew their leeks to eat at home, and also for the autumn show at the Miners' Hall. The show leeks were impressive in their size and weight, and each entrant would keep a watchful eye on their competitors' leeks growing in the trenches. 'What on earth are you putting in your feed to get them as big as that?' they'd ask each other. But the secret was kept close to each grower's heart and never passed on. Leek growing was taken seriously, almost religiously, by the pitmen in Ryhope. Adam and Henry's leeks were the best on the allotment by far. The skin of the leeks was white and pure, with just the right amount of thickness. And the leaves stood tall and proud with no hint of rust. All helped, of course, by Stella's manure, which they were buying from Davey Scott. Henry called it his magic ingredient, if anyone asked, tapping the side of his nose and winking.

One warm day in late August, with the sun high in the clear blue of the sky, Meg travelled back to Ryhope along the coast road. To her left, beyond the cliffs, the sea glittered and shone in the sunshine. Stella moved slowly, as she always did now, and Meg felt no need to gee her on. The slow pace suited them both as Meg's body gently heaved and shifted with each turn of the wheels. In the hot afternoon, Spot lay sleeping on the back of the cart, done in by the heat. Meg knew Stella would be hot too and in need of a drink.

When the spire of St Paul's church came at last into view, she directed the horse past the forge and up on to the village green. When the cart stopped at the water trough, Spot raised his head, then stood, stretched and gave himself a shake. Meg slowly climbed down and led Stella to the trough. As the horse drank, she stood under the shade of an oak tree, the air still warm on her face and her arms.

'Hey, Meg!' a call went up.

She looked over at the Albion Inn to see Hetty standing at the front door, wiping her hands on her apron.

Hetty waved. 'Come on over!'

Meg left Stella and the cart on the green, and with Spot following walked slowly over to see Hetty.

'Come on through, pet,' Hetty said as she led Meg into the pub. 'I was just about to have five minutes' break and a sit-down in the sun out the back. You came just at the right time.'

Meg followed Hetty through the bar and into the kitchen. Another door led from the kitchen into the yard. Wooden beer barrels stood against the brick walls and boxes were piled high. In the middle of the yard were two stools taken from the pub.

'It's not much, but on a day like today, I like to sit out here. It's my bit of breathing space,' Hetty said. 'Sit down and I'll get us a lemonade each.'

Meg was grateful for the drink, as was Spot, who slurped from a bowl of water Hetty brought into the yard for him.

'I've been thinking,' Hetty said at last. 'There's something we should talk about, Meg. Something that your mam would have wanted me to say to you.'

Meg took a long, slow sip of her drink and waited to hear what was on Hetty's mind.

'You need to stop going out on the horse and cart,' Hetty said at last. 'The baby's due mid September and you can't put yourself at risk. What if you're out in the middle of nowhere – down the docks or, God help us, at the market – when your waters break?'

'But I need to work, Hetty,' Meg pleaded. 'We need the money.'

Hetty shook her head. 'Love, if your mam was still alive, she'd be telling you the same thing. Course, I can't make you do anything you don't want to do; heaven knows you're too headstrong for that, just like your mam always was. But you have to take it easy, you know, for the sake of the little one.'

'I know, Hetty,' Meg sighed. 'I was thinking . . . well, I could ask Davey and Gert if they can look after Stella a bit more for me, make sure she's fed on the days I can't get up to do it myself.'

'Well, that'd be a start, I suppose,' Hetty replied. 'I'd heard Davey had offered to take the horse from you for the knacker's yard.'

'How do you know that?' Meg asked, surprised that the news had made its way to Hetty.

'Gert told me. Nothing stays secret for long in Ryhope, pet, you should know that by now. It might be a good idea to think about it. You won't want to be going out on the horse and cart after the baby comes, and you really should be thinking of giving it up now. All those bumpy cobblestones you're travelling over every day, it can't be good for you or the bairn.'

Hetty's words hit Meg hard. Giving up on the horse and cart – giving up on Stella – would mean the end of the way of life she had grown to love. It would mean the end of her freedom.

'But what would I do?' she said out loud, more to herself than Hetty.

'You could take in a lodger,' Hetty suggested. 'There's always fellas in the pub wanting somewhere to stay that offers a decent meal.'

Meg shook her head at the thought. 'I need to look after the baby when it comes . . . and Tommy. Not someone I don't know, not a stranger.'

'Well, there's always washing you could take in,' Hetty said. 'I'm sure you could find another poss tub down at the market and bring it home on the cart, couldn't you?'

Meg shrugged.

'Or sewing – folk always need things mending and stitching. You need something you can do at home now, Meg, not out in all weathers with a horse that's beyond its best.'

'But . . . but I like the market,' Meg said. 'I'd miss it if I didn't go there. I'd miss meeting folk if I didn't do my rag-and-bone collections. Folk expect me now, they know when I come calling. And my friend at the market, Florrie, I'd miss her too. I'd miss the lot of them.'

Hetty sighed. 'That market's got a lot to answer for,' she said, nodding towards Meg's stomach. 'All I'm saying, love, is that you need to think about your baby now. It's no longer just you and the old horse and this flea-bitten thing here.' She lifted her foot in the direction of Spot, who was lying on the warm ground with his tongue out, panting in the sunlight.

Just then, the back door of the pub was flung open. It was Jack Burdon, looking most displeased.

'Hetty, I'd be grateful of your help when you're ready to come back to assist behind the bar,' he said drily. 'The warm weather's bringing people out in droves. Mining and farming are thirsty work here in Ryhope and I've only got one pair of hands, which are proving inadequate to serve up the refreshment required.'

He disappeared back into the pub and Hetty stood up.

'I'll have to get back to work, Meg,' she said. 'But you will think on what I've said now, won't you?'

Meg opened her mouth to reply, but her words were lost as the scream of a siren went up around the village. Again it sounded – and again. Three times, three blasts.

Hetty's hands flew to her heart. 'The pit! My God! The pit!' She ran from the yard, leaving Meg to follow her as quickly as she could.

Spot was alert now, walking close at Meg's side. By the time she entered the pub through the back door, the men who had been sitting drinking there just minutes before were running too. The pub was empty but for card games and dominoes abandoned beside pints of ale. Meg knew she couldn't run, being so heavy with the baby. She returned to Stella and calmed her, nuzzling her head against Stella's own, stroking her and telling her everything was all right, although she knew things were anything but. It was the first time she'd ever heard the emergency siren go up at the pit. She had to know what had happened, had to know Tommy was all right.

The cart moved slowly, but it was still quicker than those running from the village to the pit. 'Jump aboard!' Meg yelled as she weaved her way through the crowds running up the colliery. Men shouted to each other, and a handful of them hopped on to the cart. Women cried and crossed themselves. The Reverend Daye flew from St Paul's and joined the mass of folk heading up the bank. As the crowd drew closer to the mine, news was shouted back and shared, each word sending ice into Meg's heart.

'A prop's gone!' she heard. 'Stone fall.'

'Anyone dead?' a yell went up from the back. 'Who's dead? Let us through! Let us help!'

Meg pulled Stella to a stop at the side of the crowd. She could feel the horse's nerves through the reins, the first time she'd ever felt her jitter. The sharp blast of the pit siren had spooked the animals too. From her elevated position on the cart, she peered above the heads in the crowd. Men, women and children pressed forward, crying, shouting, wanting to know what had happened, needing to know if their loved ones were still alive.

Suddenly there was movement at the front of the crowd beside the wooden fence at the pit entrance. Meg saw the crowd begin to part and a trickle of pitmen, shocked and blackened, started to walk out into the street.

'There's Johnny!' a cry went up. 'Dad!'

Shouts rang out from wives and children, mothers and sisters, grandmothers and aunts, all desperate to know what had happened and who was still alive. Meg scanned the crowd for Tommy, for any sign of her brother. She felt a touch on her arm and looked down to see Evelyn standing by her cart.

'Adam's in there too,' she said.

'But . . . but I thought he wasn't on the day shift today.' Meg was confused.

'They called him in,' Evelyn said as she reached for Meg's hand. 'One of the gaffers asked him to cover for a fella off sick.'

The two girls held tight to each other's hands, straining to see who was walking out of the pit alive. One miner collapsed into the arms of a woman who stood close to Meg and Evelyn, and they listened as he described what had happened.

'A sleeper got lowered in wrong and it hit a prop,' he told those around him, wiping away tears across his coal-blackened face. 'Stone fell, some planks . . . He didn't have a chance to escape, it all came down on top of him.'

'The poor bugger,' the woman cried, hugging the pitman to her breast.

'Who was it? Is there a name?' an older man asked, but the miner shook his head.

More cries went up as more pitmen came walking from the mine, but there was still no sign of Tommy or Adam.

The crowd parted respectfully as the miners walked through the mass of people. Some were heading straight home, some to the pubs to take the edge off their shock.

Evelyn squeezed Meg's hand tighter still. 'Where are they?' she whispered. 'Where are they?'

Meg scanned the crowd again, hoping to spot her brother's light brown hair and Adam's lanky gait, but another little piece of her heart broke each time she looked and could see neither of them.

'There are still men coming out,' she told Evelyn. 'They could be anywhere in there.'

Another ten minutes went past, fifteen, then thirty. It was when the bells of St Paul's chimed the hour that Meg finally caught a glimpse of her brother.

'He's there!' she cried to Evelyn, and then yelled over the crowd: 'Tommy! Tommy!'

Behind Tommy walked Adam.

'And Adam . . . Evelyn, they're both alive!'

Evelyn pressed forward into the crowd, determined to get to Adam and Tommy, leaving Meg sitting on the cart. Adam reached out for his sister as soon as he saw her and flung his arms around her. Then Evelyn turned to Tommy to hug him too, and that was when she saw the tears streaking his coal-stained face. She held tight to Adam's hand on her right and to Tommy on her left, and the three of them walked towards Meg, all of them crying now.

'It's Micky,' cried Adam, still holding tight to Evelyn's hand. 'He shouldn't have even been underground. He wanted to see what it was like. I told him not to go, Meg, I told him not to. It's Micky that's dead, Micky Parks.'

He let go of Evelyn's hand and raised both arms towards

Meg. She bent forward to return his embrace, and felt his tears as his cheek brushed hers.

A whisper floated across the crowd with the dead miner's name passed from man to woman to child. 'He was just a boy . . .' they said. 'Just a boy.'

Meg straightened herself and took Stella's reins in her hand.

'Spot, here,' she directed the dog, who took up his seat next to her at the front of the cart. She turned to Adam and Tommy, both barely able to comprehend the shock of what had happened to their colleague, their friend.

'Hop on the back of the cart,' she said. 'I'm taking you both home.'

It was standing room only at Micky Parks's funeral. Reverend Daye had seen nothing like it before and felt the grief of those packed into the pews at St Paul's only too keenly. He was careful in his sermon not to apportion blame for the boy's death, but neither did he shy away from saying that he prayed such an act of neglect would never happen again. His words about the strength of community struck the right balance with the miners who had come to mourn the loss of such a young life. Micky's mam was silent all the way through the funeral, silent and dignified until the very end of the service, when she wailed out her grief. The echoes of her cries rang up to the rafters as the mourners filed out in procession.

After leaving church, the congregation walked silently up the bank to the pit, the scene of Micky's death. The large group stood in silence, heads bowed, at the pit entrance. Afterwards, they made their way to the wake at the Colliery Inn. Drinks were supped in silence and a plate of sausage rolls, baked specially, went untouched. All that is, except for two, which found their way into Lil Mahone's handbag. She knew how fond Bob was of sausage rolls, and they might just put a smile on his face and stop him from giving her a telling-off when she got home. He'd told her he didn't want her going to the lad's funeral, but she'd defied him once again.

As the heat of August began to cool into the first days of September, Meg went out less on the cart and spent more time at home. Her body sank heavily into her mam's chair while her nimble fingers danced across laces and linens she stitched and sewed in the kitchen at Tunstall Street. It was all the work she could manage, and she bitterly regretted never taking up her mam's offer of teaching her how to knit. There was only Tommy's wages from the pit coming in now, with the little bit of cash that Meg earned from taking in sewing. Otherwise they were fully reliant on the kindness of their friends.

Adam's mam Jean called in daily, Hetty every other day. Even Florrie travelled by tram to the village and then walked up the colliery bank to visit Meg. She brought her men's shirts from the market to wear over her swollen belly. Over mugs of tea in the kitchen, Florrie filled Meg in on all the gossip from the market. Billy Shillen had been spotted, but there'd still been no sign of Clarky. Derek, the chief butcher, who ran the meat aisle, had developed a limp. And Florrie was sure that Lucy Atkins from the stall next to hers was having it away with John Stuart, the man who sold paper and pens. Meg relished hearing the news and loved knowing what was going on beyond the confines of the back lanes of Ryhope. But when Florrie shared some of her own personal news, Meg's smile began to fade.

'I'll be going away,' Florrie began. 'Not for very long, just a couple of weeks. Oh, don't worry, I will be coming back and I'll come and see you again when I return.'

'But where are you going?' Meg asked, intrigued.

Florrie took a sip of her tea. 'Well, it's a bit delicate really, and if I tell you, it mustn't go any further, you understand?'

Meg nodded.

'I've a gentleman friend who wants to take me to meet his family, in Yorkshire.'

Meg's eyes widened. 'You never said anything about having a . . . a boyfriend,' she smiled.

'Oh, I'm too long in the tooth for him to be called my boyfriend, pet,' Florrie said. 'It's not the first time around the block for either of us. But we've become friends, good friends, since my husband passed on, and he's taking me to the Yorkshire coast, to Scarborough, to meet his family.' She paused. There was more to tell the lass, much more. But there was no need to worry her yet.

'I'll head off soon,' Florrie said at last. 'I don't want to miss the tram from the village. And by, lass, it's a bonny village too. You're lucky to have it there.'

'I don't go there much,' Meg said. 'Just to the Albion pub – Hetty works there. And my friend Evelyn works in one of the big houses on the green. The village isn't really for the likes of us who live up on the colliery.'

'Well, it's a fair little place,' Florrie said. 'Pretty, with the trees and the houses around the green and the sea beyond. When I got off the tram earlier, there seemed to be something going on at the green.'

'Oh?' Meg asked. 'What sort of thing?'

'Some sort of fair setting up, I think, by the look of things. There were lots of tinkers around. And it looked like there was a ribbon seller with his pony, and a fortune teller too.'

Meg smiled. 'A fortune teller? Touting for business to anyone daft enough to listen.'

'Lots of people seek comfort that way, Meg,' Florrie said quietly. 'Those who've lost loved ones in the war especially. Does the fair come to Ryhope often?'

'Every September,' Meg replied. 'They bring their horses and ponies, but they don't stay long, just a day or two, and then they move on, further down the coast to Murton and Hartlepool.'

As Florrie gathered her handbag and stood to leave, Meg was struck by an idea.

'I'll walk with you, if you like, down to the tram stop in the village,' she said. 'I've got to take this sewing back to Hetty at the Albion and it's still nice out, so I might as well get some fresh air. Truth is, I've been feeling a bit uncomfortable sitting here all day. My back's hurting and I could do with stretching my legs.'

The two women set off together through the back yard at Tunstall Street, heading down the colliery to the village. Spot walked obediently by Meg's side. The September weather still had traces of summer in it, and Meg relished the feel of the warm air on her face. Once they were in step together, Florrie held out her arm and Meg took it, grateful for the support as the pain in her back worsened.

When they arrived at the tram stop, Florrie checked the timetable on the board.

'It's not due till ten past,' she said. 'Is there a seat round here I can wait on until it comes?'

Meg pointed to a bench on the village green and they headed towards it. The green was busy with the fair, the bright patterns of the horse caravans made more colourful in the sun. Meg caught sight of the ribbon seller and asked Florrie if she would like to take a look. 'Not bad quality,' Florrie said, running her hands over the rainbow of colours in all different sizes and widths. 'How much?'

When the price was given to her, she shook her head and smiled. 'Too much, my friend. Too much.'

The price was dropped immediately and the bartering began. Meg watched in awe as Florrie bargained hard for a stripe of fat white ribbon. She won it, too, at a price far lower than either she or Meg had expected, and handed over the pennies for it with a smile.

As they turned to walk away, a mischievous smile played around Florrie's lips. 'Come on, let me treat you,' she said to Meg, walking towards the fortune teller.

Meg winced.

'Are you all right, pet?' Florrie asked.

'It's my back playing up again . . . I'll be all right,' she said. 'But Florrie, I can't let you waste your money on a fortune teller. None of what they say is true. They only tell you what you want to hear.'

'I insist,' Florrie said. 'My treat. Go on, have a bit of fun. It's only pennies after all. You never know, you might learn something.'

Meg reluctantly took her seat opposite the fortune teller under the shade of the oak tree in the middle of the green. Florrie paid the price requested, and Meg sighed and held out her hand, palm turned upwards. The fortune teller was an old man, his face pinched and darkened by years spent working and living outdoors. He was thin, his clothes hanging loose on his skinny frame, and short, too; even sitting in his chair, Meg could see he wasn't much taller than she was. He had a head of thick black hair that was greased back from his forehead, and his eyes were hooded and dark.

He took Meg's hand and his touch was as light as air. His fingers stroked the palm and each of her fingers in turn. He lifted his gaze briefly to meet hers, and then his eyes flickered back to her palm, his fingers circling it slowly.

'Other hand,' he barked.

She looked up at Florrie.

'Give him your other hand,' Florrie nodded, and Meg did as she was told.

The same strange ritual went on with her left hand, the same circling of the palm and stroking of her fingers.

'You will have a good baby,' the man said at last, still avoiding her gaze. 'Strong baby.'

Meg looked at Florrie again and rolled her eyes. Florrie shook her head to dismiss her scorn.

'There is a woman. She . . .' The fortune teller dropped Meg's hand and looked her straight in the eyes. 'A bad woman will come.'

Meg looked from the fortune teller to Florrie and back again, unsure of what was going on.

'Is that all I'm getting for my money?' Florrie asked him. 'Come on! Where's the tall, dark, handsome stranger coming into her life and whisking her away to live in a posh house on the seafront at Roker? That's what we want to hear, isn't it, Meg? That's what I paid my money for.'

'No more,' the fortune teller said. 'Now go. Both of you.'

'I told you they were frauds and charlatans,' Meg said when she and Florrie had made their way to the bench to sit and wait for the tram. 'You shouldn't have wasted your money.'

Florrie kept quiet. She'd seen something, just a flicker that had passed over the fortune teller's face. It was a flicker that Meg hadn't seen, intent as she was on watching his fingers dance on her hand. But Florrie had seen the way it made the fortune teller wince. Had he seen something ahead for Meg?

'Is he any good, then?' a voice asked. It was Lil Mahone, who came scuttling over to Meg and Florrie. 'The fortune teller? Is he any good?'

'No,' Meg laughed when she saw her next-door neighbour. 'But I dare say that won't stop you from believing every word he says.'

'I always put great store by their words,' Lil huffed. 'My mother had the gift, you know. Oh yes, she could see what was coming a mile away and it never did me any harm to know what was around the corner.'

'He's good,' Florrie said quietly. 'Go and see him. Learn your future, if you must.'

The tram rumbled into view by the village school and Florrie took her leave, promising to visit Meg as soon as she returned from Scarborough. Meg called in at the Albion and dropped off the bag of sewing for Hetty, who was hard at work behind the bar under Jack Burdon's steely gaze. With her friend too busy to stop for a chat, she headed back up the colliery, intent on calling in to feed Stella at the stable. As she walked up to Davey Scott's house, she saw rows of pickers in the rhubarb field. As the plants matured, the luscious red sticks of fruit were picked freely by anyone who cared to take it. And the more it was picked, the more energy the plants put into regrowth, so that they could be harvested four or even five times over the summer and into September.

'Afternoon, Davey!' Meg called out as she walked past the kitchen door to Stella's stable. 'Afternoon, Gert!'

The top half of the kitchen door was open, as it usually was when the weather was fine. Davey waved from the doorway and then disappeared inside. Spot was first into the stable, ahead of Meg, and she watched as the dog walked straight towards Stella and nudged her with his head. Stella moved away to one side and gave a swish of her tail. Meg could tell immediately that Davey had fed her that morning – he'd kept his word about looking after the old horse until Meg could go out on the cart again. She stroked Stella's nose, soothing and calming her, and then, without even realising she was doing it, she started to softly sing. '*Stella, sweet Stella, what fella could want a finer horse?*' Stella turned her head and nudged her nose into Meg's hair. Meg responded by singing the line over and over again, and each time she sang it, Stella nudged further towards her.

Suddenly a spasm down Meg's back made her call out in pain. She cradled her back with her hands, pushing against the pain, waiting for it to ease, but it only worsened. Spot circled her, waiting for instructions. None came, just another cry as Meg's body cramped with pain. Spot barked, once, twice, then ran to Davey and Gert's back door and barked again, over and over, until the door flew open and Gert stood there in a blue apron covering her black skirt and blouse.

'What on earth's all this racket about?' she said. 'Spot? What's the matter, boy? What is it?'

Spot ran back to the stable, still barking, and Gert followed.

'Holy Mary Mother of God!' she cried when she saw Meg, doubled over with the pain. 'Let's get you into the house now. Come on, girl.'

She half carried, half walked Meg into her kitchen. Meg was gasping for breath.

'The baby's coming . . .' she whispered. 'My waters broke in the stable. The baby's coming, Gert.'

'In here,' Gert said, leading Meg into the front parlour. 'Come on, one step at a time, let's get you somewhere decent. A kitchen floor's no place for a child to be brought into the world.'

Meg let herself be guided by Gert's strong and experienced hands to a large blue clippy mat on the parlour floor.

'I'm scared, Gert,' she said. 'I'm really scared.'

'Davey!' Gert yelled. 'Davey Scott! Get yourself in here now.'

A few seconds later, Davey appeared at the parlour door. 'Bloody hell, what's happened here?'

'The baby's coming. Go and get Dr Anderson. Now!'

'Right away, love,' Davey said, turning to leave.

'Davey!' Gert barked.

'What, love?'

'We need hot water. Fill the kettle and put it on the fire before you go.'

'Eeh, love . . .' Davey began. 'I don't think the lass is in any fit state to have a cup of tea.'

Gert turned towards her husband with a face full of fury. 'You stupid bugger, it's not for tea, it's for sterilising stuff in case the doctor needs anything. Now go, and be as quick as you can.'

Davey turned to leave again, but Gert wasn't finished with him yet.

'Oh, and Davey?'

'What now?'

She pointed towards Spot, hovering by the parlour door. 'Get that bloody dog out of here or I swear I'll swing for it.'

Davey took Spot into the kitchen and then ran like the clappers to the village surgery to fetch the doctor.

Gert stroked Meg's brow. 'Don't you worry, love. Everything's going to be all right. I trained as a nurse, you know, worked at the hospital for years before I married that daft lump that goes by the name of Davey Scott. Just you take it easy there, breathe in, breathe out . . .'

But her words offered Meg more reassurance than Gert herself felt. In all her years working at the hospital, she had dressed wounds and strapped up broken bones. She'd seen strep throat, lazy eye, jaundice, fever and gout. But she had never, not once, delivered a baby. Still, she had gone through the births of nine of her own, seven of whom had survived, so she knew what to expect and would help Meg as much as she could.

Meg gripped Gert's hands each time the contractions rocked her body.

'Keep breathing, Meg, keep breathing,' Gert told her. 'Come on, Meg, breathe in . . . and out . . .'

Meg was drenched in sweat, writhing on the rug, when Dr Anderson burst in through the parlour door with Davey and Spot in tow. The doctor wasted no time. He knelt down immediately in front of Meg and Gert, rolled up his sleeves and opened the large black bag he'd brought with him.

'Get that thing out!' Gert yelled at Davey when she caught sight of Spot by the door. 'Then bring the hot water in. And we'll need towels and blankets too, as many as you can find – they're in the ottoman box upstairs. Now, Davey!'

Davey did as he was told, and then waited nervously in the kitchen, pacing the floor with Spot at his heels. As the hours went by Davey tended to Gert's calls for more water, more towels. Davey closed his eyes and with a bowed head offered up a silent prayer for the safety of Meg and her child. And then there was silence, no more screaming from Meg, no more cries of encouragement from Gert, just silence. And then a cry, a wail, the unmistakable sound of a newborn child right there in Davey's house. He put his hands together and raised his eyes to the ceiling above.

'Thank you,' he whispered. 'Thank you.'

Chapter Twelve

Grace

Hetty came quickly to visit the new baby. She called at Davey and Gert's house as soon as she was told the news by Tommy that the baby had arrived. Gert was in her element. She loved cuddling the baby, cooking for Meg and showing her how to feed her new child.

'I've gone through this with seven of my own, love, and umpteen grandbairns,' she kept reminding her. 'Take it from me, I know what I'm doing.'

And Davey wouldn't hear of Meg leaving any sooner than she felt ready.

'Your dad would have wanted us to look after you,' he insisted each time she said she felt able to go home. 'And anyway, we love having the little 'un in the house, don't we, Gert?'

Gert smiled. 'We do that, Davey lad. If I wasn't the age I am now, I might say that having a new bairn here is even making me feel a bit broody!' On the day Hetty called to see Meg, she brought with her a bag of baby clothes, folded neatly and wrapped in tissue paper. She handed the bag to Meg, who unwrapped each item with care. She didn't have to be told that the clothes had once belonged to Philip, Hetty and Jack's son.

'I didn't know I'd kept them,' Hetty said as she watched Meg smoothing out a tiny vest. 'I found them when I was sorting through some boxes in the attic at the Albion. I'm grateful the mice hadn't nibbled at them. Heaven knows, they'd worked their way through a pair of curtains I'd stored away up there. Chewed to bits they were.'

She laid her hand atop a cotton jacket and bonnet. 'There's blue piping on this one,' she said softly. 'But I don't think it matters, does it? And this one . . . there's a little boat on the sleeve. She won't mind wearing that, will she?'

Meg reached out for Hetty's hand. 'I'm more grateful than you'll ever know, Hetty. And I'll look after them all, thank you.'

Hetty picked up a tiny blue-and-white short trouser suit. 'And if you wrap her in a shawl, no one will know they're boys' clothes, no one will see.'

'I'll be honoured for her to wear these, Hetty,' Meg said. She noticed that Hetty's eyes were full of tears. 'And I'll tell her about Philip when she's old enough to know. I'll tell her of his bravery and how he fought for his country and for Ryhope.'

'And she's welcome at the Albion any time you want to bring her in, Meg. You're a friend of mine, and if you want to come calling with your baby, you go ahead. There'll always be a welcome for you both in the pub, no matter what anyone else in Ryhope says.'

Meg glanced over at her daughter, who had her eyes tight shut, sleeping on the chair opposite. 'What do you mean, no matter what anyone else says? Have people been talking about me?'

Hetty shook her head and tutted loudly. 'Just the usual gossip. You know what folk are like around here. It's not as if you're the first young lass to get caught out, and heaven knows, you'll not be the last. If anyone speaks unkindly of you and I get to hear about it, I'll flaming well make sure they stop their vicious tongues. Just you mark my words.'

'Thanks, Hetty,' Meg said.

The baby gave a quick jerk of her feet as she slept, and both Meg and Hetty turned to watch.

'Have you thought of a name for her yet?' Hetty asked.

'Grace,' Meg said without hesitation. 'It was my grandma's middle name.'

'Oh, I remember your Grandma Lacey,' Hetty smiled. 'Now there was a woman not to be messed with! Your mam was always trying to please her when we were lasses growing up. But no matter how hard she worked, no matter how well she did in school, your grandma would never let on how proud she was of her. She ruled that household with an iron rod, I remember. It's what made your mam as stubborn as she was, God bless her soul. And I dare say there's a bit of Grandma Lacey in you too, Meg. Strong-willed, the lot of you, on that side of the family. And this little one here . . .' She stood and walked across to the chair where the baby was sleeping, leaning over and stroking her face with a light, gentle touch. 'I hope this little one's got it too, because by, lass, she's going to need it.'

She turned back towards Meg. 'Is there anything you want me to do, Meg? Anything that needs doing down at the house for Tommy?'

'Well, there is one thing . . .' Meg replied.

Hetty sat down on the sofa next to her. 'Whatever it is, just ask.'

Meg glanced behind her to ensure that the parlour door was still closed. She knew that Davey and Gert would be in the kitchen, so she kept her voice low.

'I need to go home,' she said. 'Davey and Gert have been wonderful. I couldn't have got through it all without their help, and the food – it's been more than I could have dared hope. But I want to go home, Hetty. I want Grace to go home. Gert's been great, but I want to feel that my own mam's around me.'

'You miss her a lot, love, don't you? We all do.'

'Not a day goes by when I don't think of her,' Meg replied. 'More so than ever since Grace was born.'

'Can't you just up and leave?' Hetty asked.

'Not after all they've done for me. I don't want to sound ungrateful, but they're killing me with kindness. Dr Anderson says I'm well enough to go home; he says the baby's doing well and I'm feeding her fine. I just want to get back to my own life, to just me and Tommy and the baby.'

Hetty thought for a moment. 'I've known Gert since I was in short socks and pigtails. Our families lived next door to each other at the back of the cattle market down Scotland Street. I'll go and have a word with her. She'll understand. Just you leave her to me.'

Hetty stood, smoothed down her skirts and headed out of the parlour, closing the door gently behind her. Through the thin wall Meg heard the two women talking in the kitchen next door, and then Davey's voice cutting in with words of kindness and concern. But it was Hetty's voice that did most of the talking, and by the time she had finished, she had managed to convince Gert and Davey that it was their own idea to let Meg go home.

Meg heard the parlour door open behind her, and she turned to see both Hetty and Gert standing there.

'You'll let me come every day with something from the oven for you and Tommy?' Gert said.

'Of course,' Meg replied. 'I was hoping you might.'

Davey walked into the room with a small leather purse in his hand. 'Here,' he said, handing it to Meg. 'You'll be needing this. It's the last lot of money I got from the lads at the allotment for Stella's manure.'

'But what about Stella's food?' Meg said. 'I can't take this, Davey. It's kind of you, but you're paying from your own pocket to look after my horse, and I can't have that. It's not right.'

'Never you mind what I'm paying for and what I'm not,' Davey replied, glancing at Gert. 'I made a promise to your dad that Stella's manure money was yours and yours alone. Take it, before Gert here goes up to the Colliery Inn and blows it all on a jug of ale and starts baring her arse in front of the Co-op window.'

Gert walloped Davey playfully on the arm.

'Take no notice of him, love, he knows fine well I haven't touched a drop of drink in years. But take the money, please. It's what we both want.'

Meg did as she was told, grateful for the cash.

'Davey will walk you home after you've eaten,' Gert said. 'I've got panackelty in the oven and I'll not see you go hungry. You too, Hetty, you'd be welcome to stay for tea. And there'll be some left over for Tommy, Meg; you can take it home for him in a dish.'

Hetty accepted the offer and the four of them sat around the kitchen table to eat the hearty stew, soaking up the juices and wiping their plates clean with stottie bread Gert had baked. Grace slept through it all. It was only when Meg picked her up when she was ready to leave that the baby began to mewl and cry.

'She'll be wanting a feed as soon as you get home,' Gert reminded her. 'Now you know what to do with her, don't you?'

'I do, Gert, thank you,' Meg replied.

'Well, you'll be on your way then,' Gert said, wiping her hands on a cotton towel. She leaned over to Meg and kissed her on the cheek. Then she kissed the tip of her index finger and planted it gently on the baby's nose.

'I'll be down to see you tomorrow,' she said as Meg followed Davey and Hetty out of the kitchen door.

'Tomorrow,' Meg smiled in reply.

She walked slowly away between Hetty and Davey. And tucked inside her brown jacket, she cradled Grace close to her heart. Standing at the kitchen door, Gert watched them go with tears in her eyes.

The cottage at Tunstall Street was cold, the fire burned out in the hearth.

'I'll get it going before Tommy comes in from work,' Meg said when she saw it.

'You'll do no such thing,' Davey remarked sharply. 'I'll do it for you. You get settled in with the bairn. Hetty, come and help bring some water and coal in.'

Hetty and Davey worked quickly to get the fire going and the kettle on to boil. Meg sank into her mam's chair by the fire, still holding her baby close. Spot came towards her, his back legs almost lifting off the ground as his tail wagged nineteen to the dozen.

'Spot, stay,' she said gently, holding a hand up towards the dog. Spot did as he was told, his gaze fixed on the baby, his nose sniffing at her unfamiliar scent.

'Right, you're all set,' Davey said at last. 'Gert will be here in the morning, and you've got Hetty here to help too. Anything you need, you be sure to let us know.'

Meg nodded. 'Thank you,' she said. 'Thank you both. There's no need to stay on. Tommy will be home soon and we'll be a family again.'

'There's just one thing I need to do before I go,' Hetty said. Meg turned to look at her, but Hetty was already walking out of the kitchen and into the back yard. A few seconds later, raised voices, women's voices, could be heard through the thin wall from Lil and Bob Mahone's house next door. Then there was silence and Hetty returned with her face flushed.

'Lil will be doing all the netty cleaning for the next few weeks,' she told Meg. 'I've explained the situation, told her that you're to be allowed to rest with the baby. And she'll call in every morning to make sure you're all right, too.'

Meg smiled. 'How on earth did you get her to agree to all of that? She never usually lifts a finger if she can help it.'

'Let's just say there's a jug of ale with her and Bob's name on it at the Albion Inn once a week on a Friday night from now on. But if I hear from you that she isn't keeping her side of the bargain, then the offer is taken back straight away. Jack can say what he likes when I tell him what I've done.'

Hetty and Davey finally took their leave with promises to call in as soon as they could. Once they had gone, the kitchen was silent apart from the crackle of the firewood and the flames licking up around the coal. Meg looked down at Grace, and the baby's eyes opened and locked on to her own.

'It's just you and me now, Grace,' she whispered.

In that instant, Meg made a solemn promise that she would love her baby in the way that her mam had loved her. She would do whatever it took to make sure there was always food, always nourishment and above all, always love. It was what Mam had done for her and Tommy. And she would pass on her dad's spirit and his courage, so that Grace would never be afraid.

Meg gently stroked the baby's face. 'Just you and me.'

By the time Tommy returned from work, hungry and tired, Meg was in her bedroom upstairs. His heart sang when he saw the dish of panackelty left for him in the kitchen. As he brought in more water and bathed in front of the fire, the dish warmed in the oven, so that by the time he was ready to eat, it was piping hot. He called up to Meg, but there was no answer. Quietly he climbed the stairs, determined not to wake the baby, and knocked at his sister's bedroom door. Meg called for him to enter and Tommy tiptoed in. Meg was lying on top of the bedclothes, fully dressed.

'I'm not sleeping, just watching the baby,' she said. 'Come and see.'

Tommy walked around the bed to where he could see his dad's old army coat bundled up into a heap beside Meg. Cradled inside the coat was his baby niece.

He sat on the side of the bed, taking care not to disturb the sleeping infant.

'She looks like you,' he said. 'She's got your nose.'

'I'm going to do right by her, Tommy,' Meg said. 'I'm going to make sure she never goes without.'

Tommy took a deep breath. There was something he had to tell Meg, something important. News had arrived in a letter pushed under their front door while she had been staying at Gert and Davey's house. It had turned Tommy's blood cold when he read it, printed there in black ink under an official crest at the top of the page. But it was news that he would keep from Meg until the morning, after she woke from a night's sleep in her own bed.

The next morning, both Meg and Tommy were wakened early by a loud banging at the back door. Spot barked and stood alert by the door. Tommy ran downstairs to see who it was while Meg pulled a shawl over her nightgown and stood at the top of the stairs.

'Is Mrs Sutcliffe at home?' she heard a man's voice say.

'You need to come down, Meg,' Tommy called up to his sister.

Meg returned to the bedroom and lifted Grace, cradling the sleeping baby to her chest.

Standing at the back door was a short man, not much older than Tommy. He wore a smart black jacket with trousers and a matching tie. On top of his head was a hat the likes of which Meg had never seen. It looked like an upturned pudding dish, and it was black too. In one hand was a board covered with a sheet of lined paper, and in his other hand a black pen.

'Mrs Sutcliffe?' he said politely, addressing Meg directly.

'Yes . . .' she said, then shook her head. 'No . . . I mean, no. I'm Miss Sutcliffe, Sally Sutcliffe's daughter.'

The man glanced at the notes on the board in his hand.

'From what I understand, Sally Sutcliffe passed away some time since. And you're the head of the household now, miss?' he asked.

Meg glanced at Tommy. 'I suppose I am, yes.'

'Then you'll have read the letter that our agency sent to you earlier this week.'

'What letter?' Meg asked.

Tommy went to the sideboard and picked up an envelope.

'This letter,' he told her. He turned to the man at the door. 'You'd better come in.'

'What's going on?' Meg asked, panicked now, hugging Grace tight to her. 'Tommy?'

'No need to alarm yourself, miss,' the man told her. His face broke out into a smile, but there was a coldness to it that Meg didn't like the look of. 'I'm here representing James Jackson, your landlord. Mr Jackson has become . . . shall we say, incapacitated of late since the disappearance of his brother and has been unable to collect rent from many of his tenants. He has appointed our agency, Messrs Benjamin Ferry and Co., to collect the rent on his behalf from now on. But of course, an intelligent girl like you would have read the letter we sent you and will already know all this.'

'Meg, I . . . I was going to tell you,' Tommy said. 'Honest I was.'

Meg stiffened. 'So we pay the rent to you now instead of Jim Jackson?'

The man nodded. 'It's all there in the letter, in black and white. And according to my records, you've got a payment due today, hence my call this morning. I like to do my collections early, see?'

Meg shot Tommy a look. 'But . . . but we don't have it. We haven't been able to save it this week.'

The man from Messrs Benjamin Ferry and Co. consulted his board again. 'Nor for the last few weeks, it says here.'

'I get paid on Friday,' Tommy piped up. 'I'll bring it to your office then.'

The man shook his head. 'I'm afraid that will never do.' He glanced around the kitchen, taking in the meagre sticks of furniture, as baby Grace let out a small cry. 'I see you've got your hands full with a little 'un,' he said to Meg. Was she mistaken, or was there a gentleness to his voice that hadn't been there before?

He looked from Tommy to Meg and back again.

'I've got three children of my own, two boys and a girl, you know.' His gaze fell to the baby in Meg's arms and he gave a long sigh. 'Friday, you say?'

Tommy nodded.

'Friday it is. Just this once, mind you. And if you miss any more payments, you'll be dealing with people from the agency who are a lot less amenable than me, if you catch my drift. They'll have the power to take things from your house, furniture and the like. But then you'll know that already, it's all in the letter, like I said.'

'How are we going to pay the back rent, Tommy?' Meg said, sinking into the chair by the fire with Grace in her arms.

'We could ask Hetty?' he suggested shyly, but Meg shook her head.

'She's already doing enough for us, cooking for us and feeding Spot. Gert and Davey are doing the same, and feeding Stella for me. And Adam's mam and dad are calling in to look after us too. We can't ask any of them for money on top of all their kindness.'

'There's always Adam,' Tommy said. 'I know he'd want to help if he knew we were struggling.'

'We can't, Tommy. We can't ask him, not Adam of all people. It just wouldn't be fair. Anyway, I haven't seen him in ages.' She looked down at the baby in her arms. 'Not since Grace was born. Now go on, get yourself ready for work. I'll think of something.'

'I'm sorry, Meg. I should have told you about the letter. I just didn't want to worry you, not with the baby and everything.'

'Give it here,' Meg said, holding out her hand. 'I suppose I should find out what's really going on.'

Tommy handed over the envelope and then headed upstairs to get dressed and ready for work. Sitting in the kitchen with the baby cradled in her arms, Meg read the letter from Messrs Benjamin Ferry and Co. It was written in a language that was cold and unfriendly, and left her in no doubt that if the rent wasn't paid, then bailiffs would come to the house and take away their furniture. Worse still, if non-payment continued, they could be thrown out on to the street.

She folded the letter and set it aside. Then she took a deep breath and straightened up in the chair. She knew there was only one way to keep the roof over their heads, and that was for the rent to be paid, in full and on time, every single week from now on. Tommy's wages wouldn't cover it, she knew that. She looked down at her baby in her arms.

'Mammy's going back to work, Grace,' she whispered. 'And you're coming too.'

* * *

Later that morning, Gert was at the kitchen sink washing up the breakfast pots when she saw Meg and Spot walk past her kitchen window. Meg was wrapped in her dad's army coat, cradling the baby within. Gert watched as she made her way to Stella's stable.

'No . . . no . . . she can't be,' she said aloud.

'What's that, love?' Davey said.

Gert quickly dried her hands on her apron and flew from the kitchen with Davey following behind wondering what on earth was going on. In the stable, Meg stood close to Stella with Grace in her arms.

'Oh love, what on earth do you think you're doing?' Gert asked, her heart racing. 'You can't be thinking of going out on the horse and cart.'

'I've got to, Gert,' Meg replied. 'We're behind with the rent. There's an agent coming calling for it now, and if we don't pay, they'll chuck us out on the streets and—'

'And nothing!' Gert said firmly. 'That bairn's not big enough or strong enough to breathe in the mucky air round here. She should be indoors, where it's warm.'

She walked towards Meg. 'Now, you can do whatever you feel you have to, and you know that me and Davey will support you. But I cannot stand here and let you take that bairn out on the horse and cart with you. I won't do it.'

Meg felt the sting of tears and a lump rose in her throat. 'I've got to, Gert. What else am I to do? I can't leave her at Tunstall Street on her own.'

Gert glanced at Davey, who was standing by her side now. 'You can leave her with us, can't she, Davey?'

If he was taken by surprise by his wife's suggestion, he never let on.

'Course she can,' he replied.

Gert held out her hands to take Grace, but Meg just pulled the baby tighter to her.

'Bet she hasn't even been fed this morning, has she, poor love?' Gert said, walking closer still. 'Me and Davey . . .' she continued softly, 'that little house, why, it's an open house for all of our family, it always has been. And it's an open house for you too. You know fine well we'll look after Grace in there for you. You bring her to us on a morning when you get Stella and the cart. We'll feed her, Meg. We'll look after her. We'll love her as if she were our own. We've always got our grandbairns coming and going, so what's another mouth to feed? And at the end of the day, when you finish on the rag-and-bone, you can come and collect her from us when you bring Stella back to the stable.'

Meg dropped her gaze to the floor.

'Come on, love,' said Davey. 'Gert's right. Down the docks and at the market? That's no place to take a baby.'

Gert reached out again, and this time, Meg allowed her to take the baby from her arms.

'Davey'll help you get the horse bridled up and the cart ready, won't you, love?' Gert said.

'Course I will,' Davey replied. 'And the sooner we get it done, the sooner you'll be out earning some money.'

'And the sooner you'll be home to see this one.' Gert smiled, giving Grace a kiss on the cheek.

Meg felt the threat of tears again, and when Gert turned to give her a kiss too, she had to wipe her eyes with the back of her hand.

With Davey's help, Stella and the cart were soon ready. When Meg drove out of the stable and away past the kitchen door, she waved at Gert, who was standing there with the baby in her arms. And as soon as Meg and Stella were out of sight, Gert wrapped the baby in a blanket and laid her in an open drawer in the sideboard, just as she'd done with all seven of her own bairns. When Grace was comfortable, tucked in amongst the soft blankets in the drawer, Gert set to warming a pan of milk by the fire to feed the baby when she woke.

All day Meg's thoughts were with her baby. Would she be warm enough? Would she sleep? Would Davey and Gert feed her enough? But deep in her heart, she knew that there was no place she would rather Grace be while she was at work. And work she must, for the rent had to be paid if she and Tommy were to keep their home.

She called out long and loud from the cart as she made her way around Ryhope. 'Rag and bone!' she sang. And with every call there was a clang from the heavy bell as it swung through the air. 'Any rag and bone!'

She made her way to the village green, glancing up at the big house where Evelyn worked, not expecting to see any of the maids there but hoping that she might. It was Evelyn herself who heard her cry from the road, and she waved at her friend from the upstairs bay window. Meg directed Stella to head to the back of the house, as her dad had always told her to do. By the time she climbed down from the cart, the back door was already open and Evelyn was standing there in her black-and-white starched uniform.

She beckoned Meg inside the hallway. 'What are you doing here? Where's the baby?'

Meg brought her up to date on the events of the morning. 'Well, there's a whole lot of clothes we've been waiting to give you,' Evelyn said at last. 'The housekeeper says you're to come in and help me remove them from Mrs Patterson's room.'

'Doesn't Mrs Patterson want them any more?' Meg asked, confused.

'She can't leave the house,' Evelyn whispered. 'Ever since I started here, she's been ill in bed. Mr Patterson told us this week that she's not got long to go.'

'Seems a bit harsh getting rid of all her clothes, though,' Meg said.

Evelyn shrugged. 'It's odd, I agree. But they're a very peculiar lot who live down here in the village. More money than sense.'

She headed along the dark hallway and Meg followed her up three flights of wooden stairs.

'These are the staff stairs,' Evelyn whispered as they made their way up. 'The front stairs have carpet on them, as soft as snow underfoot.'

They came to a square landing where the walls were painted white. Evelyn pushed open a door that led to a much larger landing, this one carpeted and wallpapered. Meg followed her friend as Evelyn opened another door. This one led into a bedroom.

It was the scent that Meg noticed first, the smell of roses from the perfume bottles that lined the dressing table. In the middle of the room was an empty bed, stripped bare of its blankets, and on it were clothes laid in neat piles.

'Is this her room? Mrs Patterson's?' she asked.

Evelyn shook her head. 'It used to be. She's in the living room on the ground floor now; they turned it into a sickroom for her. She can watch from the window there and see people walking by while she's lying in bed.'

'And does your friend Michael . . . does he help look after his mam?'

'They've sent him away, to a college in Durham. I haven't seen him for weeks, but . . .' Evelyn glanced towards the bedroom door before she carried on, 'he writes to me, Meg. Every week he writes to me at Tunstall Street. He's a good friend; my best friend. Apart from Tommy, of course.'

Meg smiled. 'Come on, let's get this lot on to the cart.'

It took three trips up and down the back stairs with piles of clothes in their arms before all the dresses, blouses and skirts were loaded.

'What does the housekeeper want in return?' Meg asked when they were done. 'I've got plenty of clothes pegs if she needs them.'

'The housekeeper does indeed need clothes pegs,' boomed a voice from behind Evelyn, who stiffened at the sound of her boss.

'Back to work, Evelyn,' the woman said abruptly when she reached the two girls. Evelyn dipped her head slightly, smiled at Meg and disappeared along the hallway.

Meg went to the cart and fetched a bag of clothes pegs. The housekeeper took them from her hands, then closed the door in her face without a word of thanks, leaving Meg staring at the wooden door. Yet she wasn't at all upset by the woman's rudeness; it was what she had come to expect. More than anything, she felt a sense of overwhelming freedom, knowing that she had no one to answer to but herself, and would never be at the mercy of a boss like the one Evelyn worked for.

She rounded up Spot, climbed back on to the cart and directed Stella to the main road. After just an hour of collecting around the streets in Ryhope, her cart was already more heavily laden than she'd ever known it to be.

'We've missed you!' women called out from their cottages when they heard her approaching. 'We've been saving all our rags for you!'

And not only did Meg receive rags and bones to sell, but there were hand-knitted clothes for Grace, an apple for Stella and a meat bone for Spot, along with good wishes and kindness extended to Meg's new baby girl. One woman even held Meg to her as if she was her own daughter, and with tears in her eyes handed her a shilling.

'For the bairn,' she said.

With her cart heaving, there was barely enough space for Spot to sit there. Meg decided to offload the bones at the Railway Inn before she headed to the market to sell Mrs Patterson's clothes. When she pushed open the door of the pub, she spotted Big Pete straight away, sitting in his usual seat by the bar.

'Here she is!' Pete cried to the barmaid when he saw Meg at the door. 'The rover returns! Told you she'd be back in business once she'd had the bairn. Good to see you, pet!'

Meg gestured to him to come outside and help her lift the bags of bones from the cart. The two of them took a bag each, dragging them along the stone floor of the pub to the table where Pete's pint of beer was waiting. Pete flopped down into his seat and dug in his trouser pocket for the coins to pay her. She waited while he heaved his body up in order to get his hand right down into the lining, his stomach straining against his waistcoat. It was the same checked waistcoat with most of its buttons missing that he had worn the first time Meg had met him. And it was the same waistcoat that he'd worn every single time she'd seen him since. As Pete counted out the coins from one hand to the other, a thought struck her.

'I'll be right back,' she said. 'I think I've got something on the cart you might like.'

When she returned to the pub, the coins were piled up on the table, ready for her to take.

'What's that you've got?' Pete asked.

Meg stood in front of him and held up a brown waistcoat she'd been given earlier that morning on her rounds.

'It's yours if you want it,' she said. 'Looks about your size, too.'

Pete ran his hands across it, taking in the quality of the material. He turned it over and did the same at the back.

'It's got all its buttons,' Meg smiled.

He opened the waistcoat, then raised his eyes to her. 'And a lining, too. By, lass, this is a top-class waistcoat and no mistake. I'd be honoured to take it.'

He put his hand back in his trouser pocket and added more coins to the pile he had arranged in payment for the bones. She took the money and put it safely into her skirt pocket while Pete stood, took off his old waistcoat and put the new one on.

As Meg turned to leave, the barmaid called her over.

'A woman came in here looking for you,' she whispered.

'Me?' Meg said. 'Who was it?'

The barmaid shrugged. 'Not seen her round here before. She wasn't a Ryhope woman, that's for sure. She was shortish, dark hair, curls, about my age.'

'Did you tell her where I live?' Meg asked.

The barmaid shook her head. 'What do you take me for? But I saw her asking a couple of the fellas before she left and I can't say what they might have told her. Just thought you'd better know.'

Meg felt a sudden coldness and thrust her hands into the pockets of her dad's army coat, more for protection than any need for warmth. She left the Railway Inn and climbed back up to the cart. All the way along the coast road to the docks she wondered who the woman was. She didn't recognise the description the barmaid had given. So who had been looking for her, and why?

When she reached the market, she spotted Derek the butcher by the door.

'Need a hand, Meg?' he shouted.

Without waiting for a reply, he walked towards the cart. When he saw it piled high with clothes, he turned and yelled back down the meat aisle.

'Bobby! Sam! Come and give us a hand. Grab this lot from the cart and take it over to the lasses up the clothes aisle.'

'Thanks, Derek.' Meg smiled as she made her way through the market. As she reached the clothes aisle, the first thing she noticed was that Florrie's stall was empty. She stood with an armful of clothes, staring at the bare table in front of her.

'If you're looking for Florrie, she's still away with her fancy man in Scarborough.' It was Lucy, who worked the menswear stall next door.

Meg dropped the clothes on to the empty table, her arms aching from carrying the heavy dresses.

'Do you know when she's coming back?' she asked, but Lucy shook her head and went back to serving a customer with underpants and socks.

Just then, the butchers Derek had commandeered to

help Meg bring in the clothes from the cart appeared at her side.

'Do you want these on here, then?' Bobby asked her. Without waiting for a reply, he dumped the clothes on the table. Before Meg could say a word, Sam followed suit and she was left with all of Mrs Patterson's clothes in a large heap. One of the shoppers in the aisle sidled up to her, stroking the material of the dresses and turning them over one by one.

'By, lass, these are bonny frocks,' she told Meg.

Meg shook her head. 'No . . . they're not for sale . . . they're not mine to sell,' she said, positioning herself in front of the dresses so that no one could touch them. The woman tutted and walked away.

'Not for sale?' Lucy cried. 'Don't be daft, lass. Florrie isn't here and her table's going spare. You've got the goods so you might as well sell them if there's folk wanting to buy.'

'But . . . what about Florrie? I was going to sell them to Florrie.'

'Never mind about Florrie. Just give her a bit of cash for the rent of her table next time you see her.'

'You're sure she won't mind?'

'She'd mind if you went home empty-handed, that's what Florrie would mind. Now get yourself behind that table and sort the frocks into colours, or sizes, any way you choose. Just make them easy for the women to find what they're looking for. And keep your eye on them when they start raking through. They're sneaky beggars, the lot of 'em; they'll swipe anything that's not nailed down.'

Meg did as Lucy told her and walked behind the table. Spot lay down underneath it with his head resting on his front paws. She took off her dad's coat and dropped it on the floor, then rolled up her sleeves, pushed her hair behind her ears and started arranging Mrs Patterson's frocks, laying them out beautifully by colour, the reds and pinks on one side and the blues and greens on the other. In the middle she placed a white jacket with a feathered collar. The display was dazzling and soon drew a crowd of women, elbowing each other out of the way so that they could be at the front for the best pickings.

'How much will you take for this one?' a woman asked, picking up a white lace blouse. Meg named her price, the blouse was sold and coins were handed over. Lucy caught her eye and raised one palm, pushing it skywards to the market's high ceiling. Meg smiled in acknowledgement of the unspoken advice, and the next sale she made brought more coins to her pocket.

News of the fancy frocks spread quickly around the market, bringing a crush of shoppers to Florrie's table for the rest of the day. Meg's skirt pockets sagged with coins and she transferred some of them to the pockets of her dad's coat when no one was looking. Relief flooded through her, knowing that she was now able to pay towards the back rent that she owed. So busy was she selling the clothes that she never noticed a man in a pair of red trousers keeping watch at the end of the aisle. A short woman with dark curly hair stood next to him, both of them watching Meg.

'Is that her?' the woman asked.

Billy Shillen simply nodded in reply.

Chapter Thirteen

Beattie

'Happy birthday, Meg!'

Adam raised his cloth cap with one hand. With the other he handed Meg a small parcel wrapped in newspaper and tied with garden string. She unwrapped it slowly, taking care to untie the string to use again. Inside the package was a small, square wooden frame. And inside the frame was sea glass laid in rows of blue, green and white.

'It's supposed to be the beach,' Adam said, pointing. 'I made the frame myself from driftwood I found when I've been fishing. See there, that's the sea, those blue stones, and then there's the sky and the sand . . .'

'It's beautiful,' said Meg. Her fingers caressed each glass pebble in turn. 'It's really beautiful.'

'This time last year we all went to the beach for your birthday, do you remember?' Adam asked.

Meg smiled. 'Course I remember. At least the sun's shining today. We had to wait for the rain to stop last year before we went out.'

'It's been a bit of a year, all things considered,' Adam said softly.

'Me with a bairn now, who'd have thought it?' Meg smiled. 'And I like to think Mam's looking down on us from somewhere up there, keeping her eye on us all.'

She nodded towards a chair at the kitchen table. 'Do you have time to sit with me a while, Adam? I haven't seen you in ages, not since Grace was born.'

Adam took the seat offered and stretched his long legs out in front of him, warming them by the fire. From under the table Spot let out a long, low sigh.

'Is Tommy still in bed?' he asked.

'He's always in bed,' Meg smiled. 'Seems he's at an age when he's asleep more than he's awake. His snoring just about shakes the house sometimes!'

'Meg . . .' Adam began hesitantly. 'I haven't called on you because I didn't know if you'd want me to. I wasn't sure how things were between us, not really. I didn't want to say the wrong thing again and risk our friendship like I did before.'

Meg met his gaze briefly, then turned to watch the fire in the hearth.

Adam picked at his fingernails, unsure of what to say next. 'Mam says the baby's a little smasher.'

'And I'm grateful for her help,' Meg said. 'I don't know how I would have coped without her, and Hetty and Gert too.'

'Everyone wants to help, Meg, you know that. They all love you and Tommy. We all love you . . .'

Adam stopped himself from saying anything further. The word sat between them, loaded with so much they could say, but neither could find the words.

'Would you like to see her?' Meg said at last.

Adam straightened in his chair. 'The baby?'

Meg nodded. 'She's upstairs sleeping, but you can see her if you'd like to.'

'We won't wake her, will we?' Adam asked.

'Come on,' said Meg, and she led the way from the kitchen. On the landing, Tommy's bedroom door was tight shut.

'He's still sleeping,' Meg said, nodding towards the door. 'But I'll wake him in time for work.'

Adam followed Meg to her bedroom door.

'You can't see her from there, silly,' Meg said, beckoning to him.

Slowly he walked into the room, his attention on the bundle in the middle of the bed. Meg gently moved some of the old clothes she'd used to build a makeshift cot. Inside was Grace, with her eyes tight shut.

'Hey, Grace,' she whispered. 'Look who's here. Adam's come to see you.'

Adam stood by the side of the bed looking down at the baby.

'She's beautiful,' he said at last, and then he glanced at Meg. 'She looks just like you.'

'I think she looks like my dad,' Meg said, not taking her eyes off her daughter.

'Does she . . . does she look like him? Like . . .'

'Clarky?'

Adam nodded.

'I don't think so,' Meg said. 'I can't see it. Not yet, anyway. She might do when she's older, but by then I'll have forgotten all about him. But what does it matter anyway? He'll never know her and I'll make sure she never knows him.'

'You've not heard from him since?' Adam asked.

'And nor do I want to,' Meg said defiantly. 'I know now just by looking at Grace what real love is, what it feels like to make a connection with another human being. A real connection. I know that whatever I felt for Clarky wasn't real, it was just part of my growing up, a daft crush I had on some fella who took me in and deceived me. And I was young enough and stupid enough to fall for him. No, it's just me and Grace now, and I'll do all I can to look after her.'

She glanced at Adam. 'Funny, isn't it?' she said. 'People call me brave and tough for looking after Stella and going out working on the cart, but when it comes to this tiny baby, this little thing, I wonder if I'm strong enough to cope. I just wish Mam was here. I miss her more every day since Grace was born. She'd know what to do. She'd tell me how to look after my baby.'

Adam walked around the bed and laid his arm gently across her shoulders. Meg welcomed his touch and laid her head against his chest. The two of them stood quietly together, watching Grace sleeping, but the moment was shattered too soon.

'Meg? Meg!' It was Gert's voice, urgent, yelling up the stairs. 'Meg! You've got to come. Now!'

It was Adam who was first to the top of the stairs. If Gert was shocked to see him coming downstairs from the bedroom, her face never showed it. What Meg got up to in her own time wasn't her business, she knew that.

'It's Stella,' she breathed. 'Davey's gone to get Vic at the forge; he's seen it before, he'll know what to do.'

'What is it? What's happened?' Adam asked.

'Stella's not well, pet. She's been restless all night, pacing up and down. And when Davey went to feed her this morning, she was pawing at the floor. You need to come, Meg, you need to help calm your horse.'

'I'll go, Meg,' Adam said. 'I think I know what it might be. If I'm right, I've seen it before with the pit ponies.'

'I'm coming too. I want to. I need to see Stella,' said Meg. 'She'll be all right, won't she?'

Adam couldn't bear to give her the answer she needed for fear of lying to her. One of his pit ponies had thrashed itself to death with colic, and it sounded as if Stella might have the disease too.

Meg ran back upstairs and wrapped the baby in a shawl. By the time she had put on her coat, Adam was already running along the back lane at Tunstall Street, determined to reach Stella as quickly as he could. Gert and Meg followed on behind, Meg walking as quickly as she could with Grace in her arms. When they reached the stable, Adam was already with the horse, watched over by Davey and Vic.

'We need to be quiet,' Adam said. 'She needs to be calm. Davey, have you given her anything to eat this morning?'

Davey shook his head. 'I was trying to feed her but she wouldn't let me anywhere near.'

Adam breathed a sigh of relief. 'I think we've caught her before the colic's taken hold too badly. I need you all to go indoors and leave her be. I'm going to walk her gently up and down the rhubarb field. I've got to get her moving, get her belly working to digest any food that's inside her. I've done it before with the ponies. Now go, the lot of you, please. You too, Meg.'

'Come on in, love,' Gert said, putting her arm around her. 'There's nothing you can do. Just leave the lad to it.'

Meg watched as Adam threw a rope around the horse's

neck. After a great deal of gentle persuasion, Stella began to move slowly from the stable. She kept twisting her neck as Adam led her across the road to the field. Once there, he walked her up and down the same track, over and over, until both he and the horse were almost dropping from exertion. Meg watched from outside Gert's house. Inside, Gert brewed up strong tea for them all and warmed milk to allow Meg to feed Grace.

An hour passed, then another, until finally Adam returned to Gert's kitchen, exhausted. Gert brewed more tea and offered her home-made rhubarb jam on freshly baked stottie bread still warm from the oven. Adam accepted the food gratefully.

'What's to be done, Adam? Anything more?' Davey asked.

Adam shook his head. 'Could've been bad oats she's eaten. Ask at High Farm next time you go there. Make sure you only get the good stuff, not the oats that have been at the back of the barn far longer than they should have. I'll have a word with the pit vet, see if he's got time to come and check her over. But I reckon she'll be fine.'

'You did well, lad,' said Davey.

'I just did what anyone with a bit of knowledge about horses would've done,' he replied. 'After seeing the way the pit ponies suffered with colic, I knew that if I could get to Stella before it gripped her too hard, there was a chance of saving her.'

'Then I'm more grateful than you'll ever know,' Meg told him. 'You've saved her life, Adam. And you've saved my livelihood too.'

'You need to let her recover for a few days before you take her out again,' he said.

'But I need—'

'Never mind what you need. Whether it's money for your rent or food for your table, you're not to take that horse out until she's fit and well. Whatever you need, you just let me know.'

Gert and Davey exchanged a look. Adam's words reminded Gert to tell Davey later about where she'd found the pair of them at Meg's house earlier that day.

'Now if you'll excuse me, Gert, I'm going to have to head home and get ready for my shift at the pit.'

'I'll walk back with you,' Meg said, gathering the baby to her and wrapping the shawl around them both.

Meg and Adam set off for the walk back to Tunstall Street. They walked close together and in silence for much of the way. As their street came into view, it was Adam who finally spoke.

'I mean it, Meg. Whatever you need, be sure to let me know. Mam will call in on you when she gets back from work.' And with that, he disappeared into his back yard, leaving Meg to finish her walk alone.

As she headed back to the cottage, Meg thought of the chores that lay ahead, relieved at least that she didn't need to do the netty cleaning. Hetty's bribe of free ale had proved too strong for Lil Mahone to resist. But there was tidying and cleaning to do once Grace was asleep. Her thoughts turned to Adam and the birthday gift he'd made for her, his bravery with Stella. And she thought about how she had warmed to his touch when he'd laid his arm around her. The way it had made her feel inside had surprised her, confusing her and causing her mind to whirl, wondering just what he really meant to her. He was just Adam, wasn't he? The boy she'd grown up with, the boy she'd played in the snow with in the back lane at Tunstall Street in the harsh winters of their childhood. The boy who . . . the boy who had turned into the man who had offered himself to her in marriage. She had spurned him, thinking his words weren't real. For how could they be? There'd been nothing between them then, nothing at all, not on Meg's part at least. But now Adam had matured into a man who cared deeply for her, who had never once said a word against her when she went off with Clarky. Instead, he'd waited patiently for her, willing to take Grace on too, another man's child.

Meg stepped into the back yard and pushed open the kitchen door. In all the excitement of leaving the house earlier that morning, she'd forgotten to lock it behind her. The first thing she did was settle Grace back into the bundle of clothes on her bed. When she was certain the baby was sleeping, she knocked lightly at Tommy's bedroom door but there was only the sound of his snoring to be heard. Meg quickly nipped across the back lane to use the netty. She was gone two minutes, maybe three, no longer than that. But it was long enough for her world to turn upside down.

When Meg came out of the netty, the door slammed shut behind her and she heard a dog barking. She knew immediately that it was Spot; she'd recognise his bark anywhere. She flew across the back lane, but as she entered the yard, a woman no taller than Tommy stepped out from the kitchen door. She was clutching baby Grace to her chest.

Meg screamed with the shock and the woman cowered against the brick wall. Meg grabbed for the baby, but the woman moved too quickly. The two of them circled each other in the yard as Spot barked wildly. Meg was scared, yes, but angry too, and determined that this woman wasn't going to take her child. Spot bared his teeth and a growl rose in his throat.

'Who are you?' Meg demanded. 'Give me my child. Now.'

'Your child?' the woman sneered. 'Call yourself a mother? I've been watching you, Meg Sutcliffe. I've been watching you for some time. You leave your baby in the house on its own when you disappear to God knows where. You're not fit to raise a pig, never mind a baby. I'm taking the child to its father, where it belongs, with its family.'

There was something about the woman that Meg recognised. In the darkness of her eyes and the way her mouth closed with a cruel smile, there was something that reminded her only too keenly of someone she had been trying her damnedest to forget.

'Clarky?' she whispered.

'Aye, I'm his mother. A proper mother. A mother who loves her son enough to get his child for him.'

Meg couldn't believe what she was hearing. 'You're Beattie? Clarky's mam?'

Beattie backed away towards the open back gate. Meg lunged towards her and Spot barked again.

'Get that dog away from me now or I'll drop the child,' Beattie warned her, sidling through the gate and into the back lane. Meg ran at her again, desperate to take Grace from her grip. But she was no match for Beattie, who was whippet-thin and moved as quickly as any prize-winning dog. She darted from the yard, slamming the gate in Meg's face.

By the time Meg got into the back lane, all she saw was a figure running away. A small green van was parked at the side of the road. Meg ran faster than she thought possible, her heart bursting, her face wet with tears. The door of the van was flung open and Beattie disappeared inside with the baby in her arms. With Spot beside her, Meg kept running as hard as she could until the van disappeared from view past St Paul's church, turning left at the village school and heading on to the road to Sunderland.

She stopped for a second to catch her breath, her chest heaving from the exertion and her face wet with tears. She glanced at Spot beside her, his tongue hanging from his mouth, his ribcage moving up and down with the force of his breath.

'Come on, Spot,' she said, picking up the pace again, heading this time to the Albion Inn to let Hetty know what had happened. If anyone would know what to do, it would be Hetty.

At the Albion Inn, Big Pete was standing at the bar showing off his new waistcoat to anyone who cared to look. Not that many did, but they all feigned interest, knowing it was best to stay on the right side of Big Pete, just in case. Behind the bar stood Jack Burdon, drumming his fingers on the counter top while a foaming pint of ale slowly filled a glass. Hetty was beside him, wiping down beer spills with her dishcloth, when the pub door flew open and Meg burst in with Spot behind her.

'Get that dog out of here!' Jack yelled.

Hetty saw the state of Meg and knew immediately something was up.

'She's gone . . .' Meg panted, holding herself steady at the bar for fear she was about to keel over.

'Who?' asked Hetty.

'Grace has gone.'

'What is it with you Sutcliffes?' Jack hissed. 'Always running in here with your problems! This is a pub, not a—'

'Jack! For heaven's sake, can you not see the state of the girl?' Hetty snapped. Jack turned back to the pint he was pulling as Hetty wiped her hands on her apron and took Meg to one side.

'What is it, love? What's happened?'

Gasping for breath through her tears Meg told Hetty about Clarky's mam stealing the baby. With each word, Hetty's resolve became more steely, her anger more direct. At the bar, Jack was pretending not to listen to their conversation.

'Jack!' Hetty called. 'Brandy for the lass. Now! She's in shock.'

Meg sank into a chair at the bar. Jack did as requested, dribbling the smallest amount of amber liquid into a glass and handing it direct to Meg. She gulped it down in one go, feeling it burn in her throat. 'We've got to get her back, Hetty. I've got to find her,' she sobbed.

'We will, love. We will,' Hetty replied more calmly than she felt. 'Do you know where this woman lives, Clarky's mam?'

Meg shook her head. 'He never took me there. He said his dad used to beat him so he left home, and his mam wasn't well, in the head like.'

'Well that might help explain why she stole the baby. And what about Clarky, do you know where he lives?'

'He never took me there either,' she sobbed. 'I think he shared rooms by the docks with his friend Billy, that's all I know.'

'We've got to tell the police,' Hetty said.

Meg sat up straight in her seat and wiped her eyes with the back of her hand. 'No!' she cried. She couldn't have the police involved. She'd done her level best to avoid them since the night of Hawk's death. 'This is between me and Clarky. I know he's behind it. I'll have to find him. I've got to get my baby back.'

'I'll help you, love,' Hetty said. 'But we're not going to get very far if we don't know where he lives. Now, is there anyone who would know?'

Meg took a deep breath and thought for a couple of moments. 'There'll be folk on the market who might.'

'Then we'll go there,' said Hetty. 'First thing in the morning, we'll go there and we'll bloody find him and his mother and get your bairn back.'

Meg's shoulders sank. 'Tomorrow? Can we not go tonight? I need to get her back, Hetty. I need her now. What if they harm her?'

Hetty laid her hand on Meg's arm. 'Look, love. There's no point going anywhere tonight – they'll have packed up by now. We'll head off first thing in the morning and get there when the market opens. And try not to worry about Grace. If it's Clarky's mam who's taken her, I think the last thing on her mind will be to harm the child. I'm not certain what's going through the poor woman's head, but if she's as poorly as Clarky told you she was, then she'll have her own reasons for wanting the bairn. But no, she won't harm her.'

'Are you sure?' Meg asked.

Hetty held on to Meg's hands and gave them a gentle squeeze. 'I'm sure. Now listen to me . . .'

She cast a glance towards the bar, where Jack was trying to serve three customers at once. Meg sniffed back her tears.

'Just in case there's a chance that this woman brings the bairn back tonight . . . and I'm not saying she will, but you never know what's going through her mind . . . just in case, we'll walk back up to your house now and I'll stay the night with you.'

Meg opened her mouth to object, but Hetty shook her head.

'I won't hear any arguments. You're in no fit state to be on your own. Is Tommy working the night shift?'

Meg gasped.

'Tommy! I need to tell him what's happened,' she said. 'I left him sleeping at the house, I ran out, I wasn't thinking . . .'

'If he's working the night shift then it's all the more reason for me to come and stay with you, then. We'll get the first tram to the market in the morning.'

'You'll do no such thing,' a voice boomed over Hetty's shoulder. It was Big Pete. Hetty swung round to find him standing right behind her.

'How long have you been listening in?' she asked.

'Long enough,' he replied. 'I'll borrow my mate's van and drive you there myself in the morning. You'll have to sit in the back, though, and I'm warning you now, it's not comfortable, but it'll have to do.'

'Thanks, Pete,' Hetty said. She turned to Meg. 'Come on, let's get you home.'

The two women stood to leave.

'Where on earth do you think you're going now?' sighed Jack from behind the bar.

'She needs me, Jack,' Hetty replied. 'She needs me more than ever. Her baby's been stolen, taken by that Clarky lad's mother. I'm going to stay with her overnight. I'll be back here first thing in the morning. Big Pete's going to run us down to the market in his van and we'll do what we can to find Clarky or his mam and get the bairn back.'

'You'll be calling in at the police station to report this, surely?' asked Jack.

Hetty shook her head and shot Meg a look. 'She doesn't want the coppers involved. We've got to respect her decision.'

'No police,' said Meg, staring hard at Jack.

'Well go on then, the pair of you,' Jack said. 'And Hetty . . .'

Hetty sighed. 'What now?'

He reached behind the bar and pulled out a bottle of brandy, which he handed to his wife.

'Take this with you. Give the lass another drink for the shock when you get up to Tunstall Street. And one more before she goes to bed to help her sleep.'

Jack's gesture both surprised and gladdened Hetty.

'Thanks, love,' she replied.

'See you at first light,' Big Pete said. And with that, Hetty slipped her arm through Meg's and supported her as they walked slowly back to Tunstall Street.

In the kitchen Meg found Tommy sitting at the table eating stale bread. She sank into her mam's chair by the fire as she explained to Tommy everything that had happened while he'd been asleep. Hetty opened the brandy bottle and rummaged around until she found two earthenware cups, which she half filled with the amber liquid.

'Here, drink this. It'll help take the edge off your shock,' she said.

Meg took the cup and held it with both hands. 'What if she sells her?' she said softly.

'What do you mean?' Hetty replied.

'Florrie told me once; she said there were women who buy babies, women who can't have their own. It's good money too, she said. What if Clarky's mam has stolen Grace to sell her?'

Hetty pulled a chair from the kitchen table and sat directly opposite Meg. Between them the fire crackled around the coals.

'Oh love, you mustn't think like that. You mustn't. Listen, whatever problems Clarky's mam suffers from, there's one thing you must never forget. She's the bairn's grandma, she's got that bond. She'd never hurt her and I doubt very much she'll be looking to sell her.'

Meg took a sip from her cup, letting the brandy burn inside her mouth and down her throat. 'I don't know how to be a proper mam, Hetty,' she said softly. 'I never have known. I've got no one to show me, no one to tell me what to do. I've always been terrified I might hurt her, that I might drop her, that I won't be able to afford the food to feed her . . . All of these things I worry about, all of them, and now this . . . I can't keep my child safe from harm.'

A knock at the back door made her jump in her seat. She flew to the door, and when she opened it, Adam was there in his work clothes with his bait box and his water bottle in his hands.

'Come to collect Tommy for work,' he smiled but when he saw Meg's ashen face and Hetty sitting with her, he became concerned. 'Is everything all right?'

'No, lad.' It was Hetty who replied. 'Everything's not all right. That Clarky fella from the market has turned up like the bad penny he is, or at least his mother has.'

'His mother? What's she got to do with anything? Meg,

what's going on?' Adam stepped into the kitchen.

'She's taken Grace,' Meg said, as calmly as she could. 'We're going to get her back. First thing in the morning, we're heading to the market to get her back.'

'Then I'll come too,' Adam said. 'As soon as night shift is over, I'll come with you.'

Tommy stood from his chair at the table. 'And me too,' he said.

'You'll be exhausted, lads,' Hetty said. 'Big Pete is coming, and there's likely some fellas on the market that can lend a hand too if we need them.'

Tommy glanced at Meg. 'I want to help. If Grace is in danger, I want to help.'

'I think Hetty's right,' Meg replied. 'If you and Adam come, it could make things difficult. I might need to speak to Clarky privately, to get his mother to see sense. If you're both there, it might make things worse: he might feel threatened and there's no telling what he might do.'

Adam nodded slowly. 'I see . . . Well, if you need me, Meg, you come for me and I'll do what I can. I'll call in on my way home tomorrow.'

'Thank you. I'll see you out,' Meg said, walking towards the kitchen door. Tommy followed behind, ready to head off to the pit with Adam for the night shift.

Once they were in the back yard, Adam whispered, 'What about the police? Have you called them?'

Meg shook her head. 'I couldn't. I can't risk having them sniffing around. I can't bear the thought of having them here, in the house where Hawk . . .'

'I understand,' Adam replied. 'Of course I do. You've done the right thing. Good luck in the morning. I'll be thinking of you, Meg.'

Tommy pulled his sister towards him and gave her a kiss on the cheek before he too said his goodbye.

That night, with Meg's shock and pain dulled by the brandy that Hetty insisted she drink, she and Hetty fell asleep in their chairs by the fire. Neither of them slept well; each time they closed their eyes, it seemed they were awake again, alert to the task ahead of them the following day.

When Tommy arrived home from work in the morning, dirty and covered in coal dust, he insisted again on coming with her to the market, but Meg wouldn't hear of it and made him promise to stay at home in case Clarky's mam turned up there with Grace. It was a slim chance and she knew it, but finally Tommy agreed. Meg and Hetty left him to his ablutions in front of the fire and headed back down to the Albion Inn. But on their way down the colliery bank, a jalopy of a black van drew to a halt in front of them. At the wheel was Big Pete, and beside him in the passenger seat Hetty was shocked to see Jack.

The van stopped and Jack's long legs stretched out of the door.

'I'm coming with you,' he told Hetty, then he turned to Meg. 'I still think you're wrong for not calling in the police on this matter, but as Hetty said yesterday, we've got to respect your decision. I'm coming with you to help you get your bairn back.'

Hetty looked at Jack and saw the tears in her husband's eyes.

'You're coming with us?' she gasped.

Jack nodded. 'No one should suffer the pain of losing their child,' he said. 'No one. Now come on, get in.'

'But what about the pub?' Hetty asked. 'You're seriously telling me you're not opening the pub today?'

'Some things are more important, love,' was all Jack said in reply.

With Big Pete at the wheel of the van and Meg beside him in the front, Hetty and Jack sat in the back amongst wooden crates and fishing gear. When they reached the market, the day's trading hadn't yet begun; the stallholders were just setting up. Fishermen were unloading their catch and butchers were splitting meat carcasses into chops and steaks. The stone flags on the floor of the meat aisle were being hosed down, the water turning pink from animal blood.

Derek, the chief butcher, looked up from his stall when he saw Meg run into the market hall followed by Hetty, Jack and Big Pete. Meg didn't stop to acknowledge him; she ran straight past without stopping, heading for Florrie's patch. But the stall was empty again, with no sign of her friend.

Meg spun around at the sound of Lucy's voice behind her.

'She's still away, love. Still in Scarborough.'

Lucy was busy unfolding clothes from bags and laying them out on the table in front of her. When she saw the state of Meg, she stepped out from behind her stall and held her arms out to the girl.

'What is it?' she asked. 'What on earth's the matter, pet?'

'He's taken the baby,' Meg sobbed. 'Clarky's mam came and took the baby.'

Lucy hugged Meg tight and glanced towards Hetty standing with Jack and Big Pete by her side.

'Is there anyone here who knows where Clarky lives?' Hetty asked her. 'There must be someone, surely?'

Lucy released Meg and laid her hands on her shoulders. 'There is someone who might know.' She pulled her empty money purse towards her. The day's business had yet to begin. 'Maggie!' she yelled to the woman at the next stall. 'Keep an eye on things for me, will you? I'll not be long.'

With Lucy leading the way, they hurried to the meat aisle, where Derek was now wrapping his white apron around his fat belly. Once Lucy had explained the situation, it took little persuasion from her for Derek to reveal the address where Clarky's mam lived.

'Do you want me to come with you?' he asked. 'I've known Clarky since he was a little lad. If he's there when you get to Beattie's house, he might just listen to me.'

Meg nodded, and Derek pulled on his overcoat, ready to join them in the search for the baby. Just before they left the market, he bent low under his stall. Big Pete noticed the movement and watched as Derek slid a butcher's knife into his coat pocket.

'Just in case things turn nasty,' Derek muttered when he realised he'd been seen. 'Bobby! Sam! Keep an eye on the stall for me. I'll be back as soon as I can.'

They strode out of the market into the morning light. Beattie lived in one of the rows by the docks, just a few minutes from the market. They walked in silence, following the riverside path, where mucky puddles of rainwater gathered. When they finally turned the corner into the street, Meg wasn't the only one surprised at how tall the houses were. They weren't like those on Ryhope village green: grand houses with gardens at the front and big bay windows. These were four storeys high, thin, mean-looking blackened houses with six chimney pots on each roof. Steps led up to the front doors, with fancy iron railings along each side. On the same level as the front doors were windows to front parlours, where Meg saw patterned curtains hanging.

'This is the place,' Derek announced as they stopped on the pavement outside a house in the middle of the row. Just then, the front door opened and a woman bustled out, a smart-looking woman dressed in a skirt and jacket with a tidy hat on top of her straw-coloured hair. She carried a basket on her arm. The front door banged shut behind her as she made her way down the steps.

'Is that her?' Derek asked Meg.

Meg shook her head.

When the woman saw the group gathered on the pavement, she stopped in surprise, taking in the sight.

'Is this where Beattie lives?' Derek asked her.

The woman's eyes darted from Derek to Meg, from Hetty to Big Pete, from Jack to Lucy. She hesitated before she spoke.

'It's a lodging house,' she said. 'But yes, there's a woman by the name of Beattie in there. She needs locking up, if you ask me. Something wrong with her, all that screaming that goes on. And last night there was even more screaming too, sounded like a baby crying.'

Meg flew up the steps and hammered on the imposing black front door with her fists. Beside her, Jack, Lucy and Hetty were peering into the parlour through the window. Big Pete gave Derek a discreet nod.

'Round the back?' he suggested.

The two men disappeared. Meg banged harder at the front door.

'I know you're in there!' she yelled, but there was no response. She cupped her hand to her mouth and yelled again. 'Open up now or I'll call the police!'

She threw her fists at the door again over and over, desperate to reach her baby. The door finally swung inwards and Meg raced inside, not even stopping to notice that it was Clarky himself who had opened it. The hallway was dark and the house smelled damp, cold and unloved. 'Where is she?' she called. 'Where's my baby?'

Hetty and Lucy were opening doors, checking every room. Meg ran upstairs, taking the steps two at a time, pulling herself up on the handrail.

'Grace!' she cried. 'Grace!'

'She's here, love!' Hetty called. 'She's here!'

Meg's hand flew to her chest and she headed downstairs just in time to see Big Pete and Derek walking into the hallway from the back of the house. In front of them was Beattie, with Grace in her arms, the baby fast asleep. Another woman was with them, younger than Beattie but with Clarky's dark hair and his looks. Beside her was a short man, his eyes darting about in shock.

'I'm Clarky's sister, Barbara,' the woman explained. 'And this is Ronnie, my husband.'

The short, nervous-looking man at Barbara's side nodded towards Meg.

'I told Mam . . . I told her not to do this, not to get involved!' Clarky shouted.

Meg looked from Beattie to Clarky, finally taking in the sight of him. The very cruel sight of him.

'You'll hand the child over, missus,' Jack Burdon told Beattie.

Beattie hugged Grace tighter still. 'I'll do no such thing.

This is my grandbairn and she belongs with me and her dad. Doesn't she, son?'

She stared long and hard at Clarky, but he turned from her gaze.

'Mam, do what the fella tells you,' Barbara said softly. 'You've got to let the bairn go. You're not well, you know what the doctor told you. I know you're hurting, I understand that. But do you not think I'm suffering too? Do you think I don't lie awake at night and cry? I'm the one that can't carry a child to term, Mam. Is it not enough for me to have to go through losing bairn after bairn? Is it not enough that this house is full of heartbreak for me and Ronnie as it is without you taking it on yourself to go and steal a back-street baby?'

'Come on now,' said Jack. His lanky frame towered over Beattie. 'Come on,' he repeated. 'Just hand the baby over. That's all we want. Just give her back to her mother, back to Meg.'

'Clarky! Son!' Beattie implored. 'You can't let them do this to me. You can't!'

Clarky shifted uncomfortably but still didn't say a word. Meg looked at him, then back at his mother. She saw how tight Beattie had hold of her baby. It was clear she had no intention of letting her go. She straightened and walked towards Clarky. Standing just inches from his face, she poked him, hard, in the chest. 'You!' she spat. 'You tell your mother . . . now . . . to hand me back my baby. Otherwise my friends here are going to go and find a copper to sort this out. Is that what you want? Any of you? Because if a copper comes calling at this house, I dare say he'll find more to report than a missing child. Isn't that right, Clarky?'

He turned his face away.

'You can't even look at me, can you?' she spat. 'And you've every right to be ashamed. I know it was you who stole my dad's war medals.'

'Mam!' Clarky cried. 'Just give her the bairn.'

'But son—'

'Give her it! You know I never wanted it. You just wanted it for yourself. You've behaved like a woman on the edge for years now, but I never thought you'd stoop so low as to steal a bairn.'

Meg turned from Clarky and walked towards Beattie. This time the woman offered no resistance, and within seconds, Grace was back in Meg's arms, still sleeping. Meg showered her with kisses, her tears falling on to the baby's face.

'Promise you'll not bring the coppers round?' Barbara pleaded. 'We can't have them here, not with our dad in jail. He was locked up last month and it's set Mam off again. She's not a bad woman, not really, you have to believe me. She's just troubled, that's all. She forgets to take her pills. If you promise not to call the coppers, I'll tell you what I know about the medals.'

'Where are they?' Meg demanded.

Barbara took a deep breath. 'I knew he'd nicked them from somewhere but I didn't know they were yours. He tried selling them on the market but they knew they were stolen and wouldn't touch them, not war medals of all things.'

'Where are they?' Meg repeated.

'He got rid of two of them to someone down at the docks, but I know there's one left, in the sideboard. I've seen it. I'll fetch it for you.'

She disappeared into one of the rooms at the bottom of

the stairs, and came back after a moment with the medal still attached to its ribbon. It was Hetty who held out her hand to retrieve it from Barbara and placed it safely inside her handbag.

'Well then,' she sniffed. 'Looks like we'll promise to keep the coppers away if you promise to keep your mam from coming anywhere near Ryhope again.'

'And if I catch you at the market, lad,' Derek told Clarky, 'I'll have your guts for garters, you hear me?'

'I think we're all done here,' Hetty said, and she led the way to the front door.

Once they had gone, Beattie dissolved in tears, sliding down the wall to the hallway floor, where she sat sobbing.

'You stupid bugger,' Clarky's sister spat at him.

'I never wanted it,' Clarky sneered. 'It was her, it was Mam who wanted to keep the bairn, not me. She's mad, our mam, she needs locking up! Do you know, she offered Billy Shillen cash if he helped her? Well I'm done with her. I'm done with the lot of you. And I don't want anything to do with that Ryhope lass either.'

Barbara shook her head. 'I know she's not the first girl you've got pregnant round here. But it's the first time I'll say this about any of your tarts. That lass that's just left here with your baby in her arms, she was far too good for you. Far too flaming good.'

That evening, back at Tunstall Street, Meg set to bringing in buckets of coal for the fire. After the emotional events of the last day, it felt good to lose herself in the routine chores, but she still felt on edge. In the back yard, she lifted the tin bath from the wall, ready for a long, relaxing soak in front of the fire. There was a noise in the back lane and she froze. As the sneck on the gate lifted, she stood stock still, holding the bath in front of her, a shield ready for battle.

It was hard to know who got the biggest shock when Adam walked into the yard. Meg heaved with relief, the shock draining from her. She dropped the bath and it clattered to the ground. It was Adam who picked it back up.

'Mam's told me about today. She says you got Grace back safely,' he said softly. 'I've been worried sick, Meg. I just wanted to check you were all right, that Grace is all right.'

'We're fine,' Meg smiled in reply. 'But it's been a day I'll never forget – and for all the wrong reasons.'

Adam beckoned her into the back lane. 'I've got something for you. Here . . . look.'

In the dark of the back lane it was impossible to see what it was. But once Adam had wheeled it into the back yard, under the glow of the kitchen fire and the oil lamps, Meg gasped in surprise.

'It's just an old one, like,' he explained. 'One of the fellas brought it down to the beach hoping to collect sea coal in it when I was down there fishing. But the daft lump had come down when the tide was in and he was just going to abandon it, so I asked him if I could have it and . . . well, it's yours now, Meg, if you want it.'

Meg stared at the pram in front of her, lost for words.

'Mam's given it a good clean, of course,' Adam went on. 'And I've fixed the wheels so they'll not come loose. Dad's got the hood working. Look, it goes all the way down, and when it's raining you can bring it up again to keep the bairn dry. And Evelyn's made a blanket and she's stitched the letter G in yellow in the corner there. You might have to wait till the morning before you can see it properly, like.'

Meg felt the hot sting of tears again, threatening to fall. 'Adam, I . . . I don't know what to say . . .'

'No need to say anything,' he said. 'It's yours. Well, it's Grace's, but you know what I mean. Listen, can I help with anything else while I'm here before I turn in for the night?'

Meg shook her head.

'Well, you just shout if you need me, you hear?'

Meg ran her hands over the canopy of the pram then took hold of the handle, giving it a little push to and fro. 'Adam . . . thank you,' said Meg.

'What for?' he laughed.

'For . . . everything. For always being here. For caring. For being you.'

Adam inched towards her and brought her face close to his with his fingertips. They were so close they could almost taste each other, smell each other.

Meg stood on tiptoe and kissed Adam, briefly but firmly, on the lips. She pulled back just in time to see a smile widen on his face.

'I'll be seeing you, Meg Sutcliffe,' he whispered into the dark of the night. Then he raised his hat and disappeared into the back lane.

Chapter Fourteen

Strike

1921

The winter of 1920 was as harsh as any other for the residents of Tunstall Street. The thin walls of the cottages provided only just enough protection against the biting wind and the sleet. And at Meg's cottage at the end of the lane, the fire roared in the hearth constantly, in order to keep some warmth about the place. By now, Meg was reliant on the kindness of her friends for food for herself, Tommy and Grace and for helping her keep a roof over their heads. She went out working on the rag-and-bone with Stella less often now, the old horse unable to walk far any more. But on the days when she did work, she left baby Grace with Davey and Gert, who looked after her as if she were one of their own. And there was a closeness between her and Adam now, a bond far tighter than there ever had been before. No more was he 'just Adam', the boy she had grown up with. Her feelings for him had been strengthened by everything they had been through together. Grace grew and flourished, a happy, healthy baby, and Meg slowly grew in confidence as a mother to her child. At Christmas, when Tommy took his holiday from the pit, he and Meg and the baby spent the day with Adam's family, where Jean Wilson served up one of the best meals Meg had ever eaten. And when the new year turned, it was Adam who was first foot into Meg and Tommy's cottage as the bells of St Paul's chimed twelve. He brought with him a single lump of coal in his hand, a symbol of good fortune in the mining community. But just a few weeks into the new year of 1921, a twist of fate brought even more poverty and hardship to Ryhope, and to Meg's door.

It was a cool spring day at the end of March. Meg was bathing Grace in the tin bath by the fire when she heard a scraping sound at the back door. She turned and saw Tommy standing there, still dressed in his pit clothes.

'What are you doing back from work so early?' she asked, surprised at the sight of her brother. 'You've not taken ill, have you?'

Tommy laid his lunch pail on the floor and took off his cloth cap. He leaned one hand against the kitchen table. 'We've gone on strike, Meg.'

'Strike?' Meg whispered. 'You've walked out of your job?'

'I had no choice. I had to do what they said.'

'How long will it go on?'

Tommy shook his head. 'It's hard to know. There's nobody left there. A notice has gone up and we're not to return until we hear otherwise from the pit.'

He sank into a chair at the kitchen table and his gaze

dropped to the floor. 'I won't get paid, of course,' he said quietly. 'There's a couple of weeks' wages in back pay, but that's it, Meg. There'll be no more while the strike is on.'

'But what's going on?' Meg asked. 'Why are they striking?'

'More wages, they tell me,' Tommy replied. 'And safer working conditions underground. It's not just in Ryhope they're striking, it's all over the country. I need to do something, Meg, I need to find work. I can't be relying on you for money. None of the lads at the pit would do that, and I can't allow it to happen to me.'

Meg lifted Grace from the warm water and held her to her chest, wrapping a linen cloth around her tiny pink body to dry the water from her skin.

'Is Adam on strike too?' she asked.

'We all are,' Tommy replied. 'But Adam and a couple of the other lads are still working today. All the pit ponies have to be brought up to the surface and put out to grass while the strike's on. Some of them haven't seen daylight in years; it'll take them a bit of getting used to, being outdoors.'

Meg stood with Grace in her arms, holding the baby close to her and gently kissing the top of her head. 'But what will we do, Tommy? When your wages stop coming, what will we do?'

Tommy raised his eyes to meet hers. 'Well, I was thinking . . . I could come out on the rag-and-bone with you.'

'The two of us?'

Tommy nodded. 'Two pairs of hands on the cart means we can fetch twice as much stuff. Mind you, we'll have to go further afield than Ryhope. Folk round here won't have much to spare once the strike begins to pinch at their pockets. And I was thinking we could—'

'Now hold on a minute,' Meg said sharply. 'Just hold your horses. I need time to think about this, Tommy, about how it might work.'

'Gert and Davey are happy enough looking after Grace when you're working, aren't they?' he asked.

'Yes, but—'

'Well then. What's there to think about? Let me help you, Meg. You can show me the market and the paper mill and all the places you go to with Stella and Spot. I want to help. I've got to earn some money somehow while the pit's closed. I'll see to Stella for you too. I'll do all the jobs at the stable you haven't been able to do lately. I'll clean her hooves, I'll take her to the forge and see if Vic can give her new shoes. I'll brush her like Dad used to do. I'll feed her the good oats from High Farm so she doesn't get sick again.'

Meg took a deep breath, taking in her brother's words.

'Please, Meg. Go on, let me help you,' he pleaded. 'The two of us working on the cart together. Just until the strike's over, please?'

Meg sat down in her mam's chair by the fire with Grace in her arms. She nodded towards Tommy and then looked down at Grace's face. The baby's eyes were fixed firmly on her own.

'What do you think, baby Grace?' she smiled.

Grace gave a smile in return and kicked her feet at the sound of Meg's voice.

'Looks like Grace approves of your madcap idea,' Meg told Tommy.

'Then we'll start tomorrow,' Tommy declared.

In the coming weeks, the effects of the pit strike hit Ryhope hard. There was no money to be spent in the shops and the pubs as there had been before. Unable to feed their families, striking miners dug over allotment patches for vegetables to be grown for the table. And under dark of night, desperate men went poaching for pheasants and rabbits to be brought home and cooked. With the pit silent, the coal heaps sat untouched and the fires in the cottages could no longer be fuelled. Stealing coal from the pit was a desperate act and one that could lead to jail if the culprit was caught.

For the wives desperate to keep their families fed and watered, food was bought on tick from the Co-op with repayment promised as soon as the strike ended. And as humiliating as it was for them, some women even went begging along the coast to Seaham, but the story there was the same, with the Seaham pit on strike too. Reverend Daye opened the doors of St Paul's, offering shelter to anyone who needed it as the effects of the strike took hold. With Hetty's help, he set up a soup kitchen inside the church for those not too proud to use it. Food parcels from the poor relief came into St Paul's to help the striking miners and their families, with the bairns always fed first. Reverend Daye even managed to talk the farmer at High Farm into contributing his produce for free. Breakfast in the soup kitchen was a mug of beef tea with a buttered slice of bread, when bread was available. For dinner there was a bowl of broth or potato soup.

Ryhope came together like never before, those with little enough to start with helping others to survive. It was a long strike, a hard strike that would last a full three months into the summer. And as it continued, Tommy was true to his word, working with Meg on the rag-and-bone round every single day, never letting her down once. He looked after Stella, giving the horse the care and attention that Meg had been too busy to provide since Grace had been born. And working outdoors in the spring and early summer gave him a chance to shine in a way he'd never had at the pit. He smiled more, Meg noticed. He sang as he worked, and his face glowed from the sun as the pair of them roamed the streets on the cart. His deep, strong voice travelled further than Meg's too.

'Any rag and bone!' he called, as Meg had told him to do. 'Any rag and bone!'

Meg lifted her bell after each of Tommy's cries and then brought it down sharply again, ensuring that they were heard as far away from the main roads as they could be, into the back streets and lanes. But since the strike had begun, there were slim pickings in and around Ryhope, with little being given to them any more.

'We're going to have to go further out,' Tommy told Meg as they made their way through the village with an empty cart.

'But it's just the same down at Seaham and up at Silksworth,' Meg replied. 'If folk haven't got anything to give here in Ryhope, things won't be different elsewhere.'

'Then we'll go further still,' Tommy replied. 'We'll go somewhere in Sunderland that folk have got a bit of money. Up to Barnes, or Ashbrooke.'

'We can't go there!' Meg cried. 'They'll just laugh at us. A couple of colliery kids with a horse, traipsing round the posh streets of Ashbrooke?'

She felt something nudge at her shoulder and turned to see Spot there, resting his chin in the gap between her and Tommy. She laughed.

'And you too, Spot. We'll be a couple of colliery kids, their horse . . . and a dog.'

Tommy stroked Spot under his chin.

'What choice have we got, Meg?' he asked, serious now. 'If we don't earn money, we don't eat. It's as simple as that.'

'We have to do it,' he urged. 'We've got to try. And who knows, we might even get some decent stuff from the posh houses too.'

Meg bit her bottom lip. 'It's a new area, one I'm not familiar with. But if we keep to the main roads so we don't get lost, it might just work.'

She took a deep breath and straightened up in her seat on the cart. 'Walk on, Stella,' she called to the horse. 'Walk on.'

But Stella paid no heed to the command and simply continued at her own steady pace as Meg and Tommy smiled at each other. Meg directed her along the familiar road that she travelled on each time she went to the market, but when the road split, this time she turned to the left instead of carrying straight on. Up the cart went, along Queen Alexandra Road, towards the leafy outskirts of Sunderland. An expanse of green came into view, a park dotted with trees, with heavy iron gates at its entrance.

'To keep the likes of us out,' Meg noted as they travelled straight past.

Around the park was a narrow road with trees on either side, their branches reaching across and almost touching overhead. Green shoots on the branches bore the promise of summer leaves, and Meg urged Stella on under the canopy. Behind the trees at each side of the road stood a honey-coloured stone wall, the same colour stone as Florrie's home, Meg remembered. And behind the wall, tucked well away from the road, were houses the likes of which Meg and Tommy had never seen. In Ryhope the big houses on the village green were close together; neighbours could call out to one another over garden fences. But here in Ashbrooke, the houses were set apart, and in their own grounds.

'Will they hear us if we call?' Tommy asked, looking around. Only the roofs and top storeys were visible over the wall.

'I don't think we should,' Meg said. 'It doesn't seem right to, not here. The people in these houses aren't going to take kindly to us shouting. I've got a bad feeling about this, Tommy.'

Tommy put his hands to his stomach. 'And I've got a bad feeling here. I'm starving, Meg. And I know you must be too. We've got to do it. We're here now, we've got nothing to lose. If no one comes out, we'll go and never come back. But we've got to give it a chance.'

Meg bent low to the floor of the cart and picked up her bell. She shot Tommy a look and he was off, crying as loudly as he could, 'Any rag and bone! Any rag and bone!'

The bell echoed around the leafy street, the noise of Tommy's call bouncing off the stone walls and coming straight back to them. Meg let Stella trot forward a few steps and they called again, over and over. She glanced up at the top windows of the houses, hoping to see a maid in one of them, as was the custom in Ryhope. But there was not a soul to be seen, on the street or behind the large windows of the houses.

'Keep going,' Meg called to Stella. 'Keep on.'

Another lane appeared, and another. Winding streets led to more narrow lanes, each one as pretty with trees as the next. Clumps of wilting daffodils, now past their best, stood to one side.

'Call again,' Meg urged Tommy. 'We're here now, keep going, keep calling.'

'Any rag and bone!' Tommy called over and over.

Finally a movement caught both Meg and Tommy's eye. In front of them to the left was a green wooden gate set into the stone wall. The gate was flung open into the road and a man stood there, an old man, holding a pile of clothes with both hands. He waited for the cart to pull to a stop, then handed Meg the clothes.

'Where's the usual fella?' he asked.

'Who?' said Tommy.

'The big fella that comes around here with his horse and cart.'

'He's not well,' Meg said, glancing quickly at Tommy.

'Ah, tell him I hope he recovers soon,' the old man said. And with that, he turned and disappeared back through the gate.

Meg looked at the pile of clothes she'd been given. They were men's clothes, a jacket and shirts, good quality too.

'What did you have to go and say that for?' Tommy asked. 'You know Mam never liked us telling fibs.'

'Didn't you hear what he said? We're on someone else's patch. There's another rag-and-bone man who does these streets, and he'll not be happy if he finds out we're stealing his business.'

'But they're not *his* streets, are they? I mean, they're anyone's streets.'

'And how would you feel if someone else came into Ryhope and roamed the streets there, taking clothes from Evelyn that she was saving for me at the big house?'

Tommy thought for a moment. 'Maybe we should try somewhere else.'

'There's no maybe about it,' Meg said. 'I think we should scarper, and quick. That old man said it was a big fella who does these streets. And I don't want to be here when he turns up, do you?'

'Let's take these clothes to your friend at the market,' Tommy said. 'All we need to do is remember how to get out of here; all these winding streets look the same.'

The cart trundled on with Stella leading the way and Meg and Tommy sitting in silence. Behind them, Spot barked.

'Shush, boy,' Meg said.

She kept her eyes on the road, concentrating on finding her way out of Ashbrooke and back on to Ryhope Road. But if she had turned around, she would have seen a man, a big man, wide with muscle and fat. He had an unruly crop of black hair that never lay flat no matter how many times it was brushed. His face was weather-beaten from a lifetime spent working outdoors, making him look much older than his years. Minto Davis had worked as the rag-and-bone man in the streets around Ashbrooke ever since he'd been a boy. The Davis clan had never taken kindly to anyone who tried to muscle in on their patch, and if a couple of young kids, one of them a lass too, thought they could steal their business, then they had another think coming.

Minto scratched his fat belly and set off after the cart, hidden by the line of trees. He'd heard stories of a lass working on the rag-and-bone from his mates at the market, but it was the first time he'd seen her with his own eyes. And with a little help from his market pals, he knew it wouldn't be too difficult to find out where she lived. He'd give her a warning, that was all. Just a little warning that would leave her in no doubt where things stood when it came to his lucrative patch.

* * *

The next day, Minto started asking around at the market to see if anyone knew where the rag-and-bone lass lived, but there were few who would give him the information he required. All he was told, by Derek the butcher, was that she came from Ryhope. But it was enough for Minto. Working the streets all his life meant he knew every pub, every shop, every inn and miners' hall in Sunderland, and it wouldn't be long before he tracked the girl down. He and his brothers had worked hard, very hard, outdoors in all weathers collecting rag and bone, working their way up from the back streets and lanes to the big houses in the avenues. Ashbrooke wasn't a patch that Minto was willing to share. All he wanted was a word with the lass to make sure that she knew how things stood.

Leaving his horse, Dusty, in her stable, Minto took the tram to Ryhope village and headed straight to the Albion Inn, the nearest pub to the tram stop. Behind the bar, Hetty and Jack were working together in companionable silence. Hetty was cleaning glasses while Jack was lifting bottles from a wooden crate and positioning them on the shelves behind the bar. Minto walked into the main bar, casting his eye around to see if he recognised anyone. A handful of men were sitting without drinks in front of them, playing dominoes or cards; with the strike still going on, there was no money for ale now.

Minto walked the length of the room before turning and heading back to the bar, intent on buying a drink and waiting to see who turned up. Maybe there would be someone with information on the lass with the horse. But just as he was standing waiting for Hetty to serve him, a movement outside the pub window caught his eye – and there she was! A black horse, moving slowly up around the village green, with two kids sitting at the front of the cart.

'Hetty!' Jack said when he saw Minto waiting. 'Customer needs serving.'

Hetty put down her glass cloth and smiled across the bar. 'What can I get you?'

Minto stared out of the window, watching the horse and cart disappear up towards the village school, then he turned and started to walk towards the pub door.

'I'll be back this afternoon,' he called to Hetty. 'Just remembered I've got a bit of business to do first.'

Hetty and Jack passed a smile between them and each returned to their work.

Minto walked from the pub, keeping his eye on the horse ahead. He quickly caught up with the cart, and followed it at a comfortable pace. He watched the way the horse moved, guessing the age of it from its gait and its speed. He studied the back of the girl and boy sitting close together on the cart, the lass's long dark hair hidden inside her coat. Behind them stood a skinny white dog, facing backwards, keeping watch as Minto followed.

The cart was moving so slowly as it made its way up the colliery bank that he had to slow his pace so that he wouldn't overtake it. He wanted to see where the lass was going and what streets she was working. But there was no crying out from the cart, no bell-ringing as he'd heard up in Ashbrooke when he'd first come across her. She was quiet now, her only words those of encouragement to the horse, which he could hear as he walked behind.

'Come on, Stella,' she said in a sing-song voice. 'Come on, Stella, sweet Stella.'

Minto hung back a little, giving the cart a chance to move ahead of him, but the horse was tired through, he could see that, and he knew it couldn't walk on much further. Yet still the lass was urging it on, sweetly and gently singing to the beast and with every line of her song, every 'Sweet Stella,' that she sang, the horse shuffled forward a few feet more. Minto watched with frustration. He'd been around horses since before he could remember. He'd grown up with them, ridden them as a boy and respected them as his livelihood now. He knew them in a way that this young lass could never learn. But he had to admire her, and the old nag too, for continuing on when the horse was so tired and worn.

He stepped up his pace so that he was walking level with the cart.

'She's an old one, eh?' he called up to Meg, pointing towards Stella.

Meg looked down at the stranger walking by her side, but it was Tommy who replied.

'She's old, all right. But she works hard.'

'I can see that,' Minto said. 'She's a strong horse, a good worker.'

'She's not for sale, if that's what you're after,' Meg said.

Minto laughed out loud and shook his head. 'No, love, I wouldn't give you ha'pence for that old thing. I just want to speak to you, to both of you. And I think your horse could do with a rest, don't you?'

'We don't speak to strangers,' Tommy said as Minto continued to walk alongside the cart.

'Oh, I think you'll want to talk to this one,' Minto replied grimly.

'What about?' Meg asked.

'About rag-and-bone collecting,' Minto said. 'Up in Ashbrooke. About stealing someone else's patch. My patch.'

Meg and Tommy turned to each other.

'Give us half an hour,' Meg said. 'I've got to stable the horse, then we'll talk.'

Minto nodded. 'Where?'

'At yon end of Tunstall Street, up there.' Meg pointed up the colliery bank. 'Half an hour.'

By the time Meg and Tommy returned home, Minto Davis was already waiting at their front door. Meg cradled Grace in her arms and headed inside, while Tommy called for Minto to come around to the back. Meg sat by the fireside in her mam's chair, with the sleeping Grace on her knee. She'd been asleep since Meg collected her from Davey and Gert's house earlier. Normally she woke at the sound of her mam's voice, but not today. Tommy stood beside Meg, his hands balled into fists by his sides, ready for whatever Minto had to say.

When Minto walked into the kitchen, he stopped, taking in the state of complete emptiness in front of him. He'd never seen anything like it before. In the hearth was just a grey pile of ashes with no fire going to heat or light the small room.

'I didn't know you had a bairn, miss,' he said when he saw Meg with the baby. 'You're not much more than a child yourself. And you, lad, how old are you?'

'Old enough to be on strike from the pit. But never mind about us, what do you want?' Tommy said, his words coming out more assertively than he felt.

Minto put his hand to a chair at the kitchen table.

'Can I sit down?' he asked, and without waiting for an answer, he pulled the chair towards him and sank his bulk down on to it. Tommy and Meg stared at him as he ran a hand through his thick black hair. Spot sat next to the chair, alert, looking from Tommy to Minto and back again.

'This has fair taken the wind out of my sails,' Minto said quietly. 'I was all set to come here and give the pair of you a right old rollicking.'

'For working up at Ashbrooke?' Meg said.

Minto nodded. 'It's my patch. I've been working those streets for decades, me and my brothers. My dad worked them when he was a lad, and his dad before him, my Grandad Ted. And there's a rule out there, an unwritten, unspoken rule of the rag-and-bone man, that you do not, under any circumstances, tread on another fella's route. You got that, the pair of you?'

'We only did it the once,' Tommy said. 'It's slim pickings around Ryhope at the minute, because of the strike.'

'We had no choice,' Meg explained. 'We've barely any money coming in and there's the three of us to feed, on top of the rent.'

'Aye, I can see how you're fixed,' Minto said, his eyes scanning the kitchen. 'And I admire you, the pair of you, but if I catch either of you up at Ashbrooke again, there'll be trouble, you hear?'

'What else are we to supposed to do?' Tommy said, his anger rising now. 'How are we supposed to eat? You want us to starve just because you think those roads belong to you? We've got just as much right—'

Minto sprang from his chair and grabbed hold of Tommy's jacket with both hands, shaking the lad.

'Get off him!' Meg yelled, but Minto paid her no heed.

Even at the sharp sound of Meg's voice, Grace carried on sleeping.

'Now listen, sonny,' Minto growled. 'I came here to give the pair of you a warning. You hear me? But I see there's a bairn to feed, and the circumstances you're living in, well, they aren't the best I've ever seen. And so I'm going to go easy on you this time.'

He dropped his hands from Tommy's jacket. 'But let me tell you this. If I see you . . .' he turned to Meg, 'or you anywhere you shouldn't be, there'll be trouble. Got it?'

Tommy looked him straight in the eye. 'Got it,' he said.

'And you, lass?'

Meg simply nodded, her attention focused now on Grace.

'Right then,' said Minto. 'Then I'm glad we've got that sorted.'

Spot stood and followed Minto out of the house and into the back yard. As the big man lifted the sneck on the gate to head out into the lane, the dog ran a ring around his feet, once, twice.

'Get out of my way, you stupid dog,' Minto hissed.

Spot continued to dance around his legs and feet, without growling, without barking, as if he was simply playing with a new friend. Minto tried to walk on, but it became increasingly difficult. His feet were caught up in Spot's game until he lost his balance and fell on his fat backside in a puddle of mud. Only then did Spot return to the back yard with his tail wagging, heading to sit beside Meg.

Meg breathed a sigh of relief and she and Tommy exchanged a smile as the tension of Minto's visit began to recede.

'I reckon we've had a lucky escape,' she said. 'And I've learned a valuable lesson never to work anyone else's patch again.'

'I wasn't scared of him,' Tommy said, standing tall. 'I reckon I could have taken him on if he'd come looking for a fight. Working at the pit now, I'm stronger than I ever was before. I reckon I can handle myself if I need to.'

'Tommy, look . . .' whispered Meg. She had pulled back the blanket in which Grace was cradled on her lap.

Tommy looked down at his niece as Meg rolled up one of the baby's sleeves.

'It's on both arms, look. It's all red. And she's burning up too.' Meg stood, gently rocking the baby in her arms. 'She hasn't woken since we left Davey and Gert's earlier, and now the rash is spreading. I've never seen her like this before, Tommy.'

'Shall I fetch Hetty?' Tommy asked, trying to mask his panic.

Meg shook her head. 'I need to get her to Dr Anderson, quick. I'll go there now. You tell Hetty, and Adam's mam too. Ask Hetty to meet me there if she can.'

Meg half walked, half ran down to the doctor's surgery in the village. Grace continued sleeping, opening her eyes briefly only to close them again. The rash flared scarlet on her tiny arms and legs each time Meg pulled back the blanket to see.

The surgery was held in a house off the village green. Meg pushed the heavy door open and flew into the waiting room. A row of faces turned towards her.

'It's the baby . . . I've got to see the doctor straight away!' Meg cried.

'Get yourself to the back of the queue,' a woman's voice shouted.

'Some of us have been waiting for hours,' another voice said, a man this time.

A woman seated at the front jumped to her feet.

'Shame on you, the lot of you. Can't you see the girl's worried for her bairn?' She turned towards Meg. 'I'm due in next, love, you can have my place.'

Meg thanked the woman and walked towards the front of the room with all eyes on her.

'I've been waiting three quarters of an hour and I'm in a spot of pain,' a man tutted as she walked past.

'I'll give you even more pain if you don't shut up,' a woman sitting next to him said.

It was ten, maybe fifteen minutes before an old man shuffled out of Dr Anderson's office.

'Go on, love,' the woman beside Meg told her.

Meg disappeared behind the dark wooden door with Grace in her arms just as Adam, Tommy and Hetty came through the front door.

'Where is she?' Adam called out, scanning the room.

'If you mean the lass with the baby, she's in with the quack now,' a man's voice said.

Adam ran to the door of the doctor's office and there was a general grumbling amongst those waiting.

'Hey! You can't go in there!'

But it was too late. He barged in without knocking, and Tommy and Hetty followed behind. To his credit, Dr Anderson didn't bat an eyelid at the interruption, having suffered far worse in his time tending to the ills of Ryhope folk.

'What is it, Doctor? Will she be all right?' Hetty asked. She reached out and laid her arm around Meg's shoulders.

Dr Anderson listened to Grace's heart and lungs, then stood back, surveying the rash on her skin. He pondered for a while in silence, and then gave a gentle nod.

Meg stepped forward. 'What is it, Doctor? What's wrong?'

The doctor took a deep breath. 'Well, it might be a virus, in which case it could clear up within a few days. But there's also the possibility that it might be scarlatina.'

Meg gasped.

'Scarlatina, Doctor?' whispered Hetty. 'But you can prescribe medicine to make her better, right?'

'In most cases medicine will help, if the virus isn't too far advanced in her central nervous system,' Dr Anderson replied. He reached up and removed his glasses before turning to Meg. 'But I have to warn you that if the medicine I give you doesn't have an effect, we may need to admit Grace to hospital for a diagnosis to be confirmed. She'll be kept in an isolation cubicle before being moved to a general ward. And what I'm going to prescribe isn't cheap, I'm afraid.'

Adam stepped forward from his spot by the door. 'I'll pay,' he said simply. 'Whatever it costs, I will pay.'

'But . . . but you don't have any money,' Meg whispered. 'The strike . . .'

'I've got savings, Meg. I've been saving my money from the pit.'

'I can't take your savings!' Meg gasped.

'You can,' Adam said gently. 'I insist. I was saving to buy a small boat for fishing, but it was only ever just a dream. I'd never have had enough, not in a million years. I want you to have the money for Grace.'

Meg glanced at Hetty, who simply nodded.

'The lad's talking sense,' she said. 'We need to get the medicine quickly too.'

'I don't know how I'll ever repay you, Adam,' Meg said. 'But I will, I promise.'

'There's no need,' he replied.

Meg felt as if she wanted to thank Adam a thousand times, a million even, but after such a display of generosity and kindness, she didn't know where to begin.

With the doctor's note in her hand, Meg led the way back through the waiting room, Grace still sleeping in her arms.

'I'm going to get Gert,' Hetty announced as they hurried to the dispensary. 'She'll be more use to you than I could ever be at a time like this.'

But Meg hardly heard her words, so intent was she on keeping Grace safe in her arms. The thought of having to send her to hospital, to an isolation cubicle, was too horrible to consider. She would do everything she could to keep her baby at home. After almost losing her to Clarky's mam, there was no way she was going to let Grace out of her sight again.

Adam had run home to collect his savings, which he'd stored in a tin box under his bed, and he met Meg and Tommy at the dispensary. It was all Meg could do not to cry at his generosity as he handed the cash over the counter. In exchange, she was given a small box with instructions on how to administer the medicine, and a warning to keep Grace warm and to feed her warm milk mixed with cocoa. It was Adam who bought the milk and box of cocoa powder on the walk back to Tunstall Street. Meg didn't have the words to express how grateful she was. Merely saying thank you wasn't enough for the debt of gratitude she owed him.

When they finally reached Meg's house, Gert was already there, waiting at the gate in the back lane. She was carrying a black bag, which she swung gently towards Meg when she saw her.

'My old nursing bag,' she explained. 'It never let me down when I tended my own bairns when they were ill, and it'll not let me down now.'

She followed Meg, Adam and Tommy into the kitchen and then reached out to take Grace from Meg's arms.

'We need to keep her warm,' she said, taking control of the situation. 'She can lie in her pram and we'll get a fire going.'

'There's no coal, Gert,' Meg told her. 'No one's got any, not since the strike began.'

'We'll need another blanket then,' Gert directed. 'Now then, Hetty told me that Dr Anderson's prescribed something for her.'

Meg handed over the box, and Gert turned it over in her hand, reading the instructions.

'My word, but this must have cost a pretty packet.'

'Adam paid for it,' Meg said quickly.

'It was the least I could do,' he said. 'It's good of you to come, Gert.'

'I couldn't not come, lad,' she replied. 'Once a nurse, always a nurse. If there's something, anything I can do to help . . . well, I have to try.'

'What do I need to do, Gert?' Meg asked, rolling up the sleeves of her blouse.

'Nothing, lass. Leave the nursing to me. I've already told Davey not to expect to see me for a couple of days. I'm going to stay here with you and the baby until . . . well, until we see a change in her, whichever way that might be. And if we need to call Dr Anderson, if she takes a turn for the worse, we'll deal with that if and when it happens.'

'Do you think she might take a turn?' Meg asked.

Gert knew from experience that there was no point

hiding the truth from a mother in danger of losing her child.

'I think . . .' she began. 'I think you should prepare yourself, Meg. She's taken very poorly, has Grace. She's in danger of the virus and the fever, whatever it is. And if it *is* scarlatina, well, you need to be ready for what that might bring.'

'Hospital, you mean? The isolation cubicle?'

'Or worse, love,' Gert replied gently. 'I've seen babies die from scarlatina.'

Her words rocked Meg and she stepped backwards in shock. Adam reached out to hold her close. He could feel her shaking with sobs against his chest.

'Now come on, we'll not have tears,' Gert said. 'While I've got breath within me, I'm going to do everything I possibly can for this bairn. I'm going to keep watch on her night and day, Meg, until she gets well.'

'But you've just said she might not!' Meg cried.

'And if that happens, we'll fetch Dr Anderson immediately,' Gert said. She turned to Tommy. 'Now, lad. Go and fetch a bucket of water in. And Adam, I'd recommend you go home and we'll call on you if there's any change.'

Adam shook his head. 'I'm staying,' he said, holding Meg tighter. 'I'm not leaving my girls.'

Meg lifted her face and kissed him on the cheek.

'Are you sure I can't do anything, Gert?' she asked again, and this time Gert was ready with her reply.

'You can bring blankets downstairs and get comfortable in your chair. It's going to be a long night for us all.'

It was two days, two long days and two dark and sleepless nights, before Grace's fever finally broke. Meg was exhausted, as was Gert, who had refused to rest, even for a short while. Apart from when he was working on the allotment with his dad, Adam spent all his time with Meg, sitting with her and the baby until he could no longer keep his eyes open and had to head home. On the third day, Dr Anderson's treatment finally began to have an effect on the child, and although the rash was still evident, it was thankfully subdued. Meg woke to find Gert with Grace in her arms, wrapped in a shawl. She lifted the corner of the shawl to show Meg the baby's leg.

'Look, love. Look.'

Meg gasped at the sight of the clear skin. Her whole body flooded with a warmth, a feeling of reassurance after spending the last few days in such distress.

'Will she be all right?' Meg asked Gert.

'I think so, pet. It could have gone either way, you know. I didn't want to worry you, but I felt it was best to prepare you, just in case. But from the look of her now, her skin there, I think she's on the mend.'

'I don't know what I would have done without you, Gert,' Meg said softly. 'I'll never be able to repay your kindness, you know.'

'You mustn't think that way,' smiled Gert. 'She's almost like one of my own. I nearly brought her into the world, didn't I? If Dr Anderson hadn't turned up when he did, I would have had to deliver her myself.'

She handed the baby over to Meg, who stroked Grace's cheek tenderly.

'However did you manage to bring up seven bairns?' she asked. 'I'm not sure I can even manage one.'

A shadow passed over Gert's face. 'There were nine,' she said. 'Davey and me, we had nine bairns. Two of them died, about Grace's age they were.'

'Gert . . . I'm sorry,' Meg said. 'I'm truly sorry.'

'Well, it happens,' Gert said matter-of-factly. 'It happened a lot more in my day than it does now, but it still happens. And I've a lot to be thankful for. Seven healthy bairns I brought up, and all those grandbairns I've got now. I wouldn't be without them.'

'Does it get easier?' Meg asked. 'I mean . . . does life get easier when you get older? Every day I think about Mam, every single day. And I miss her, Gert, I really do. I even miss Dad. I miss his spirit, the fight in him, you know? Some days, in my heart, I don't think I'm cut out to be a mam. I don't know what I'm doing and—'

'You're doing fine, Meg. You really are,' Gert reassured her. 'And I'm always here for you, and so are Hetty and Jean and all your friends from the market. And there's Adam. He really cares for you and Grace. I've seen it with my own eyes while I've been here, him sitting with you and helping you through Grace's fever, paying for her medicine.'

'Without him, I might have lost her,' Meg said softly, gazing down at her daughter.

'And you and him together, well, you know . . . you could do a lot worse.'

Meg smiled. 'I don't think I could do any better.'

Chapter Fifteen

Florrie

The next morning saw a flurry of activity in the cottage at Tunstall Street as the good news spread that Grace was on the mend. Adam told his mam, who passed on the news to Hetty at the Albion, and soon it seemed that everyone in Ryhope wanted to check on Meg and Grace. First came Davey and Gert. While Gert fussed over and fed the baby, Davey brought up the subject again of selling Stella to the knacker's yard.

'She won't take much more,' he warned Meg. 'You've seen the way she is now. The poor thing can barely walk once around the village green, never mind to the market and back. And you know you need the money. Big Pete will take her there; he knows the lads who run the place. You can say goodbye to her properly before she—'

Meg held up her hand. 'No, Davey. Not yet.'

'Leave the lass alone,' said Gert, nodding towards her husband. 'She'll do what's right in her own time.'

After Davey and Gert left, Big Pete called in on his way

to the Colliery Inn, where, he told Meg with a wink, he was hoping to do a nice little bit of business. And then at lunchtime Hetty called with a pan of stew for Meg and a bag of scraps for Spot.

'Jack couldn't come,' she explained with a sigh. 'He's busy at the pub. But he sends his love, especially to the little one.'

'Jack said that?' asked Meg, surprised. 'Sorry, Hetty, I don't mean to tease, but that doesn't sound like the Jack Burdon we all know.'

Hetty looked down at Grace in Meg's arms. 'You remember the day Grace went missing, when Clarky's mam took her?'

'How could I forget?' Meg sighed.

'Well, when we got home that night, Jack and me, we had a heart-to-heart. We opened up about things, about Philip, and we talked, we actually talked, for the first time in a long time. And we've got you and little Grace here to thank for making us two daft beggars finally see sense.'

After Hetty had left, Meg settled Grace in the pram in the warmth of the kitchen, and the baby fell into an easy, untroubled sleep. Meg herself felt her eyes closing as she sat in her mam's chair, but her doze was interrupted by a knock at the back door. Her stomach turned. It couldn't be Minto Davis again, could it?

But when she walked to the door and opened it, her spirits lifted and a smile spread wide. Florrie was standing in the back yard.

She held her arms out and embraced Meg. 'I've just got back from Scarborough. Lucy told me what happened with the baby. I haven't even unpacked my bag yet, just left it at home and hopped on the tram to come and see you.'

'Please, Florrie, have a seat,' Meg said.

'I told you that Clarky was a bad 'un,' Florrie said as she settled herself on to a chair at the kitchen table. 'But you've got your bairn back now and he won't be troubling you any more. I've heard from Derek that Clarky's joined his dad in jail. He was caught stealing lead from church roofs around the docks. Him and that Billy Shillen lad, the two of them have been sent away for a while.'

'Church roofs?' Meg asked, her mind going back to what Reverend Daye had told her some time ago about lead being stolen from the roof of St Paul's.

'That's what I've heard,' Florrie said.

She leaned over to peek into Grace's pram. The baby was awake now, smiling and pushing her feet into the blankets Meg had wrapped her in.

'She's a grand one, isn't she?' Florrie smiled. 'And Lucy told me you'd used the table at the market while I was away.'

'You don't mind, do you, Florrie?'

'Mind? I applaud you for it, Meg. It sounds like you had a good day. Bonny frocks they were too, by all accounts. Do you think there'll be any more of that kind?'

'I'm not sure . . . but I'll get the money to you for the rent of your table,' Meg said quickly. 'I've been waiting to see you. I was going to pay it to you as soon as I could.'

'No, lass. There's no hurry to pay,' Florrie replied. 'Just mark it down in your book as an amount owing, to be paid when you can afford it and not before. Listen, love,' she went on. 'I've got something to tell you, a bit of news.'

'Oh?' Meg asked. 'Good news or bad news?'

'Depends on how you look at it,' Florrie said. 'Bit of both, I suppose. Well, at least it's good news for me, but . . .'

'Bad news for me?' Meg asked.

'Doesn't have to be, not if you listen to what I have to say.' She looked Meg straight in the eye. 'I'm going away, Meg. Moving on and selling up.'

'From the market?'

'From Sunderland. I've been asked to move down to Scarborough to live with—'

'Your fancy man?'

Florrie laughed. 'That's what Lucy's always called him. He's called George, and he's a lovely fella, Meg, he really is. We're mad keen on each other and we have been for years. But him living down there and me up here and hardly ever seeing each other, well, it's not ideal. And he's got a lovely little place by the sea, a right bobby dazzler of a house up on the cliff top with views out over the South Bay. And there's a park nearby, and oh, the tea rooms there, Meg. You would love them, you really would.'

'I've never been to Scarborough,' Meg said quietly.

'Then you must. You must come and visit and bring Grace when she's older.'

'When will you go?' Meg asked.

'Soon, pet. As soon as I've packed my boxes at the house and sorted things out at the market. I reckon I'll be gone in the autumn.'

Meg sat quietly for a few moments, taking in her words.

'Meg . . . before I go, there's something I want to ask you,' Florrie said at last. 'Now, you can say no, of course – there's no obligation – and you don't have to give me your answer right now. You can think on for a few weeks and let me know.'

'What is it?' Meg asked, curious.

Florrie took a deep breath. 'Do you recall me telling you

that when my husband died, the house came to me as his widow?'

Meg nodded.

'Well, the thing is, if I marry again, I lose it. My late husband was very clear on that in the paperwork he left when he died. And with my chap living in Scarborough . . . Well, I don't want to be putting all my eggs into one basket, and so I was thinking I'd keep the house on up here, maybe rent it out.' She caught Meg's gaze and held it. 'Rent it to you, Meg. For you to live there with Tommy and Grace, if you want to, of course.'

Meg gasped. 'How can we afford it?' she whispered.

'I don't want to make money on it,' Florrie explained. 'I just want to keep it, in my own name. It's a bit of insurance in case things don't work out with George. I'll charge you the same as you pay here, whatever it is. And there's something else I want to say . . .'

It was a few seconds before Florrie spoke again. 'I want you to take on the market stall for me,' she said at last. 'Lucy said you did well there, and I know you'll make a success of it. I'll transfer it to you through the market officials to help keep your accounts book straight.'

Meg's mouth opened, then closed again with the shock. When she could finally speak, she said, 'But we'd be away from Ryhope, from everything and everyone I know here.'

'Isn't that what you wanted?' Florrie asked. 'To move away from the dirt of the pit and the coal?'

Meg shook her head. She was confused, overjoyed and frightened all at the same time, and unable to make sense of her feelings.

Florrie stood to leave. She gathered her coat and bag to her and then leaned over the baby in the pram. From her handbag she brought out a silver half-crown and placed it gently in Grace's tight fist.

'Like I said, there's no need to give me an answer right away,' she said as she headed towards the back door. 'But promise me you'll think about it.'

'I will,' Meg replied. 'I promise.'

Florrie's offer was much on Meg's mind over the coming days, but the more she mulled it over, the more confused she became. If she moved away from Ryhope, it would mean leaving the people she knew and loved. How would she cope without Davey and Gert's support and friendship . . . without Hetty right there within reach? And how could she ever break the news to Adam that she and Tommy were moving away? Oh, it wasn't far, not really. Only a mile. Walkable in good weather, or just a short tram ride in bad. But it seemed unthinkable to leave Adam after living so close to him, growing up with him too. Of all of them in Ryhope, he'd be the one she'd miss the most.

And yet . . . Florrie's offer of her home, that lovely cottage with its stone walls that kept out the wind and the rain, with a garden for Spot and plenty of grass for Stella, was almost too good to turn down. There'd be fresh air for Grace, trees to climb as she grew up, birds singing as she played outdoors. There'd be no more screaming from the neighbours as they waged war with each other; no more collecting water from the shared tap in the mucky back lane. And there was even an inside netty! She knew she could make a go of things at the market, that was for sure. No more would she need to sell clothes she'd collected on the rag-and-bone with Stella. She'd have her very own market stall to sell clothes that other pedlars brought to her.

And Florrie had always told her that she'd make more money that way than she was bringing in at the moment.

She kept the offer to herself for a few days, twisting and turning it over in her mind, looking at all the angles and all the questions it threw up. She even kept it secret from Tommy until she felt certain in her mind of what it was she wanted. And she kept it secret from Adam until she felt certain in her heart.

The pit strike carried on through the summer. The weather was exceptionally warm, which was welcome, for there was still no coal to heat the cottage at Tunstall Street. Grace was growing now, a strong, healthy baby, but Gert and Davey were still at pains not to allow Meg to take her out with her when she worked on the horse and cart.

'But it's a fine day, and I'll have Tommy with me,' Meg said when Davey came out to the stable as she readied the horse for another day at work.

'Gert!' Davey shouted towards the kitchen. 'Get yourself out here and have a word with the lass!'

Gert came plodding out, wiping her hands on her apron.

'How many times have we told you, love?' she said. 'You know we enjoy looking after Grace. I've got the milk warming in the pan right now.'

'And your dad, rest his soul, he'd be turning in his grave if he knew I was allowing you to take his grandbairn out on the cart,' Davey added.

'I know,' Meg said. 'And I appreciate all that you do, I always have done. But I want to show her my world. She'll be safe. Tommy can take the reins and I'll sit with her in my arms. We're not going far, just to the paper mill today. Please, Davey. Just once?'

Davey and Gert exchanged a look, and Gert shrugged. 'I suppose we've got to let her go sometime.'

Meg handed Grace over to Gert while she continued readying Stella and the cart.

'Where is Tommy anyway?' Davey asked.

'Gone to a meeting at the pit,' Meg replied. 'All the miners have been called there this morning, and then he's coming straight here once it's done.'

'Hey! Speak of the devil,' Gert said, turning to see Tommy walking towards them, his face flushed red.

'I've run all the way,' he said, his chest heaving. 'We're going back, Meg. The strike's over! We're going back to work next week!'

'Well I never,' said Davey. 'Gert, I'm going to get myself up to the Colliery Inn to find out what's going on.'

Tommy jumped up on to the cart and took the reins in his hands. Meg lifted her skirts and climbed up to sit next to him, then folded her dad's army coat so that the lining faced towards her and placed it in her lap. Gert handed Grace up to her mother, and Meg wrapped the coat around the baby and held her securely on her knee.

'Come on, Stella.' Tommy urged the horse to start moving. 'And go carefully today, we've precious cargo aboard.'

'Mind what you're doing,' Gert shouted as she waved the three of them off.

The heat of the summer day made Stella walk even more slowly than she usually did.

'Davey reckons we should sell her,' Meg told Tommy as they travelled along Ryhope Road to the mill. 'And heaven knows, we could do with the money.'

'Well, she is just a horse,' he replied.

'But she's Stella . . .' Meg said quietly.

'She's just a horse,' Tommy repeated. 'And we mustn't forget that. But if we sell her, how would you do the rag-and-bone when I go back to work?'

Along the coast road on the right-hand side, the tall chimneys of the paper mill came into view.

'Let's drop the rags at the mill first, and then I've got something to tell you.'

Tommy shot his sister a look, confused, but Meg paid him no heed. Stella walked slowly on, positioning herself on the road for the turn to the right. She knew she was going to head down to the mill long before Tommy did, and he and Meg smiled at each other.

'She's just a horse, eh?' Meg said.

As they got close to the mill, Meg saw that the side door, which was usually closed, had been flung open to the warmth of the day. A cloud of cotton dust lay at the entrance.

'You miners work underground in the dark,' Meg told Tommy. 'But these lasses in here work covered in dust. Come and have a look.'

Tommy took Grace from Meg's knee and held his niece while Meg clambered down to the ground, then handed the child back to her and walked behind his sister as she headed to the open door. It didn't take long for Ruth to notice her there, and she came bounding over.

'Girls!' She turned to shout behind her into the cutting room. 'Come and have a look at this!'

Needing no excuse to stop work and take a breath of fresh air, half a dozen of the girls stood from their tables and headed towards the door. The last one out was a girl called Claire, who had long dark hair and almond eyes. She hung back a little from the others as they greeted Meg and smiled at the baby, trying to make Grace giggle and laugh. Meg handed Grace over to Tommy while she conducted her business with Ruth. As the girls from the mill fussed over the baby and Tommy, Claire watched from one side before approaching him.

'It's a lovely little bairn,' she said, holding out her hand towards Grace. Grace gripped tight hold of Claire's little finger and wrapped her fist around it. 'Is it yours?'

Tommy laughed. 'No . . . no, it's not mine. It's my sister's.' He nodded towards Meg.

'I've never seen you at the mill before,' Claire said softly.

'First time I've been here,' he said. 'Do you really work in there in all that dust?'

Claire shrugged. 'You get used to it.'

'Not sure I would,' Tommy replied.

'Not sure I'd get used to working outside with a horse.'

'I work at the pit,' Tommy said. 'But with the strike and all, I've been helping my sister.'

'Do you work underground?' Claire asked.

'Not underground yet,' Tommy replied. 'But I will soon enough. And we're going back to work next week, they tell me.'

'Oh . . . so you won't be coming here again?'

Claire leaned towards Grace and the baby tugged at her long hair, making Claire laugh. Tommy gently took hold of Grace's hand and loosened her grip.

'Sorry about that,' he said.

'That's all right. I like children. We've got three little 'uns in the house. I help Mam look after them when I go home.'

'Girls! Back to work now!'

Ruth, her business with Meg now done, was marching towards the mill door with the girls following behind.

'I've got to go,' Claire said. 'It was nice to meet you . . .'

'Tommy. I'm called Tommy. And this is Grace.'

'It was nice to meet you, Tommy. I'm Claire. Look, I'm going to have to go or Ruth will dock my wages. Maybe I'll see you again sometime?'

Tommy smiled. 'Maybe you will.'

'Bye, Tommy.' Claire turned and waved as she headed indoors. 'Bye, Grace.'

'Looks like you've made a friend there,' Meg said as she climbed back up on to the cart. Tommy handed Grace up to her and then walked around the cart and climbed into his own seat.

'Looks like I did,' he smiled in reply.

He took up the reins and was about to start Stella moving when he remembered something and his hands dropped again.

'You said you had something to tell me, Meg. You said earlier there was something . . .'

'Walk her on, Tommy. We'll stop at Hendon, on the beach road, and I'll tell you everything then.'

At Hendon beach, Meg and Tommy sat on the cart looking out to the churning sea. Sea salt blew on to their hands and faces, and Meg huddled Grace tight to her to protect her against the wind. Despite the warmth of the day, away from the cliffs the breeze whipped around them. The sea was wild, angry, dark and foamy as it crashed to the shore, and Tommy made sure that they were far from the waves so as not to upset Stella with the noise, although she seemed to take it all in her stride.

He listened to Meg's news in silence, without questions, soaking it all up. He heard her words all right, each one as clear as a bell, but he also heard her voice rise with excitement as she told him all about Florrie's house, about the inside netty and the garden at the back. He knew, without Meg telling him so, that this was what she wanted. He could see it in the way her eyes lit up, in her smile as she talked about the trees and the birds and the cobbled lane where Florrie's house sat quietly, in peace. There was no hurry to answer Meg, he knew that, for there was no hurry for Meg to tell Florrie her decision. But Tommy knew, he just knew, it was what Meg wanted above all else. Florrie's house could offer a better life, if not for Meg, then for Grace. And he knew he would follow his sister's choice, whatever it would be.

They travelled home along the coast road, with Stella slower now, slower than she'd ever been. When they returned to the stable at the back of Gert and Davey's house, they saw Davey and Vic from the forge sitting in their shirtsleeves in the yard on chairs that Meg recognised from Gert's kitchen.

'Just soaking up the sun,' Davey smiled as the cart rounded the back of the house. 'Got to make the most of it.'

Vic stood and walked towards the cart, helping Tommy unbridle Stella and fill up her water trough. Then he stood quietly watching the horse before following Meg into the kitchen. Gert reached out for Grace as soon as she saw her, fussing over the child, wanting to make sure that her ride on the cart had done her no harm. In return, Grace smiled and stretched her tiny hands towards Gert's face.

'Meg?' Vic said. 'I think you and me need to have a word about your horse.'

'She's all right, isn't she?' Meg said quickly. 'She's old, that's all. Just old and slow.'

Vic shook his head. 'Oh, she's old, and she's going to get older, and slower. You can't keep working her, Meg, not in the way that you're doing. The trips you're making to the market and the mill, they're too much for her now. You ought to think about . . .' He quickly glanced at Davey. 'You ought to think about letting her go.'

Meg shook her head. 'No. She's not ill. She's not lame. You can't take her, not yet.'

'Meg, listen to the man,' Davey pleaded. 'She's old for the work you need her to do. And if anyone knows what he's talking about, it's Vic. I've been saying for a long time that you could do worse than let her go now, while you can still get a bit of cash from the knacker for her bones.'

Meg reached her hand to the sideboard to steady herself.

'The men are right, love,' Gert said gently. 'It's time to let her go.'

'But . . . but I love Stella, she's part of my life.' Meg's words caught in her throat.

'If you love her as you say you do, then you'll do the right thing,' Vic said softly.

Meg shook her head again. 'I can't send her to the knacker's yard,' she said, looking from Vic to Davey and Gert. 'I won't . . . no . . .'

She ran from the kitchen. Davey started after her, but Vic put his hand on his friend's arm.

'Leave her be,' he said.

Meg flew to the stable, where Tommy was sorting out the hay. She put a hand on Stella's neck and gently patted it.

'Do Vic and Davey reckon she's had enough, then?'

Tommy asked. 'I heard some of what they said. They were saying it's time to turn Stella in, weren't they?'

Meg stroked the horse slowly, mulling over Davey and Vic's words in her mind. They were men who knew horses, and she only knew Stella.

'Maybe it is time,' she replied at last. 'Maybe it's time for us all to move on.'

'Move to Florrie's house, is that what you're saying?'

'I'm saying we've been given a chance, Tommy. A chance that might never be given to us again. I can work on the market and take Grace with me. No more trudging the streets in the cold and the rain.'

'What about me?' Tommy asked. 'What about my job at the pit?'

'It's only a mile away; it's not as if we'd be going to the back of beyond. And there's bound to be someone on the market who'll know where you can get an old bike so you can cycle to work.'

'Then we need to tell everyone,' Tommy said. 'Davey and Gert in there, Hetty . . . we'll need to tell them all we're moving away.'

Meg nodded. 'I know. I'll do it. I'll go in now and tell Vic he can . . . he can let Big Pete take Stella.'

'Are you sure?'

Meg nodded. 'We need the money, Tommy. We have no choice.'

'And if we move, Meg . . . if we move, what will you say to Adam?'

Meg took a deep breath. In her heart, she knew exactly what she had to say to Adam. She just needed to find the right time.

* * *

The following week, the miners returned to the pit. The workings of the coal mine that had lain quiet for three warm months of the summer roared into life again. The pit caller knocked on doors for the miners that first morning, getting them up out of bed, but Tommy needed no knock to wake him. He was up early for his first shift, eager to see his friends and start earning money again.

Adam had been at work the day before the miners went back to the pit, driving the ponies underground. From Tommy, Meg knew that he wasn't due at the pit again until the late shift of the first proper day back. While Tommy was out at work, she took Grace in her arms and walked along the back lane at Tunstall Street to the cottage where the Wilson family lived.

It was Evelyn who greeted her at the door, with a hairbrush in one hand and a chunk of stottie bread in the other.

'Sorry, Meg,' she gasped. 'I'm late for work. They'll have my guts for garters if I don't get there in the next ten minutes. I'm going to have to run all the way down to the village.'

She leaned in to Grace and gave her a peck on the cheek.

'Sorry, Grace,' she smiled. 'I'll see you soon, I promise.' And with that, she flew from the house into the back lane.

Meg stood at the kitchen door, looking into the empty room. There were footsteps on the stairs, and she turned to see Adam walking along the passageway towards her.

'This is a nice surprise,' he smiled. 'We don't often see you here. Did you want to talk to Mam about something? She's not back from work until this afternoon.'

'No, Adam . . . it's not your mam I wanted to speak to. It's you. Can I sit down?'

'Course you can, here . . .' Adam said, and he pulled out a chair from the kitchen table. Meg made herself comfortable. 'You might want to take a seat, too.'

A puzzled look crossed Adam's face as he pulled out a chair for himself and sat next to Meg. Between them, Grace sat on Meg's lap.

'Adam . . . there's something I need to tell you,' Meg began. Slowly she started to tell him all about the offer that Florrie had made, and of her plans to sell Stella too.

Adam leaned back in his chair and pressed his fingertips together, as if he was in prayer. A long sigh came from his lips, and he took deep breaths, one after another. The two of them sat in silence for a few moments as Meg's news sank in. Finally, Meg reached out to hold his hand.

'There's something else, Adam,' she said. 'Something I want to ask you this time.'

Adam sat up straight in his chair. 'Anything, Meg, you know that. You can ask me anything. If I'm going to lose you from Ryhope . . .'

'But that's just it,' she said, smiling at him and holding his hand tight. 'You're not going to lose me. Not if you don't want to, that is.'

'Not lose you? But you've just told me you're moving away.'

'And now I'm asking you to come with me. Come with me and be part of our family . . . be part of me.'

'Live over the brush?' Adam said, shaking his head slowly. 'I don't think I could, Meg. I don't think Mam would approve.'

Meg laughed. 'Do you remember, Adam, when you asked me to marry you, and I turned you down? I was so sure I could bring Grace up on my own with no help from anyone, not even you. Well, I dare say I could carry on as I am and this little 'un wouldn't suffer, because I'd always put her first. But I don't want to carry on as I am. I want to have a family. I want you, Adam. If you'll still have me, of course.'

'Are you asking me to marry you?' Adam smiled.

'Suppose I am, if you put it like that,' Meg replied.

'You'd let me be a dad to Grace?' he asked.

Meg nodded. 'You're already a brother to Tommy.'

'And a husband to you?'

'I'd like that, Adam. I'd like that very much indeed.'

Adam reached for Meg and gently, softly kissed her on the lips. He held out his hand towards Grace who gripped tight with her fist around his fingers. Meg looked deep into his face, taking in the warmth and the soul of him.

'Is there anyone I need to ask?' he said at last. 'In place of your dad, I mean, to ask for your hand in marriage. The vicar, perhaps?'

'Just Tommy,' she smiled. 'But you won't find any objection there. And we should go to Florrie's house too, so you can see it for yourself.'

'This weekend?' Adam offered. 'And we can meet with Reverend Daye too. I'll see what we need to do to book a date at St Paul's.'

Meg nodded, unable to speak now, a lump in her throat and tears in her eyes.

Adam gently stroked her hand where it lay on the kitchen table.

'I need to tell you something, Meg,' he said. 'Something I've always wanted to say but have never dared. Something I've always felt – always – but have never been able to show you, not truly. I love you, Meg. I always have.'

Meg's tears began to fall now, tears of happiness and joy that she could not control even if she had wanted to.

On Sunday, Meg took Adam and Tommy to visit Florrie's house. The three of them travelled by tram with baby Grace in her pram. Florrie welcomed them all into her home, where the unmistakable scent of freshly baked bread greeted them as soon as they stepped inside. As Meg positioned Grace's pram in the hallway, she didn't notice the look that passed between Florrie and Tommy: the discreet nod that Florrie gave and the smile that landed on Tommy's face because of it. Adam held out his hand in a polite greeting, but Florrie pulled him to her in a hug once Meg shared their wedding news.

'You'll be wanting to look around the place,' Florrie said to the two men. 'Go on, the pair of you. The stairs are there, there are two bedrooms upstairs, and the netty's just there through the kitchen door. There's a scullery and a pantry at the back and a yard with the water tap to the side. Spot could live in the yard if you want him outdoors. Course, it's up to you when you move in. If you want him by the fire in the kitchen where he's used to, then so be it.'

'Can we see the garden first, Florrie?' Tommy said urgently.

Florrie's hand flew to her chest. 'Of course, of course . . . how could I forget? We must see the garden first.'

'But it's a bit damp out,' Adam said. 'It was starting to rain when we came in.'

'No, I insist,' Florrie said. 'Tommy's right. You must see the garden.'

Florrie led the way and Tommy followed quickly behind.

'Has she got prize leeks out there she's keen to show us?' Adam whispered to Meg, making her giggle.

But as she stepped outside, she stood stock still. At the edge of Florrie's large back garden, in the shade of one of the trees that ran the length of the field, was a large black horse with a star-shaped flash on its nose. Meg flew down the field towards it, tears streaming down her face, as Florrie, Adam and Tommy stood and watched the reunion.

'Stella, sweet Stella,' Meg called. 'Sweet Stella. My Stella.'

The horse turned its head towards her call as she ran to it and flung her arms around its neck.

'I got her back from the knacker's yard just in the nick of time,' Tommy told Adam. 'They reckon she'll live a few more months, happy months grazing in the garden.'

'You did well, lad,' Adam said, laying a hand on Tommy's shoulder. 'I've always been proud to call you my friend, but I'll be prouder still to call you my brother.'

'And we don't need to worry about paying for oats and hay,' Tommy continued. 'Davey's going to get them for us from High Farm as he always did. All he asks in return is that we give him a hand breaking the stable down at the back of his house. He wants to dig an allotment patch there and get some vegetables growing. I said we'd help him. That's all right, isn't it, Adam?'

'Course it is,' Adam replied, ruffling Tommy's hair.

'Come on, you two,' Florrie said. 'Go and see the rest of the house; get yourselves acquainted with what will become your new home.'

Chapter Sixteen

Meg

Meg's eighteenth birthday passed with little fuss. She had more pressing matters on her mind. The only person who marked the day was Adam, calling into the cottage at Tunstall Street with a tiny gift wrapped in a page torn from the *Sunderland Echo*. Meg held the small parcel in her hands, turning it over.

'Go on then,' Adam smiled, watching her. 'It's not going to open itself.'

She untucked the ends of the page where Adam had folded it, envelope-like, so that it wouldn't spring open. Inside was a tiny piece of wood, no bigger than Meg's little finger.

'Turn it over,' Adam said. 'It's driftwood. I found it on the beach when I was fishing.'

'It's beautiful,' Meg said. She ran her fingers across the smooth surface of the wood, admiring the lines that had been worn into it after being tumbled in the sea for years. Then she peered closer. 'But there are flowers etched into it,' she said, glancing at Adam.

'I did those,' he said. 'Dad showed me how, with a small knife. It's not much, Meg, but it's all my own work.'

'It's beautiful,' Meg repeated. 'I'm going to put it next to my jar of shells that you gave me on my sixteenth birthday, and my sea glass picture you made for me last year too. I'll put them on display in our new house when we move, pick somewhere really special for them all.'

'Do you need any help packing? Mam and Evelyn have offered; you're just to say the word if you need them. And I'll help when I come home from work.'

Meg shook her head. 'What do we have that needs packing?' she smiled, looking around at the sticks of furniture in the kitchen. 'Clothes maybe, blankets for Grace, the pram, that's about it. Tommy's done most of it already.'

'And you're all set for tomorrow?'

Meg held out her arms and pulled Adam towards her. 'I can't wait for tomorrow,' she whispered. 'I'll be leaving this little house as Meg Sutcliffe for the very last time.'

Adam hugged her tight. 'And walking into our new home as Mrs Wilson,' he said. 'Mam's that excited for the wedding, it's all she talks about. And Evelyn's managed to get the day off work, although the housekeeper wasn't happy about it.'

'Our Tommy's bringing a friend to the wedding, a girl called Claire he met down at the paper mill,' Meg said.

'It'll be a day to remember, that's for sure,' Adam said. 'Look, Meg, I'll have to go now, get myself down to the pit for my shift. I'll see you in the morning, at the church.'

He leaned towards her and kissed her softly, full on the lips. It was a kiss that held the promise of forever, for the next time they met, they would become husband and wife.

With a last smile, he turned and headed out of the

kitchen. Spot followed until Adam turned the corner of Tunstall Street and disappeared from view. Then the dog padded back to the kitchen door, where he sank to the stone floor in the yard and closed his eyes to sleep.

He was woken by a clattering noise as a pair of shoes came walking towards his nose along the stone ground. The noise was followed by a sharp bang at the back door. When Meg opened the door, Spot darted straight inside to sit beside Grace's pram.

'Lil?' Meg said, surprised to see her neighbour there.

'I brought you this to wear,' Lil said, offering Meg a small linen bag. 'For the wedding, like. That's if you'd like it, of course. Didn't know if you'd already have one or not.'

Meg untied the ribbon around the top of the bag, letting the linen fall away to reveal a beautiful silver brooch in the shape of a tiny butterfly.

'I'll want it back after, mind,' Lil said sharply. 'It was my mother's, may she rest in peace. But I wore it on my wedding day to Bob and I'd be honoured if you'd wear it too.'

'Are you sure, Lil?' Meg said. 'I mean . . . it's very special. Are you sure you'd like me to wear it?'

'Yes, pet,' Lil said. 'May it bring you good luck tomorrow. And may you and Adam be as happy as me and my Bob have been through all our married life.'

Meg hid a smile as she remembered all the screaming matches and fights she'd heard through the walls over the years.

'You can borrow it, pet, like I said,' Lil continued. 'All you'll be needing now is something old, something new and something blue. But I expect you've got that all covered. Young lass like you, organised to the last.'

She turned to walk out of the kitchen, but as she reached the door, she stopped, with her hand on the doorknob. Meg watched and waited, expecting her to turn back, but there was no movement. There were just words, directed at the kitchen door, though Meg heard them clear enough.

'You take care, lass, you hear? Me and Bob . . . we were never blessed with children of our own. I dare say things might have been different between us if we'd been able to have bairns. Who knows, we might have got on better. Anyway, I'll miss you, Meg, when you move. That's all I wanted to say.'

'I'll bring it back to you, Lil,' Meg said softly. 'I'll be back in Ryhope soon enough, to visit Adam's mam and dad. I'll bring the brooch back to you then.'

Lil gave a sharp nod of her head and opened the door, heading out into the yard and the back lane and then to her cottage next door. But her words had left Meg with something to think about.

She sank into her mam's chair by the fire, watching Grace as she slept in her pram. Spot was lying underneath the pram now, snoring gently. The something old, Meg decided, would be the fur coat that Florrie had given her before she left for Scarborough. The coat had been the one she'd seen many times before, hanging up in the market high above the stalls, out of reach and out of price range for those who shopped there. It was upstairs now, on a hook on the back of Meg's bedroom door. She'd had to put it out in the back yard on the washing line when Florrie first gave it to her, for it had reeked of mothballs and had to be beaten to get the stench from it. But once it had been brushed, and Adam's mam had worked her sewing magic on it, repairing the holes and the lining, the honey-coloured coat looked as good as new. Well, almost. And Meg was going to wear it tomorrow, in honour of Florrie.

Her wedding dress would be the something blue. The dress had come from the market too; Meg had bought it from Lucy's stall and cleaned it up at home herself. It floated delicately around her slender frame, its sleeves falling to just below the elbow, and there were white flowers embroidered at the neck.

All she needed now was something new, but where would she get that from, and at such short notice too? She had a tiny bit of money spare, money that she'd made at the market that was still in her accounts book in the unspent column. She could spend a little of it for tomorrow of all days, surely?

Her thoughts were directed back towards the baby in the pram as Grace began to wake. At a year old now, Grace's face was plumping out, her smile enough to brighten the darkest of days. Milk that Gert had brought for them earlier was warmed in a pan on the fire, and Meg sat with the little girl in her lap, feeding her. From his place under the pram, Spot watched and waited, hoping for some milk to come his way too, but Meg shook her head at him.

As she glanced out of the kitchen window, she saw a break in the clouds, the tiniest scrap of blue in the smog of coal dust.

'How about a bit of fresh air, Grace?' she said. 'How about you and me going on a trip into town? You've never been to Sunderland before, have you, not all the way there?'

Grace gurgled and kicked at the soothing sounds of her mother's words.

'We'll go on a tram, Grace. Just you and me. We'll go on

a tram to the town and we'll buy something new for tomorrow.'

Meg waited at the tram stop at the village green, holding tight to the handles of the pram. If anyone had noticed her there, they would not have recognised her as the girl with the horse, the girl who did the rag-and-bone round. Gone was the big chunky army coat. In its place was the fur coat from the market, worn for the first time before her wedding the following day. Gone was the green knitted hat, safely packed away in one of the tea chests at Tunstall Street with the rest of their clothes, ready for the move to Florrie's house. If anyone had noticed her there, they would have remarked on what an agreeable young mother she was and how attractive she looked too.

The tram appeared at last, with its *Shop at Binns* advertising banners running the length of the upper deck and across the front too. When it came to a stop, Meg struggled to lift the pram on to the lower deck, until the conductor came to help.

'All aboard,' he cried once Meg was seated with the pram to her side. 'All aboard.'

The tram trundled along the coast road, the same road that Meg had travelled so many times with Stella. The thought of the horse brought a smile to her face as she imagined Stella grazing in the garden of her new home. It rattled past the paper mill and its chimneys, past the road that led down to the market and the docks. And as the journey continued, a plan began to form in Meg's mind. By the time they arrived in Sunderland town centre, she knew exactly what she was going to buy for her something new – and where she was going to buy it from.

The tram stopped directly outside the Binns store, so there was no distance for Meg to walk with Grace's pram. She approached the glass doors of the entrance and then turned so that she could push them open with her backside, bringing the pram in after her. Once inside, she noticed the same gentle hush that she remembered from when Florrie had brought her to Sunderland the very first time. But the panic that she'd felt on that first visit to Binns had long gone. She had money in her pocket now, money that was as good as anyone else's, and she was going to spend it wisely.

Behind the counters of the women's clothing department, uniformed assistants stood to attention. One of them, Sue Pegg, was busy helping a customer, but as soon as she saw Meg, she stopped what she was doing. There was something familiar about the lass, something that Sue couldn't place at first. She knew she'd seen her before somewhere, but where? It was the girl's bonny features that jogged her memory, although the fur coat she wore now was in sharp contrast to the army coat that Sue had seen her in the first time she'd entered the store. But it was her all right, it was definitely her.

Sue smiled at the customer she was helping, wrapped up her purchase and wrote out a receipt. Once done, she headed straight towards Meg.

'Can I help you?'

Meg stood still, holding on to Grace's pram. 'I'm looking for the tall woman,' she said. 'Tall, thin. I think her name was Miss Nichols?'

Sue smiled. 'Oh, you mean our floor manager, Miss Nicholson. Is there anything I can help you with, or is it Miss Nicholson you need to see?'

'I'd like her to serve me, please, if she's free.'

'Certainly, madam. I know she has a visitor with her today, a manager from head office who is inspecting our branch, but I'll see if she can help.'

Meg watched as Sue crossed to the other side of the long room. When she returned, she was walking two steps behind the tall, thin woman Meg remembered so clearly from her previous visit. Beside her was a man, a real gentleman, done up in a waistcoat and tie. Meg waited for Miss Nicholson to reach her.

As the floor manager approached, she began to realise where she'd seen the girl before. It wasn't every day she had to throw out a tinker, and she always remembered the ones she got rid of in case they tried to come back. And oh, she remembered this one all right, even if she was all scrubbed up in a posh coat and had her hair brushed now. And was that . . . was that a bairn in the pram beside her?

She eyed Meg all the way from her boots up. Her gaze lingered a while on the coat, her trained eye taking in the synthetic nature of it.

'You asked for me, madam?' she said, looking down at Meg. 'Although I am rather busy . . .'

'I'd like to see the quality of your ribbons,' Meg said politely. 'I wish to make a purchase and I'd like you to assist, to serve me.'

Miss Nicholson's face gave a slight twitch around the mouth. 'I'm sure my assistant, Miss Pegg, would be delighted to serve you, madam,' she said.

Sue Pegg took her cue and stepped forward, but Meg shook her head.

'I'd like you to serve me. Please.'

'Come now, Miss Nicholson,' the gentleman chided. 'If madam has specifically requested your expertise in the matter of haberdashery, then you must do all you can to help.'

Miss Nicholson took a deep breath and squared her shoulders. 'Yes, of course, sir,' she said, smiling through gritted teeth. 'Madam, please, come this way, if you would.'

Meg pushed Grace's pram behind Miss Nicholson as she followed her through the women's clothing department into the haberdashery room. Rows and rows of shelves lined the walls, with every colour of material imaginable. Silks and furs, cottons and linens were draped across tables. Fastenings and buttons of all shapes and sizes were on show. Meg pushed the pram carefully through the central aisle towards the reels of ribbons in all different widths and colours. She chose a slim ribbon, a blue one to match her wedding dress, just the right length to wear in her hair. The purchase was conducted politely and graciously, all under the gaze of the head office manager, who watched Miss Nicholson like a hawk.

When the transaction was complete, Meg thanked Miss Nicholson, gave a nod towards the gentleman by way of thanks too, and then walked from the store with her head held high. Sue Pegg ran to her aid at the exit door when she had trouble pulling the door inwards and managing Grace's pram at the same time. Meanwhile, back in the haberdashery department, Miss Nicholson excused herself, saying she needed to visit the ladies' parlour as she'd come over quite peculiar and needed a few moments of rest.

The following morning, Meg and Tommy prepared for the day ahead in companionable silence. Tommy brought in one last bucket of coal for the fire and filled buckets of water for a bath for Meg and Grace. He himself had washed the night before, cleaned behind his ears too, in readiness for the wedding. But first there was something he needed to do.

'I'll see you later, Meg,' he yelled up the stairs. 'I'll be back in time to walk you to church.'

He headed out to the yard wearing the black jacket that Meg had found for him on the market months ago, hoping that he'd grow into it one day. With his muscles building from his work at the pit, he'd grown to fit it much sooner than expected, his broad shoulders filling it nicely. He liked the cut of the jacket, and the fact that it made him feel, and look, a little older than his years. He'd even started wearing his dad's army coat to work at the pit now, the coat that Meg had for so long worn when she worked on the cart. He took pride in wearing it, not least because of the compliments that he received from his workmates. He'd taken in his dad's war medal, too, the one Meg had retrieved from Clarky's house, to show the lads at work.

He headed to the tram stop in the village, where he'd catch the tram to the paper mill to meet Claire and bring her to the wedding. He was looking forward to seeing her again, and intended to ask her to come to tea at their new house as soon as they were all settled in. As he waited, he bent down to rub a spot of muck from one of his shoes, then stood and took a moment to gather himself for the day ahead. His life wasn't a bad one, he knew that. He had a good home to live in, a sister he loved and admired and a new brother-in-law to chat to about matters that were increasingly on his mind. He needed to talk about his work at the pit to someone who knew the horrors of what it was like underground.

And he knew that if he ever needed to, he could talk to

Adam about the day that Hawk died. Because deep down, every time he thought about it, he still blamed himself for killing him, even though his mam had always told him that it wasn't his fault. He'd long ago resigned himself to the fact that the events of that awful night might never completely leave him, and he knew in his heart that he had to make peace with how he felt.

There were other matters he needed advice from Adam on – girls, for one. He liked Claire a lot but he was unsure of the new and confusing feelings and emotions that went rushing around his brain and body every time they met.

No, it wasn't a bad life that Tommy Sutcliffe had. With Adam to look up to as his brother-in-law, with his sister Meg and her fighting spirit, with the money that his job at the pit brought in . . . well, he had a lot to be grateful for. Now all he had to do was finalise the arrangements he'd been working on in secret, arrangements that would make up his wedding gift to Meg.

An hour later, Reverend Daye took up his position at the church door, ready to welcome the wedding guests. Lil Mahone was first there, bristling up the church path with Bob behind her.

'Come on, Bob,' she whispered, turning to her husband. 'I want to get in and get a good seat.'

Reverend Daye beamed a smile of joy to the Mahones as they neared the door.

'Good morning to you both!' he greeted them, handing them each a hymn book. Lil took hers from his hand and bustled into the church, heading for the front pews.

Bob raised his eyebrows as he followed her inside. 'Morning, Vicar,' he said.

'Bride or groom?' Reverend Daye asked.

'Sorry?'

'Are you with the bride's family or the groom's?'

'Oh . . . er . . . bride's, I suppose,' Bob replied.

'Be seated on the left, please. The left-hand side is for the bride's family and friends.'

'We're Meg's next-door neighbours,' Bob explained.

The vicar rubbed his chin. 'Ah . . . well, perhaps leave the front pews for family.'

'Will do, Vicar,' Bob said, peering into the dark of the church. 'Mind you, I'd best go and tell that to Lil first.'

As Bob walked down the aisle, he saw Lil sitting in the second pew. He tapped her gently on the shoulder and nodded towards the pew behind.

'But the lass hasn't got any family,' Lil tutted. 'Who's to know?'

'Lil, I'll only ask you the once,' Bob said sternly. 'Now come on, move back and let those who deserve it sit forward.'

Reluctantly Lil gathered her bag towards her and moved into the row behind to sit next to her husband.

Next into the church were Hetty and Jack Burdon, walking together, hand in hand. In Hetty's auburn hair a white flower was pinned. She glanced at Jack as he wiped at his face.

'Are you crying, Jack Burdon?'

'No,' he replied quickly, looking away. 'It's just . . . I think I've got something in my eye, that's all.'

Lil watched as the Burdons took their seats.

'I dare say we'll be going to the Albion for a drink or two once the business here is done,' she whispered to Bob as she craned her head to the door to see who else was coming in.

It was Davey next. He took his hymn book from the vicar and headed to sit next to Lil and Bob.

'Gert must be ill,' Lil whispered to Bob. 'There's no sign of her, look.'

But before Bob could say anything, a baby's cry filled the church, echoing all around. All heads turned towards the door, and there was Gert with Grace in her arms, shushing her, hoping against hope that the bairn wouldn't make a racket when Meg arrived later on.

Adam's mam Jean and his dad Henry arrived next, with the vicar directing them to the front pew on the right-hand side of the aisle. Then came Evelyn, with Michael Patterson in tow.

'Who's that with the young Wilson lass?' Lil whispered to Bob. 'He doesn't look familiar.'

'Can't say I know the lad, Lil,' Bob replied. 'Anyway, it's none of our business.'

Gert was heading to the front pew on the left-hand side.

'Come on, Davey,' she said. 'We need to be at the front.'

'But we're not family, love,' Davey said quietly.

'This little one is.' Gert smiled down at Grace, who was chewing contentedly on one of Gert's rhubarb biscuits. 'And Meg will want to see her when she says her vows.'

The left-hand side of the church began to fill as more guests headed inside. From the market there was Derek the butcher, taking a rare day off work, with his wife by his side. Ruth from the paper mill came next, done up in her best bib and tucker, with a young man by her side. She gave him a gentle poke in the ribs with her elbow as they walked into the church.

'Isn't this beautiful, Stuart? And just think, it could be

you and me next, our turn to get wed. That's if you play your cards right, of course. And remember, I want to be in a good spot to catch the bride's bouquet when she chucks it later on.'

Stuart gulped and sank gratefully into his wooden seat.

'There's folk here who aren't from Ryhope,' Lil huffed. 'I don't recognise half of these.'

Bob opened his hymn book and feigned interest in the words of the songs, trying to ignore his wife's gossip about the wedding guests.

'Ooh, I know those two,' Lil chirped when she spotted Micky Parks's mam and dad coming into the church. Mrs Parks stopped in the middle of the aisle. She raised her right hand and made the sign of the cross before taking her husband's hand and heading towards a pew.

'Can't be easy for them, losing a child so young,' Lil whispered to Bob, shaking her head. 'Nasty accident that was at the pit.'

'Lil!' Bob hissed. 'Will you have a bit of respect? Remember where you are, love.'

Suitably chastised, Lil straightened in her seat and didn't utter another word.

Big Pete was next to walk up the church path. He smiled warmly at the vicar as he received a hymn book.

'Had any more trouble with the lead being nicked from the roof?' he asked.

Reverend Daye shook his head. 'I'm pleased to say not, Pete. It cost a pretty penny to replace it last time.'

'And still no idea who the culprit was?'

'None at all. Some fly-by-night, I expect.'

'Well, if you ever need any lead, Vicar, just give me the nod. I know where I can get some on the cheap.'

'Thank you, Pete.' The vicar smiled. 'I'll bear that in mind.'

Big Pete headed inside and took a seat next to Micky Parks's dad. The two men shook hands and Pete settled himself on the hard wooden seat of the pew. Trying to make himself comfortable, he pulled at his tie to loosen it slightly and then undid the buttons on his jacket.

Mr Parks nodded towards his stomach. 'Nice waistcoat,' he said. 'It's top quality that, Pete lad.'

Big Pete beamed with pride before flicking open the silky pages of the hymn book in his hand.

The friendly chatter amongst the guests seated in the church soon turned into a hushed conversation, with one word repeated over again.

'Adam . . . it's Adam.'

The whisper went from the back of the church, from those who could see the vicar at the door with the groom, all the way to the front. Jean straightened her skirt at the sound of her son's name, knowing it meant he had arrived.

With the vicar by his side, Adam walked down the aisle. Reverend Daye positioned himself in front of the small congregation, beaming out to the guests as they readied themselves for the ceremony. Then he brought his gaze to meet Adam's.

'All ready?' he asked.

Adam nodded. 'I am, Vicar. Yes.'

Reverend Daye scanned the pews. 'Who's giving Meg away in place of her dad?' he whispered.

'No one. She wanted to do things differently. You know what Meg's like.'

'I see,' Reverend Daye said, although he wasn't really sure that he did. 'Then all we need to do now is wait for your bride to arrive,' he beamed.

Adam took a deep breath and dropped his hands to his sides. He turned his head, ever so slightly, just enough to see his mam and dad sitting behind him.

'Don't be nervous, son,' Jean whispered. 'You've got your whole life ahead of you now.'

As the congregation waited, up at Tunstall Street Meg was making her final preparations. She sat quietly in her mam's chair by the fire, with Spot lying at her feet. She watched the embers, glowing orange through the black of the coals, dying in the hearth. There was no need to keep the fire burning, no need for it to continue to warm their little home, for after today it would be theirs no more. Around her on the kitchen floor sat wooden crates filled with clothes, standing next to Grace's pram. Her mam's blackened cast-iron pan and her knitting needles were packed, along with plates and cups. In another box was her mam's enamel jug and the three-legged cracket stool, all ready to be moved to Florrie's house later that day.

Vic from the forge had offered – indeed, he'd insisted – to take their belongings to the new house while everyone was at the church. After the wedding was over, drinks at the Albion were planned, with a spread of meats and cheese that Hetty and Jack were laying on by way of their wedding gift. And when all was done there, Meg and Adam, along with Tommy, Grace and Spot, would head to their new home, leaving Tunstall Street behind.

Now all that needed to be done was for Meg to fix the blue ribbon in her hair and wait for Tommy to return. But where was he? He promised he'd be back in time to walk her down to church, but he was taking his time, wherever it was that he'd gone.

She lifted her hair from the back of her neck and threaded the ribbon underneath, tying it with a bow that fell softly to drape at her neck. Then she picked up the fur coat from the back of her mam's chair and pushed her arms into the sleeves, closing it at the front with one button. To the lapel of the coat she pinned the tiny silver butterfly brooch that Lil had loaned her. And on her stockinged feet were shoes from the market, real ladies' shoes with a tiny heel, that she was proud to show off. They pinched at her toes and she wriggled her feet in them to get as comfortable as she could.

She was ready now. Ready and keen to get to the church. She didn't want to keep Adam waiting; she wanted nothing more than to become his wife now. And she didn't want to keep Grace waiting either, as she would be hungry and ready for food. Grace had become very vocal about letting everyone know when she was ready to eat. The last thing Meg wanted was her bairn screaming down the insides of the church on today of all days.

There was a noise at the back door and Meg turned to see Tommy there, tall and broad and grown-up in the jacket she'd bought for him from Florrie.

'You ready, Meg?'

'Where's Claire? I thought you were meeting her,' Meg said.

'She's at the church. I sat her next to Hetty and Jack – hope that was all right?'

'Is Adam there already?'

Tommy nodded. 'They're all there. All waiting. Grace was falling asleep in Gert's arms when I got there. It's just you and me they need now.'

Meg headed out of the kitchen, past Tommy, and into the back yard, intending to lock the gate. But before she did, she pulled it open and took one last look up and down the back lane. The netty stood empty, its door swinging in the breeze. Weeds grew around the water tap. She closed the gate and locked it. The tin bath that had hung on the wall of the yard for as long as she could remember was now standing in the middle of the kitchen floor, ready for Vic to move it to their new home. The coal shed was empty, just a covering of black dust left for whoever would need it next. She walked back into the kitchen and closed the door behind her. Tommy handed her the key and she turned it in the lock.

'Ready?' he asked her.

Meg breathed deeply and straightened her shoulders. 'Ready,' she said.

She placed the back-door key on the hearth, which was cooling now, the fire dying. From the kitchen table she picked up her bouquet of white roses, which Adam's dad had grown on the allotment and Adam's mam had prepared for her, tied with a blue ribbon in a bow. Tommy unlocked the front door and pulled it towards him, hard. It wouldn't budge at first and he had to try again, harder this time, to get the stiffened door to move. And when it did move . . . when it opened . . .

Meg couldn't believe what she was seeing. There on the road outside the cottage stood Stella, with blue ribbons plaited down the length of her mane. Behind her was the cart, Meg's cart, ribbons streaming out from that too. Vic was sitting at the front of the cart with Stella's reins in his hand.

'Your carriage awaits,' he said, lifting his cap towards Meg.

'Here, let me help you up,' Tommy offered, but Meg was already clambering aboard to sit next to Vic. Spot ran out of the front door behind Tommy, looking from right to left before jumping up on the back of the cart.

'Don't you worry about the horse, Meg,' Vic told her. 'It's just a short walk and I've made sure she's well rested. When you're in the church I'm taking her to the forge to eat and rest again before we walk her back to the garden. It's just a few short walks, Meg, I promise.'

'A short walk . . . and her last walk,' Meg said softly.

'Hetty and Gert did her ribbons,' Tommy said. 'And Claire helped them too. But with Stella walking as slow as she does . . . that's why I was late just now. We all wanted it to be a surprise, Meg. I can't afford to buy a wedding present for you and Adam, but I knew I could do something you'd never forget.'

'Gee up there, Stella!' Vic called, but the old horse stayed where she was. He tried again, but there was still no response.

'Come on, Stella,' Tommy urged. 'We're going to be late.'

'Leave it to me,' Meg said, and then softly she started to sing. '*Stella, sweet Stella, what fella could want a finer horse?*'

At the sound of Meg's voice, as clear as a bell, Stella's ears flickered. Then she began slowly, very slowly, to move forward down the colliery, to where Adam was waiting for his bride.

out of the front door behind Tommy, looking from right to left before jumping up on the back of the cart.

'Don't you worry about the horse, Meg,' Vic told her. 'It's just a short walk and I've made sure she's well rested. When you're in the church I'm taking her to the forge to eat and rest again before we walk her back to the garden. It's just a few short walks, Meg; I promise.'

'A short walk . . . and her last walk,' Meg said softly.

'Hetty and Gert did her ribbons,' Tommy said. 'And Claire helped them too. But with Stella walking as slow as she does . . . that's why I was late just now. We all wanted it to be a surprise, Meg. I can't afford to buy a wedding present for you and Adam, but I knew I could do something you'd never forget.'

'Gee up there, Stella!' Vic called, but the old horse stayed where she was. He tried again, but there was still no response.

'Come on, Stella,' Tommy urged. 'We're going to be late.'

'Leave it to me,' Meg said, and then softly she started to sing, '*Stella, sweet Stella, what else could want – pure love*.'

At the sound of Meg's voice, as clear as a bell, Stella's ears flickered. Then she began slowly, very slowly, to move forward down the colliery, to where Adam was waiting for his bride.

Belle of the Back Streets

Bonus Material

Make your own stottie cake with Glenda's recipe!

A stottie cake or stotty is a bread which originated in the North East of England. It is a flat, round loaf about the shape and size of a frisbee – and it's delicious! Here's my tried and trusted recipe with my grandma Emily's secret ingredient.

See pictures of me making stottie cake and read my blog post online at bit.ly/BelleOfTheBackStreets

Makes 1 large stottie cake

Ingredients

- 400g strong white bread flour
- ½ teaspoon salt
- 1 teaspoon sugar
- ½ teaspoon ground white pepper
  (*this is my grandma's secret ingredient, she used to add it to just about everything!*)
- 1 sachet (7g) dried yeast
- 1 tablespoon softened butter
- 2 teaspoons sunflower oil
- 90ml milk
- 180ml tepid water

1. In a large bowl, stir the flour, salt and pepper, sugar together.
2. Add the yeast and give it another stir.
3. Add butter and oil and rub in with fingertips for a minute or so until everything is crumbly.

4. Put the milk and warm water into a jug and then pour around the sides of the bowl to distribute the liquid evenly.
5. Stir it so that the liquid combines with the dry ingredients. Turn it out to a floured board and work it all together by hand for about 5 minutes into a good dough. Don't worry if it's still wet and sticky. Turn into a bowl.
6. Cover the bowl with cling film and leave in a warm place for an hour.
7. When the dough has doubled in size, turn it on to a floured board and form into a flat, round disc shape – like a frisbee!
8. Squash it gently with another floured bread board, not too much, it needs to be roughly 2.5cm thick.
9. Place on a greased baking tray and cover with a bonny tea-towel.
10. Leave it in a warm place for 30 minutes.
11. Pre-heat the oven to gas mark 6 / 200 degrees C / 400 degrees F.
12. Squash it gently again with the floured bread board, down to approximately 1cm thick.
13. Using your finger, press down to make a hole in the centre of the stottie.
14. Put in the oven and bake for just 6 minutes.
15. Carefully turn the stottie over, return to the oven and bake for a further 6 minutes.
16. Cool on a cooling rack.
17. Cut into pie-shaped pieces and slice each one in half. Eat and enjoy. Perfect with soup.

With thanks to Barry Smith, my husband and chief cook in our house, for his help!

All About Ryhope

Ryhope is a village on the northeastern coast, south of the city of Sunderland in Tyne and Wear. The first mention of Ryhope was in 930AD when the Saxon King Athelstan gave the parish of South Wearmouth to the See of Durham. King Athelstan's name lives on in Ryhope with a street named after him – Athelstan Rigg.

The name Ryhope is an Old English name which means 'rugged valley'. Originally Ryhope is recorded as being called *Rive hope* and has also been recorded as *Refhoppa*, *Reshop* and *Riopp*.

Ryhope developed as a farming community and was popular as a sea bathing resort. However, in 1856 sinking operations reached coal seams deep beneath the magnesian limestone and Ryhope grew as a coal mining village. Ryhope had two separate railways with their own train stations, putting Ryhope within easy commuting distance of Sunderland. By 1905 electric trams also reached Ryhope from Sunderland. The coal mine closed in 1966, marking the end of an era for Ryhope.

For more on Ryhope's past, present and future, Sunderland City Council have a very interesting planning document showing historic pictures. You can find it at http://bit.ly/RyhopeHistory

And if you'd like to know more about the village of Ryhope, here are some good websites you might like to explore for historic maps, guided walks and a visit to the ever-popular Pumping Station at Ryhope Engines Museum.

A guided walk around Ryhope – From agriculture to coal
http://bit.ly/RyhopeWalk

Historic map of Ryhope
http://bit.ly/RyhopeMap

Ryhope Engines Museum
http://www.ryhopeengines.org.uk/

Historic Pictures of Ryhope
http://east-durham.co.uk/wp/ryhope/

Keep reading for an early preview of Glenda's next enthralling saga,

The Tuppenny Child

Coming soon from Headline.

Chapter One

Escape

May 1919

'Where to, miss?'

Sadie glanced behind her to ensure she hadn't been followed. Her heart hammered in her chest.

'Miss?'

'Ryhope, please,' she said, snatching another look behind her, just in case. 'Third class.'

'Single or return?' the ticket clerk asked.

'Single,' she replied. She had no intention of ever coming back.

'That'll be one and six, please.'

She lifted her small blue bag to the wooden counter. Her hands were shaking as she spilled the coins from it to the counter top. As the clerk expertly flicked each coin towards him, totting them up one by one, Sadie looked around the ticket office. It was a neat and tidy little place, with time-tables and schedules pinned to the walls, a clock ticking above an oak desk, and a small coal fire burning in the hearth. There was a quiet hush about it, a sense of order that helped calm her racing mind.

'You'll be needing the Sunderland train for Ryhope. It's due at half past the hour,' the clerk said as he handed over her ticket. 'You can wait in the ladies' room if you wish.'

'Me, sir?'

'Yes, miss. West Hartlepool railway station is proud to open its waiting room to all ladies, whatever their ticket class.'

Sadie walked out of the ticket office, relieved to see that the platform was clear apart from a porter gathering a pile of wooden crates, laying one on top of the other. He whistled as he worked, a tune that she didn't recognise. She turned and saw the sign for the ladies' waiting room and quickly walked towards it. She'd never been inside one before, but she knew it was the safest place, somewhere she could hide. Her heart continued to thump as she glanced behind her one final time to be certain she hadn't been followed. Then she took a deep breath and reached out her hand. The doorknob was cold to her touch but turned easily, and the green wooden door swung open.

It was the fire she noticed first. The roaring blaze in the huge blackened fireplace dominated the small room with its noise and heat and its musty, smoky smell. In front of the hearth was a black iron guard, wrapped around the fireplace to protect skirts and bairns. Sadie felt drawn to the fire; she wanted to walk towards it, to lift her coat and warm her backside. But a quick glance around the room at the three ladies already seated suggested that this was not the thing to do.

All eyes turned towards her as she hesitated by the door. In the centre of the room was a large table, scattered with worn magazines and a copy of *The Hartlepool Northern Daily*. On the wall high above the fireplace, the waiting room clock loudly ticked the minutes until the next train arrived.

'Shut the door, pet,' the woman closest to the fireplace barked. 'You're letting in the wind.'

Sadie moved quickly at the demand, and swung round to close the door. She gave a brief nod by way of apology, but all she got in return was a blank stare from a pair of dark and deadened eyes. She fell into the seat closest to her, landing heavily, the bench as hard on her legs and as uncomfortable underneath her as it looked. But it was warm in the room, and she was grateful for that, for although it was early May, it was cold and windy out.

She pressed her back against the wall and allowed her gaze to settle on the stone floor before she slowly lifted her eyes to fully take in her surroundings. On the wall to her right was a blue and white tiled map of the north-east coast, next to it a colourful poster advertising the twin resorts of Roker and Seaburn, with their sweeping bays and golden sands. On the opposite wall were two large windows, frosted to stop prying eyes looking in from the platform, providing the women inside with privacy. Underneath each window, on deep sills set in the stone walls, stood white enamel jugs holding golden daffodils.

Sadie glanced at the older woman by the fire who had spoken so abruptly when she'd entered. She guessed that the woman was travelling in third class too. Her boots were worn, and her flat brown hat sat askew on her head as she slouched against the wall. To Sadie's right was a young woman who looked about twenty, slightly older than her own seventeen years. But from the look of her, she would definitely not be travelling in third. The girl's clean, pretty bonnet partly shielded her unlined features, and her concentration went into reading a book with a light brown cover that she held in her small, soft hands.

To Sadie's left was another well-dressed young woman. Whether she was a mother or a maid, Sadie couldn't tell, but she had a large black perambulator in front of her with a sleeping baby inside. The pram was turned towards Sadie and she could see a baby's tiny pink face peeking out. She had grown used to seeing women with bairns over the last ten months, though it hadn't been easy at first. In those ten months her life had been turned upside down. As she gazed into the dancing flames of the fire, she cast her mind back to the Hartlepool lodging house she'd left only that morning, where she'd been living with Freda McIntyre and her son, Mick.

Sadie had been left with little choice but to move into Freda's house after the Spanish flu ravaged Hartlepool and took her parents in its deadly wake. With no relatives to take her in, she was handed over by the authorities into Freda McIntyre's care, to live as a lodger in her spare room. But there was nothing caring about Freda, as Sadie soon found out.

Freda was a woman who looked older than her years, her face made heavy from the drinking of ale. But she must have been pretty as a girl, for there was a touch of something to her features and her long dark hair that made her popular with gentleman callers. Sadie would scuttle away and hide from the men who came into the house, afraid in case any of them climbed the stairs to her room. Freda enjoyed the company of her men friends more than she cared about

Sadie's welfare. Sadie hadn't been sure, when she first moved into the house, what Freda's business was, but she soon found out when she became friendly with Mick, Freda's son. He was the one who explained to her that the men who came to the house paid to spend time with his mam, and in her bedroom too.

When she first arrived at Freda's, Mick walked Sadie to Hartlepool market each morning. He was friendly enough at the start and Sadie was glad of his companionship. She was just one of the many girls who lined up at the market, waiting for the women from the fancy houses to appraise them and pick them off one by one to work in service. If they were found suitable, a shilling would be placed in their hand to contract them for however long they were needed. Sometimes Sadie was hired for a day, sometimes just an hour. If she was lucky, she was given a job that would last all week.

She was obliged to hand over her earnings to Freda, every single penny. In return, Freda provided her with a roof over her head, a bed to lie in and breakfast and supper to eat. But it was a breakfast that Sadie had to prepare before she went out to work, and a supper that she had to cook no matter how tired she was at the end of her working day. And she was forced to cook not just for herself but for Mick and Freda too before she climbed the stairs to her cold, damp room.

She proved herself a hard worker, and word spread amongst those who hired at Hartlepool market that she was good in the kitchen. It was said she had perfect hands, cold hands, for making pastry for pies. When she was given a job with a cook or a chef in one of the big houses, she tied back her long fair hair into a plait and happily got down to work.

The warmth of the coal oven and the sweet aroma of baking reminded her of helping her mam.

She was always eager in the kitchen, always keen to know more and to learn, but when she was chosen at the market to work with a housekeeper, she dreaded her days. The endless cleaning and scrubbing were not to her liking. It was back-breaking work. Worse still were the times when a housekeeper contracted her services on a Friday, for all the girls knew that Fridays were the worst days of all, when the heaviest cleaning was done ready for entertaining at the weekends, and there were always stairs to be scrubbed.

Sadie would be given a stiff brush and a tin bucket filled with scalding water and washing soda and left to get on with it. With the houses so big and so grand, there were always plenty of stairs, wide too, with as many as four flights – and woe betide any girl if she didn't do a good job, for the work would be checked. The housekeeper would peer at each stair with a candle in her hand, and if she found dirt in any corner, she would put down the candle long enough to give the girl a tongue-lashing. After that, she'd give her another bucket of steaming hot water and make her do the stairs again, every single one of them. Only once had Sadie, unknowingly, left a scrap of dirt on the stairs. After having to clean the whole four flights again, she never made that mistake again.

© Emily Pentland

Glenda Young credits her local library in the village of Ryhope, where she grew up, for giving her a love of books. She still lives close by in Sunderland and often gets her ideas for her stories on long bike rides along the coast. A life-long fan of *Coronation Street*, she runs two fan websites.

For updates on what Glenda is working on, visit her website **glendayoungbooks.com** and to find out more find her on **Facebook/GlendaYoungAuthor** and Twitter **@flaming_nora**.